PRAISE FOR

The Single Ladies of Jacaranda Retirement Village

'I haven't laughed out loud at a book as much since I read Marian Keyes' *Lucy Sullivan is Getting Married*. Regardless of your age, I can highly recommend you snuggle up with Peggy Smart and her band of old-timers' **ESTHER CAMPION**

'The perfect blend of funny and moving; Peggy Smart had me laughing and crying in this ultimately uplifting story' **NATASHA LESTER**

'I loved this warm and witty story of an older woman learning to stand up for herself, and found myself cheering for her to succeed. A terrific feel-good read' **KAYTE NUNN**

'I loved it! I want to be Peggy when I'm older. With many laugh-out-loud moments, this book celebrates life in the later years and is sure to make you see "getting old" in a different light' **FIONA PALMER**

'Peggy Smart is Bridget Jones for retirees. Such a refreshing, warm and at times hilarious read' **FIONA HIGGINS**

'It was so refreshing to read about characters at this stage of their lives. It touched my heart and will have real staying power in the hearts and minds of readers' **VANESSA CARNEVALE**

The Single Ladies of
Jacaranda Retirement Village

The Single Ladies of
Jacaranda Retirement Village

JOANNA NELL

hachette
AUSTRALIA

hachette
AUSTRALIA

Published in Australia and New Zealand in 2018
by Hachette Australia
(an imprint of Hachette Australia Pty Limited)
Level 17, 207 Kent Street, Sydney NSW 2000
www.hachette.com.au

10 9 8 7 6 5 4 3 2 1

Copyright © Joanna Nell 2018

 A catalogue record for this
book is available from the
National Library of Australia

NATIONAL
LIBRARY
OF AUSTRALIA

ISBN 978 0 7336 4035 3

Cover design by Christabella Designs
Cover images courtesy of Shutterstock
Author photo by Kate Williams Photography
Typeset in 12/17 pt Sabon LT Pro by Bookhouse, Sydney
Printed and bound in Australia by McPherson's Printing Group

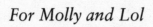

For Molly and Lol

Do Not Go Gentle into That Good Night

Do not go gentle into that good night,
Old age should burn and rave at close of day;
Rage, rage against the dying of the light.

Though wise men at their end know dark is right,
Because their words had forked no lightning they
Do not go gentle into that good night.

Good men, the last wave by, crying how bright
Their frail deeds might have danced in a green bay,
Rage, rage against the dying of the light.

Wild men who caught and sang the sun in flight,
And learn, too late, they grieved it on its way,
Do not go gentle into that good night.

Grave men, near death, who see with blinding sight
Blind eyes could blaze like meteors and be gay,
Rage, rage against the dying of the light.

And you, my father, there on the sad height,
Curse, bless, me now with your fierce tears, I pray.
Do not go gentle into that good night.
Rage, rage against the dying of the light.

Dylan Thomas 1914–1953

1

The Dance of the Seven Bath Towels

PEGGY SMART WAS NINETY PERCENT SURE IT WAS MONDAY.
She squinted at the days printed on her medication pack. What
an ingenious invention. Thanks to the individual bubbles,
she never forgot to take her pills. And more importantly,
she never missed Brian.

Armed with a fresh cup of tea, Peggy took up her usual
vantage position. She cradled the steaming brew and waited.
He was late this morning. She felt a wrinkle in her optimism.
What if she'd missed him? What if he'd left already? It would
be another twenty-four hours before she could watch him stride
to his car, striped beach towel draped around his shoulders.

Peggy turned to the sugar bowl for consolation. She
swirled another spoonful of comfort into her tea before
returning to the kitchen window. To her surprise, there he
was, standing on the footpath, holding a newspaper. He
glanced up at the window. To Peggy's astonishment, Brian
Cornell smiled. And waved.

Startled, Peggy slopped hot tea onto her slippers. She grasped the windowsill for support. He'd seen her. What's more, he'd waved. Months of doubt evaporated, leaving Peggy with a heady sense of possibility.

She stole another peek from behind the nets. This time, the footpath was empty. Brian and his *Morning Herald* were gone. Her disappointment, however, was tinged with exhilaration. That wave, however fleeting, signified a turning point in their budding relationship.

Smiling, she lined up Monday's tablets on the striped tablecloth – a tiny army of chemical soldiers waging war on the passing years. She still had bottles of Ted's pills in the cupboard, but couldn't bring herself to dispose of perfectly good medication. The heartburn tablets might come in handy, for digestive emergencies. The prostate pills were a different matter. She should return those to the pharmacy. Unless Brian had a thick prostate. Peggy pushed away an image of him silhouetted in the bathroom light. There was no point pretending life was perfect. At their age, relationships always came with extra packaging.

The first of the tablets disappeared with a swig of extra-sweet tea. She took a bite of toast and opened her calendar. It was last year's Christmas present from her grandchildren, each month bearing a different photograph of young Emily and Sam having fun without her. But Peggy Smart knew better than to complain. There was no point upsetting the apple tart where family were concerned.

Peggy flipped through the calendar to October. There was a lovely photo of Sam and Emily collecting eggs on a farm with her daughter-in-law's parents. *Goody.* A whole month to remind her of her place in the pecking order. Peggy debated blacking out Geraldine's front teeth and drawing Mike a moustache. But that would be childish for a woman of seventy-nine.

Since she'd introduced the new colour-coding system last month, to her knowledge Peggy hadn't missed a single appointment. She congratulated herself daily on her ingenuity. Red for the doctor, purple for the podiatrist and blue for the hairdresser. She'd borrowed a pen from Emily's green fluffy pencil case to write a shopping list and had forgotten to return it. The gold glitter pen now took pride of place next to the calendar and was reserved for the residents' committee meetings. First Thursday of the month. With Brian as the new treasurer, however, she hardly needed to mark the dates. When it came to matters of the heart, Peggy's memory was flawless.

Brian Cornell.

The image of him tucking into one of her special baked dinners set Peggy aquiver. She pictured his slender features in the candlelight, his hand reaching for hers across the lace tablecloth. One mouthful of her sticky date pudding and the handsome widower would be smitten.

But it wasn't something she could easily drop into the agenda. 'Evening Brian. Have you approved the budget for the driveway landscaping yet? Oh, and would you care to join me for an intimate candlelit dinner?'

It was time to face facts. Four years of small talk, a compliment on her buns, and the inevitable enquiries after health was about as far as they'd ventured. Either this was slow-burning passion on a whole new level or she was flogging a dead Dodo.

Everyone knew women became invisible at a certain age, even to men in their eighties. It was as though Peggy Smart had turned completely neutral, blending in so perfectly to the tasteful décor of the retirement village that she had all but disappeared. It was hardly surprising. She was neither exciting nor glamorous. Quite unremarkable in every way. Her fantasy was just that; a fantasy.

Peggy sighed and drained the syrupy dregs of her tea. A woman could dream, couldn't she? One day, the perfect opportunity would present itself. In the meantime, she had memories of Ted to keep her company. And there was Basil too, snoring in his basket with the remnants of breakfast peppered across his snowy whiskers.

'Just you and me now, old man,' she said.

Perhaps it was all for the best. After all, if Ted were alive, he'd be turning in his grave.

~

Twice a week, the more adventurous ladies of Jacaranda Retirement Village disrobed together in the cramped changing room at the indoor pool. Peggy always fought to disguise her embarrassment, ensuring her gaze remained at eye-level. It was hard to reconcile the abundance of naked flesh with her mother's preaching about modesty. Sheila Martin was the only woman to have apparently shared Peggy's draconian upbringing, hiding inside a locked cubicle to change, like a Victorian lady in her beach bathing machine.

Aqua aerobics was the ultimate leveller, a reprieve from the politics and power games of village life. Here in the communal changing room, the women stood shoulder to shoulder in their unmentionables – practical, cotton, in every shade of white, with industrial-strength reinforcement as standard. Peggy had always recognised the licence to wear sensible undergarments with impunity as one of the unexpected bonuses of ageing.

Comfy undies. Big undies. The kind that came in packs of three.

With all her decent pairs still drying on the line, Peggy hid her back-of-the-drawer smalls beneath her folded outerwear. Over time, they'd turned a nondescript grey but with the elastic still fully functional, she couldn't bring herself to consign them to landfill on the basis of aesthetics alone. Her swimsuit wasn't much better, the black fabric beginning to bag around the bottom, where the Lycra had disintegrated. It still covered the essentials, however, and if anything the expanding fabric was becoming more comfortable with each wear. Besides, Peggy wasn't in a hurry to replace the decrepit garment. She hated shopping. Underwear was challenging enough, but swimwear was in a league of its own. Nothing fitted, no matter what the label claimed. This one had been dubbed a Miraclesuit. The miracle was that she hadn't taken it back to the shop and demanded an immediate refund for false advertising. She wrapped a towel around her waist to disguise her drooping tail and tiptoed across the wet tiles towards the pool. On the dot of ten o'clock, Peggy Smart surrendered her aches and pains to the weightlessness of the warm water.

'Okay ladies, let's get started. Grab yourself a noodle and space out.'

Everyone loved the young instructor, Libby. None of the women could aspire to her lithe figure, but it made a change from the dimpled delights of the changing room. Libby was happy to share snippets of her life with the Aqua group: the unreliable boyfriends and exotic travel plans, along with dreams of motherhood. Peggy found it a refreshing change from the usual ailment one-upmanship.

Mavis Peacock bobbed past with a pink foam noodle. 'Morning, Peggy,' she said. 'Did you get my message about the Meet-and-Greet on Friday?'

As guaranteed Brian-time, it was already marked in gold glitter on the calendar. Peggy relished every opportunity to portray the role of an active, intelligent woman, magnanimously engaged in the running of village affairs. A modern woman. And the creator of the most renowned baked goods.

'Let's start with some jogging on the spot.' Libby bounced on the side of the pool, her pert body defying gravity at every landing. Mavis led from the front of the class as usual, creating giant whirlpools with her breasts. Sheila Martin, her sparrow's frame lacking in natural buoyancy, clung to a noodle for dear life.

Libby jogged over to her iPod and turned up the volume. 'Come on ladies, let's get those arms going.' She clapped her hands above her head and sang along, inviting them all to walk on sunshine. The taut muscles in her upper arms tensed with each clap.

Peggy's shoulder crunched, and she changed to a muted applause at chest height.

Mavis bounced herself level with Peggy. 'We have several new residents this month,' she said. With her flapping wings gaining momentum, Mavis looked set to take flight.

'Noodles under the arms now, on your backs and kick up those toes!'

'I'll put you down for the nibbles?' Mavis had a way with rhetoricals.

'I wouldn't miss it for the world,' said Peggy. *Was that a little too obvious?*

'Come on ladies! Kick, kick, kick.'

'It's good to know we can count on you to take care of the kitchen. There are a number of new female residents this time, and with so few men as usual, I've asked Jim Wilde and Brian Cornell to act as social hosts for the evening. To entertain the single ladies.'

Peggy stopped kicking. The thought of her Brian cosying up to some unattached baby-boomer while she slaved away in the kitchen made her lose her footing. Before she knew it, she was sinking, her toes scrambling for something solid. The distorted music echoed. Ribbons of sunlight marbled the tranquil blue water that folded around her like a blanket. How easy it would be to stop fighting and slip away. Like Ted.

All around her were the pale thighs of women just like her, pedalling imaginary bicycles in the chlorine. Outside the pool, they bickered and gossiped; laughed and swapped photos of their grandchildren. Down here, they were all treading water.

But after four years of struggling to stay afloat, Peggy was tired. Sometimes she wondered if it would be easier to succumb. The grandkids would be sad, but they would still have Grandma Geraldine and Grandpa Mike. Her son, David and daughter, Jenny, would no doubt put up a good show of grief, only to find consolation in her will, for what it was worth. And what about Brian? Would he even notice she'd gone?

'I haven't seen Peggy around in a while,' he might say. Eventually.

The last bubbles escaped from the corner of Peggy's mouth. She pictured her overdue library book, and the wet clothes still sitting in the washing machine. No, she wasn't ready to go yet. Peggy kicked and torpedoed to the surface.

'I was thinking vol-au-vents,' shouted the oblivious Mavis above the music, as Peggy breached with a splutter. 'And something with smoked salmon if you can manage it.'

Peggy imagined herself shoving a creamy mushroom vol-au-vent into Mavis's face and saying, 'Would you like to try the smoked salmon too?' Instead she retrieved her errant noodle between coughs and managed a smile. 'How about mini sausage rolls?'

Libby removed her tracksuit top, revealing a skimpy singlet. Her pert breasts stood to attention like two steamed puddings. 'Alright ladies, now this one's good for the old pelvic floor,' she said, bending the noodle in half and placing it between her honey-coloured thighs. 'As we all know, it's important to keep our pelvic floors toned as we get older. It's great for the love life.'

Peggy imagined that Libby had an excellent pelvic floor. But then, she hadn't given birth to two 9-pound babies. Not yet anyway. She could go on bus trips without the slightest anxiety about the next stop, or book the window seat on a plane.

'Focus on lifting up your pelvic floor, drawing up inside, tightening around your front and back passages.' Libby lay on her back, demonstrating. 'In and out, in and out.' Her thighs squeezed the noodle in time to the music.

This is ludicrous, thought Peggy. Every one of us over seventy, in our tummy-control swimsuits, concentrating hard on mythical muscles in the hope of a better love life.

Libby was gaining momentum with her noodle now. 'Imagine you are holding on to a full bladder . . .'

Not difficult, I'm always holding on to a full bladder. Or at least trying to.

. . . and wind at the same time.'

A titter rose inside Peggy and escaped through her nose. Behind her, she heard chuckling. Someone let out a snigger. Peggy tried to stifle the impatient giggles. Mavis's concerted efforts to recruit her sagging perineum only made it more comical. Soon, they were all in stitches. Eventually, Peggy noticed the corner of Mavis's mouth begin to twitch. Her eyes widened before she too guffawed.

Creased with laughter, Peggy's face ached, and her thighs burned as she clamped her knees together. Abandoned noodles floated away like beans in a minestrone. Peggy hadn't laughed like this in years. She hadn't dared to. Swept along in a moment of sisterhood, the women howled and roared, leaving the nubile Libby floundering on the poolside like an upturned beetle.

~

The Aqua girls were still laughing back in the changing room. There was an awkward moment when, slithering out of her one-piece, Mavis lost her balance and almost fell into Peggy's lap. It was a close encounter of the uninvited kind and saw Peggy marking out her territory with her elbows. It was hard to get completely dry in such a confined space. With all that wriggling and gyrating, it was like some new style of interpretive dance. Talcum powder scented the air like cathedral incense. The whole thing felt bizarrely spiritual. A sacred bonding of elders, a celebration of womanhood, wisdom and the ability to laugh at the absurdity of their lives.

She remembered an article she'd read at the hairdresser's last week. *Why women need women friends.* Something to do with oxytocin, the hormone that bonded breastfeeding mothers to their babies. It supposedly reduced inflammation in the body and produced feelings of calmness, contentment and empathy. Jacaranda Retirement Village could certainly do with more of all three.

Yet for all that the nipple-tweaking sisterhood had to offer, what Peggy really missed was intimacy, a deeper connection with another human. She'd met so many people since she'd moved to the village, but none of them had progressed beyond the foam noodles, a mince pie at Christmas or a please-pass-the-popcorn at movie nights. Even her fellow committee members were little more than pleasant acquaintances. Sadly, that included Brian.

2

God's Waiting Room

PEGGY SCREWED THE LID ONTO THE ANCHOVY JAR AND wiped her hands on the bath towel. What on earth had she done with that sterile specimen container? She made a mental note to check the fridge, followed by the microwave. It was one of many items that had gone missing recently. No sooner would she put something down, than it would vanish into thin air. If she didn't know better, Peggy would swear that someone was creeping into her unit and deliberately hiding things. Her reading glasses were the worst, turning up in the most unlikely places, including perched on the top of her head or in one or other of her hands. On the plus side, having sacrificed the jar, at least there'd be Nicoise salad to look forward to tonight. Peggy couldn't bear to throw the remaining fishy carcasses away. She hated wasting food and was good at improvising, especially when it came to discretionary items such as anchovies. Potatoes, eggs and tinned tuna. Quite an indulgence for a Tuesday.

The path from the ensuite suggested a herd of wildebeest had migrated to the bathroom during the night rather than a pair of size 7 sheepskin slippers. Peggy considered buying a new rug to disguise the wear. Ted would have disapproved. He could never see the point in superfluous soft furnishings. But he was gone now, along with the pile in the carpet.

Peggy wrapped the tiny glass bottle in tissues and hid it in the bottom of her handbag. The last thing she needed was to bump into Brian carrying her mid-stream sample.

The hill seemed much steeper than usual and Peggy stopped to catch her breath halfway. Ahead, a team of removalists was lugging furniture down a ramp from a large van into an empty ground floor unit. A cube-shaped man balancing an oversized velvet sofa across one shoulder smiled at Peggy as she stepped into the road to pass the van.

'Morning, love,' he said.

Peggy wasn't sure whether to be flattered or offended. She was so used to being ignored, he'd caught her completely off guard. 'You shouldn't park across the footpath. It's very dangerous for someone of my age,' she said.

His face dropped. Immediately, she regretted the outburst. He was only trying to be friendly. Grumpy old fool, he must be thinking.

The slope flattened out in front of the community centre. As the hub of the village, it was where residents exchanged pleasantries and tittle-tattle in equal measure. The manicured foyer was brochure perfect, but Peggy was yet to meet anyone who matched the airbrushed seniors in the adverts. Brian was the exception. He was hot. Positively gas mark 7 in Peggy's oven.

On the far side of the community centre was the medical clinic. For Peggy, the convenience only marginally outweighed Dr Szczpanski's bedside manner. Or lack thereof. She would have asked David to take her back to the old family GP, Dr Steele, but she'd already outlived him.

The waiting room was heaving. Silver-headed residents lined the walls like strings of Christmas baubles. Some looked like they'd been waiting for decades.

Sheila Martin glowered from behind a planter box in the far corner of the waiting room. It was best not to react. The committee secretary had friends in high places, and the last thing Peggy wanted was a repeat of the infamous Scrabble Night that split the village.

The air was stuffy, making Peggy warm and woozy. She needed somewhere to sit, preferably before she ended up on the floor.

'Here, be my guest.'

Peggy turned to see Brian stand and offer his seat. Her heart paused then booted her behind the ribs. She knew all about Brian's knees. They'd spent several delicious minutes at the last residents' committee meeting comparing their joint replacements. Naturally, a professional man like Brian had had both his knees replaced in a private hospital under a double-barrelled surgeon. On the other hand, Peggy had gone public for hers. Her specialist had had only one surname, and she'd shared a bay with another lady who screamed all night. But for all the minor inconvenience, Peggy was grateful to go home with a perfectly serviceable hinge joint. She was still waiting patiently for the other.

'I couldn't possibly,' said Peggy.

'I insist,' said Brian, waving a blushing Peggy towards his seat. 'I always stand for a lady.'

Peggy forgot to breathe.

In his paisley bow tie, Brian looked particularly distinguished today. Judging by the other admiring looks, Peggy wasn't the only one who thought so. The venom in Sheila Martin's glare seeped like mustard gas from behind the dusty ficus leaves. Again, Peggy pretended not to notice.

It wasn't as if she'd planned to fall for Brian. In fact, lust had been the last thing on her mind when she began the 1000-piece jigsaw depicting a Venetian gondola. It was a rainy afternoon in the residents' lounge and she'd been concentrating on straight edges for several minutes when, without warning, someone leaned over and slotted a three-tab into her Bridge of Sighs. Outraged, Peggy steeled herself to rebuke the perpetrator only to discover, magnified through his varifocals, the limpid blue eyes of Brian Cornell. Widower. Chartered accountant, she later discovered. Lexus driver.

All of a dither, Peggy had dropped the top right-hand corner. It tumbled under the table and was never found. Someone later crossed out 1000 pieces on the outside of the puzzle box, and wrote 999 instead. It was as though she'd been looking for that missing piece ever since. That Brian-shaped piece to complete her puzzle.

'Why don't you squeeze in here next to me?' said Mavis Peacock, shuffling to one side. Brian declined with a polite wave and turned his attention to an emergency evacuation notice on the wall.

'Is she running late again?' asked Peggy, hoping to engage Brian in small talk as she settled in his vacated chair. The heat from the fabric travelled up through her like flames from a fire. She felt something ripple inside, and wondered if she might need the bathroom again.

'Dr Cranky-Pantski isn't even here yet,' said Celia Davenport from behind *The Senior.* 'Some of us have better things to do than waste our precious last hours waiting for that sourpuss to arrive.'

'What do you have on that's so important?' said Mavis, her school principal voice shrill above the chatter. 'More spark plugs to polish?'

Celia rustled her paper between her oil-stained fingers. She muttered something just out of Mavis's earshot that made Brian grin. Peggy liked Celia. She was a straightforward bread-and-butter kind of woman. Rumour had it that the young Lady Celia, faced with a debutante ball and the obligatory season of social niceties designed to find her a suitable husband, had taken the boat train from London Waterloo to Southampton and set sail for Australia instead. Cut off from her inheritance, she'd trained as a mechanic and made something of a name for herself in mobile tractor repairs.

Peggy often wondered what such a robust-looking woman as Celia needed to see a doctor about. Brian too. She glanced him over, searching for clues. Hopefully it was just a check-up. At our age, she thought, you could never have too many check-ups.

Heads swivelled as the village manager, Christine, appeared in the waiting area. She always looked like she'd stepped out of a catalogue. 'Ladies and gentleman, Dr Szczpanski won't be coming today after all,' she announced.

A Mexican wave of disgruntlement skirted the waiting area.

'My appointment was at ten o'clock,' said Mavis, closing the zip of her handbag with a huff. 'This simply isn't on.'

'But,' Christine continued, smiling through her perfect make-up, 'I'd like to introduce Dr Stephen Lim to you all. He'll be taking over as our regular GP here at Jacaranda Retirement Village, on Tuesday and Thursday mornings. I hope you'll make him feel welcome.' Behind her stood a young man wearing dark-framed spectacles and an open-necked shirt.

Dr Lim followed Christine into the consulting room, carrying a large black doctor's bag. He looked very young to be a doctor. Anyone would after old Dr Steele.

Mavis turned to the lady next to her. 'I'm not sure about having a male doctor. They're not very good at listening.'

'Who'd want to listen to your whingeing?' Celia folded *The Senior* and crossed her arms. 'I don't care, as long as he knows his stuff.'

'But what about more . . . intimate problems?' said Mavis in a stage whisper.

'He's a doctor, not the bank manager,' said Celia.

Peggy caught Brian's eye. He winked and stifled a chuckle. Peggy's amusement was tinged with apprehension, however, as she too contemplated handing her anchovy jar to a stranger barely out of puberty. She opened her book and tried not to think about what lay ahead.

The smell of toasted sandwiches from the coffee shop distracted Peggy from her paperback, just as she was reaching the good bit. It must be nearly lunchtime and she was the only one left in the waiting room. Peggy folded over the corner of her page in anticipation. She'd read this particular one so many times already, she knew it almost by heart, which was just as well, having once again mislaid her specs. *White Coat Rogue. Six-foot-three of chiselled jaw and smouldering blue eyes, world-famous cardiothoracic surgeon Dr Sebastian McBride spends his life mending hearts, and breaking them.* It wasn't like that in real life, but every woman needed a little escapism.

'Peggy Smart?' Dr Lim stood in the doorway, smiling straight at her.

She stuffed the book into her bag and, after rocking backwards and forwards, gained enough momentum to stand up. The doctor's hand was smooth and warm as Peggy shook it, like a child's.

'My name is Dr Lim, but you can call me Stephen if you prefer.'

Peggy considered this for a moment. He looked even younger close up, like he'd borrowed his father's spectacles. There was a pimple on his chin. She was old enough to be his grandmother. What a strange world she was living in. Every year, her generation was left further and further behind as time accelerated away. Yet here was the perfect opportunity to demonstrate she could move with the stampeding times.

'Thank you, Dr Stephen.' The words seemed perfectly natural on her lips. 'Call me Peggy.'

'Okay. How can I help?'

Peggy retrieved the tiny glass jar from the depths of her bag, unwrapped the tissues and placed it gingerly on the desk. The sample was past a Chardonnay and verging on a Vermouth. She couldn't meet the young doctor's gaze, as if it were a severed limb sitting there, and braced herself for the inevitable antibiotic that would do little more than make her nauseated for seven days. Why couldn't she just say it, have the confidence to ask for help instead of hoping that a miracle would somehow stumble across her? She was a grown woman, a mother of two – three if she included Basil – and a grandmother, but old habits were hard to break.

Dr Stephen cleared his throat and fell silent. He inspected the computer screen, using his mouse to click between pages of Peggy's medical records. After several minutes, the doctor sat back, balancing his elbows on the armrests, delicate fingers tented in front of his face.

'Being a doctor is a little like being a detective,' he said. 'It's all about looking for clues.'

'Like *Midsomer Murders*, you mean?'

'In a way, yes.'

The clues were all there. The curled toes, the bitten lip, the wringing of hands. Not to mention the glass jar on the desk.

'The diagnosis is all in the history. It's the first thing I learned as a medical student.'

Peggy was worried. History had never been her strong subject. Ted had liked to watch endless documentaries about the wars: the World Wars, the American Civil War and the Vietnam War. 'I'm more a geography girl, really,' she said.

Dr Stephen cleared his throat. 'No, I mean in the history of the complaint. When it first started, what makes it better, what makes it worse. That kind of thing.'

'Yes, of course.'

'Let's go back to the beginning. How long have you been having trouble with your waterworks?'

A series of ugly scenes popped up like bubbles from Peggy's subconscious. She pushed them away.

I will not feel sorry for myself. I will not break down in front of this lovely young man.

'As long as I can remember. I've always been different to other people. My mother used to punish me for my accidents when I was a child, which only made it worse. She told me I was defective, that there was something wrong with me.'

'And you've never had any treatment for it?'

'I've been too embarrassed to tell anyone until now. I assumed my mother was right and that I must be some sort of freak. I suppose I just learned to hide it.'

'That must have been very hard for you, suffering in silence all these years.'

'I must have done a good enough job, pretending to be normal. Enough to get married and raise two children, that is. Unfortunately, it all went downhill once I hit the mental-pause.' Along with everything else: the palpitations, the sweats that saw her changing the sheets every morning and the hot flushes that rose out of nowhere and erupted across her neck and chest. Poor Ted must have felt as if he was living with an impostor, the body of the woman he married inhabited by a sweaty stranger who would fly off the handle at the slightest setback.

In spite of herself, Peggy felt a tear breach and trickle down one cheek. Dr Stephen handed her a box of tissues and she blew her nose with a honk. Why, after all these years, was she worrying about it now? Was it something to do with meeting Brian? If the plucky heroines in her paperbacks were anything to go by, modern women were much more forward than her generation. She was the one who needed to make the move. But somehow, a giant absorbent pad had soaked up all her confidence.

Dr Stephen passed the wastepaper bin and listened as

Peggy told her story. By the time she got to the part about losing Ted, the bin was full of soggy tissues.

'I'm so sorry. I'm not usually this overemotional.'

Dr Stephen placed his hand over Peggy's. 'I'd like to help you,' he said. 'If you're willing to trust me.'

Peggy nodded. What choice did she have? For the first time in her life, there was a glimmer of hope.

'I'm not promising anything, but there are things we can try,' said Dr Stephen.

Peggy leaned forward in her chair, poised for the magical formula that would transform her from a self-conscious old lady with a shameful secret into a confident mature woman who could stay out of the bathroom long enough to ask Brian over for dinner.

'I'm ready,' she said.

'Good. First, I'll need to examine you.'

Peggy swallowed. *Examine her?* She presumed he wasn't referring to a quick peek at her tonsils. Hell's bells, she hadn't been expecting this, but as Celia had pointed out, he was a doctor, not the bank manager.

By the time the doctor snapped off his gloves into the pedal bin, Peggy had mentally rearranged the terracotta pots on her patio and decided on a new outdoor setting for under the mini-pergola. She'd planned her trip to the garden centre, the one where she could sit in the café amidst the seed packets and weatherproof knick-knacks.

When he'd finished, Dr Stephen left the curtains discreetly drawn while Peggy dressed.

She was worried she'd taken up enough of the doctor's time already, so she balled her pantyhose and shoved them into her handbag on top of *White Coat Rogue* before taking her seat once more.

'Do I need an operation?' She hated hospitals, especially after what had happened to Ted. 'Only I overheard Marjorie Cousins in the changing room talking about a vaginacologist she'd consulted. Apparently, he'd promised her the pelvic floor of a Romanian gymnast.'

'I'm afraid surgery won't fix this.' Dr Stephen went on to explain, in detail, the affliction that was surprisingly common and nothing to be ashamed of.

'You mean I'm not alone?' It wasn't the sort of thing Peggy had ever thought to discuss over morning tea.

Dr Stephen gave her a wry smile and handed her a booklet. There were some anatomical diagrams and enough technical jargon to suggest she might need a lawyer rather than a doctor. On the front page, a grey-haired couple were riding bicycles. But for the toothpaste-commercial smiles, they could have been her and Brian.

'One in three women experience incontinence at some stage in their lives. You'd be surprised how many young women suffer too. I see it all the time.'

'One in three?' Peggy mentally scanned the busy waiting room she'd just sat in. Which of her fellow residents were hiding the same embarrassing affliction?

'I want you to see a specialist continence adviser. Here's her phone number.' Dr Stephen handed over a business card. *Sister Slack*. Peggy was already dubious. The biggest challenge would be keeping a straight face.

'Thank you for being so kind.' Peggy only just refrained from hugging the young doctor. Instead, she pumped his hand and dabbed at a fresh crop of tears.

Back in the waiting room, Peggy opened her handbag to check on her hastily concealed hosiery. The paperback tumbled out and, bending over to retrieve it, Peggy tipped the entire handbag upside down, sending the contents spilling onto the floor. She managed to rescue her wallet and keys, but the pantyhose made a dash for freedom and rolled across the carpet. With her vision still foggy from the tears, Peggy's fingers fumbled in vain over the pattern in the carpet.

'Here,' said a woman's voice. 'You dropped these.'

Someone pushed the balled-up pantyhose into Peggy's hand, followed by *White Coat Rogue*. An icy finger traced its way down Peggy's spine. She shivered with the cool chill of recognition.

Peggy's heart broke into a canter like a startled colt.

After all these years.

Could it really be her?

Angie.

3

The Latchkey Crisis

DISCOMBOBULATED. IT WAS PEGGY'S FAVOURITE WORD, AND twenty-five Scrabble points. She was still waiting for the perfect moment to drop it into conversation with Brian and impress him with her vocabulary.

'Are you alright?'

'Hmm?' Peggy couldn't remember how she came to be standing in the middle of the foyer. She looked around, searching for clues in the silk flower arrangements and framed watercolours.

Where am I?

Christine led her towards a chair, guiding her gently by the shoulder. 'Here we go. Sit down for a moment and gather yourself.'

Gather yourself. Re-combobulate yourself. Find the missing pieces and pull them together, quickly. The last thing she needed to appear was vague. Peggy put on her most un-vague face and smiled at Christine. 'I love your jacket,' she said.

Christine frowned. 'Would you like me to call David?'

There was no pulling the cotton wool over her eyes. 'No, I'll be fine,' said Peggy.

'Jenny? Shall I call Jenny then?'

'No! Definitely not Jenny.' Not her daughter. She couldn't risk it. A single concerned phone call from Christine and the next thing she knew, Jenny would be turning up and taking her for a 'little drive', never to return. Peggy would find herself parked in an aged-care facility with a cup of tea and a shortbread finger in time for *Antiques Roadshow*.

'Shall I ask Dr Lim to check you over?'

'I've just come from seeing him,' said Peggy, clutching her pamphlet and the contact details for the bladder lady.

'Do you think you might be having a *mini-stroke*?'

Christine had dropped her voice, but they were within hearing-aid distance of the coffee queue. News of Peggy Smart's 'turn' would be all over the village by afternoon tea. This place was like Bletchley Park when it came to secrets.

'I'm fine.' *Try harder, but not too hard.* 'I've had a bit of a shock, that's all.' In truth, Peggy wasn't sure what had been the greater shock: stripping off her not-so-smalls for someone young enough to be her grandson, or hearing that voice again.

Angie Valentine. International jetsetter. Fabulous fashionista. A glamorous career woman who'd worked for *Vogue*. Peggy had read an article about her in a magazine a few years ago. At first, she'd been excited to see the familiar face again, and while the podiatrist's receptionist was on a call, Peggy had torn out the page and kept it. She must have tucked it into her diary and eventually thrown it out, because she hadn't thought of Angie again for a long, long time. Until today. What would someone like Angie Valentine be doing at such an utterly un-glamorous and un-international place as Jacaranda Retirement Village?

Christine offered Peggy a glass of water. Why did people do that? It was the very last thing she needed, the mere sight of the clear liquid enough to curl her toes.

'How about I run you back to your unit?'

Please, no. Anything but the golf buggy. That really was the beginning of the slippery end.

'I'm feeling much better now, thank you. I think I'll head home and let Basil out. Before he starts to worry.'

Christine glanced from side to side then leaned closer to Peggy.

'I thought I'd give you the heads up about a tiny issue that's come to light,' she whispered, measuring the scale of the problem between her thumb and index finger.

There was no such thing as a tiny issue in Jacaranda Retirement Village. World wars had started over less. 'What issue?'

'It's about Basil. There has been a complaint.'

Peggy's hackles rose. 'What kind of complaint?' The poor little Shih Tzu was deaf and virtually blind. He only ever left the unit to cock his leg and he rarely barked, except at the postman.

'Well, it came in the form of a request for clarification of the rules regarding pets.'

'What sort of rules?'

'Health and safety.'

How on earth could Basil threaten anyone's health or safety? Peggy knew the day would come when she'd have to put him to sleep. She'd always assumed David would take her to the vet's, but he was so busy these days, with work and the children. Being married to Mel was a full-time job in itself. She could always ask Jenny. But her daughter lived so far away in the country. Peggy knew the journey well. It was a six-hour round trip, with fourteen toilet stops.

'I don't understand. When I moved into my unit, I was told I could keep Basil until he died.'

'The wording was that you could keep Basil as long as no-one *complained*.' Christine tilted her head in corporate sympathy. 'Someone's complained.'

'Who?'

'I'm not at liberty to say. You will receive an official letter in due course, but suffice it to say, unless the residents' committee votes otherwise at the next meeting, Basil is on notice.'

'Notice?'

'Of eviction.'

'How long?'

'Four weeks.'

~

The automatic doors stalled as Peggy stormed towards them. She backed up a couple of steps and waved her arms at the sensor until they opened. Hot air blew through the foyer like a hairdryer. There was a chorus of grumbles from the coffee shop.

Grumpy so-and-sos.

Sometimes she hated this place, regretted selling the family home so soon after Ted died. Jenny's words haunted her. 'Think of all the activities, Mum,' she'd said. 'And lots of other people your own age.'

That was just the problem. The cavalcade of walking frames was a constant nod to her own mortality. It was like waiting for a train, one that may not come for years, or thunder through without warning. She was in limbo: too old to be young, and too young to be old.

The wind was getting up as Peggy crossed the car park. It blew grit into her eyes and throat, making her cough. *Poor Basil.* What cold-hearted person would complain about an innocent pooch? She'd make him a special dinner tonight. Mince and potatoes. His favourite.

At her front door, Peggy thrust her hand into her handbag and searched for the key. She shook the bag a couple of times, listening for the jingle. Where was it?

With growing irritation, she discarded the bulkier items into a little pile at her feet. Pantyhose. Wallet. Dog-eared paperback. Reading glasses ... *so that's where they went.* No key.

A familiar tingle in her bladder invited her to hurry. Basil scratched on the other side of the door, his urgency to get out matching hers to get in. Peggy checked the inside pockets and bounced on her heels to distract herself.

With the lining of the handbag clearly visible and no key in sight, Peggy contemplated relieving herself in the gardenias like Basil often did in the mornings. She half-jogged and wiggled on the spot, clenched her jaw and rifled through all the outside pockets of her bag.

Nothing.

Peggy sensed someone behind her.

Please go away, whoever you are.

'I think you dropped these.'

Peggy turned to see Brian walking towards her. 'I've been calling after you all the way from the car park, but you mustn't have heard me.'

Of all people, not Brian.

'Thank you.' Peggy snatched the keys from his hand and smiled, her back teeth clamped together. Brian hesitated. Was he waiting for an invitation to come inside or worried she'd contracted lockjaw? Peggy pictured the fruit loaf on the cooling rack next to the kettle. It would be lovely with a cup of tea, and Brian.

She put the key into the lock. There followed spasm upon spasm, each more demanding than the last. She couldn't hang on any longer.

'Sorry Brian, I have to dash.'

Brian's dark eyebrows twitched in confusion. His hair, what little was left of it, was completely white, yet strangely, his brows had kept their colour. Peggy risked a split second to picture him as a handsome young man.

'Well, then,' said Brian. 'I'll leave you to it.'

He tipped his Panama hat and walked away.

4

Sweet or Dry?

HOW WAS IT THAT FROM THE SHELVES OF HER LARDER, Peggy could conjure up dozens of potential dishes, each with exciting flavour combinations, and yet when it came to putting clothes together, her mind went completely blank? Her wardrobe resembled the racks at Vinnies, so stuffed with mismatched garments it was impossible to distinguish one piece from another, let alone pull together an actual outfit.

It was all too hard. No wonder some folk in the village gave up and wandered around in nighties or pyjamas. Why couldn't she be one of those women who always got it right? Forget that, Peggy Smart would settle for occasionally, even once in her life, getting it right. Naturally stylish, fashion-conscious women like Angie Valentine seemed to know instinctively what suited their figure and what went with what. It must be in their DNA, Angie part of a subspecies of women who were genetically predisposed to pick just the right accessories for an elegant and sophisticated look. Not like a bag lady or a drag queen.

The advice was all there in *Women's Weekly*: dress for your body shape, mix and match key pieces, avoid horizontal stripes. One article had suggested the over sixties avoid black except for a funeral. She'd been to a few of those since she moved to the village. In fact, she'd met more people at wakes than Happy Hour. On the plus side, mourners nowadays were often invited to wear the favourite colour of the deceased. With such an active funeral scene at the village, it explained the kaleidoscope of primary colours at one end of her otherwise neutral wardrobe.

Hearing Drive Time on the radio in the kitchen, Peggy started to panic. Time was running out. There were still the canapés to prepare for tonight's Meet-and-Greet. She had to hurry, but the open wardrobe was an impenetrable jungle standing between her and the salmon blinis.

Basil watched her from the bed, paws outstretched like a snowy sphinx.

'Please tell me what to wear.'

She longed for Ted to pick something out, zip her up and tell her she looked fabulous. With him, she could wear a potato sack and still have his rose-tinted approval.

Peggy closed her eyes and plunged her hand into the wall of clothes. Whatever came out, she would wear. Add a squirt of perfume and be done with it. Besides, with Brian busy entertaining the single ladies, he would be too busy to notice her.

After the incident with the key, Peggy wasn't ready to face him yet anyway.

~

The kitchenette at the function centre was broiling. Rivulets of sweat ran down Peggy's neck and soaked the wad of tissues stuffed in her cleavage. At first, the plunging neckline hadn't worried her. The dress she'd plucked from the rail was a passable colour, though she couldn't recall which of her deceased acquaintances had loved royal blue. Squeezing her flesh into the fabric reminded Peggy of massaging the icing to the tip of a piping bag. Thankfully, the dress still covered her knees.

Things took a turn for the worse, however, once she set to work in the kitchen. The dress seemed to shrink in the steamy heat. Now vacuum-packed around her body, the clingy material rode up her damp thighs with each step. Suddenly, Peggy was fearful of greeting the new residents with more than just a savoury nibble. There was no way she could risk bumping into Brian looking like this. She would have to hide in the kitchen all evening.

'You've outdone yourself as usual.' Jim Wilde swiped a vol-au-vent from the platter. Wherever there was free food or a well-turned ankle on display, he could be relied on to push the boundaries.

'Hey, hands off, they're for the new residents.'

'Are you sure you won't marry me, Deidre?' Jim popped the entire pastry case in his mouth and winked.

'Thank you for your kind offer as always, but no.'

Not in a million years.

Jim was perfectly harmless, terrible with names but that was part of his charm. He was one of the livelier ones in the village. He had a trim figure for a man of his age, and an expensive set of veneers. In his jeans and leather jacket, he looked every bit the ageing rock star, exactly what he was. His dodgy hearing and ashtray voice were testament to a life lived at both full speed and full volume. Sadly, the only singing he did nowadays was in the shower. His long-suffering neighbours called it 'Jim's water music', though the tunes were more Hendrix than Handel.

'I do love Meet-and-Greet night,' said Jim, pinching another vol-au-vent. He smouldered from beneath his whiskery eyebrows. With an Elvis-curl of his top lip, Jim not-so-Wilde-anymore swaggered away, crooning to himself. He paused after a couple of steps to rub the back of his leg. Poor Jim. His plumbago must be playing up again. Peggy wondered how many other women he would call Deidre tonight.

From her vantage point at the serving hatch, Peggy watched the residents arrive in ones and twos. Early arrivals included Mavis, resplendent in cerise, and Sheila Martin, scurrying behind in navy blue. For some reason, Peggy thought of David Attenborough. *See how the stork rides on the back of the oblivious water buffalo.* She shoved a vol-au-vent into her grin.

The place was filling fast. Jim took up position at the door and triaged the arrivals into single women and couples, passing the latter on to Mavis to entertain. With the usual dearth of unattached males, new or otherwise, he was taking full advantage of his novelty. Peggy was torn between watching the spectacle unfold and attending to her catering duties. It was fascinating, watching a true pro like Jim in action, scanning the room for his next prey. Again, David Attenborough sprang to mind.

Celia walked in as Peggy took a breather between batches of sausage rolls. She'd ditched her perennial overalls for a pair of jeans and a clean T-shirt and Peggy imagined her as a young woman, raising eyebrows astride her beloved motorcycle. They were of the same vintage and both surprisingly well preserved for their age, but it was the machine's throaty roar that quickened men's pulses these days rather than the runaway debutante.

Heading straight for the serving hatch, she announced, 'I need a drink.'

'Make yourself useful and pass round the sherries.' Peggy nodded towards a tray with rows of identical glasses. 'Sweet on the left. Dry on the right.'

'Right-o. Might polish off a couple of these myself first. Bloody clutch went on the Enfield. What a bore. Sometimes I think the old girl's more trouble than she's worth.'

Celia lived a few doors away, and Peggy was accustomed to the revving noises. Bits of disembowelled engine spilled from Celia's garage and often littered the front path. No-one seemed to object. To Peggy's surprise, Brian appeared more interested than most. She'd spotted him on numerous occasions, stopping outside the garage to admire Celia's stripped-down parts.

With a tray of savoury tartlets browning in the oven, Peggy sneaked another peek through the hatch. The Clubhouse was full now. There was no sign of Brian. Relieved, Peggy plated the last of the hot sausage rolls and filled her own glass with the dregs from the sherry bottle. The glass was millimetres from her lips when Sheila appeared in the doorway.

'Mavis says we need more smoked salmon, and can you bring out the vol-au-vents now?'

Peggy mumbled something about slaves and handed Sheila the sausage rolls instead. 'We've run out of salmon.'

Sheila made a noise through her nose. She looked as if she'd been to the hairdresser in preparation for tonight, and Peggy could swear she saw the freshly permed curls tighten against her scalp.

It was all very well for Mavis, demanding gourmet finger food on a party-pie budget. Peggy hated being taken for granted and vowed to say something at the next committee meeting. Would Brian, as treasurer, back her up?

Half Peggy's bodyweight seemed to have precipitated around her ankles over the course of the evening. Leaning against the work surface, she inspected the swollen flesh, trussed up like a butcher's joint by her strappy sandals.

Cankles, as Sam and Emily liked to call them, meaning where calves and ankles blend into one. *Granny's cankles*. Peggy scooped the last spoonful of creamy mushroom mix into her mouth and washed it down with a sip of sherry.

Washing up piled neatly on the draining board, Peggy wiped her hands and then her face on the tea towel. The Clubhouse had fallen eerily silent. Peggy poked her head through the hatch to see what was happening. There, silhouetted in the doorway, was a figure in a long floaty dress. Peggy couldn't make out who it was at first, but as a breeze caught the diaphanous sleeves, she saw an angel.

A hand reached inside and wrung out Peggy's guts like an old rag. Any remaining doubt evaporated. The woman in the waiting room, the one who had witnessed her tear-streaked face and handled her pantyhose, was unmistakably the very same Angie she'd once known.

Peggy glimpsed her own steamy reflection in the metal tea urn, and panicked. Her cheeks were ruddy and there were two giant damp patches under her arms. This wasn't how she wanted to meet someone like Angie again, after more than fifty years. Not if she was going to retain any shred of self-respect.

The thrum of conversation resumed, punctuated by that strained laughter of awkward social events. Peggy peeped through the hatch again but saw only Mavis brandishing a half-eaten sausage roll as she talked at a new couple. There was no sign of Angie. And still no Brian.

Her sigh of relief was only half-exhaled when the crowd parted. Heading straight towards her was the beautiful, confident and self-assured Angie. In an instant, Peggy's crippling insecurity and jealousy were back, as bruising as if not a day had passed.

The angel was almost at the hatch when Jim swept in from stage left, separating her from the crowd, like a Kelpie mustering sheep.

Bless you Jim Wilde, you horny old goat.

There was still time to slip away without being noticed. Before Brian arrived. Before Angie recognised her.

5

The Sugar-free Pill

'I INSIST, DAVID,' SAID PEGGY. 'I ALWAYS MAKE SAM'S
birthday cake.'

'We couldn't ask you to do it again this year, Mum.'

'It's no trouble at all. I thought I'd do a pink sponge with
buttercream icing this time.'

The recipe was there in front of her on the kitchen table.
She'd already written a shopping list on the back of Dr
Stephen's pamphlet. In glitter gold.

'It sounds . . . lovely. But Mel is quite adamant that you
shouldn't go to the trouble. She thinks it would be too much
for you.'

'It almost sounds like she doesn't want me to make
it.' Peggy dangled a buttered crust for Basil. The old dog
surveyed it with his good eye before giving it a dismissive
sniff. He sighed and waddled back to his basket.

'Mum, you're being oversensitive again. It's just that she
had something different in mind this year.'

'I'm assuming I am actually invited to my own grandson's party?'

Peggy desperately wanted to ask David the date. She must have written it down somewhere, but sadly not on the calendar.

'Of course you're invited. I gave you the invitation last week, remember?'

He did?

'Hi Granny!' There was a different voice now on the end of the phone.

'Sam, is that you? How lovely!'

'Did you like the invitation? I wrote it myself.'

'Oh darling, I loved it. Thank you.' She'd gone and done it now.

'It's a *Star Wars* party. Grandma Geraldine and Grandpa Mike will be there too. Dad says it will be good for you to have some other old people to talk to.'

She bet Mel's parents hadn't lost Sam's invitation. It would have pride of place on that ridiculous oversized fridge of theirs, as if it had won the Archibald Prize. No doubt they also knew a *Star War* from a Space Invader.

'I can't wait,' said Peggy.

'It's a shame you're not allowed to make my cake, Granny, only Mummy says it has to be tasteful this year.'

~

Peggy studied the doctor's face as he listened through his stethoscope. She glanced at the numbers on the machine as her pulse tapped inside the Velcro cuff.

'One sixty-five over ninety.'

'That's good for me,' said Peggy. 'It used to be much higher with Dr Szczpanski.'

'It's still too high. The increased pressure puts strain on your blood vessels and your heart. Hypertension increases your risk of heart attack, kidney failure and stroke.'

How cheery.

Peggy considered the options. Given a choice, she'd go for the heart attack. Why not? She'd known plenty of folk from the village who'd suffered one and they'd all bounced back in no time. Except for the ones who died.

A stroke was a different kettle of worms altogether. It was the loss of independence Peggy feared the most, having to rely on her children for everything. She never wanted to be a burden, on them or anybody else for that matter. Her own father's half-melted face still haunted her, as if he'd been left by the fire for too long. He'd never been a talker – not with Peggy's mother there to correct his every utterance – but his stoic silence was more upsetting than if he'd raged against the injustice of it. Fifty years old. What a waste.

If I ever have a stroke, thought Peggy, make it a big one and be done with it.

'The good news is that, judging by your last blood results, your kidneys are working normally, and you don't have diabetes.' Dr Stephen turned the computer screen and pointed out the rows of numbers.

'Good,' chirped Peggy.

'Yet.'

Peggy subsided. She was *trying*, she explained, hoping she didn't sound too whiney. She went regularly to her Aqua class, never smoked and drank only an occasional glass of sherry. 'And I never touch illegal drugs,' she added for some reason.

'It's your weight,' said the doctor, his lovely smooth forehead now puckered in a frown.

A pout stole Peggy's smile. She'd tried just about everything, every diet going. Nothing worked. Even Jenny Craig had thrown up her hands in despair. It was the same story every time: she'd lose a couple of kilos, but the effort made her irritable, and some minor setback would have her rooting about in the cupboards.

Peggy braced herself for the inevitable lecture.

'People overeat for different reasons. Some just don't recognise when they're full, some snack on high sugar foods between meals, and others are emotional eaters, meaning they eat to reward themselves, or in times of stress or upset. Does any of this ring a bell for you?'

Ding, ding and ding. She ate because she was hungry. Simple. The problem was that she was *always* hungry.

'I lost all my willpower after Ted died. Not that I had much when he was alive. Now I'm on my own, I get bored and lonely. Food is like a friend to me.'

Dr Stephen leaned over and squeezed her shoulder. 'Let's pop you on the scales and make a plan.'

Peggy liked Dr Stephen. He was a good listener, and he gave good advice. This time she was determined to make it work. For him as well as herself. And if she was going to run into Angie again, as seemed inevitable in a place like Jacaranda Retirement Village, she wanted to be fit and fabulous, and prove she hadn't lost her self-worth under a pile of terry-towelling nappies.

The doctor clicked the top on his ballpoint pen and turned the sheet of paper towards Peggy. She fished in her handbag for her glasses case, relieved to find it this time, and peered down at the list of instructions.

'My approach to weight loss is a little different. First, it's best to focus less on actual weight loss and more on improving overall eating habits and fitness. We need to make sure you don't gain more weight.'

Peggy was puzzled. 'You're not going to put me on a diet then?'

'Diets don't work. Think about it, if they did, everyone who'd ever been on one would be an ideal weight. In fact, there are some studies showing that once they reach eighty, women who carry a bit more weight may actually live longer than thinner women of the same age.'

Peggy was sure to file that statistic away for future use. Mel's underfed mother Geraldine was always harping on about carbs.

'I want you to start eating mindfully.'

'I know all about mindlessness,' said Peggy. 'I tried it once in a yoga class here at the village. We had to focus on the sensations in each part of our body.' Peggy remembered she'd got as far as her bladder and it had all gone downhill from there. She might have been able to will her way back to the zone if it hadn't been for Marjorie Seaton snoring like a Sherman tank on the next mat.

'Good. I want you to think about every single thing you put into your mouth. I want you to taste it as you chew it and listen to your body, so you can work out when you've had enough.'

'But that's the problem. It doesn't know when to stop.'

'Only eat until your hunger is satisfied. Don't wait 'til you're full or the plate is empty.'

Peggy's shoulders slumped. She wanted a pill or a quick-fix diet, not some new-fangled mumbo-jumbo.

Dr Stephen continued, writing down a list of instructions. 'Eat plenty of fresh fruit and vegetables, and avoid anything white or processed. Sugar, flour, rice, bread. Especially sugar.'

Peggy mentally scanned the shelves of her larder. 'So chocolate's okay then?' This was going to be easier than she'd expected.

'Sugar.'

'Yoghurt?'

'Natural unsweetened Greek yoghurt is fine.'

'With honey?'

'Still sugar.'

Peggy's heart sank when she read the next item on the list. *Exercise.*

'Walking, every day, twenty minutes to begin with, increasing week by week.'

'But what about my other knee? I'm still only half fixed.'

'Swimming then.'

'Breaststroke *especially* hurts my knee.'

'Water activities such as jogging in a pool are great for arthritis.'

'I already do Aqua twice a week.'

'Good. I'd like you to increase that to three times a week, and jog in the pool on the other days.'

Peggy wasn't so sure she liked Dr Stephen anymore. He was beginning to sound like Dr Cranky-Pantski. Only with slightly warmer hands.

'There's something else I've noticed in your records,' said Dr Stephen, scanning the computer screen in front of him. 'How long have you been on these?' He pointed to the list of current medications.

Peggy hadn't a clue. The pharmacy delivered her blister packs and she took the tablets. They all looked the same, small, round and white. They should make pills in the shape of tiny hearts or kidneys or prostates, so people would know what they were taking and why.

'These are diuretics,' said Stephen pointing to something on the screen, 'designed to excrete fluid through the kidneys, and these here are calcium channel blockers. They'll make your ankles swell.'

They both stared at Peggy's cankles, spilling over her lace-ups.

'You mean—?'

'Yes, they could be causing your ankle swelling, and aggravating your . . . other issues.'

'They're not exactly helping my blood pressure.'

'It's time to change, Peggy. I'll ask the pharmacy to make the necessary adjustments.' Dr Stephen tapped away on his keyboard. Jenny was always prattling on about how doctors were all in cahoots with The Big Farmer. Perhaps he was getting a more lucrative kickback with some expensive new drug instead.

'You do realise I'm on a pension, Doctor. It's costing me a fortune to live this long.'

'You know something, Peggy? I bet if you follow my advice about diet and exercise, you could stop nearly all these tablets.'

Stop them? Her relief at the reduction in her monthly pharmacy bill was tinged with apprehension. Without her tablets, she could potentially lose track of the days – and more importantly, Brian – altogether. Her mornings would be thrown into chaos. She wouldn't know whether she was coming or going, whether she was Arthur or . . . whoever. Either way, David and Jenny would have the perfect excuse to put her in a home.

6

Fall is a Four-letter Word

WITH HER CAR ONLY RECENTLY BACK FROM THE MENDERS, Peggy was reluctant to venture too far, but if she waited any longer for David to set up that internet dating thing for the groceries, as he'd promised, she'd starve to death. The rustic-looking fruit and veg shop on the beach road was her only option. She could pull up right outside the door. No circling the car park looking for a space, no reverse gear, and no invisible Mercedes. Honestly, the accident had shaken Peggy up as much as the other driver, and she relived the sickening crunch of metal over and over in her mind. He had been gracious about it, in the end. Once he'd calmed down.

The selection of produce on display was a pleasant surprise. The colourful fruit looked so appetising, lined up in the cardboard trays. And not a single piece of white food in sight. The young man behind the counter was very friendly, and even carried Peggy's shopping to the car for her. You didn't get that at Coles or Woolworths.

The sun was experimenting with an early summer and with Smooth FM playing on the radio, Peggy couldn't face going straight back to the village. Over the tree-tops she saw a carpet of diamonds as the sunlight reflected on the ocean. When was the last time she'd driven down to the beach? She'd heard they'd redone the surf club and opened up a new café. Could that be where Brian disappeared off to every morning? Her arms tingled with goosepimples.

The salty breeze blew in through the open windows as Peggy wound her blue hatchback down the narrow road towards the beach. She turned Lionel Richie up to full volume and sang along. She glanced at the bananas sitting on the passenger seat. Feeling reckless, she'd thrown caution to the wind and bought a whole bunch. It was good to be alive. And Peggy Smart wasn't about to give up her independence – or her bananas – without a fight.

Peggy's elation deflated a fraction when she arrived in the car park. The actual beach was hidden behind rows of parked cars – rows and rows of them. This was worse than the supermarket. She was about to abort her mission when she spotted reversing lights.

It took three attempts but at least she'd avoided the cars on either side. There was even enough room to squeeze out through the driver's door. Peggy decided to take the bananas with her in her handbag. At that price, she couldn't afford to take any chances. Her plan was to stroll down to the ocean pool for a quick look, then head to the café for a coffee. Black, of course. With the public conveniences situated across the car park, it would be the perfect outing.

Weaving between the rows, Peggy noticed a familiar car. Silver, with four shiny black tyres, it was as solid and reliable as its owner. What's more, it was the kind of vehicle that hinted there might be more under the bonnet than met the eye. Peggy flushed as she read the numberplate. She couldn't remember the four-digit passcode for her new phone, but she knew these letters and numbers by heart.

It was Brian's Lexus.

So this was where he came every morning. All along, the perfect opportunity to accidentally bump into Brian, away from the prying eyes of the village gossips, had been staring her in the face.

Was this the beginning of the rest of her life, a second chance at love and happiness? Or was it a monumental mistake? What if he didn't recognise her outside the familiar surroundings of the village? What if he recognised her but pretended not to, or accused her of *stalking* him?

Worst-case scenarios charged at her: she'd have to resign from the residents' committee, change her name, move away from the village, even put herself into a home.

Rooted to the spot, Peggy dithered with indecision. The last few days had drained her. Her get-up-and-go had got up and gone. She was turning eighty soon. There'd be a party of sorts, a revoltingly tasteful cake arranged by Mel, and cards with glittery exclamation marks on the front.

You're 80!

In a few weeks, she would be officially old, the cue for David and Jenny to step in and take over. Her children would smother her and call all the shots. They'd tell her what she needed and, eventually, wanted. Peggy's life would be curated and managed until it was no longer hers.

Peggy could see the swimmers in the distance plodding

up and down the lanes. One of them must be Brian. Her legs slackened.

She'd spent her whole life trying to please others, being the good girl. It was time to do something daring. Fate had handed her this golden opportunity, and Peggy Smart was never one to look a gift horse in the eye.

~

She was still some way from the pool when Peggy noticed a couple walking towards her. On the left was a thin woman wearing a broad-brimmed hat and celebrity sunglasses that obscured her face. A lean-limbed man in a Panama hat walked by her side, carrying a striped towel around his gently stooping shoulders. They were chatting and laughing. As they moved closer, Peggy could see the man in more detail. There was a tangle of white hair in the centre of his chest. His skin hung like wet washing. One look at the scars on his knees and Peggy knew instantly who he was. Who they both were.

Fight or flight?

She knew all about survival in the wild. Stay and face the threat, or run away. Unfortunately, the message didn't reach Peggy's feet in time as her body turned to flee. She listed to starboard, as if she'd run aground, and for a moment she was airborne before the darkness wrapped around her.

When she opened her eyes, Peggy wondered if she'd fallen asleep, but instead of her bedroom ceiling, a flock of noisy seagulls circled overhead like vultures. Was she dead? She hoped she was.

For a few seconds nothing happened. Then came the pain in her wrist. *Not dead after all.*

Lying spatchcock on the ground, Peggy had a fleeting moment of mental clarity. This was why people of her age wore earthy tones. Stone, sand, pebble. Was there any chance she was so perfectly camouflaged that no-one would notice her?

'Give her some air.' A woman's face appeared, silhouetted by the sun. 'Peggy Smart. It *is* you! I thought I recognised you the other day in the waiting room.' The woman's face swam in front of her eyes until her brain reassembled the features. Peggy groaned. Could this possibly get any worse?

'Do you two know each other?' It was Brian, his lovely face wrinkled with concern.

'Oh yes, we go way back,' said Angie.

'Are you hurt?' asked Brian from the corner of Peggy's right eye.

Peggy wiggled her toes. At least she hadn't severed her spinal cord.

'Do you want to try to sit up?' Brian again. He was standing awkwardly, half-squatting, half-kneeling. Peggy remembered when he'd finally bent his new knee past one hundred degrees. It was six weeks after his operation and she'd toyed with baking him a special cake to celebrate, but changed her mind, not wanting to appear too forward.

At Brian's suggestion, Peggy experimented with a sitting position. A wave of nausea knocked her back and she succumbed to the safety of the solid ground once more. A crowd of concerned onlookers had gathered by now and with the help of two young lifeguards, Peggy finally managed to stay upright.

She was mortified. For some reason she thought of her mother, scrubbing her grazed hands with iodine and telling her to stop crying. Peggy could hear the old bat now, 'Get up this minute, young lady. You're making such a spectacle of yourself.'

'I'm fine,' said Peggy, struggling to her feet like a newborn foal. 'Look.' She spread her arms wide to demonstrate her fine-ness, and wobbled.

'Whoopsie-daisy.' Brian caught her and cushioned her descent. This time, Peggy's landing was somewhat more elegant. Thanks to Brian.

Oh, how she wanted to melt into those arms, but there was too much at stake. She had to appear stoic and the very opposite of frail and broken in front of both Brian and Angie.

'There,' said Peggy. 'No harm done.'

'What about that?' said Brian pointing to her left arm.

Peggy looked down at her wrist. It was bent into the shape of a dinner fork. 'It's nothing,' she said, waving the deformed limb. The pain was excruciating as the bones crunched beneath the rapidly expanding skin.

'That's it. Someone call an ambulance,' said Angie. She hadn't changed a bit. Same old bossy Angie. Resistance was futile.

'But what about the bananas?' Peggy looked down at her crumpled handbag on the ground where she'd landed. Mangled banana oozed from within. *What a waste.* She must have a recipe for banoffee pie somewhere.

'Your friend is right. You do need to go to hospital, my dear.'

My dear. Peggy felt giddy and light in the head.

'Not in an ambulance.' Not if she was going to keep this quiet from David and Jenny.

'What if I drive you?' Brian's frown turned into a smile.

Such lovely teeth.

Peggy nodded obediently.

'If anyone's going to take you, it should be me,' said Angie.

Peggy's bottom lip began to tremble. 'But Brian . . .' She reached for him, knocked back by a wave of pain from her wrist. The dream was fading. Brian was slipping through her fingers. Her rapidly swelling fingers. This wasn't how it was supposed to end.

Angie leaned over and, grasping Peggy by her good arm, hauled her unceremoniously to her feet.

'Come on,' she said, softening her voice. 'I hear the nurses are really nice.'

~

Peggy tried to piece together the series of events. It had started with Lionel Richie and somehow ended with her lying on a plastic-wrapped mattress in a hospital gown. Everything in between was a muddle. There was the nice man in the veg shop and something about bananas. More worryingly, she still couldn't recall if she'd returned *White Coat Rogue* to the library. Best not let on about the library book, in case the doctors decided to do that memory test they all talked about back at the village. If you scored less than twenty out of thirty, they put you in a home. Peggy made a mental note to start practising, just in case. Now, what were those three objects they asked you to remember? She'd heard all about it from Dorothy White before she disappeared. Poor Dorothy. She'd been so looking forward to her daughter taking her for a drive. Little did she know she'd never return. The suitcases and removal van should have given it away.

'Apple, table, penny,' muttered Peggy.

'I see the happy juice has kicked in.' Angie was sitting on a plastic chair next to the bed.

'Crikey, what are you doing here?'

'Lining up for Beatles tickets. What do you think?'

'The Beatles are back together?' Peggy wondered just how long she'd been unconscious.

'No, you silly mare. I brought you here to get your wrist looked at, but I think I should get them to X-ray your brain while they're at it.'

Peggy studied her friend. The skin on her face reminded Peggy of inflated bubble gum, her expression frozen in a look of faint surprise. The perfect make-up and symmetrical teeth only added to the astonishing realisation that Angie had barely aged in five decades. The look was unsettling, eerie even.

'You look peculiar,' slurred Peggy. 'What's wrong with your face?'

'Charming. I've missed you too.'

Around them, doctors and nurses, clerks and porters marched like ants in determined paths. Everywhere Peggy looked, there was white. From the blankets and pillowcases, to the walls and furniture; the endless sheets of white paper on white clipboards, even the little white straw sticking out of the white plastic cup on the table next to her. She remembered Dr Stephen's prosaic words, 'I want you to avoid anything white.'

'What happened?' asked Peggy, still trying to make sense of it all, as if she'd walked in halfway through a movie.

'You had a fall.'

A fall.

A fall was fine when you were a toddler, but catastrophic for someone of her age. How many of the colourful dresses in her wardrobe had been worn to farewell someone who had *had a fall*. Stay upright seemed to be the mantra of her age group. For some reason, Peggy pictured Elizabeth Taylor in *National Velvet*, begging her sick horse to get up. Or die.

Peggy lifted her head off the pillow and was immediately knocked back by the pain behind her eyes. 'I need to get home to Basil.'

'Don't worry about the dog. Brian is taking care of him.'

'Brian?' She'd forgotten about him. He'd witnessed the whole clumsy, foolish event. A new wave of despair crashed over Peggy.

'Yes, tall fellow from the village. I met him at the pool, about five minutes before you did your swan dive. He's quite a hottie, for an oldie.'

It was all coming back to her now. Peggy tried to sit up again. She needed to check her handbag to see if there was any hope for the bananas.

'Lie down. Relax. You've got concussion and we're waiting for the orthopaedic doctor to give you the all clear.'

Peggy noticed for the first time that her left arm was encased in plaster of Paris from the elbow to her knuckles. More white. 'Where are my clothes?'

'Down here,' said Angie retrieving a pink plastic bag from under the trolley. Peggy's stomach turned watery. It was identical to the one she'd carried home from the hospital containing Ted's things.

'My wedding ring!'

'Don't worry. I've got it here, all safe.' Angie opened her palm to reveal the gold band, now a broken circle. 'They had to cut it off before they put the plaster on. Your finger was so swollen, it was cutting off the circulation.'

A tear burst from the corner of Peggy's eye. 'I've had that ring on my finger since my wedding day.'

'I know,' said Angie, handing Peggy a box of tissues. 'I was there.'

She'd forgotten that. Peggy wondered if Angie remembered the kerfuffle at the church when Ted couldn't force the ring over Peggy's chubby knuckle and she'd had to suck her own finger to slip it on. Everybody had laughed. Except Peggy's mother, of course, insisting afterwards that it was an omen.

Peggy studied the bare finger. There was a groove in the pale flesh as if Ted had branded her all those years ago. It was as though every part of her had grown apart from the skin under that ring. Her gaze shifted as Angie leaned over the bed to place the tissue box on the bedside table.

'What's that?' asked Peggy, pointing to a circular lump tenting the skin on Angie's bony chest. It was a bit small for a breast implant and there was only the one. As she looked closer she noticed a pale scar running down the middle of Angie's breastbone. It looked like someone had zipped her up.

'It's a pacemaker. I had it put in when they did my bypass.'

'A pacemaker?' Peggy felt guilty. Here she was with nothing more than a broken wrist and a bruise on her backside, while a battery-powered device was keeping Angie alive. 'I'm sorry, Angie. I had no idea.'

'Don't be silly. You weren't to know. We lost touch a long time ago. It's no big deal, it's not like I'm carrying an atomic bomb that might go off.'

Behind the bravado, Peggy glimpsed the vulnerability. No amount of Botox or vegetable peels could disguise the fact that Angie's body was ageing too, with the scars to prove it.

'How much longer do you have left in your battery?' Peggy managed a wan smile.

'Don't you worry about me. I'm bulletproof.'

Peggy shivered in the disinfected air. Angie pulled the blanket up over her shoulders. 'Thank you.'

'Don't mention it.'

'This is all so humiliating,' Peggy picked at the edge of the blanket with her good hand. It was like she couldn't trust her own body anymore, as though someone had reprogrammed it for a cheap laugh. 'Sometimes, I'm sick of being me,' she said.

'Well, suck it up, sweetheart,' replied Angie, 'because everyone else is taken.'

Peggy smiled in spite of herself. Part of her had missed Angie and that no-nonsense attitude. She'd never admit it. Peggy Smart still had her pride. In this case, it had come after the fall.

A nurse appeared between the curtains with a small plastic cup containing a painkilling tablet.

'Here,' she said. 'Take this. It'll help the pain.'

Peggy popped the little white pill into her mouth and leaned forward to take a sip of water.

Angie clinked the side of Peggy's polystyrene cup with an identical one, filled with what looked like vending-machine tea. 'Cheers.'

'Bottoms up!' replied Peggy.

Sensing the irony, the women smiled at each other.

~

'We usually recommend that elderly patients living alone stay in hospital overnight after an episode like this,' said the orthopaedic registrar when he finally arrived.

Elderly? Episode? Peggy supposed he was referring to her. After all, she was the one lying in the bed with her arm in plaster.

'But I don't live alone. I live with Basil.'

The registrar looked at Angie for clarification.

'Dog.'

'I see. Well, that's not the kind of help I was thinking of. You'll need assistance with things like washing and dressing for a few days. We could always arrange carers in the community.'

Carers? Peggy pictured officious women in rubber-soled shoes. Before she knew it, there would be an army of strangers marching in, making weak tea and rearranging the kitchen. It was bad enough having a fall, but to have some complete stranger handing her the soap really was the limit.

'I'll be fine. I'm not staying in hospital and I certainly don't want carers. I'll discharge myself if I need to.'

'Would you like me to call your family?' The registrar looked like he hadn't slept in days. 'We have a David Smart listed here as next of kin. And a Jenny.'

'No!' Peggy snapped.

'I'll have no alternative but to inform your family if you go home against medical advice. So, what is it to be? Hospital or carers?' The registrar's pen hovered impatiently above the clipboard.

Angie stood up and turned to the registrar. 'I'll stay with her.' Before he had a chance to protest, she added, 'Just put a little tick in your box, and send someone to help me dress her.'

'I couldn't ask you to do that.'

'You're not asking, Peggy. You don't have a choice.'

'But Angie—'

'Don't worry. You can do the same for me one day.'

7

It's Not Beige, It's Taupe

THERE WAS A SOFT TAP AT THE BEDROOM DOOR AND ANGIE
appeared, holding a steaming cup of tea. 'Don't worry, I've
cancelled your 9 am kickboxing class,' she said, a twinkle
in her eye.

What time was it? Peggy lay on her back, staring at
the bedroom ceiling, trying to get her bearings. Her head
pounded when she tried to lift it from the pillow and she
ached all over. Then she remembered.

You've had a fall. It was the dawn of her new life as an
old person.

Angie placed the tea on the bedside table and with one arm
under Peggy's shoulder, hoisted her into a sitting position.

'Thank you,' said Peggy, her brain rolling inside her skull.

What bizarre twist of fate had brought her oldest friend
to Jacaranda Retirement Village of all places? Perhaps this
was one of those weird cheese dreams. Any moment now, she
would wake up in front of *Who Wants to Be a Millionaire*

with Basil on her lap. Then she remembered the removal van, the velvet sofa and the look on that poor young man's face when she told him off for parking on the footpath. This was no casual encounter, a quick hello and how've you been. Angie Valentine – *the* Angie Valentine – was now living only a few doors away, in an identical unit to Peggy's.

Angie sat on the end of the bed. She was wearing a simple black linen dress with a chunky glass-beaded necklace. Her make-up was once again immaculate.

'Still sleep on the same side of the bed?' she said.

Peggy nodded. She'd never thought to change. Though she downgraded to a double when she moved into the unit, there was already a hollow on one side of the mattress while the other half remained pristine. She and Ted had rarely spent a night apart during their marriage. Bed had become such a lonely, empty place.

'That's just the problem. I can't sleep,' said Peggy. 'I'm an insomno-maniac.'

'Tell me about it. After Bill died, I tried sleeping in the middle, but I kept rolling over in the night. I ended up with vertigo and had to buy a new bed,' said Angie.

'Bill? Your husband?'

'One of them.' Seeing Peggy's eyes widen, she added, 'Drink up, Pegs. Breakfast is nearly ready, and we've got a lot of catching up to do.'

~

Peggy shuffled into the kitchen in the towelling gown and slippers Angie had left for her on the bed. She kept her best slippers and a brand-new dressing gown in the wardrobe, in case she was admitted to hospital. The whole idea seemed ludicrous now. If there was ever a genuine medical emergency, the last thing the paramedics would do would be root around, asking her whether she wanted the silk slingbacks or the sheepskin moccasins. They were destined to gather dust, along with all the scented candles and fancy smellies she was also keeping for a special occasion.

'Buckwheat pancakes, fresh fruit and black coffee.'

Angie had found Peggy's best china and laid it out for two at the tiny kitchen table. She'd pictured setting it out for her and Brian for their special dinner, but after the events of yesterday, that particular fantasy seemed further away than ever.

'You shouldn't have gone to all this trouble,' said Peggy staring dubiously at the stack of pancakes and bowl of chopped fruit. She usually had toast with butter in the morning. And tea. Lots of tea.

'Sorry, it looks like you're out of bananas,' said Angie with a wry smile.

Peggy noticed her handbag soaking in the kitchen sink. Her only handbag. Next to Angie's huge designer thing, it looked rather pathetic. What on earth did the woman keep in there? She and Ted went on their honeymoon with a smaller bag than that.

'Where did you sleep last night?'

'On the couch. Bloody uncomfortable and darling, let me tell you, jacquard went out with the Ark. Don't worry, while you were still away with the fairies, I popped home for a quick shower and threw some clothes on.'

Threw some clothes on? Give her a hat and she'd be ready for the Melbourne Cup. It was the same at school: Peggy in a hand-me-down dress that almost reached her ankles and

Angie showing off her legs in a rebelliously short skirt. Peggy had always wondered how they'd ended up as friends. Yet they'd become two sides of the same coin. And here they were again, over fifty years on, having breakfast together.

'Very nice,' said Peggy after her first mouthful of buckwheat. She contemplated drizzling honey over, but out of the corner of her eye, she could see the doctor's list of instructions on the fridge. 'Honey is still sugar,' he'd said.

'It's low GI.'

Peggy wasn't sure what American soldiers had to do with pancakes. She nodded, not wanting to appear ignorant.

'Very . . . healthy.' Peggy tried to co-ordinate a swallow, but it was like chewing a dry face washer.

'I haven't eaten any processed food since my last heart attack.' Angie placed a carefully dissected morsel into her mouth.

Peggy's fork clattered to the table. '*Last* heart attack?' Here was a woman who looked at least ten years younger than her age and weighed less than a bag of shopping. She didn't look the heart-attack type. 'But you're—'

'Female? C'mon Pegs, women get heart disease too.'

'Skinny. I was going to say skinny.'

'Don't be so naïve. You can't fight genetics. I'm the climax of the family curse, I'm afraid.'

Peggy thought about her own family history. Her father had died from pneumonia following a stroke, a mute and helpless end. Her mother, on the other hand, had simply grown old, an ancient wizened creature in a nursing home. She didn't relish either as an ending.

'It happened after my marriage broke down,' said Angie, forking a cube of pineapple.

'Hang on, I thought you said Bill died?'

'He did. I've had four husbands. Only one died, though I wished it on the other three towards the end.'

Peggy's head was spinning. She was losing count of the heart attacks, and the husbands. What an unremarkable life she'd led by comparison. One husband. No heart attacks. At least now she'd broken her wrist and given herself concussion. Life had become infinitely more remarkable since Angie arrived.

'I've got high cholester-oil too,' said Peggy. It was like being thirteen again, desperate to fit in with the crowd. What she lacked in spouses, she could make up for with ailments. 'I'm on the little white oval tablet. The one that makes your legs ache and stuffs up your memory. What's it called again?'

Angie chuckled. 'You're so witty, Peggy.'

Basil appeared from under the table. He wagged his cotton-wool tail, but exhausted from the effort, flopped down on the tiles panting.

'Meet Basil. The man in my life.'

She'd almost forgotten about Basil's impending eviction, what with the fall and the trip to hospital. That bang on the head must have cost her valuable brain cells, ones she simply couldn't spare, and Angie's mysterious arrival in the village had well and truly scrambled the rest. He was only a dog, but life without her faithful companion was unimaginable to Peggy. When she'd moved to the village, there was a lady a few units down who'd owned a dog like Basil. It used to sit on the back of her sofa and yap at passers-by. The woman's husband died suddenly, but somehow she carried on, throwing herself into bowls and bridge with a new lease on life. When the dog died from a tick a year later, however, the old dear went downhill so rapidly, it was as if she too had contracted deadly paralysis. She was gone within days.

'Hello, Basil.' Angie stretched out her hand towards him. To Peggy's amazement, the little dog struggled to his feet and began to lick her hand. Some things never changed. Men just couldn't resist Angie. Even the old codgers like Basil.

'He's not long for this world,' said Peggy, 'but he's all I've got. I can't bear to part with him just yet.' Angie broke off a piece of buckwheat pancake and offered it to him. He sniffed it and turned up his nose. Peggy felt the tiniest bit pleased. 'He's a bit fussy. I cook him a hot dinner most days. Though I have to cut everything up very small for his teeth. And he only drinks full-fat milk. I think I've spoiled him.'

'I reckon he's got plenty of life left in him,' said Angie. She leaned over and tickled Basil behind one ear.

'He's fifteen now. That's over a hundred in dog years.'

'Age is just a number, Pegs. I stopped counting at fifty. That way, I can call myself vintage rather than antique.'

'Seriously though, don't you worry about getting old?'

'The older I get, the older old is. No, honestly, I don't think about it. What's the point?'

Peggy stroked the cast on her wrist. The shattered bones throbbed. 'There'll be hell to pay if my children find out about my little mishap.'

'If?' Angie lined up the bangles on her wrist and cleared her throat. 'Try when.'

'What do you mean?'

'David phoned this morning while you were asleep.'

~

'Are you sure you don't want me to come in with you?' shouted Angie through the bathroom door. She'd taped a plastic bin liner around Peggy's plaster cast, laid out the towels and adjusted the water until the shower was just right.

'Quite sure, thank you.' Peggy had to draw the line somewhere.

She heard Angie shout from the bedroom. 'Good God, woman. It's like an archaeological dig in here. When's the last time you went shopping?'

For some reason, Peggy found the sight of Angie rifling through her wardrobe when she returned from the bathroom even more confronting than stripping off in front of her for the shower.

'Right,' said Angie, rubbing her hands together. 'Let's get you dressed.'

In too much pain to argue, Peggy untied the robe and let it fall to the floor.

'What do you call this?' said Angie tugging at Peggy's bra. It was the one Peggy had been saving for a special occasion. It still had the tag attached. She couldn't let Angie see her in her greying minimiser.

'It's a balconette bra.' Peggy wondered if it had shrunk in the drawer. The label assured her it would create lift and cleavage, but that was some years ago. The flimsy lace now appeared defeated by the challenge.

'My first unit had a smaller balcony than this,' said Angie, hauling up the shoulder straps. 'You could fit a table and chairs on these girls and still have room for the neighbours.'

She attempted to squash Peggy's pendulous breasts into the dainty cups. Compared to Angie's modest chest, Peggy felt like she was carrying a couple of spare cushions around.

Of the two friends, Angie had been the first to buy a bra. At that time, her breasts hardly warranted the purchase, but Angie wore it more as a badge of honour than a means of restraint.

Peggy, on the other hand, fiercely resisted her mother's attempts to have her properly measured and fitted at Blake's Department Store. Still coming to terms with her breasts' sudden and uninvited appearance, Peggy had taken to hunching her shoulders forward in a futile attempt to disguise her bosom. While Angie stuffed her tiny brassiere with cotton wool, Peggy attempted to flatten her voluptuous figure by binding her chest with the muslin cloth her mother used to drain curds. Eventually, she conceded, out of sheer necessity.

To Peggy's horror, the boys from St David's soon noticed her precocious development. Every week, the girls had to run the gauntlet of wolf-whistles as they passed the school on their way to swimming class. It wasn't long before one or two of the braver chaps started waiting for them outside the gates.

One in particular became a regular. He was taller than the others, with thickly quiffed hair and a swagger.

'What's your name?' he shouted, leaning against the brick wall.

'Keep walking,' said Peggy, eyes fixed on the footpath ahead.

'Wouldn't you like to know?' Angie's walk slowed, filling Peggy with panic.

'Come on, Angie. We'll be late.'

'Why don't you stop and act friendly, huh?'

Peggy sensed the boy following them. She could feel his eyes on her body, appraising it beneath her formless tartan pinafore and thick stockings. She pulled her rolled-up towel into her chest. To her horror, Angie stopped and turned back. She stood square-on to the boys with her hands on her hips and her chest puffed out, bold as brass. Peggy noticed for the first time how short Angie's skirt was. There'd be hell to pay if the nuns found out she'd taken a needle and thread to it. They'd all be lined up, made to kneel to make sure their skirts touched the ground. But Angie was never one to conform. Never one to wear the uniform the way all the other girls did.

'What's your name?' asked the boy again.

'Angie. Are you going to ask me out?'

'If you like.'

'What's her name?' Another lad stepped forward, turning his head towards Peggy. He was slight, with mousy brown hair that covered his eyes.

'She's Margaret,' said Angie.

'Peggy for short.' Peggy surprised even herself. Her voice sounded small and squeaky next to Angie's and she knew her face was flushed pink. She kicked a pebble with the tip of her scuffed shoe. The mousy lad smiled at her and blushed too.

When Peggy's mother got wind of the goings-on, she stepped in before matters – in her own words – got out of hand.

'Mother, really, please don't make a fuss,' Peggy pleaded outside the principal's office.

'Safeguarding the virtue of my underage daughter isn't making a fuss. We scrimp and save to give you the very best, and this is how you repay us. You've fallen in with the wrong crowd.'

Peggy presumed she meant Angie. Not exactly a crowd, given she was pretty much the only friend Peggy had. She prayed the principal wouldn't summon Angie to the inquisition. Peggy pictured her friend through her mother's eyes: all legs and attitude.

'It's nothing. Just a bit of harmless fun,' said Peggy, thinking about the inane banter with the mousy-haired boy. Compared to Angie's eager forays into heavy petting, it was quite innocent.

To Peggy's surprise, her mother turned and gave her the stare. 'Harmless fun is the reason you're here in the first place, my dear. I don't want you making the same mistakes I did.'

Peggy's eyes widened at the thought of her parents ever having any fun at all, harmless or otherwise, but the subject of premarital relations was enough to bring the conversation to a rapid close. As the principal opened the door and ushered them in, her mother's words hit Peggy like a punch to the solar plexus.

Peggy Weaver. Mistake.

It all made perfect sense now.

～

Near naked, Peggy stood like an artist's model while Angie inspected her from all angles.

'Not bad,' said Angie eventually. With that, she patted Peggy's bottom and turned her attention back to the wardrobe. She rifled through the straining rack, pulling hangers out at random and examining each at arm's length as if it was infectious.

Too young.

Too old.

Too fitted.

Too shapeless.

Garment after garment, all consigned to the growing reject pile on the bedroom carpet. With each piece of discarded clothing, Peggy's shoulders dropped a little further.

'Do you have anything that isn't in hearing-aid beige?'

'It's not beige, it's taupe.'

'Beige, taupe, biscuit, whatever. It's all hideous.'

'I've always thought neutrals were timeless.'

'If you're a dinosaur, maybe. It's so ageing, Peggy. Don't you have anything in an actual colour?'

'There's my funeral collection.'

'What? Dear God, this is worse than I thought. Is it too early for a drink?'

After what seemed like hours, Angie stumbled upon a pair of navy pants and a plain white top. Peggy couldn't remember seeing these clothes before, but she had a habit of splurging in the sales and buying multiple items that she never wore, simply to save herself money.

'Try these.'

As she guided the navy fabric over her feet, Peggy noticed her ankles looked considerably slimmer this morning. Dr Stephen's medicinal adjustments were starting to work already. By some miracle, the pants fit. Angie helped her with the button and zip.

'Okay, now for the top.'

Peggy held up her arms and allowed Angie to slip the garment over her head. A few minor adjustments, and she was dressed.

'There. Not bad, though I think we could lose the bag,' said Angie untaping the bin liner.

Peggy turned and looked in the mirror. If she ignored the giant cast on her wrist, she looked almost presentable. But one thing troubled her. 'Do you think I should risk white at my age?'

Angie thought for a moment before pulling a scarf out of the pile on the floor. She tied it round Peggy's throat and pulled the knot to one side, like French women did.

'Women of a certain age need colour next to their face. Rule number one.'

'You don't think it shows up my broken veins, do you?' Peggy frowned. The reds and russets of the scarf had given her face a vaguely boiled appearance.

Angie held her head at an angle and squinted. 'Nah, a touch of concealer under your foundation and it's a winner.'

Peggy's gaze dropped to her feet.

'You do have concealer, don't you?' said Angie, as if Peggy were missing a kidney. 'Foundation?'

Peggy untied the knotted scarf and slipped it off. She tossed it back onto the pile of discarded clothing on the floor. A gloom descended and her earlier optimism evaporated.

'Try the green spotted scarf instead.'

'It's not the scarf.'

'How about a nice necklace then?' Angie rummaged through the jewellery box on Peggy's dressing table.

'Stop, please.'

'What's the matter?'

'It's no good. You can't make a silk purse out of a sow's ear.' Her mother's favourite saying. In Peggy's mind, the scratched record had played over and over again until it was impossible to unbelieve those stinging words.

'What are you talking about?'

'I don't see the point at my age. Who's going to look at me anyway?'

'Well, if that's your attitude, go ahead and throw yourself a pity party. You may as well knit yourself a shawl and a pair of booties right now.'

'I'm a seventy-nine-year-old widow with a broken arm and a body like day-old rice pudding. It's time to face facts. I'm past it.'

'In case you've forgotten, our birthdays are five weeks apart. That makes me seventy-nine too. And I'm a widow. Do I look like I'm past it?' Angie flicked her dark hair back off her face, and struck an exaggerated model pose. Peggy softened a fraction at that ridiculous pout, remembering her friend's legendary impersonations of the nuns. Her depiction of Sister Philomena with her distinctive limp was particularly memorable, and had landed them both in detention.

'You're a nutter, Angela Valentine.'

'You shouldn't be so hard on yourself. It's all about attitude.'

Peggy's gaze settled on the necklace Angie was wearing. The glass beads in blues and greens reminded her of the boiled sweets they used to buy at the little corner shop on the way home from school. Angie was so full of dreams back then, telling Peggy how she planned to travel the world. Peggy would listen to her with wonder, mouth stuffed with Cobbers or Jaffas, trying to imagine her own future. She saw a handsome husband and two beautiful blond children, a perfect house in the suburbs, holidays to the coast. Neither of them had ever imagined themselves turning eighty.

'I think you're right. A necklace might suit me better,' said Peggy.

'Here,' said Angie, reaching around the back of her neck for the clasp. 'Try this.'

The beads sat just above the open neck of the white shirt. They seemed even more vibrant on Peggy than on her friend. Angie noticed too. 'It brings out the blue in your eyes.'

Peggy admired herself then moved to unclasp the necklace.

'No,' said Angie. 'Please keep it. I've so many necklaces and my new unit is like a shoebox.'

'Are you sure?'

'I'm sure. Anyway, it looks so much better on you.'

Peggy wasn't sure how to react. It was as though they were improvising on stage, without a script. 'Just imagine you're two childhood friends who haven't seen each other for fifty years and you discover you're living virtually next door,' the director might say. 'Imagine there's something unspoken between you, a secret perhaps. Let's see where it takes us.'

It didn't take a fashion genius to see that Peggy had let herself go. Not quite the grieving widow dressed in black, but close enough. Four years was a respectable period of mourning, surely? Ted hadn't asked her permission to exit their marriage so suddenly and so permanently. She hardly needed to ask his approval to buy a few new clothes.

'I'd love it if you'd take me shopping,' said Peggy.

'It's a deal. On one condition.'

'What condition?'

'We start with some decent foundation garments.'

The two women looked at each other, the memory stirring in both of them.

'Yes, Mr Haw-ley,' said Peggy in a sing-song voice.

They both began to laugh, transported in an instant back to 1957.

~

Mr Hawley licked his lips as he appraised his new trainee. Peggy felt the colour rise in her cheeks. She wasn't comfortable with this kind of scrutiny from men, aware that her hourglass figure was beginning to attract admiring glances. She knew that even the starched blouse and dark gabardine skirt of the Blake's uniform did little to detract from her ripening womanhood.

'I can assure you Mrs Weaver that I will take care of your daughter *personally*,' said Mr Hawley, licking his lips as he moved to stand between Peggy and her mother.

'She's so shy,' said Peggy's mother. 'I'm hoping you might be able to do something with her. Heaven knows, I've tried.'

'I can assure you that here at Blake's, we pride ourselves on introducing young ladies to the adult world.'

For a moment, Peggy considered grasping her mother's hand and begging to go home. But she was almost nineteen and seeking a life of her own, free from her mother's interference. She'd thought of becoming a teacher – she'd always loved reading and poetry – but with her father gone, she needed a job to help her mother with the bills, not years at college to add to them. A friend of her mother's had put in a good word for Peggy, and the job, when offered, was too good to turn down. Girls of her age would give their right arm to work in fashion at such a prestigious place as Blake's Department Store. In their flagship store, no less.

Mr Hawley led Peggy away towards the staff elevator. Her damp fingers tore the brown paper bag containing the limp sandwich her mother had prepared that morning.

'Follow me, Miss Weaver. I like to see the new girls in Lingerie first,' he leered, titillated by his private joke.

The elevator doors closed and the floor jerked as they began to ascend. There were two other staff members in the lift, a stern-looking woman in a grey suit, and a young maintenance worker, wearing smart khaki overalls. He caught Peggy's eye from behind his ladder, and grinned. Peggy blushed.

The grey-suited woman disembarked at Drapery, leaving Peggy with Mr Hawley and the workman. Peggy caught the young man's eye on several occasions. Each time he pulled a funny face and made Peggy giggle. When they arrived at Furniture and Homewares, he tried to exit with his ladder widthways across the doors. It reminded Peggy of a clown she'd seen at the circus and she laughed out loud in spite of herself. He turned and winked before disappearing behind a display cabinet.

Mr Hawley cleared his throat and glowered. 'We do not encourage fraternisation between members of staff, Miss Weaver.'

'No, Mr Hawley.'

'Do I make myself clear?'

'Yes, Mr Hawley.'

Peggy watched the numbers flash as they passed each floor. With a ding, the lift came to a halt at the fourth floor. Several moments passed yet the doors remained firmly shut.

Out of the corner of her eye, Peggy noticed that Mr Hawley's thumb was pressed firmly against the button. A sudden squall of panic blew through her, heading straight for her bladder.
Not now!

Something brushed against Peggy's leg, coming to rest on her buttock. The saliva evaporated from Peggy's mouth. A spasm tore through her pelvis and she instinctively clenched her buttocks. She noticed Mr Hawley smile. He gave her bottom a squeeze and withdrew his hand just as the doors opened.

'Peggy Weaver!'

To Peggy's surprise, standing there, in an identical uniform of white shirt and dark skirt, was Angie. The relief at seeing her old friend was short-lived, however.

'Sorry, I need the ladies' room.'

Sensing the urgency, Angie took her by the hand. 'I'll show her.'

The girls scurried away, leaving Mr Hawley to stroke his moustache.

'I can't believe it's you,' said Peggy as she dried her hands with the rotating towel in the bathroom.

Angie leaned against the tiled wall, smoking a cigarette. She offered it to Peggy, who coughed and shook her head. 'Yeah, I started as a Saturday girl, not long after you left St Catherine's,' said Angie.

She looked different. It wasn't just the cigarette. With her neatly styled hair and full, shaped eyebrows, she reminded Peggy of Jean Simmons. In the mirror, Peggy tried to flatten her own hair to match. Full of natural wave, however, it protested in a rebellious frizz around her face.

'I'm sorry I didn't get a chance to say goodbye.' Peggy hung her head. 'After Father died, my mother couldn't afford the school fees or the mortgage and we had to move away. She wouldn't let me keep in touch. She told me it was for the best, otherwise I'd make myself miserable.'

She felt she owed Angie an explanation for disappearing without so much as a goodbye, but it sounded pathetic as excuses went. On the verge of adulthood, the time had come to start making her own decisions. She no longer needed her mother's approval when it came to choosing friends. In fact, now was the perfect time to make a stand. Angie was exactly the kind of girl her mother had tried to steer her away from. Which made her exactly the kind of girl Peggy wanted to hang out with.

'You want to watch Hawley.' Angie flicked her cigarette butt into an empty toilet bowl and pulled the chain. 'He's a right one. Stick with me and I'll show you how to handle him.'

Angie pulled out a lipstick from the pocket in her skirt. Peggy watched as her friend moved the creamy red stick around the outline of her lips, before filling in their fullness.

'Here, want some?'

Peggy nodded and took the lipstick in her right hand. Concentrating on the mirror, she copied Angie and spread the colour around her bare lips. She used the corner of her folded handkerchief to wipe away where the colour bled. She'd never worn make-up before, but standing back to admire the result in the mirror, she was astounded by the transformation. She grinned at Angie.

'Whoops, teeth,' said Angie laughing at the stains across Peggy's chaotic front incisors.

Mr Hawley was waiting when they returned, staring at his pocket watch with a scowl. 'I trust that this won't become a regular habit, Miss Weaver. Staff breaks are strictly allocated and unscheduled trips to the . . . powder room will not be tolerated. Do I make myself clear?'

Peggy nodded, trying to ignore a new quiver in her bladder. It was a long time until lunch. 'Yes, Mr Hawley,' she said in barely a squeak.

'Miss Valentine, you will instruct Miss Weaver in how the Foundation Wear department operates. Miss Weaver, at this point you will observe *only*. You will not talk to customers directly until such time as I am satisfied. Do you understand?'

'Yes, Mr Hawley.'

'Your willingness to co-operate in whichever way I see fit will greatly assist your promotion here.' As he said it, he moved towards Peggy, pretending to squeeze past. His eyes glazed and his lips parted a fraction.

In the blink of an eye, Angie swung around, holding a wooden drawer full of frilly undergarments. Mr Hawley let out a groan and doubled over, clutching his groin.

'Oh sorry, Mr Hawley, didn't see you standing there.'

Peggy stifled a giggle. Angie was nobody's fool. She was a survivor. And Peggy wanted to be just like her.

'Spencers in this section, slips in this one . . . full slips here, and lace-trimmed in here.'

Peggy studied the bewildering array of intimates. Her own were invariably white, functional and purchased by her mother. Not a lace trim in sight.

'Cream, skin-tone, honey-beige, mid-beige and smoky.'

The silky fabrics were cool to Peggy's touch. Rayon, silk, cotton and nylon. There were delicate shoulder straps and flounced hems; Swiss embroidery trimmed in pink, pearl or powder blue. A whole new world was opening up to her.

'Now I'll show you the nylons.'

Angie knew about all this stuff. She was a sophisticated woman of the world. Like Jackie Kennedy.

'Waltz Dream by Hilton are twelve shillings. Elation are more expensive. Are you taking any of this in?'

Peggy's shoulders slouched. It was no use. None of it made any sense to her. Girdles with zips or hooks-and-eyes; corselettes; snag-proof nylons with Nyoseal; Kayser, Berlei, Hilton. It was like double-Dutch to her. Peggy still had her heart set on a career in teaching. Blackboards and exercise books made far more sense to her than brassieres and slumber sets. But it was out of the question, the dream slipping further from her fingertips with each unpaid gas bill. Peggy couldn't let her mother down.

'Look, we all have to start somewhere, Pegs. I'm not planning to stay here forever either. My sights are set on high-end fashion.' Angie nodded towards a small display of knitwear across the carpeted walkway. 'Keep a watch for me, would you?' she said and headed towards the mannequin.

There was no sign of Mr Hawley but, in the distance, Peggy noticed a well-groomed lady in a white hat and matching gloves, stepping out of the elevator. She was heading straight for them.

Angie slipped a yellow cardigan off the mannequin and draped it around her own shoulders. 'All the way from New York comes this elegant cardigan in pure Merino wool. Team it with a simple sweater in emerald or Windsor pink.' Angie sashayed along her imaginary runway, stopping every now and again to pose and aim a sultry pout at Peggy.

The woman in the hat was getting closer. If she noticed Angie prancing around in the display clothes, they'd both be in trouble. Peggy tried to warn Angie by pointing towards the elevator and pulling a face. But Angie was too busy knotting a Hermès scarf around her shoulders.

'As seen in the latest edition of *Vogue* . . .' By the time Angie had worked out what Peggy was trying to tell her, it was too late.

'I'm looking for a girdle.' The woman was already at the counter. 'And some nylons.'

Peggy remembered the look of horror on Angie's face as the girl with her sights set on Paris and Milan peered out from behind the naked mannequin.

8

A Dog with Fleas

WITH ONE WRIST IN PLASTER, IT WAS DIFFICULT FOR PEGGY to hold the *Women's Weekly*. It was an old issue but if she had read any of the articles before, she couldn't remember them and consumed the glossy pages with fresh eyes. She consoled herself with the thought that if she were going senile, she'd save herself a fortune in magazines.

Days later, the village was still abuzz with the news of Peggy's fall. So many concerned residents had stopped Peggy on her way to the medical centre that she feared she'd miss her appointment. Gossip spread faster than the flu in Jacaranda Retirement Village and, in the tradition of Chinese whispers, the details of Peggy's accident had been exaggerated with each telling. She'd grown weary of setting the record straight, reassuring well-wishers that she hadn't fractured her skull, or ended up in intensive care. Nor would she be moved to a nursing home, that she knew of.

It was as though there was a script that everyone followed. 'If there's anything I can do, just let me know.' She was inundated with offers of help, none of which would ever materialise into anything useful like hosing out the wheelie bins or unblocking her U-bend.

'Thank you, but I'll be fine.' Peggy knew she was as much to blame. She'd told Jenny the same when the phone rang at precisely eight o'clock that morning. There was only one person who ever phoned her at that time, as if checking Peggy had survived another night.

'Mother, I've been worried sick.'

'Hello, Jenny. How are you?'

'It should be me asking you the same thing. Why didn't you call me?'

Where do I start? thought Peggy. 'I didn't want to—'

'Worry me? I'm your daughter. I should be the first person to know in case of an accident.'

Peggy carried the phone over to the kettle. She'd have to multitask if she was going to get to her doctor's appointment on time. Make tea and placate Jenny. It was a tall order, but she'd had plenty of practice at both.

'Hang on a moment, Jenny, I'm just putting the kettle on.'

Peggy could feel the tension building at the other end of the line. She braced herself.

'What are you doing making tea? You should be in bed, resting.'

'I've broken my wrist, not my neck. The rest of my body is working perfectly normally.'

'You were very lucky, this time,' said Jenny. *Lucky. This time.* The words stung like nettles around bare ankles. She wasn't finished. 'It's time to face facts, you're not as young as you used to be. It's nothing to be ashamed about. And at your age, most people need a bit of help.'

'Help?'

'Cleaner, gardener—'

'Butler, Jenny? Shall I appoint a housekeeper and a couple of footmen while I'm at it?' The kettle began to rattle on its stand. Peggy poured a little of the half-boiled water into the teapot, swirled it around and emptied it into the sink one-handed. 'I am perfectly capable of cleaning my own unit, and my garden is the size of a postage stamp.'

She looked out of the window at the overgrown gardenias and the path to her front door, covered in gum leaves. Next month it would be carpeted in jacaranda blossom. Pretty but a slippery death trap if she didn't keep on top of the sweeping. Inside wasn't much better. The laundry basket was overflowing and there was a ring of scum around the shower tray that she could see even without her glasses. If only she'd got to it with the Gumption *before* she'd had the fall.

'I've decided to come and stay for a few days,' said Jenny. 'To help you out.'

'Stay? Here?'

'I don't mind sleeping on the couch. I'll give the whole place a good going over, sort out a few things. It'll be good for us to spend some quality mother–daughter time together.'

The kettle boiled, fogging the kitchen tiles. Peggy froze, teabag poised over the pot. 'You really don't need to do that, darling. I know how busy you are.'

'It's no trouble at all. I have a few appointments that I can reschedule, and I'm sure Eve can manage the animals on her own. Then there's the trip to the ashram, but I can cancel that. Once my car is serviced and they've finished laying the new road, I can be there straightaway.'

Peggy released the teabag into the pot and scalded it with hot water. Switching the phone to her other hand, she carried the pot and then the milk jug to the kitchen table. With a sigh, she said, 'That'd be lovely.' She hoped the garage would take its time with Jenny's car. Was it too much to hope the council would run out of road base too?

~

There were one or two new faces in the waiting room. Word must be spreading about the lovely Dr Stephen. Peggy had been careful not to overshare praise for the young doctor. She didn't want him swamped with moaning Minnies, and turn into Dr Cranky-Pantsky. Peggy wanted Dr Stephen all to herself, like the Queen with her personal physician.

'Peggy, come through,' said Dr Stephen, ignoring the other waiting patients. Peggy could hear the grumbles start before she was even out of earshot.

'My appointment was at 9.30.'

'Mine was 9.15 and I'm still waiting.'

'Well, I was here before all of you.'

'Yes, but you're not until 9.45. It's not our fault if you've come at the wrong time.'

Dr Stephen waited until Peggy sat down. 'I hope you don't mind me calling you in ahead of the others,' he said, 'but I've just had a call from the fracture clinic. Here,' he said signing a piece of paper and sliding it across the desk towards her. 'I've written you a referral letter. Can you be down at the hospital outpatient clinic at twelve o'clock?'

'How did you hear about my little misadventure?'

The doctor turned the computer screen around so Peggy could read the discharge summary from the hospital. There, in black and white, were the words *Geriatric Fall*.

'*Geriatric?*' Peggy squinted at the screen. 'Are they referring to me?'

Dr Stephen nodded soberly.

'I tripped, that's all.'

'Did you feel dizzy or light-headed before it happened? Any palpitations or chest pain? Shortness of breath?'

Dr Stephen peered over the top of his spectacles, fingers hovering above the keyboard. Peggy worried it was a trick question. If she said yes, she'd be off to all sorts of specialists for tests. On the other hand, if she said no, it would confirm her official status as a clumsy old fool.

'I slipped on a banana,' she said avoiding direct eye contact.

'Ri-ght,' said Dr Stephen.

'It won't happen again, I can assure you. Not at that price.'

'I see.'

'You can take my blood pressure now.' Peggy rolled up the sleeve of her good arm. She'd noticed how Angie's assertive style seemed to get her what she wanted. It was time to give it a try.

Dr Stephen wrapped the Velcro cuff around Peggy's upper arm and pressed the automatic button. She held her breath and concentrated very hard on having low blood pressure. She felt cautiously optimistic as the digital numbers flashed on the machine. Air gushed from the cuff. Dr Stephen raised his eyebrows and pressed the start button again.

'It must be difficult for you, doing everything one-handed,' he said eyeing the plaster on her wrist. 'You must be careful not to overdo things, Peggy.'

'My friend Angie Valentine is helping me. She's very . . . capable.' In other words, bossy, overbearing and domineering.

'If you need more help, we could arrange—'

'Carers? No thank you. I have Angie.'

'But what about your children?'

'It's a bit complicated, Doctor.'

It hadn't always been that way. Once upon a time, it had been simple: she was the parent, David and Jenny the children. They were fully-grown adults now, but in Peggy's mind, they were still her children. It was her job to love and protect them, always. She'd been worrying about them since they were babies and she would continue to worry about them. There was the guilt too. It overwhelmed her in the dark hours when she lay awake, ruminating over her failings as a mother, convinced that she alone was responsible for their happiness – or otherwise – as adults.

'Well, you and Angie seem to be managing so far,' he said with a smile. Peggy was grateful he didn't pursue it. Perhaps hers wasn't the only complicated family after all.

'I think the change in medication is working, Doctor.' Peggy circled her new ankles. 'Look, no cankles.'

'The blood pressure is looking better too. 138 over 75. Spot on.' Dr Stephen looked very pleased with himself, as he turned the machine to show Peggy. 'Any improvement in the waterworks?'

Peggy didn't want to burst the doctor's balloon, but she owed him the truth. The poor nurse at the hospital had barely concealed her irritation at Peggy's constant requests for a bedpan. Then there was the front door incident with Brian.

'I get so little warning.'

'Like putting the key in the lock, for instance?'

Peggy's cheeks burned. Had he somehow seen her bolt for the loo, leaving poor Brian abandoned on the doorstep? Or was the young doctor a mind reader with psychopathic powers?

Dr Stephen must have registered her alarm. 'Don't worry, it's a common phenomenon, part of something known as Overactive Bladder Syndrome. It happens because the nerve endings in the bladder are oversensitive, sending signals at the wrong time. Stress and worry can make it worse.'

Peggy was secretly impressed. She'd never had a syndrome before. She tried to imagine the nerve endings, all arguing and trying to talk over each other. 'It sounds rather like one of our residents' committee meetings.'

'The good news is that retraining exercises can make a big difference, even after a lifetime of problems.'

An image of Libby pulsing the giant noodle between her thighs sprang to mind. Peggy knew they were all supposed to do the 'lift and squeeze' exercises every time they came to a red traffic light or road junction. It might explain why the traffic was so slow around the village, and why she'd seen Mavis pull onto the roundabout without signalling the other day.

'Have you contacted the continence nurse?'

'It's top of my list.' Peggy bit her lip. In truth, it sounded too much like hard work. She'd flicked through the brochure, determined to keep an open mind, until she got to the bit about retraining and exercises. Willpower had never been her strong suit, as she'd proved when Jenny bought her a gym membership one Christmas. The place was worse than a cult, using all sorts of mind-bending tactics to prevent her from leaving. When she did eventually manage to terminate her membership, she'd been so worried about being discovered that she'd kept a packed gym bag by the front door for months, in case Jenny happened to drop by. Besides, she'd already had quite enough prodding and poking down there from Dr Stephen.

'What about hypnotism?' She preferred the idea of lying down for an hour while someone spoke softly to her. She'd seen it on the TV, and it seemed to work. A hypnotist had managed to convince a woman in the audience that she was naked, and a man that he was in fact a dog with fleas.

'Mmm,' said Dr Stephen. 'You could try acupuncture, I suppose.'

'Can they do that without needles these days?'

Dr Stephen looked dubious. 'Look, there are some specialists who are even using Botox for this.'

'Botox?' Peggy remembered Angie's still-life expression. Admittedly, from a distance she looked great. But the closer Peggy got, the more disconcerting she found it. It was impossible to read Angie, to tell what she was thinking or feeling. Peggy had experimented in the mirror by stretching her own cheeks to see what she'd look like. The skin had moved a surprising distance, giving her a startled and frankly, embalmed look.

'I believe it can be very effective, but it is quite expensive and only lasts a few months.'

Peggy wondered what Angie really looked like once her injections wore off. It seemed an awful palaver to look younger, and she was sure Brian would disapprove of such vanity. He was such a no-nonsense type – a roast potato of a man.

There had to be an easier way. 'Isn't there a medication you could prescribe to calm my nerve endings down a bit?'

Jenny would disapprove. The last time she'd visited, she'd tried to talk Peggy into stopping all her tablets.

'They're poisoning you, Mum,' she'd said as she read the list on the back of the Webster-pak. 'All these man-made chemicals can't be good for you.'

'They're keeping me alive,' Peggy had replied melodramatically. She had no way of knowing if it was true, not game enough to put it to the test.

The mother–daughter skirmish had stalled at that point, and despite Jenny's last-ditch salvo – blaming sugar for all Peggy's woes – had ended in a stalemate.

Dr Stephen clicked the end of his ballpoint thoughtfully. 'There is something we can try. A tablet. It reduces urgency.'

Peggy's jaw plummeted. 'You mean to say that all these years of shame and embarrassment, and I could have been popping a pill instead?'

She glimpsed another life, a parallel universe full of possibility and opportunity in which Peggy Smart could have done so much more. Been so much more. One in which she'd travelled the globe and lived an utterly fabulous life. A life like Angie Valentine's.

Why hadn't anyone suggested this before? Peggy had lost track of the number of samples she'd handed to Dr Cranky-Pantski, and to old Dr Steele before her, in search of a cure. She'd dropped enough hints. If only she'd had the courage to bring up her lack of control, she might have been spared this life of misery. If only they'd asked.

'Hold on a minute. Let's not get carried away.' Dr Stephen held up his hand as if he was stopping traffic.

Peggy fidgeted with her cast. She so wanted to get carried away, for once.

Dr Stephen swivelled nervously from side to side in his desk chair. The motion made Peggy feel queasy.

'Look,' he said, 'I'm not a big fan of prescribing medication as first line treatment. That goes for any medical condition – high blood pressure, depression, or arthritis. At least not until we've exhausted all the non-pharmacological options. That's especially true in this situation. The drug doesn't work for everyone, and there can be unwanted side effects.'

'Such as?'

'Dry mouth, blurred vision, falls . . .'

She had the dry mouth already, the blurred vision too, whenever she misplaced her reading glasses. No big deal. The potential for another fall was the real concern. One fall was bad enough, but a repeat performance would be the final nail in the coffin.

It was so unfair, thought Peggy. When David fell playing soccer, tearing the ligaments in his knee, nobody tried to put him in a nursing home or treated him like an invalid. He was off work for weeks following his deconstruction operation, just as Mel was starting back at work again after her maternity leave.

Peggy had tried to help out as best she could, dropping in endless meals and taking Sam to Jungle Jim's on a Monday. It had cost her a fortune in fuel and dried lasagne sheets.

'. . . Constipation, dizziness, tiredness.' The list of potential side effects went on. And on.

Peggy's mind wandered back to the accident. She recalled the seagulls flying overhead and the fluffy-edged clouds wafting across the sun. She felt the pain in her arm, and pictured the poor bananas. But there was also Brian, his lovely face full of concern and kindness. His eyes were the same colour as the ocean. *My dear*, he'd said. Not *oh* dear or *old* dear, but *my* dear. *His* dear.

'I'll risk it,' said Peggy. With her eightieth birthday looming, there was no time to waste. 'Just write me a prescription.'

~

Peggy scuttled out of the office, clutching her prescription like a cheque from the Lotto. Dr Stephen called after her. 'Don't forget your referral letter.'

'Referral letter?' Peggy's mind was a blank.

'The fracture clinic. At the hospital.' Dr Stephen handed her a sheet of paper as he ushered through his next patient.

What fracture clinic?

Celia had advised her to request a waterproof lining when they changed the plaster at the fracture clinic. That way she could still go to Aqua. Now Peggy remembered.

'How will you get to the hospital?' Dr Stephen shouted across the waiting room.

'I'll drive,' replied Peggy, a touch irritated. It went without saying.

'No. You can't drive with that cast on your arm. Someone will have to take you.'

9

The Granny Nanny

PEGGY LUNGED FOR THE FINISH LINE. 'PEGGY SMART . . . twelve o'clock,' she wheezed, leaning on the reception desk for support. 'I'm so . . . sorry . . . I'm late.' She panted by way of exaggerated apology.

Unfazed, the receptionist handed her a clipboard. 'Take a seat.'

'Only we had trouble finding a parking space,' puffed Peggy, waiting for the woman to look up.

They'd circled the hospital perimeter three times, looking for a spot close to the outpatients department. Angie insisted on driving her Mini the wrong way past a one-way sign, forcing an ambulance to back up and let them through. In the end, the only available space was right against a wall, and Peggy had to clamber out through the driver's door. There was a tricky moment when, straddling the gear stick, she got stuck and Angie had to flag down a passing porter to help with the extraction. By the time they arrived at the clinic, they were barely speaking.

'I see.' The receptionist glanced up then returned her attention to a pile of X-ray packets.

'It was a long way to walk. For someone of my . . . in my condition.'

Peggy felt a tug on her sleeve and turned to see Angie glaring at her. 'Were you about to say what I think you were?'

'Really, you'd think they'd have special parking spaces reserved for senior citizens.'

Seeing Angie and Peggy looking for somewhere to sit, a woman prodded her teenage son to stand and offer his chair. The lad smiled weakly from beneath his foppish fringe as he rose then returned to his mobile phone. He too had a plaster on his arm.

'Skateboards,' said the woman, rolling her eyes.

'No, I slipped at the beach actually,' said Peggy.

'I think she means him,' said Angie indicating the boy.

Peggy sat down in the vacated seat. 'Thank you,' she said, 'but my appointment was at twelve, so we won't be waiting long.'

'So was ours,' said the woman.

'And mine,' said another man cradling a pair of wooden crutches.

The other nodding heads suggested it would be a long wait.

'Christ alive,' said Angie. 'You stay here and fill the forms in. I'm off to find the bar.'

Welcoming the distraction, the other patients watched Angie sashay towards the exit, dwarfed by her enormous designer handbag.

'That's my friend,' said Peggy to the woman sitting next to her. Part apology, part brag. 'We've known each other over seventy years.'

The woman's eyes widened. 'You must be very close.'

Peggy found herself mulling over the woman's comment. Were they close? Close enough to skip formalities, certainly. Enough shared backstory to skimp on the small talk. But in many ways, she and Angie were as good as strangers. Once the catching up and reminiscing were over, what would they have left to talk about? Would they land on common ground or would an awkward silence take over from the banter, once the novelty wore off?

Peggy tried to concentrate on the form attached to the clipboard. It was the usual stuff, name, address and date of birth. At first she filled in her old address – the family home – by mistake. Peggy was too embarrassed to ask for a new form, so she crossed it out and wrote Jacaranda Retirement Village underneath. Her nerves were playing havoc with her concentration. She was anxious about seeing the specialist, but even more so about the shopping trip.

By the time Angie returned with two plastic cups of steaming brown liquid, Peggy was rifling through her carrier bag, looking for her Medicare card.

Angie pulled a face as she took a sip from her cup. 'Tastes like shit.'

The teenager looked up from his phone and smirked.

'Angie! Keep your voice down. What will people think?'

'I couldn't give a toss what people think. Women should swear more.'

A young mother speared Angie with a look and covered her little girl's ears. Angie turned to her and said, 'Take my advice and teach your daughter a few profanities while she's still young. It's very empowering, especially for girls.' All eyes were on Angie now. 'See? At least people pay attention when women swear.'

Angie fidgeted in her chair and checked her watch. 'Arabella closes at five. At this rate, we'll miss her.'

'You go on without me,' said Peggy, unzipping her wallet.

'No way. You can't wriggle out of this. You don't know Arabella like I do. She won't take kindly to being stood up.'

There was no sign of the Medicare card in Peggy's wallet. It was stuffed full of loyalty cards for stores she never visited, and a whole stack of redundant bankcards for which she'd forgotten the PINs.

'Allow me,' said Angie, taking over.

'Try the flap, behind my driver's licence.'

Angie held a green card at arm's length and squinted at the numbers.

'Here,' said Peggy. 'Try these.' She handed her reading glasses to Angie.

'That's better.'

'Where are your glasses?'

'Don't need any. The only things I ever read were the price tags in shops, and I stopped needing to do that after husband number three.'

'What about books?'

'Darling, haven't you heard of audiobooks? I play them in my car.'

Peggy recalled David saying he did something similar in his new BMW. The car was cleverer than she was. Apparently it even had blue teeth.

'Isn't it amazing what technology can do nowadays?'

Angie experimented with the reading glasses, closing one eye then the other, examining her hand at close range then staring off into the distance. 'Bloody marvellous,' she muttered.

After a few minutes, the receptionist came to collect the clipboard. 'Not long left now,' she said cheerfully, indicating the shrinking line of patients ahead. Peggy wondered if she said this to all the elderly patients.

As Angie tucked the Medicare card back into its slot she paused, staring at the photograph in the outside flap of Peggy's wallet.

'Are these the grandchildren?'

Peggy smiled. 'That's Sam. He's turning six soon. And this little cutie is Emily. She's three and a half. They're David's children.'

Angie studied the picture, lost in some far-away thought. 'Do you see much of them?'

'Yes, and no.'

Peggy didn't know where to start. Somehow, Angie had found her Achilles tail. Naturally, young Sam and Emily were the rosy apples of her eye, two cheeky cherubs who could do no wrong. Grandparents and their grand-offspring – it was a unique bond that straddled the decades and leap-frogged the generations. It was a second chance at a less austere childhood for those who, through no fault of their own, had grown up during the war. There was something about a shared silliness, about not taking each other too seriously, that bound them, and a healthy sense of what really mattered in life. Like ice-cream and tickles, stories and old-fashioned games. It was about walks in nature and funny faces. It was being able to say, 'I love you.' It was sacred, and at the same time fragile. And it came with one enormous hairy-legged fly in the ointment, or more accurately two of them. Their parents.

When Mel first talked about going back to work, Peggy had volunteered to have the children one morning a week at her place. She wanted to help them out, since they were always dropping hints about how tight finances were. Mel treated motherhood like an Olympic event, and Peggy feared her over-parenting would see the poor kids burn out before they even reached high school. They'd had their differences about parenting, and Peggy soon learned to keep her opinions to herself. But as a grandmother, she had to do something, before it was too late.

At first, Mel was reluctant to abdicate responsibility, hovering in the kitchen when she dropped them off and enquiring what activities Peggy had planned. Sam and Emily came with an instruction manual – an actual flow chart as it happened – indicating naps and meal times. There were flashcards to recite and strict instructions for no commercial television. Of course, from the start, Peggy never had any intention of following Mel's regime. In those precious hours together, she was free to spoil and indulge, as was every grandparent's right. Kids were kids, and Peggy had already raised two. One of whom, she wanted to remind her daughter-in-law, had turned out well enough for Mel to marry.

Peggy began to cherish every precious moment alone with her grandchildren. Time with them had a pace all of its own. She taught Sam to roll pastry and cut little scalloped cases to fill with jam. They raided her drawers and jewellery boxes in search of treasure then laughed at cartoons together.

The local ducks gained so much weight they could barely waddle, let alone fly.

There was a patience and tolerance that only came with age. An unhurried meander through the day without deadline or goal that let grandchildren be grandchildren, and Granny be Granny.

What was strange was that Peggy had so few memories of day-to-day motherhood with David and Jenny. It was as though she'd lived those days under a light anaesthetic. But the years were there, plain to see, in a series of grainy photographs. Peggy, Ted and the children, all smiles. Christmas trees and birthday cakes. Tight-skinned summer days with buckets and spades. Memories strung together like bunting, with nothing in between. Now she had a second chance to relive the best bits, minus the sleepless nights and bone-crumbling weariness of life as a new mother. It broke her heart that Ted was missing out, but that was the way the cookie curdled.

Before she knew it, one morning became two, then three. Mornings stretched into afternoons as Mel had her nails done or popped to the hairdresser after work. At first, Peggy absorbed it like a sponge, moulding her own life around her grandchildren, or rather her daughter-in-law's refurbishment schedule. It was only when Sam and Emily arrived with a basket of ironing one Wednesday that the granny realised she had become the nanny.

With her own life on hold, she began to harbour a secret resentment. She'd already given up her quilting class and resigned from the choir. Where once she'd looked forward to seeing her grandchildren, planning special trips to the park and the zoo, she began to dread their arrival. It was exhausting without Ted to share the load, not to mention expensive, by the time she'd bought extra biscuits and cordial. Eventually, the perpetually snotty noses and endless tummy bugs took their toll.

A deep sigh escaped.

'What's the matter?' asked Angie.

'I feel like I'm between a rock and the deep blue sea,' said Peggy.

'How come?'

'It's David, my son, or rather Mel, my daughter-in-law. Ever since I told her how tiring it was for a pensioner to look after two small children all day, she's been funny with me.'

'I've never had a daughter-in-law myself, but I've been one enough times to know how prickly that relationship can be.'

'She told me that if it was too much for me, she would make other arrangements.'

'That's fair enough.'

'I suppose so. But it hurt. I still want to look after Sam and Emily, but I just didn't want to be tied down to regular days. I don't want to be taken for granted. It was weeks ago, and I feel like I've been begging for scraps under the table ever since.'

'She sounds like a pain in the arse to me,' said Angie.

'Angie!' Peggy grinned. 'That's my daughter-in-law you're talking about.'

Angie drained her plastic cup and shuddered. 'Still not sure if that was coffee or tea.'

Peggy fought to swallow unbidden tears. 'And the worst thing is, they've been treating me like an old lady ever since, dropping hints about care homes. I think they're deliberately punishing me.'

'Are you sure you're not being oversensitive?'

'They told me I shouldn't be driving.'

'That's outrageous. I remember you driving your mother's old Holden back in the fifties. You were perfectly safe behind the wheel. As long as you didn't have to park.'

'How could I ever forget that old heap?'

'That's no way to talk about your mother.'

'You're terrible.' Peggy dabbed under her eyes with a tissue.

'I don't understand. What's the big deal? It's not like you crashed your car with her precious kids inside is it?'

Peggy stared at the floor. 'Not crashed . . . exactly.'

'You didn't, did you?'

Peggy nodded, a fresh crop of tears welling. 'It was more of a nudge really, a minor miscalculation. No-one was hurt. I swore Sam to secrecy, but he let it slip.'

'Oh no.'

'Yes, he told David he couldn't wait to go in Granny's bumper car again.'

'Bloody hell, Pegs.'

'And now they want to take the car away from me. They treat me like I'm incapable of doing anything. Like I'm an invalid.'

'You're not an invalid,' said Angie, patting Peggy's plaster cast.

At that moment, a nurse in a blue uniform appeared in front of them with a wheelchair.

'Mrs Smart? Hop in.'

~

The orthopaedic registrar did a double-take. He appeared to be wearing the same crumpled shirt from the day of the fall. He was certainly still wearing the same world-weary expression.

'Mrs Smart and Mrs Valentine. We meet again.'

Unprompted, Peggy said, 'We're managing very well, thank you.'

'Excellent,' he said, addressing her broken bones.

He produced an enormous pair of scissors and cut through the somewhat shabby cast. He prodded the bruised swelling that was her wrist.

'Ouch.' Peggy winced.

'Excellent,' said the registrar again.

'How long before she can go skateboarding again, Doctor?' Angie sniggered into her compact mirror as she applied a fresh layer of lipstick.

Peggy apologised. 'Sorry, Doctor. It's a joke.'

The registrar wasn't smiling. He wrote on a form and handed it to the nurse. 'Four weeks, with a new X-ray,' he said. 'Do you drink milk?'

'Just a splash, and one sugar please.' Peggy was pleasantly surprised. She hadn't anticipated refreshments. But then, it had been a long wait.

The registrar was taken aback. 'Calcium, in dairy products. I'm talking about strengthening your bones.'

'My doctor told me to avoid anything white.'

'Tinned salmon, green leafy vegetables, almonds then.'

Peggy didn't like to tell him about the problem she had with nuts and her teeth. She'd stick with the tinned salmon instead.

'You need vitamin D too. One capsule every day.'

The nurse jumped in, adding, 'Don't forget the sun is an important source of vitamin D.'

'Especially for older or institutionalised patients,' said the registrar, delivering the winning punch.

Older? Institutionalised? Did he assume because she had a cast on her arm and had arrived by wheelchair that she lived in an institution? It wasn't fair. Angie – dressed in a satin jumpsuit with an arm full of brightly coloured ethnic bangles – didn't look like she lived in an institution. At least, not in an aged-care one.

'In that case, I'd like a waterproof cast,' said Peggy. There was one place she could get her daily dose of sun. And Brian.

'Make it any colour except beige,' Angie added.

10

The Chamber of Horrors

'I THINK WE SHOULD GET CRACKING. WE WASTED ENOUGH time at the fracture clinic,' said Angie briskly.

'I'm not sure I can face this on an empty stomach.' Peggy stared at the display of cakes and muffins and then at the other shoppers, sitting enjoying their coffee and sweet treats.

'Let's have a teeny tiny little look in Arabella's and then come back here for a nice cup of tea. How does that sound?' Angie's tone sounded as if she was trying to placate a fractious toddler. It was the same voice Peggy used when she attempted to lure Jenny into a dress shop when she was four. There was still an atmosphere between them, and sometimes Peggy wondered if Jenny still held the whole ghastly Broderie Anglaise debacle against her.

'Alright. You win.' Peggy slumped a whole inch. To argue would be petulant, now that Angie had already sacrificed precious hours of her own life drinking vended tea at the fracture clinic. Of all the possible options, bus, taxi or phoning David, asking Angie for a lift had been the least unappealing.

Yet again, she found herself in Angie's debt. It was as though she was fighting some unscrupulous loan shark, where every favour granted sank Peggy deeper and deeper in arrears. What's more, Angie was starting to get on her nerves.

It seemed like a lifetime ago and yet the fall was only days ago. Angie had wasted no time in stripping the remaining items from the wardrobe, and the drawers. With the majority of her clothing now consigned to bin-liners, Peggy quite literally had nothing to wear. Not content with her assault on apparel, Angie had confiscated the biscuit tin and hauled Peggy off the couch for a walk, just as she was settling down to watch *The Chase*. What's more, the inside of the fridge was unrecognisable. It looked like Angie was composting in there, with strange plants filling the cheese and cold-cuts trays. Then there was her obsession with chia seeds; tiny specks of misery that burrowed under Peggy's gums, and the anaemic-looking milk that barely coloured her tea. With pots of yoghurt containing millions of actual bacteria, the whole kitchen was fast becoming a health hazard. It was a wonder Angie had lived so long on this fandangled diet, and a miracle she hadn't contracted wisteria along the way.

Basil, on the other hand, was positively thriving in Angie's company. Somehow, she'd persuaded him to eat tinned food – albeit some fancy organic stuff that cost a fortune – and Peggy had never seen his tail wag so furiously.

It would be weeks until she could have her independence back. If things carried on like this, Peggy would be forced to move out of her own unit.

'Do hurry up, Pegs.' Angie was almost trotting towards the expensive end of the shopping mall. She was a woman on a mission. Peggy feared *she* was that mission.

With her stomach growling, Peggy trailed behind, a plodding draughthorse to Angie's show pony. With wall-to-wall designer boutiques and homewares stores, this was uncharted territory. It was a parallel universe in which Angie seemed completely at ease, navigating the familiar route like a spawning salmon.

'I think I need to go to the loo,' said Peggy, struggling to keep up.

'You can't possibly need to go again,' said Angie spinning around on her kitten heels. 'You only went five minutes ago. It's all in your mind.'

Peggy remembered she was carrying Dr Stephen's prescription in her bag. The new calming pills for her neurotic bladder. She'd made up her mind to give it a try. Her heart quickened, sensing a major turning point in her life. It was an opportunity to take control of her life, or at least her storage capacity. She was at the edge of a precipice. As long as she could get to the pharmacy before it closed.

Arabella's was the very last shop. *Typical.* Peggy paused outside to catch her breath. She'd used up her full repertoire of excuses and delaying tactics. It was time to face the firing squad.

The shop was empty apart from a petite woman with platinum hair, who was busy folding sweaters on a table. For a clothes shop, there were surprisingly few actual clothes on display.

'What are you waiting for?' Angie grabbed a stiff-limbed Peggy by the arm and dragged her through the door.

'Angela, darling.'

'Arabella, you look exquisite, as always.'

Peggy felt as though she'd just walked onto the set of *Real Housewives*. She squirmed, trying to hide the green eco-shopping bag she was using as a handbag while Angie and Arabella exchanged air-kisses and lightweight compliments.

'Let me introduce my friend, Peggy. We were at school together, and we worked together at Blake's a million years ago.' Angie prodded Peggy as if she were parading her at a livestock market.

Arabella fell into silent appraisal. She stood back, moving between different vantage points to take in every aspect.

Peggy hadn't felt like this since her third-grade teacher hauled her out in front of the class.

'Shyness will get you nowhere, young lady,' the teacher had bellowed, his jellied eyes bulging with indignation. 'Why can't you be more outgoing like your friend here?'

Peggy wondered if Angie remembered it, since she had been the outgoing friend.

'So Arabella, can you work your magic?' asked Angie.

'I like a challenge.'

The two women herded Peggy towards the fitting room at the back of the shop, where they confiscated her shopping bag. Shivering behind the heavy velvet curtain, Peggy pulled her cardigan over her cast and draped it over a hook on the wall. Her wrist ached and she was desperate for a cup of tea. Having missed lunch, her empty stomach was inconsolable. Why ever did she let Angie talk her into this? It was all a huge waste of time and money. Money she simply didn't have to spare.

Every now and again, Peggy caught a snippet of conversation from beyond the curtain. 'I say let's just start from scratch.'

'More like a sixteen, I'd say.'

'Tailored. Must be tailored with those knees.'

'Definitely no stripes.'

'Forget sleeveless.'

Sensing the activity outside, Peggy cowered in the fitting room, by now dressed only in her underwear. Surrounded by full-length mirrors, she was trapped in 360 degrees of purgatory. When was the last time she'd actually looked at her body?

At first, Peggy looked anywhere but at her reflection. The revulsion she felt at the sight of her own body filled her throat. The shame stung her cheeks. She covered her eyes with her hands, yet through her fingers she could still see the dimpled thighs, the lumpy whorls of purple veins on her legs and the folds of skin hanging from her shoulder blades. Every part of her disintegrating body was another chapter in the story of her life. The scar on her shin, the legacy of an old hockey injury, was a reminder of a vibrant youth, and her pale skin, pebble-dashed with brown warty things, testament to a childhood under the Australian sun. Peggy dropped her hands to her belly and traced the lacework of silvery stretch marks: the story of motherhood.

Ted had loved every inch of her. He'd told her often enough, both in words and his search for her soft folds beneath the bedclothes. The waist that had forgotten it was a waist; the sagging breasts. She missed his touch and cherished the memory of his ever-hopeful advances, so rarely reciprocated.

Suddenly the air was too thin. Peggy drew breath after breath, each one longer and deeper than the last. No matter how hard she sucked the molecules into her lungs, she couldn't get enough air.

There were no windows or doors in the fitting room, no possible means of escape. She was trapped inside this torture chamber, waiting for her tormentors to return.

'We'll start with a few wardrobe staples.' Angie appeared between the curtains, a pile of garments draped over each arm.

All potential exits were now blocked by tailored separates. Peggy debated running out of the shop shouting, 'Help me, I've been kidnapped!'

Held prisoner in a suburban shopping mall? No-one would believe her. Her only option was to plead for the mercy of her captors.

'Can I powder my nose first?' she said in a small voice.

'No. You're not leaving until you've tried these on.'

Arabella appeared behind Angie with more clothes on hangers. 'And these.'

Peggy folded her arms in defiance, the effect diminished by the comical blue of the new waterproof cast on one wrist. Blue was her favourite colour, but the shade she'd ended up with at the fracture clinic was more child's poster paint than the tasteful cornflower she'd envisaged. She looked at her own clothes hanging on the hooks – frumpy, dated, and flecked with blond dog hair – then at the two polished and sophisticated women with the hangers.

'I need a cup of tea.'

'One outfit,' said Angie firmly. 'One outfit and then we can go for tea.'

'And cake?'

'Two outfits and you can eat what the hell you like.'

'Promise?'

Peggy pulled the giant curtain across. It was one thing to stand there virtually naked, it was another to have a complete stranger watch as you struggled to fit into a pair of pants.

The first item off the hanger, a pair of black crepe pants, slid up her legs with surprising ease. She braced herself for the usual tug of war with the waist-fastening business. Elasticated waistbands were so much more practical, and comfortable.

To her astonishment, Peggy slid the button through the buttonhole and fastened the zip without any of the usual sucking in or squeezing. She daren't look at herself yet.

'Try the pants with the cream blouse,' a voice shouted from outside.

She slipped the blouse across her shoulders, the silky coolness of the fabric little more than a whisper against Peggy's skin. The tiny pearl buttons proved too great a challenge one-handed, and sensing the growing impatience beyond the curtain, she left the cuffs undone with the fabric hanging loose over her cast.

'Are you ready yet?' called Angie.

'Okay,' said Peggy, stepping outside the fitting room.

The two oppressors primped and preened, adjusting seams and doing up the tiny buttons at the cuffs. Angie appeared from nowhere with a necklace of giant pearls in multiple strands. She choked Peggy with it before letting it sit just inside the neckline of the blouse.

Very slowly, Peggy's eyes rose to meet her reflection in the mirror. Accustomed to the years of disappointment, what she saw took her breath away. Instead of a pensioner camouflaged in fifty shades of beige, she saw an elegant, mature woman with a figure.

'Team this with a cream blazer for a stylish lunch outfit, or a silver clutch for evening.' Arabella draped the blazer around Peggy's shoulders and thrust her feet into a pair of black patent shoes with a tiny heel. 'Every woman needs a pair of beautiful wide-leg pants. You can dress them up or down.'

There wasn't much call for lunch outfits at Jacaranda Retirement Village. Usually it was a quick ham sandwich at the kitchen table with Basil, or sometimes a wrap in the coffee shop after Aqua with the girls. She tried to picture their reaction if she turned up in this outfit. She imagined Mavis, speechless for once. It'd be worth the effort just to see her face. And Brian's.

'That's a yes then,' said Angie, pushing Peggy back into the changing room for round two.

The next outfit was an inky-blue shift dress that finished just below Peggy's knees. The hem concealed her knee-replacement scar and the sleeves ended at the most flattering part of her upper arm. Angie pulled the zip up at the back. The dress fit perfectly.

The seed of a smile germinated on Peggy's lips.

'Very Helen Mirren,' said Arabella, throwing a matching chiffon wrap around her shoulders.

'Now there's an idea. I've seen a fantastic photo of Helen on the front cover of *Women's Weekly*. That's how I'm going to get Alessandro to do your hair.'

Peggy stared at Angie. 'Alessandro?'

Angie was already unzipping the back of the dress. It was all going too fast, the merry-go-round speeding up before she was ready. Peggy hadn't even had time to check the price tags, usually the first thing she looked at. These clothes were all very well, but when would she ever get the chance to wear them? She spent most of her time pottering around the village in easy-care fabrics. Her steam iron had been gathering cobwebs in the laundry for months. The idea of getting all dolled up just to take Basil for his daily widdle was absurd. She had to put an end to the situation, before it got any more out of hand.

'I'm really more of a casual girl,' she said, realising her mistake.

'Not to worry. Leave it to me.' Arabella scurried off for more hunting and gathering.

Angie leaned against the wall of the fitting room. 'Are you okay with this, Pegs?'

The tears fogged Peggy's reflection. She swept them away with the back of her right hand. 'I don't know why I'm crying, silly old fool. It's not that I don't appreciate what you're trying to do here. It's just that, I think I'd resigned myself to getting old. I could never see the point of making an effort. Just finding something in the wardrobe that didn't have food stains down the front was an achievement.'

'But can't you see the potential? Why hide that great figure of yours?'

'Angie, don't.' Peggy retrieved a tissue from the sleeve of her cardigan and blotted under her eyes. 'I feel so confused, like I don't know who I'm supposed to be anymore.'

'You're you, you daft mare. Wonderful, warm, funny Peggy. The person inside doesn't change just because a few years have passed.'

'I think it's going to take more than a new wardrobe to bring Ted back.'

Angie placed a hand on the dimpled skin of Peggy's arm. 'You have to accept that Ted's gone now. But you're still here, and there's a lot of life left to live. Start living it.'

'It's easier said than done.'

'We all have to start somewhere. I just want you to see the potential you have inside. By the time I've finished with you, everyone else is going to see it too.'

Peggy smiled at the idea of herself in the utterly fabulous shift dress clinking Waterford flutes with Brian, dressed in his signature casual ensemble of light-coloured pants and collared shirt.

Arabella appeared carrying several more hangers. 'I was thinking classic cotton chinos, and a crisp shirt.'

So was I, thought Peggy.

~

She couldn't afford everything. In fact, she couldn't afford any of the items. Peggy fretted in the changing room as she squeezed back into her old clothes. The frumpy woman in the mirror pleaded with her. *The black pants. You have to have them. Go on. Ple-ase? But then you won't have anything to wear them with. Unless you get the cream blouse too? The dress, oh my, the dress. Brian, the Waterford crystal, and the dress.*

When Peggy finally emerged, ready to apologise for wasting everyone's afternoon, she found half a dozen matching bags lined up on the counter, each filled with parcels of tissue paper.

The floor turned to quicksilver. She couldn't possibly afford all of this. She'd given up the mental tally when the dress had appeared.

Peggy's vocal cords froze as she opened her mouth to protest.

'Lovely to meet you,' said Arabella, taking a mute Peggy by the shoulders and planting a kiss on one cheek, then the other. 'Our summer range is due in soon. Do come back and have a look.'

'Grab your bag, Pegs. Even I'm dying for a cup of tea.' Angie handed her an expensive-looking handbag. The smell of the soft mocha leather filled Peggy's nostrils, and she had an irresistible urge to cradle it like a newborn baby. Nestled in the pristine silk lining were her wallet and phone, alongside the prescription.

'Where's my shopping bag?'

'In the bin darling, where it belongs,' said Angie. 'Now I just have one word of warning – this bag may be Italian but is most definitely not designed for fresh produce.'

'Don't forget these,' said Arabella, loading Peggy's one good arm with purchases.

'Ciao.' Angie blew Arabella a kiss and held the door open for Peggy.

'I need to pay,' squeaked Peggy, reaching for her wallet.

'No, you don't,' said Angie. 'I'll explain later.'

~

Angie carried the tray of teacups and a jug of milk to the table where she'd already dumped the shopping bags. Peggy followed, grateful to sit at last and rest her aching legs. Operation Peggy was beginning to take it out of her. Angie, on the other hand was like a dynamo, like one of those Energiser bunnies that went on and on. She seemed not in the least bit fatigued by their marathon shopping trip. But then again, she was the pro.

Peggy divided the tea between the two cups one-handed and used the knife to halve the slice of toasted pear and walnut bread. At least Angie had let her pay for the refreshments. It was the least she could do.

Peggy sipped her tea and placed the china cup back onto the saucer with a grateful sigh. She looked at Angie, hoping the right words would form on her lips. Instead, the syllables crashed into each other in a rush for the exit. In the end, all she could manage was, 'Thank you.'

'You don't have to say anything. It's my treat. Well actually, that's not strictly true. It's my ex-husband's treat.' Seeing Peggy's look of confusion she added, 'Fourth and final. All I'll say about Richard is that there is sweet poetic justice in using his money to make a woman feel good about herself again.'

For all the tragedy and heartache that she must have endured along the way, Angie was every bit the consummate professional when it came to divorce and widowhood.

'I don't care, it's still way too generous of you.'

'It's a long story,' Angie sighed. 'Let's enjoy the spoils of war, and I'll fill you in on the rest over a bottle of bubbles some time.'

Peggy caught Angie ogling the young waiter as he collected the empty cups on the next table. He caught her eye and smiled.

'He's a bit young for you,' joked Peggy.

Angie turned back to her friend. 'There's no harm in admiring the scenery. Besides, I prefer to see myself as middle-aged.'

'Middle-aged if you're planning to live to a hundred and sixty,' said Peggy. They laughed before falling silent again. 'Do you get lonely?'

'Sometimes.'

'Seriously, does it frighten you, being on your own?'

'If I stop to think too hard about it, I get scared, like I'm looking down at my life from a great height. I have to face facts: I am alone. I have no family. I've spent more time with my lawyers than my friends in the past thirty years. Which is why it was so wonderful to find you again after all this time, Pegs darling.'

Something made Peggy feel uneasy. She couldn't quite put her finger on it. 'Yes, fancy.'

'I never forgot you.' Angie patted the back of the blue cast with her perfectly manicured fingers. Peggy's own nails were a mish-mash of shapes and lengths. She'd always intended to grow them, but when one broke she had to start all over again. There was a pair of yellow washing-up gloves under the sink. They were still in the packet. Ashamed, Peggy curled her fingers into her palms. She wondered if Angie saw her purely as a project. Yes, they'd been friends a long time ago, but today, all they really had in common was their fear of being alone.

'I never thought I'd cope on my own after Ted died,' said Peggy, corralling some crumbs with her fingertip. 'I suppose I've finally come to terms with being alone. I still have Basil, but even he's on his last legs, poor old thing. I've made a few friends in the village, more acquaintances really. It's difficult to make those really deep friendships when you're our age, don't you find? No sooner have you got to know each other than you're wearing their favourite colour and singing *Abide With Me*.'

The two women looked at each other, expressions fixed with concern, each wondering who would be the first to crack. Angie snorted into her Earl Grey.

Peggy giggled and squeezed her knees together. 'We are awful, aren't we?'

'You have to laugh darling, because the alternative is too depressing.'

'We always enjoyed a good laugh, you and me. We never took ourselves too seriously, did we? Marriage, kids, moving to the village. Sometimes I think growing up took away all the fun.'

'Now you're depressing me, not to mention cramping my style.' Angie called the young waiter over to the table, and ordered another pot of tea. Peggy watched her in action, fluttering her eyelashes and touching his arm quite unnecessarily. To Peggy's surprise, he didn't recoil in horror or regard her with distaste. In fact, he took it in good humour and winked as he went off to fetch the tea. Peggy couldn't help feeling she was being treated to a masterclass. But then, Angela Valentine had had plenty of practice.

Part of Peggy wanted to hug Angie and tell her how much she'd missed her, but she was wary. A tingle in her bladder urged caution, however much she longed to dive straight back into their friendship. She wanted to trust Angie but didn't want to end up broken and disappointed if it all went sour. People could change in fifty years. Who knew what secret hurts the undivinable Angie Valentine had hidden up her leg-of-mutton sleeves?

'Do you think you'll ever get married again?' Peggy tested the idea out loud. It was all very well to dream about a life with Brian, but could she ever pledge herself to another man after Ted? It was so final. There'd be no changing her mind later if he snored or objected to her cold feet.

The tea arrived and this time, Angie played mother. 'I think I'm done with marriage,' she said as she poured. 'Wasn't it Albert Einstein who said the definition of insanity was doing the same thing over and over again and expecting different results? No, I've finally got my shit together, and I'm not prepared to compromise for anybody.'

Peggy wondered if there was still time to get her own shit together, before it was too late.

Angie continued. 'What about you? Got any plans for a new husband?'

'Me? Of course not.' Peggy forced a little laugh. She couldn't let on about her secret crush lest Angie make it her next mission to play matchmaker. *A closed mouth gathers no feet.*

'Even if you met Mr Right?'

'I couldn't possibly. What would David and Jenny say?'

'What, those two middle-aged people you call your children? It doesn't matter what they think. It's about what you want.'

'It's not as simple as that.'

'Don't you want to feel the touch of another human again, skin against skin?'

'I go to the podiatrist every six weeks.'

'I'm not talking about your feet. What about sex?'

Peggy was poised to insert the last chunk of pear and walnut bread into her mouth but rested the fork back down on the plate, her mouth suddenly dry.

'I think I'm a bit too old for all that nonsense.'

'Too old for sex?'

A young couple on the next table turned around. Peggy could hear them giggling.

'I'm seventy-nine, Angie, and unless I'm very much mistaken, so are you.'

'So?'

Peggy became aware that a grey-haired man on a nearby table was peering over the top of his newspaper in their direction.

'Do you mean to say you're still having it?' she asked, leaning in and lowering her voice to a whisper.

'Why not? It's very good for women of our age. I still enjoy it, so why should I stop?'

Peggy was reluctant to point out the obvious. 'With whom?'

'Mostly with myself these days, sadly.'

'Isn't there a law against that kind of thing?'

'What, masturbation? It's not like we're talking murder.'

We will be in a minute, thought Peggy. 'Angie,' she pleaded, 'keep your voice down.'

The man with the newspaper began to cough, and Peggy wondered if his panini had gone down the wrong way.

'I'm not ashamed. I've always enjoyed a healthy sex life, and I don't intend to stop now, just because society thinks it's icky or even worse, quaint somehow.' Angie swivelled round to address the young couple who were making gagging gestures behind her back. 'FYI, old people are having sex. A lot of it.'

They stood up to leave.

Some more than others, thought Peggy, pouring the dregs of the tea into Angie's cup.

'Use it or lose it,' said Angie. 'Besides, it's great for the pelvic floor and I sleep like a log afterwards.'

Peggy remembered the prescription in her bag. 'It's late. I think we'd better be getting back to the village. Do you mind if we stop by the pharmacy on the way?'

'Sure, but first, tell me something. What does Peggy Smart do for fun these days?'

Peggy looked for inspiration in her empty teacup. Aside from Aqua class and coffee mornings, what *did* she do for fun? There was Happy Hour on a Friday. Bingo, bridge, Tai Chi. It would be a challenge to entertain Angie after her glamorous life in New York, London and Paris. There was however, one event on her calendar she'd like to see Angie liven up. It was there in glitter gold.

'If you're free, tomorrow night is the residents' committee meeting,' said Peggy.

11

The Collapse of Modern Civilisation

PEGGY CRADLED THE SHERRY GLASS AND BASKED IN HER impeccable timing. Side-stepping the crush at the Clubhouse bar, she'd used the sympathy vote to pinch the last packet of salt and vinegar chips. They were called something fancy nowadays, balsamic vinegar and sea salt, or some such rubbish. All salt came from the sea, didn't it?

'Ladies and gentlemen, I'd like to call the meeting to order.' Mavis Peacock's high-pitched voice cut through the din. The ding-ding of a spoon against a china teacup sparked a game of musical chairs, with committee members bobbing up and down like silver-haired meerkats. Peggy took a sip of sherry and wondered if it would be too forward to save Brian a seat.

'Do hurry up. I'm sure none of us wants to miss *MasterChef*,' said Mavis, breathing onto her lenses and polishing them on a lace-trimmed handkerchief.

'It's a wonder she doesn't set them on fire,' said a man's voice. Peggy swivelled round to see Brian standing behind her. She giggled in spite of herself. Brian was always so witty.

Peggy imagined him entertaining guests at supper parties with amusing anecdotes about tax returns.

'Mind if I snuggle in next to you?' Brian dragged a chair from a nearby table and squeezed it into the circle.

'No, snuggle away.' Peggy cringed at herself. She took another swig of Harveys Bristol Cream and wondered if it was too late for a refill.

Brian opened a packet of roasted nuts and offered it to her. 'Fancy a nibble?'

Peggy felt like she'd been electrocuted. Brian Cornell was flirting with her. Flames of desire tore through her body, erupting across her décolletage. She fanned herself with a copy of the minutes and glanced around the group to see if anyone else had noticed.

Peggy watched Vince Livingstone take a swig of his beer leaving a yeasty moustache on his top lip that he licked away with the tip of his tongue. His wife Sylvia nibbled a restrained corner from the wedge of King Island brie. Peggy wondered if the Livingstones still enjoyed a spot of rumpy-pumpy between the flannelettes. Immediately, she regretted the thought – the unwelcome picture of the committee's power couple with a post-coital glow now flourishing in Peggy's desolate short-term memory.

'How's the arm?' whispered Brian. 'I've been thinking about you all week.'

I've been thinking about you all week too.

'Much better, thank you,' she replied. 'I'm a tough old bird.'

Old bird? Peggy mentally kicked herself.

Brian was wearing a new shirt; the creases still visible down the front. A wife would have ironed those out for him.

She imagined the two of them getting dressed together in their bedroom. 'You can't go out like that,' she might say in mock outrage. 'Let me press your shirt for you. And take those pants off. I'll give them a going over too.'

Peggy flushed again. She was getting carried away. Ever since her little chat with Angie, she'd been thinking about sex more than was healthy for someone in a retirement village. She'd found herself rereading the steamy scenes in her latest library book, and lying awake imagining Brian next to her under the Sheridan duvet cover.

Mavis cleared her throat and rustled the papers on her lap. 'Do we have any apologies?'

Celia raised a grease-stained hand. 'Yes, Pat Pritchett sends her apologies. She's just had her cataracts done and things are still a little hazy.'

'Things are always a little hazy for Pat,' whispered Brian, 'especially after Happy Hour.'

Peggy sniggered, spilling sherry down the front of her new top. She rifled through her handbag to find a clean tissue. It was the first outing for the navy Capri pants and striped boat-necked tee with the three-quarter sleeves. Peggy wondered if Brian had noticed her new outfit. She slid her gaze towards him, but he was looking at Celia as she swigged from her sherry glass, oblivious.

What did Brian see in Celia, thought Peggy? Her close-cropped hair was almost white; deep lines framed her eyes like quotation marks. Below the neck she was sturdy and straight-limbed, her skin tanned from the outdoors. Celia was peculiarly ageless. Peggy imagined her looking no different at forty or fifty. She was great company, but kept her cards close to her chest. She wasn't the marrying type, she'd told

Peggy one day while they were waiting for the new girl to operate the coffee machine in the community centre. She had a niece who visited occasionally. Beyond that, nothing. Celia seemed more at ease in the company of machinery than people. Peggy hoped that included Brian.

'Moving on,' said Mavis, glowering over the top of her half-moon spectacles. 'I will assume everyone has read the minutes from the last meeting.'

At that moment, the door opened and Angie walked in. 'Is this the residents' committee?' she said. In a red, belted shirt-dress and elegant sandals, she looked fabulous.

'Can I help you?' Mavis scrutinised the new arrival as if deciding whether to spray her with Mortein, or squish her in toilet paper and flush her away.

Peggy stood up. 'This is Angela Valentine, an old friend of mine. I invited her to the meeting.'

'There's a spare seat over here,' said Brian, jumping up to fetch another chair, tripping over the wheels of a stray walking-frame in his haste.

'Not so fast, Brian,' said Mavis. 'Section 14-3 of the rulebook states that any person who is not a member of the committee must not attend a meeting unless invited by the Chairperson.'

Secretary Sheila Martin chewed the end of her pencil thoughtfully.

Celia's BBC vowels rose from behind a copy of the Rules and Regulations. 'I think you'll find Mavis, that section 8-3 says that any resident at the meeting can nominate themselves or another resident to be a committee member.'

Peggy wondered if Celia had designs on the committee's top job. Was she planning a coup to oust the incumbent

Mavis? Once upon a time, Peggy had contemplated seeking her own nomination for the presidency, seeing it as an opportunity for some top-drawer Brian-time. But she wasn't one for political shenanigans, and the thought of speaking in public was sufficient to dissuade her.

Mavis narrowed her eyes.

'In that case, I'd like to nominate Angela as a candidate for the residents' committee,' said Vince Livingstone, waving his hand in the air like a drowning man. Sylvia gave him the look that wives have for their husbands.

'I second the nomination.' It was Brian.

Peggy's heart dropped to her knees, the moment rushing away from her like ripples from an atomic bomb.

~

'Are we all in agreement?' Mavis looked up from her agenda. There were no challengers. 'Good. Madam Secretary will record for the minutes that in the interests of fiscal restraint, the Village Wellbeing Committee will dispense with *Get Well Soon*s and only send *In Sympathy* cards in future.'

Peggy noticed Brian appraising Angie's tanned legs as she crossed them demurely at the ankles. Peggy looked down at her own legs. There had been a noticeable improvement since the change of tablets, but next to Angie's petite pins, they still looked doughy. Perhaps she should go back onto the water tablets? It was that or support stockings, but trying to imagine Brian peeling them off seductively, she decided against it.

'We'll need to book Jerry and the Toe-Tappers,' said Mavis, returning Peggy abruptly back to the moment. They must have moved on to the next item on the agenda: the Annual Dinner Dance.

A hush descended over the Clubhouse.

'What is it?' asked Mavis.

Sheila Martin looked up from her notepad. 'Jerry had a stroke.'

'He won't be tapping any toes this year,' whispered Brian, making Angie giggle girlishly.

'What about The Diamond Duo then?'

'Divorced,' said Sylvia Livingstone, glancing sideways at her husband.

'Surely there must be somebody? What about Sandy's Smooth Tones? They stood in the year Jerry had his hernia done.'

Several members cleared their throats before Sheila leaned in towards Mavis and, in hushed tones, reminded her that the Wellbeing Committee had sent Sandy's widow an *In Sympathy* card back in January. Along with a shepherd's pie.

'Do any of you have a suggestion? Hmm?' Mavis's face turned puce.

Everyone examined his or her shoes, trying to avoid eye contact. Peggy noticed Brian was wearing odd socks. Poor love.

'I do.' It was Angie who raised a hand. 'I know I'm only new here, but I wondered if I might suggest something a little more modern. Like a disco or karaoke?'

'Karaoke?' bellowed Mavis, as if Angie had suggested naked mud wrestling. 'May I remind everyone that the Annual Dinner Dance has been a regular fixture since the village first opened. Same music. Same menu. You can't just go changing things willy-nilly.'

'Why not?' Angie asked.

'I'll tell you why not. *Tradition.*' Mavis was virtually apoplectic.

'I think Angie has a point,' said Brian. 'I don't think I could face chicken Kiev and bombe Alaska again this year. It's about time we spiced things up, moved with the times, so to speak. I think karaoke is a top-notch idea.'

Peggy feared Mavis was on the verge of a major cerebral event. She saw Vince Livingstone's shoulders twitch.

'Come on, Mavis,' said Celia. 'Wouldn't you enjoy a bit of singalong?'

Vince inhaled Tooheys through his adenoids. Peggy couldn't help herself either. She had to squeeze her knees together and clench her toes as she pictured Madam Chair under a glitter ball, belting out 'My Way'. She also pictured herself singing a duet with Brian, like Kenny Rogers and Dolly Parton.

'I'm glad you all find it so amusing. Madam Secretary, would you please record for the minutes that we have a volunteer to organise this year's social event, our newest member, Mrs Valentine. To be discussed in more detail at next month's meeting.'

'That's a little unfair on Angie,' said Brian.

He was so gallant, thought Peggy. *A little too gallant.*

'And,' blustered Mavis, 'we have a volunteer to help her. Our very own Treasurer, Mr Cornell.'

Peggy's insides tumbled. Mavis had just stolen Christmas. The idea of Angie having one-on-one anything with Brian was as unwelcome as shingles. Angie didn't wear a wedding ring; ironic considering the number she must have collected. Was it the kind of detail men noticed? Peggy fingered the imprint of her own missing wedding ring. Would it disappear with time, or would Ted forever stake his claim from beyond the grave?

'Moving on to item 6.4 on the agenda. The library,' said Mavis.

The Clubhouse echoed with groans and tuts. Several members checked their watches or yawned. Only Sheila hung on Mavis's every word, as though they were delivered on tablets of stone.

Mavis ploughed on, undaunted, towards *Masterchef*. 'There have been reports of vandalism in general fiction.'

'Vandalism?' said Peggy, suddenly worried.

'Some readers have been deliberately folding down corners . . .'

Celia yawned. Peggy swallowed hard.

'. . . and, a number of dust jackets have been torn.'

Vince Livingstone struggled to contain himself.

'Furthermore, a person or persons unnamed have demonstrated reckless disregard for the Dewey Decimal classification system.'

'Really Mavis, we're talking about the residents' library, not the collapse of modern civilisation here.' Brian was on his feet now, brandishing his nuts with contempt.

Mavis emitted a derisive snort. 'Madam Secretary will note, for the record, that we have a volunteer to reorganise the library. What a busy little bee he's going to be.'

Sheila scratched furious notes across her pad. 'Do we have any other volunteers to give Mr Cornell a hand?' Mavis scoured the faces for any takers. Sheila's pencil hovered.

Peggy looked at Brian. He was smiling straight at her, his face paused in expectation. In that moment, it was just the two of them in the room, alone.

'I'd like to volunteer to help Brian restore law and order,' she said.

Peggy tried to rein in her erratic breaths as it all sank in. The air fizzed with endless possibilities. She had visions of her and Brian enjoying a slice amidst the periodicals. At last, Peggy had a legitimate excuse to get Brian alone. It was time to start polishing the Waterford.

~

'You were right, that was a hoot,' said Angie.

Peggy rocked to her feet from the low chair.

'Would you like some help?' Brian offered his hand.

Peggy was torn between the warm touch of his skin against hers, and not wanting to appear a complete invalid. 'No, I'm fine, thank you.'

Peggy's fingers had swollen during the meeting and looked like little cocktail sausages sticking out of the end of her cast. Her neck itched from the label in her boat-necked top and her new shoes were rubbing against her corn. She longed to strip off and settle down in front of the television in her pyjamas with a block of Dairy Milk. Mavis had stormed off at the end of the meeting, Sheila scurrying behind her with her pad and pencil. The other committee members had returned to their units and villas, leaving just Peggy, Angie and Brian.

'Thank you for your support back there. I think I might have upset our Madam Chair.' Angie touched Brian's forearm as she spoke. Brian didn't react, but a hot spear of jealousy ripped through Peggy.

'I can tell you're a passionate woman, Angie. I like a woman who knows her own mind. I'd be game to help you with the social event planning.'

Stomach acid surged and burned the back of Peggy's throat. Her legs turned to water and she reeled. Brian caught her before she collapsed and helped her back into the chair.

'Are you feeling alright?'

'I think I just got up too quickly,' she said.

'Here, let me fetch you a glass of water.' Brian marched towards the sink on his titanium knees.

'You don't look well, Pegs. You've been overdoing things.'

Overdoing things? That's what old people did. They *over*did things. Peggy bristled. Only yesterday, Angie had been encouraging her to think young, have more sex even. Now she was implying she should slow down and act her age.

'Here, drink up.' Brian handed Peggy a glass of water. Dare she drink it? Her bladder was already full and impatient. Stay and drink the water, or go home to Basil, leaving Brian and Angie to plan their own karaoke duet?

'I've been thinking,' said Angie. 'What this place needs is a social committee.'

'But there's the Wellbeing Committee,' said Peggy.

'It's time to think beyond memorial services and fruit baskets. We can share ideas and spread the workload. Come on, you two. It'll be fun!' Angie clapped her hands together.

On the one hand, any excuse to spend more time with Brian would be a bonus, thought Peggy. But if history was anything to go by, Angie was bound to steal the attention. On the other hand, could she afford *not* to get involved? *Think, woman.* How was she going to get out of this one?

'I'd love to, of course,' said Peggy, 'but I think Brian and I are going to be tied up in the library.'

'Ah yes, the crisis of the folded corners,' chortled Brian.

'In that case, I have an even better idea.' Angie looked as if she'd just discovered radium. 'How about we *combine* our efforts? I propose we form the Jacaranda Retirement Village Library *and* Social Committee.'

'Well, I for one think it sounds like an excellent idea,' said Brian rocking back on his heels with enthusiasm. 'The more the merrier.'

Or three's a crowd.

'I knew I could count on a man like you, Brian.' Angie touched his arm again.

Peggy sucked her teeth.

'I suggest the three of us meet in the morning to discuss tactics. Say nine o'clock? We can take a look at the Armageddon in the library, and all go for a coffee afterwards,' said Brian.

Tactics. Peggy was busy thinking up some of her own.

Keep your friends close and your enemies closer.

12

Would You Like That in a Welsh Accent?

BRIAN WAS ALREADY IN THE LIBRARY WHEN PEGGY ARRIVED.
She'd planned to be on time, relishing some undisturbed
Brian-time before Angie turned up. It dawned on Peggy
that Angie's perpetual lateness was purely attention-seeking
behaviour. She wouldn't put anything past that woman. Years
ago, the lady from the puppy training school had advised
her to ignore Basil when he jumped up. She should try it
with Angie.

'I'm sorry I'm late,' said Peggy. Sorry she'd already wasted
precious time.

She'd squandered precious minutes wrestling with an
unruly section of hair in the bathroom mirror. In the end,
she'd resorted to a few strategically placed hairpins to hold
it in place. It was doubly tricky on account of the cast on
her arm. The final look reminded her of her grandmother.
Her strict mother's strict mother. Although she had died
when Peggy was only small, the old lady's stern scowl had

continued to haunt her from the mantelpiece. Perhaps it was all those pins sticking into her scalp that had made her so sour.

'Good morning. Do relax and get your breath back. Besides, I was early,' said Brian. His arms were full of books and Peggy noticed how his glasses had fallen to the tip of his nose. She wondered if she should adjust them for him, but held back, fearing the gesture too intimate. It was the sort of thing she and Ted would have done for each other. Along with plucking stray eyebrow hairs.

The shelves were half-stripped, and the floor already covered in piles of books. 'Library' was rather a grand term for a few shelves in the corner of the Leisure Centre, but there were a couple of comfy chairs and a borrowing system of sorts. In the middle stood a table spread with newspapers and magazines. Mainly golf and quilting. It could certainly do with freshening up. Looking through Angie's eyes now, Peggy could see how dated the whole place looked. She'd started to see a lot of things through Angie's eyes.

'You've done so much already,' said Peggy, squinting through a blizzard of dust motes as Brian lifted another book from the shelf.

'I have to confess, I've been here since six. I don't sleep that well,' said Brian.

'I wake up at four, regular as clockwork, and can't get off again. It's so frustrating.' Peggy felt a tiny and unexpected thrill. They had something in common. She imagined Brian in his pyjamas tossing and turning. How much better they might both sleep cuddled up together.

'I think all us old folk are the same, judging by the number of lights on around the village in the early hours.'

Old folk. Is that how Brian saw her? In his eyes, no doubt she was just another leaky old lady. Yet she was only seventy-nine, wearing straight-leg white pants and her new chambray tunic top. She may as well have been 109, wearing leg bandages and the remains of her lunch. If she was going to ask Brian for that dinner, she'd have to try harder.

Peggy placed her new handbag next to Brian's Panama on the newspaper table.

'It looks like you have a system worked out,' said Peggy perusing the piles of books. 'Just point me in the right direction and I'll get stuck in.'

'Okay, this box is for the no-hopers, books too damaged to put back on the shelf,' he said, dragging a cardboard box already filled to the brim. 'This one is for books in good condition but no-one takes out. I thought we'd donate them to charity, give them a last chance.'

'Good idea,' said Peggy. 'In fact, there's a Lifeline book sale on at the high school on Saturday afternoon. We could take our rejects and pick up a few new titles while we're at it.'

There, she'd done it without even thinking. Peggy Smart had asked Brian out. It wasn't dinner. There would be no Waterford crystal or inky-blue chiffon with the matching wrap. But it was a chance to get Brian alone for an hour or two. Innocuous enough an invitation if he declined, and an exciting opportunity to get to know the captivating widower if he agreed.

'Splendid. I'll write it in my diary.'

At last, she was in Brian's diary. Peggy fluttered in anticipation.

For goodness sake, woman, pull yourself together. Look busy for a start.

'What about this pile over here?' she said, picking up a book from the top and scanning the pages.

'They're old but still have plenty of life left in them. They can go back on the shelves once we've dusted them.'

'Which pile do you think we belong in then?' Peggy smiled at Brian, wondering if he got the joke.

'I'd say we've plenty to offer to the right reader, wouldn't you?'

Peggy blushed. Any minute now, she'd wake up. It'd be 4 am and she'd shuffle towards the bathroom in her sheepskin slippers. It was all going too well to be anything other than a delicious dream.

Peggy knelt and began pulling books from the lower shelves.

'Are you sure you can manage down there with your wrist?'

'I'm better down here. I don't think I could reach those top shelves with my cast.'

'Then we'll make a great team, Peggy.'

It was true. Between the two of them, they made a fully functioning human being. It struck Peggy as strange that no-one ever considered the practicalities when forming a couple. Walking down the aisle at twenty-three, she and Ted had never considered what might lie ahead. At that age, 'in sickness and in health' meant little more than making chicken broth or rubbing in Vicks. They, like every other doe-eyed couple, assumed they were compatible, never taking into account which joints might need replacing, or the infirmities they might develop later on. Nothing had changed. Young folk these days still put more thought into choosing breakfast from a menu than a husband or wife. They certainly never paused to consider that the pair needs a minimum of one set of functioning limbs, and at least one reliable memory – one to remember the shopping list and one to carry the bags.

'So, have you worked out who the culprit is yet?' said Peggy.

'You mean our phantom corner folder?'

'Are we looking for the same suspect for dust-jacket ripping as for misfiling, do you think?'

Brian chuckled. 'Well, Miss Marple, the evidence seems to suggest that our corner folder is a fan of romantic fiction.'

Peggy bit her lip. She was always careful with the books she borrowed, unfolding all the corners before she returned them. There was one occasion when she'd accidentally left a book on top of her wet swimming costume in her bag overnight. She'd thrown the pulp in the bin under some potato peelings the following morning. The library ran on an honesty system, so it was unlikely her crime would be uncovered.

'Do you think that Madam Chair is a romance reader then, seeing as she noticed it?'

The idea that Mavis harboured secret yearnings was quite titillating. Perhaps she had more in common with the dour Chair than she realised.

'A delicious deduction,' said Brian, scanning the library to make sure they were alone. 'Although I have to confess, I wouldn't have thought she was the type.'

Type? Peggy wasn't sure whether to rebuke him for assuming stereotypes or to laugh it off. What was wrong with enjoying a happily-ever-after? Imagining yourself into another world was a harmless pastime. Only the other day, she'd heard a discussion on the radio. She'd been creaming butter and sugar at the time, and had paused to consider it before she added the eggs. Something about the miracle of a reader living an alternative life, simply through the words in a book.

Peggy had never imagined a life beyond the perfectly satisfactory years she'd shared with Ted. Every marriage had its up and downs. But of the many romances she'd read, the stories of passionate kisses and lustful temptation, Peggy had only ever shared her bed with one man. She'd never had cause to doubt Ted's fidelity either, in all their time together. Theirs, she considered with pride, had been an exclusively monotonous marriage.

Brian threw a mildewed hardback into the no-hoper box, bringing Peggy abruptly back to the moment. 'Then again,' he continued, 'the books with the torn dust jackets were all science fiction or fantasy novels, and the ones that had been misfiled were crime thrillers. They were everywhere.'

'Perhaps the thriller readers were so shaken, they didn't notice what they were doing.'

'Or do we have an innumerate Agatha Christie fan in our midst?' There was an easy smile on Brian's face. He looked as if he was enjoying himself.

'Mmm, that narrows it down somewhat. I see you have cleverly ruled yourself out.'

'What do you mean?'

'I think you're deliberately trying to throw me off the scent, Mr Cornell. Retired accountant, committee treasurer. No-one would suspect you, of all people, of such a misdemeanour.'

'Assuming I wasn't trying to call your bluff, that is.'

Peggy revelled in their light-hearted banter. That's what it was, wasn't it? Banter. Or was it flirting? It was over half a century since she and Ted had exchanged surreptitious looks across the nylons counter at Blake's, since he'd allowed his fingers to brush against her hand in the staff elevator.

Young folk were so forward nowadays, sending each other photos of their private parts from their phones. Peggy shuddered and hoped Brian wouldn't expect anything like that. Besides, she couldn't even make outgoing calls let alone use the camera thingy. David would help her, of course. Once she'd plucked up courage to ask. Peggy had to be careful not to admit to too many memory lapses, what with the party invitation fiasco and the fall. No, if she were to share any images of her anatomy, it would be done tastefully. In soft focus. With the old Kodak. Assuming they still made film for it.

'I would have put you down as more the historical type,' said Peggy, sitting back on her heels and appraising Brian. 'Yes, wars, crusades, famous explorers like Shackleton and Scott of the Antarctic.'

'Ah, Miss Marple, that's where you're wrong.' Brian tossed a Gough Whitlam biography into the charity box. 'You're stereotyping me.'

'Stereotyping?'

'Yes, assuming that because I'm a man of a certain age, I read nothing but war stories. It's just as bad as assuming that as a woman, you read nothing but romance novels.'

Peggy was piqued. It was true, but she didn't like being pigeonholed any more than he did. She grasped the shelf for support with her good hand and stood up. She adjusted her hairclip and tugged a loose strand behind her ear.

'As a matter of fact, I read quite a wide variety of books. I don't have a particular genre.'

It was true. She'd somehow fallen between the genres. Everywhere she looked, people were defined, conformed to the conventions of their particular genre. Brian the educated, handsome widower; Jim the ageing Lothario; Celia the capable tomboy. Even Angie had never wavered from her man-eating temptress persona. It made them who they were: individuals. Real people. Peggy did have her own identity, even if she didn't like it. Overweight, self-doubting. She was a nondescript person, an elasticated waistband of a human being.

Brian had opened a dusty plain-covered book and was reading it closely. Peggy heard him sigh.

'So, Professor Mysterious, what is your preferred reading matter then?'

Brian fell silent, staring intently at his book. His bottom lip quivered, and Peggy wondered if she'd been overfamiliar with the Professor bit.

Then his lips parted around the words as he recited them by heart:

'*Do not go gentle into that good night,*
Old age should burn and rave at close of day;
Rage, rage against the dying of the light . . .'

Brian's eyes were closed, and his voice faded to little more than a whisper.

'That's beautiful.'

'Dylan Thomas.'

'I wouldn't have guessed you were a poet, Brian.'

'My father always frowned upon it. Reading poetry wasn't what real men did. I used to sneak away from football practice and hide behind a tree with Wordsworth or Yeats.'

'A rebel!' laughed Peggy.

'You could say that,' said Brian. 'Always rebelling against my father. He wanted me to join the Navy like him, so I became an accountant.'

'A chartered accountant, no less.'

'I know, ridiculous isn't it? Kids today have so much more freedom. What would you have done Peggy, if you hadn't been a secretary?'

It was strange to think that if she'd done what her mother wanted, she'd have stayed at Blake's and worked her way up from women's foundation. Perhaps she'd have ended up like Angie, travelled to Paris and Milan, footloose and fancy-free, with a string of husbands in her wake. But then, she wasn't Angie. They were like chalk and cheese. As different as two friends could be: salt and pepper, bitter and sweet, naughty and nice.

'I always dreamed of being a teacher.'

'My wife Phyllis was a teacher. Did I ever mention that?'

Peggy shook her head. She pictured Phyllis in cap and gown, then holding thirty tender minds in chalk-covered hands. Peggy imagined philosophical conversations over the Cornell dinner table, discussing politics and current affairs. She imagined Brian reciting poetry to his beautiful wife as they lay naked between crisp white sheets.

'Do you miss her?'

What a stupid question.

'Every day,' said Brian, eyes looking into nowhere. 'As I'm sure you miss your husband. Ted, wasn't it?'

Peggy nodded. She still felt his presence, like a phantom limb, the pain of which was so severe that at times it could not be soothed. Waves of grief would rise out of nowhere and crash over her. In the beginning, they came so often that she thought she would drown beneath the sadness and loneliness. After a while, she learned to breathe through each memory as it consumed her like a labour pain, then passed.

'You never think you'll survive it, do you?'

'Not at first, no. But now I've come to realise that Phyllis would want me to go on with my life, just as I would have wanted her to go on with hers if I'd been the one to die first.'

'I think Ted would want the same for me,' said Peggy.

What would have happened to Ted if she'd gone first? The idea of him wasting away on his own brought a strange relief that she'd outlived him. For all his faults, she could only hope he'd have found some homely woman to look after him and keep him company. He was the type of man who needed a good woman in his life. What's more, Peggy was in no doubt that the ever-practical Ted would have found himself one.

Brian chewed the arm of his spectacles. 'You know, I could see you as a teacher, someone I'd have gone to with my poetry, perhaps.'

Peggy rearranged her face into a smile and tried to disguise the wobble in her voice. 'Now young Master Cornell, I'd like you to read the rest of the poem to the class.' She lowered her voice and peered over the top of her spectacles. 'Do I pass?'

'Would you like that in a Welsh accent, Miss?'

'Of course! Now what are you waiting for?'

Brian cleared his throat.

'*Good men, the last wave by, crying how bright*
Their frail deeds might have danced in a green bay . . .'

Peggy sat down on a chair at the library table and listened to Brian recite the words he knew by heart. She imagined his father thundering in to his room while he was practising them in front of the mirror, face full of disdain.

'Wild men who caught and sang the sun in flight,
And learn, too late, they grieved it on its way,
Do not go gentle—'

Brian paused.

Peggy looked up to see Angie walking towards them. She was wearing a loose cotton dress over what looked like a black one-piece swimsuit. She was hugging a rolled-up towel under one arm. Her sudden presence seemed to fill the space, sucking the molecules out of the air, stealing every precious word that Peggy and Brian had just exchanged.

Peggy felt Brian slip away from her. The spell had been broken.

'Sorry, did I interrupt something?' Angie jangled her car keys in one hand.

'Oh no, it was nothing,' said Brian, straightening himself up.

'You two bookworms coming for a swim? I met Celia in the hall, and she suggested we all have a quick dip followed by a coffee down at the beach.'

'I thought we were planning a committee meeting this morning,' said Peggy, sulking.

'Still can. Let's have it at the beach instead. Brian, are you in?'

He wasn't a big man – far from – but Peggy was sure she saw Brian suck in his stomach.

13

À Bout de Souffle

At first, Peggy failed to notice the woman standing behind her. It was only when she saw Ted turn his head mid-sentence that she followed his gaze to the slim figure not three feet away. It seemed strange for the woman to be wearing dark sunglasses inside the cinema foyer. Paradoxically, if she was trying not to be noticed, she had succeeded only in drawing attention to herself. When the woman removed the glasses, peeled away her silk headscarf and shook free her close-cropped platinum hair, however, Peggy recognised immediately who she was.

It felt like only yesterday that they'd worked together at Blake's, but their worlds were now light years apart. One had launched herself into a stratosphere of chic sophistication, leaving the other with her ever-practical lace-ups planted squarely on terra firma.

'Hello Peggy. It's been a while.'

'Gosh, you look so different.'

Angie looked cool, superior and slightly bored. She glanced at the ice-cream in Peggy's hand and raised her eyebrows. It was starting to melt in the heat of the foyer, vanilla goo dripping down Peggy's hand and onto her feet.

Angie opened her handbag and offered Peggy a handkerchief to mop up the mess. 'Are you still at Blake's?'

'No, I'm at secretarial college now,' replied Peggy, licking around the edges of the ice-cream cone in an attempt to contain the landslide. With the money she'd saved from working at Blake's and a bequest from her dead aunt, Peggy had been able to secure a place on the course. *Shorthand and typing.* It had sounded so exotic when she rehearsed it in her head. *A secretary.* All of a sudden, Peggy's dream job sounded parochial and utterly dull.

'Hello,' said Angie. 'I recognise you from somewhere.'

'Oh sorry, let me introduce you. Angie, this is Ted. Ted, meet Angie.'

Ted shook Angie's hand. Peggy noticed his cheeks colour.

'I remember you from Blake's. I fixed that wobbly drawer for you.'

'Ah yes, I remember you now. So, since when are you two an item?'

They'd flirted for weeks over the counter and in the elevator, until Mr Hawley had intervened and dispatched Ted back to the works department with a flea in his ear. They'd started with afternoon tea, then a picnic, before moving on to the cinema. To Peggy's surprise, Ted had turned out to be something of a film buff. Far from skulking on the back row with the other courting couples, Ted always splashed out on the very best seats and lapped up every moment. He could recite all the best bits word for word. On several occasions, he dragged Peggy along for a second viewing if he'd particularly enjoyed a movie. Peggy was simply happy to be with Ted. On their six-month anniversary, Ted borrowed his father's dinner jacket and took Peggy to a fancy restaurant. The jacket was far too big, and she tried not to laugh when he caught his sleeve in the crème brûlée. She didn't want to hurt his feelings. She was becoming rather fond of him.

When her mother told her she should set her sights a little higher, Peggy took her at her word and set them on the highest place of all – the altar.

'A couple of years now,' said Peggy. She linked arms with Ted, smearing ice-cream on his shirt. He hadn't exactly proposed yet, but she'd begun dropping hints. Peggy was prepared to wait. Like a good fruit cake, Ted couldn't be hurried.

Angie pulled a cigarette out of her bag and held it to her lips. Ted broke free of Peggy's grip and reached into his pocket, pulling out a silver lighter. He flicked the lid and held the flame to the unlit tip of the cigarette. Angie inhaled and blew the smoke over her shoulder.

'I wouldn't say we were an item,' said Ted, putting the lighter away. 'Do you know you look just like Jean Seberg?'

Angie took another long drag on her cigarette and smiled. 'So they say.'

There was a poster of the glamorous actress on the foyer wall directly behind them. Angie had the same impish features and blonde pixie haircut. The resemblance was striking. Ted wasn't the only one to notice. A number of other cinema-goers had turned to stare at her, most of them men.

'I love French cinema,' said Ted, his back now turned to Peggy. 'Peggy was a bit worried about seeing *Breathless* until I told her about the subtitles.'

'*À bout de souffle*,' purred Angie.

'You speak French?' Ted's eyes widened.

'I picked up *un petit peu de Francais* when I was in Paris.'

'Paris?' Peggy manoeuvred herself between Angie and Ted. 'Last I heard you were going to London.'

'After I left Blake's, I worked my way up to fashion buyer at Grantchester & Co. I'm overseas most of the time. I'm only back in Sydney to see my mother, then I'm off to Milan.'

Peggy remembered Angie hiding behind the knitwear mannequin as she struggled to find a girdle for one of Blake's most respected customers. Mr Hawley had had plenty to say, once he'd appeased Mrs Asquith with a spray of Chanel No. 5 and a complimentary scone in the tearooms. Angie was dismissed and escorted from the premises with barely time to fetch her coat, let alone say goodbye. According to one of the girls from Haberdashery, she'd secured an excellent reference, after managing to convince Mr Hawley that her uncle was on the board at Blake's, and threatening to spill the beans on his lascivious initiation practices.

～

The Odeon foyer was almost empty by now, with couples handing their tickets to the doorman before being shown to their seats by the usher with a flashlight. Ted and Angie were still busy chatting about their favourite films. Peggy was beginning to worry they'd miss the start of the film.

'We mustn't hold you up,' said Peggy, kissing Angie on both cheeks, a smile straining every muscle in her face. 'It's been lovely to bump into you again.'

'We can't have you sitting on your own,' said Ted. 'Would you like to join us, Angie, or should I say, *Jean*?'

A sudden and unexpected spasm gripped Peggy's bladder. She managed to clench her muscles sufficiently to avert an unscheduled leak, but faced with sitting in the middle of a row with no means of escape, Peggy knew she couldn't wait.

'I wouldn't want to play gooseberry.' Angie inclined her head in a coquettish pose.

Tears threatened to spill from Peggy's eyes as she tried to dismiss the insistent calls from her urethra.

'Not at all. We insist, don't we Peggy?'

Peggy opened her mouth to politely object, but the only sound that escaped was a strangled squeak, followed by, 'Excuse me.'

Shrinking behind the locked door of the end stall, Peggy surrendered to the hot sting of tears as they tumbled down her cheeks.

By the time the usher showed her to the only free seat in the Odeon Cinema – several rows behind Ted and Angie – the film had started. In the dark, Peggy tried to fill the deep emptiness inside her with ice-cream. She wondered why she wasn't like other women. What cruel fate had handed her a vital storage organ the size of a walnut instead of Angie's seductive confidence?

14

It's Lovely Once You're In

'I DIDN'T GO THROUGH ALL THAT PALAVER AT THE FRACTURE clinic to get you a waterproof cast for you to stand there and tell me you're not coming with us to the pool.' Angie folded her arms and tapped one foot on the terracotta kitchen tiles.

'But I washed my hair this morning.' Peggy knew she was losing ground, her pathetic excuses no match for Angie's determination. She was scraping the barrel with the hair thing. There was no way Angie would fall for it.

'Here,' said Angie fishing around in her beach bag. 'You can wear mine.'

Angie tossed a red bathing cap towards Peggy. It was covered with rubbery flowers, a fashion statement in itself, unlike Sheila's tight-fitting latex cap that made her head look comically like a prophylactic.

Peggy sighed in defeat. Her procrastination arsenal was exhausted. 'Give me a minute, I'll get changed.' She sloped off towards the bedroom, cap in hand.

'Now that you mention it,' Angie called after her. 'I've been wanting to talk to you about your hair.'

'What's wrong with my hair?' said Peggy, poking her head back around the bedroom door. Instinctively, she began to comb her grey hair with her fingertips, smoothing it down around her neck and ears. The hairclips must have fallen out somewhere between the library and her unit. The rebellious strand she'd attempted to tame this morning was making a last-ditch attempt at escape.

'Nothing. Back in 1986, perhaps. I'll make you an appointment with Alessandro for next week.'

'But Louise always does my hair. Trim, first Wednesday of the month. Wash and set every other week.'

'Since when?'

'About 1986,' said Peggy with a sheepish grin.

'What *am* I going to do with you?'

Peggy stood in front of her wardrobe, perusing the co-ordinating staples that Angie and Arabella had picked out. There was just about every occasion catered for: just about every point on the social spectrum, including cocktail, black tie, tennis, lunch and polo. Then there was *The Dress*, sitting there ready for dinner with Brian. It wouldn't feel right to wear it beforehand. With pride of place in the centre of her ultra-organised closet, the luxurious fabric and the glorious colour served as a talisman, a gentle reminder of the life she still aspired to.

'Here, throw this on over the top,' said Angie appearing behind her. She leaned across and pulled a dress from a hanger in the far corner. Through some miracle, it had escaped last week's cull. Peggy was relieved. She liked to keep contingency items in case of any significant body weight changes, including several garments for when she finally achieved her target weight. If, on the other hand, she suddenly doubled in size, then this was the dress. It *had* been in a sale, and therefore a bargain, regardless of whether it fitted.

Angie kicked a pair of rubber thongs in Peggy's direction.

'I can't wear those. The podiatrist says my arches are too flat.'

Angie sighed. 'We're walking from the car park to the pool, not trekking the Kokoda Track.'

Peggy pushed the rubber strap between her toes. There was no use trying to hide them, she had her mother's feet. In the mirror she noticed Angie recoil at the thickened toenails. The podiatrist didn't seem particularly bothered. More than likely, the fungus hitching a ride on Peggy's feet was keeping Fresh Steps in business. She'd already spent a small fortune on special products from the pharmacy. The whole process was so time-consuming, with all that sanding and painting. It reminded her of Ted and the weeks he'd spent in the shed making a cubby house for Jenny's sixth birthday.

'Ready?'

Ordinarily Peggy would have paid her respects to the bathroom before she left, but that would mean taking off the dress, then the one-piece swimsuit, and getting dressed all over again. Angie wasn't the patient type.

'Give me one minute,' said Peggy. She scuttled into the bathroom, opened the cabinet door and took out the box of Dr Stephen's magic bladder medicine. She'd asked the pharmacist to leave them out of her Webster-pak for the time being. She needed time to think. The information leaflet in the box was a disturbing read, and on several occasions, she'd considered throwing the box out. Perhaps Jenny had a point. Even Dr Stephen himself had been reluctant to prescribe them at first.

Peggy pushed the first of the little white pills from the foil. It looked harmless enough. Was this tiny pellet the panacea she'd been searching for, the key that would unlock her self-confidence and help her find her inner temptress? Or would she suffer the entire smorgasbord of side effects, including a fall?

Out of the corner of her eye, Peggy spotted the framed cross-stitch she'd given Ted for his last birthday. It had taken her months to sew the blue and white fishing boat. It was moored to the jetty by a rope embroidered in golden thread and was meant to represent his favourite saying, the one he used to justify everything from taking on the big house they couldn't afford, to trying out the new Italian restaurant around the corner.

'A ship is safe in harbour,' he would say, 'but that's not what ships are for.'

Peggy popped the pill onto the end of her tongue and swallowed it with a handful of water from the cold tap.

~

The big surf had attracted a crowd of tradies' utes and it took two circuits of the car park before they found a spot. The sun had broken free of the clouds and welcomed the day with a sultry start. Peggy recognised the silver Lexus across the car park, but didn't let on.

'I'll get the ticket,' she said. It was the least she could do, given all the driving Angie was doing at the moment. The closest meter was miles away and Peggy regretted her sudden generosity. By the time she'd schlepped there and back in her thongs, there were watery blisters on each foot. Grains of sand the size of golf balls had already worked their way under the rubber straps, and her attempts to dislodge them were drawing curious looks from the café.

The smell of freshly roasted coffee wafted across the car park. 'Can't we skip the swim and go straight for coffee?' said Peggy while Angie displayed the parking ticket on the dashboard of her Mini.

'Where's your sense of adventure? You'll love it once you're in the water. The others are already there, let's hurry.'

Peggy scanned the figures as they swam up and down the lanes in the pool, their rhythmic strokes like metronomes through the blue-green water. None of them appeared fazed when a large wave broke over the far corner and swamped the pool.

Peggy shuffled behind Angie towards the pool. She'd never been a great swimmer. Why ever had she let Angie talk her into this? She was beginning to feel like a duck out of water.

Indeed, she was surprised Angie hadn't brought up the fiasco of Mr Durkin's swimming class. Her own recollection of events was limited to regaining consciousness on the side of the pool with an ashen Mr D pumping the water out of her stomach, while the rest of the class looked on in a combination of horror and mild amusement.

'I've never known anyone to actually sink like that before,' Mr Durkin had said as he covered his half-drowned student with a towel. Peggy was sure the experience must have contributed to his unscheduled retirement a few months later.

That was back in 1950, but Peggy had always maintained a cautious approach to entering the water ever since, preferring to sit hot and sandy on the beach like a human schnitzel while Ted splashed about in the ocean with the kids.

Brian was standing in waist-deep water when they arrived, adjusting his goggles. Peggy tried to act nonchalantly, but with the man of her fantasies, not six feet away, virtually naked, she found it impossible to remember how a normal human behaved. She fidgeted and fumbled with her bag, and struggled to work out what to do with her arms and legs.

She snuck a peek at Brian, a mental keepsake. His upper body was lean and pleasingly muscular, but about a size too small for his skin. His chest reminded Peggy of her vacuum cleaner when she'd cleaned up after Basil, and his skin was pebble-dashed in dark brown age-spots, the standard geriatric camouflage. In Peggy's eyes, however, Brian was perfect. An Adonis.

When he saw her, he waved and grinned. 'It's lovely and warm in here,' he shouted. Peggy imagined Brian holding up the edge of her duvet and patting the mattress beside him. She felt a rush of blood to her head and almost lost her balance.

Ted had always made a point of warming her side of the bed in winter while she brushed her teeth and creamed her face. When she returned, trussed up in her nightie, he would roll back to his own chilly hollow, and still be asleep within seconds. They could have invested in an electric blanket but Peggy always cherished Ted's thoughtful act. As long as he warmed her sheets, she knew he still loved her. She smiled back at Brian, wondering if his feet were as warm as Ted's.

Meanwhile, Angie was busy reapplying lipstick.

I swear that woman will be wearing a full set of make-up on her deathbed.

Peggy moved away from Angie as they disrobed. The last thing she wanted was to be compared side by side: one as skinny as a minute to six, the other with a backside the size of Denmark. Peggy worked out she could stop eating completely and still be twice the size of Angie by Christmas. Was it really worth it for a body like that? Surely all that buckwheat and kale couldn't be good for her insides?

With the last strands of hair safely contained inside Angie's swimming cap, Peggy took a deep breath, and tucked her overgrown nails over the poolside. She tried to circle her arms above her head as she'd seen them do on the telly. Far from limbering up, the muscles went into spasm and sent an urgent memo to her brain, reminding her not to do it in future.

Brian was already halfway up the pool, his unusual arm action surprisingly effective at propelling him through the water. He reminded her of the little water boatmen she used to catch down at the creek when she was a kid.

Angie dived in, breaking the surface with barely a ripple. Naturally, she emerged looking photo-shopped perfect.

'Are you going to stand there all day?' she called from the water.

The sounds of the pool and the beach – the crashing waves, the chatter from the café, the cry of a sea eagle overhead – waned to a pulsating throb in Peggy's ears.

Above the thrum of her own heart, she heard the sirens sing.

In a Welsh accent.

Rage, rage against the dying of the light.

~

Peggy recalled standing on the poolside, imagining she was Dawn Fraser. The next thing she remembered, Celia was hauling her up from the depths by her shoulder straps.

'Crikey,' said Celia, who was wearing black goggles around her neck and a metal nose-clip. 'I've never seen anyone sink like that before.'

Peggy's eyes smarted from the salt, and she couldn't keep them open. Sopping tendrils of hair fell across her face, but between blinks, she could just make out the bathing cap floating away like a flaccid jellyfish. As her vision cleared, she saw Brian gliding towards her.

'I say, are you alright?' he said, his lovely face etched with concern. He handed her two triangles of black foam that turned out to be the bra-cup inserts from her bathing suit.

'I'm fine!' lied Peggy, trying to stem the torrent of seawater sluicing from her sinuses. Instinctively, she reached for the balled-up tissue she kept up her sleeve. Instead, her fingers found the hard, rough surface of the cast. She could hardly blow her nose on that.

I should just drown myself now and be done with it.

'It's lovely once you're in, isn't it?' said Peggy, forcing a smile through her chattering teeth.

~

After the near-drowning incident, Angie seemed to soften a little. She even turned a blind eye when Peggy bit the end off a sachet of sugar and stirred it into her cappuccino.

Angie pulled the towel over Peggy's bare shoulder and gave it a pat. Peggy pulled away. It was one thing to be helped, quite another to be babied. The constant fussing was beginning to get on her nerves. She was going to have to say something. Or find a way to disconnect Angie's pacemaker.

'Here,' said Celia, producing a small stainless-steel flask from her beach bag. 'Have a drop of this.'

Peggy sniffed the contents and recoiled. 'Isn't it a bit early for the strong stuff?'

'Brandy is good for shock,' said Celia, leaning across the table and pouring a measure into Peggy's coffee. Peggy imagined Celia in a Girl Guide uniform, always prepared.

'I'm feeling shocked too,' said Angie. She snatched the hip flask and poured the amber liquid into her long black. 'Brian looks a bit peaky as well.'

'Now that you mention it,' said Celia, who was next around the table, 'I'm not feeling so crash hot myself.' She poured a large measure into her own cup then lifted it towards the centre of the group. 'Here's to the Jacaranda Retirement Village Library and Social Committee.' She grinned, revealing a suspiciously perfect set of teeth.

A middle-aged couple on the next table gaped at the chorus of cheers, giggles and clanking crockery. Peggy saw the man roll his eyes, and imagined what David and Jenny would say if they could see her drinking spirits at the beach café so brazenly on a weekday. The thought was as intoxicating as her cappuccino now was.

'How about we get down to business?' Brian put his spectacles on and pulled a notebook from his bag. His thin hair had dried into a halo of white fluff. It looked like a bushfire had taken hold on his weathered head. 'Item one on the agenda,' he continued, testing his ballpoint pen inside the cover of the notebook. 'The karaoke machine.'

Brian's face was a study of concentration as he wrote the date at the top of an empty page. He looked up and smiled across the table. Peggy's chest tightened with longing, crushing the air from her lungs. She wondered if she might have angina.

'Does anyone even know how much these things cost?' Celia poured out the last drop from her hip flask and slurped it from a teaspoon.

Angie blew the steam on her long black and took a sip, her lipstick still perfect. 'I did some research last night,' she said. 'It's not just the machine. There are the speakers, microphones and turntable to go with it. Few hundred bucks at least.'

'Do we really need a turntable?' said Peggy, her mental image of a cosy duet with Brian morphing into a nightmarish scenario of him boogie-ing on the dance floor with Angie. Angie had always been such a good dancer. Such a good everything.

'If we have our own gear, then we only need to hire a DJ for functions.' Angie looked quite pleased with herself. 'We could hire the Clubhouse out for private functions. Discos and the like.'

Brian clapped his hands together. 'Marvellous idea!' Peggy wondered if he'd ever even been to a disco.

'I hate to be a party pooper,' said Celia, 'but just how are we going to come up with the cash for this?'

'I'd suggest another bring and buy sale,' said Brian, 'but we only raised eighty-seven dollars from the last one. The problem was that everyone brought and no-one bought.'

Peggy smiled. His modesty and self-defaecating humour were the things she admired the most. She and Ted had always laughed together, at comedy shows on TV, and other people's jokes, but *he* never really made her laugh. He used to tell her that she was the funny one, with her funny little sayings, whatever that meant.

'How about a sponsored swim?' They fell silent and stared incredulously at Celia. She seemed quite serious. Peggy calculated they must have a combined age of well over three hundred. '*Me*,' said Celia reading their faces. 'I'm talking about sponsoring *me*. I swam the English Channel when I was sixteen. I reckon I've still got what it takes.'

Peggy wished she'd share it round.

'I think we have to be more imaginative,' said Angie, butting in.

'Think outside the envelope you mean?' Peggy looked around the table, an idea swelling inside her. 'How about a cake sale? I could make my special recipe muffins.'

Celia might be able to swim the Channel, but everyone knew the way to a man's heart was through his stomach. She pictured herself feeding a blindfolded Brian, teasing his lips with her warm raspberry muffins.

'I, for one, always relish your sumptuous wares, Peggy, but I think we have to think a little bigger,' said Brian.

'There's always my famous Battenberg cake. If I use the extra-large tin, and slice it very thin . . .'

A toddler ran past the table, smearing ice-cream across the back of Peggy's beach dress. The cold made her gasp. She braced herself for Angie and a handful of tissues, but for once, she hadn't noticed, too busy pouting into a compact mirror.

Irritated, Peggy waved her hand in front of Angie's face.

'Hello. What do you think? After all, the whole karaoke thing was *your* idea.'

Sometimes there was nothing she wanted more than to shove a large bun down that skinny throat.

'We need something the whole village can take part in.' Angie positioned the empty notebook in front of her and took possession of Brian's poised ballpoint. 'Ideally, something that will raise the money we need and be fun to organise.'

'Something that Mavis will really disapprove of,' added Peggy, inviting a nod of approval from Brian.

'Absolutely,' said Celia, clinking coffee cups with Peggy's at the suggestion. 'I'd love to see that stiff-haired despot and the sanctimonious Madam Secretary brought down a peg or two.'

Brian looked over the top of his half-moons, his bottom lip twitching. 'Indeed.'

Peggy was torn between rebuking Celia and offering her own twenty cents' worth. However good it felt to have the upper hand, she knew how it felt to be on the other side.

Meanwhile, an oblivious Angie was sketching on the notebook. At first, Peggy was annoyed, but as she craned her neck to get a better look, she watched a long, willowy shape come to life on the blank page. It was the silhouette of a woman with high cheekbones and anatomically impossible limbs. With practised strokes, Angie clad the figure in a full-skirted dress and gave her a tiny cinched-in waist.

What on earth was she doing? Was it another attention-seeking ploy by Angie? Peggy had to admit, that watching her create such beautiful images from the end of a pen was mesmerising. There was no end to this woman's talents.

When she'd finished, Angie turned the paper around to show the group.

'Ladies and gentleman,' she announced triumphantly, 'I would like to propose the inaugural Jacaranda Retirement Village Fashion Show.'

15

At Your Age

'I WISH YOU'D CALLED ME. I COULD HAVE LEFT WORK AND taken you to the hospital myself. I *am* your son.'

Peggy imagined herself sitting in the car park at the beach with her wonky wrist, waiting for David to finish his meeting and battle the traffic from the city. She pictured him pacing up and down the corridor at the hospital, pestering the staff. *What was happening? How much longer?*

Mel would phone him every half an hour, asking what time he'd be home. He'd cover the mouthpiece and smile at Peggy, 'Mel sends her best.' Peggy would mouth, 'Thank you', while Mel instructed David to order his mother a taxi.

Peggy steadied the Lean Cuisine carton with her cast and ripped off the cellophane using her good hand. The freezer was full of ready-made meals thanks to Angie, who'd decided it was time for Peggy to broadcast her self-sufficiency to her family. In fact, Angie had gone from smothering Peggy to abandoning her almost overnight. She had a new project to focus on now: her precious fashion show. It was only a matter of days until the next committee meeting. Already, Angie was a woman on a mission, persuading Arabella to loan the outfits, and stalking potential models. Word had spread, naturally, and there had been a noticeable change in the standard of attire at Jacaranda Retirement Village. Suddenly, the coffee shop looked more like the foyer at the ballet and apparently Louise at Dazzling Dos had been booked solid. It seemed everyone wanted to be in on the action, the committee members inundated with volunteers to act as models. But Angie was keeping her cards close to her chest. In fact, she was becoming a control freak, refusing to delegate anything to do with the actual fashion side of the event, leaving the others to merely tinker around the edges.

In addition to the catering, as a gesture of goodwill Peggy had agreed to a single lap of the catwalk in an outfit of Angie's choosing. Her only stipulation was that it should be in green. That way, if the whole thing went pear-shaped, she could always hide in the bushes.

'Hang on David, I'm going to put you on loud-hailer,' shouted Peggy at the phone. Balancing the phone under her chin with her head to one side had brought on a bout of vertigo. She pushed the button shaped like a horn and rested the phone in the fruit bowl between an overripe mango and a Granny Smith. 'Can you still hear me?'

'I was just saying that you should have called me.' David sounded like he was driving home from the office. He must be talking on his arms-free phone. Peggy could hear the car radio in the background. That Richard Glover had such a lovely soothing voice. Perhaps she should record his program and use it to help her fall asleep.

'There was no point worrying you. Angie drove me to the hospital in her Mini,' said Peggy.

Such a nippy little thing. Both of them.

'Is that who I spoke to on the phone?'

'She's been very kind to me.'

Overbearing, controlling and domineering but always with a smile.

'I haven't heard you mention an Angie before. Is she new?'

'Not exactly.' Peggy felt coy, as if Angie were a new lover she was trying to keep under wraps. 'She moved in recently, a few doors away. The funny thing is, she's an old school friend of mine. I haven't seen her in years. It's a small world, isn't it?'

A small world indeed. Not so small since Angie had arrived. Peggy's horizons had expanded beyond the manicured hedges at Jacaranda Retirement Village in ways she couldn't quite bring herself to share with her son. It crossed her mind to ask David what he knew about karaoke machines, but she decided against it. The same went for the cost of a new Mini Cooper on part exchange. As for the new wardrobe, the look on Mel's face would give Peggy something to look forward to. Mel obviously had her own idea about what 'women of a certain age' should be wearing, judging by all the patterned cardigans and printed scarves she'd given her mother-in-law over the years. They were all hideous, but Peggy had stored each item with care and worn them in dutiful rotation at family functions. Thanks to Angie, there were now three bulging bin-liners full, destined for the charity shop. It was quite liberating.

'I'm so pleased for you, Mum. I expect you have so much in common.'

'So much,' echoed Peggy.

Except that I've spent five decades cooking, cleaning and changing nappies, babysitting and doing cross-stitch, while Angie is an anorexic, four-times-married, globe-trotting sex-maniac.

'I hope you're not getting up to any mischief, Mum. We all know what goes on in those retirement villages.'

He was joking of course, judging by the tone of his voice and forced laughter. He and Mel loved to tease her about it, as if there were something quaint about her actually having a life of her own. Behind the gentle goading was the unspoken fear of a generation left to navigate the ill-advised second marriages and new blended families of their elderly parents. Assets divided and shared. Amended wills and probate: the new taboo of Sunday lunchtime conversations.

'I do wish you wouldn't patronise me, David.' Peggy surprised herself. She was so used to being the passive one, bending under the weight of other people's expectations. To correct her son, challenge him even, was uncharted territory. Far from providing new fodder to ruminate over in the early hours, Peggy found it quite invigorating.

'I'm sorry, I didn't mean to imply ... Look, Jenny and I were worried sick.'

Jenny. So, they'd spoken. Peggy sensed the silent countdown to her daughter's wrath, like a gathering storm beyond the horizon. On the one hand, she should be grateful that her two offspring were at least on speaking terms again. Something had happened, and a state of frostiness ensued over the past couple of years. Peggy had her suspicions. David would be keeping tally of all the errands he was running for her, all the hours he so selflessly sacrificed to care for their mother while Jenny was off finding herself in the country with Eve, the free-spirited vegan.

'I can't manage the farm on my own,' Jenny had explained when Peggy enquired why she needed a lodger. They weren't fooling Peggy. She wasn't born yesterday. Or even the day before. Peggy had always thought of herself as broadminded. Up until she and Angie had casually discussed masturbation over tea and walnut bread.

'I hope you told Jenny I am managing,' said Peggy, placing Mongolian Beef with Wholemeal Noodles onto the rotating glass plate in the microwave. The last thing she wanted was Jenny taking over. She made Angie look docile. At least Jenny had calmed down a bit since she'd met Eve. Perhaps it was all that tofu.

'Your daughter has a right to know when there's a crisis.'

'Crisis? We're not talking about the outbreak of Ebola or civil war here,' said Peggy. 'I tripped.'

'You have to be more careful,' said David. Peggy held her breath, waiting for him to say it. 'At your age.'

It was a game of geriatric bingo. *Take it easy. Elevate your legs. Drink more water. At your age.*

No wonder she had high blood pressure. All she needed was a good scream. Let it out.

'David, I wish you'd stop going on about my age. I could live for another twenty years, you know.'

The enormity of Peggy's words must have hit them simultaneously. Peggy heard David crunch the gears of his precious BMW. Twenty years. Crikey. That was a lot of trips to the podiatrist and the doctor. And a lot of trips to the bathroom.

'Right, well, you'd better start taking care of yourself then.' David sounded like a man who'd just recalculated his inheritance. 'Don't overdo things.'

Bingo.

Peggy had no intention of slowing down. She felt full of energy, full of fight. In fact, she felt quite unlike her most recent self, the distance between the age of her body and how she felt inside increasing with each passing day. From this all-new perspective, she surveyed her lengthening past and shortening future with a sense of optimism.

Woe betide anyone who tried to stand in the way of the new, improved Peggy Smart.

Richard Glover had gone. David was home, no doubt parked in his driveway behind Mel's armoured four-wheel drive.

'Give my love to the children.'

'I will. And talking of which, any chance we could drop Sam and Emily at your place for a couple of hours on Saturday? Mel and I have been invited to a lunch. Strictly no kids.'

It reminded her of the Rubik's cube she'd fretted over many years ago. About to congratulate herself on having all the colours lined up, she'd noticed a rogue red square on the yellow face. That was so like David to do this, just as she was gaining the upper hand.

The fact that her babysitting services were once again in demand signified a thaw in the previously frosty relationship. She'd be a fool to turn down an opportunity to spend time with her only grandchildren. But she had a right to feel peeved. One minute being treated like a child, the next expected to mind them. Peggy had other responsibilities to consider too. The shelves in the library wouldn't fill themselves. She couldn't possibly expect Brian to manage all that on his own. He needed help and moral support, not to mention morning tea.

'I'm sorry, David. I'm busy on Saturday,' said Peggy.

'Busy? You? On a Saturday?'

Peggy opened the door of the microwave. Steam rose from the edge of the cellophane, but a quick prod with a fork proved the meal was still frozen in the centre. Ignoring the instructions on the packet, Peggy turned the power dial up to maximum and pressed the button.

'Yes, darling,' she said. 'I'm going out with Brian.'

There was silence on the other end of the phone and Peggy assumed they'd been cut off. And you'd better get used to it, she told the fruit bowl.

'Mum, are you still there? Who's Brian?'

Basil was sitting to attention at Peggy's feet, enticed by the smell of Mongolian Beef wafting through the microwave vents.

'He's my new . . . friend.' Peggy winked at Basil. He smiled back through his whiskers, a slippery trail of dog-drool escaping his jowls and pooling on the tiles. Peggy wondered if she'd gone too far but it was strangely satisfying. She felt reckless and empowered.

'*Friend*. Right. Not to worry.'

Peggy could hear Mel in the background asking if he'd remembered to buy milk. 'How about I pop in on Wednesday? I'm working from home that day.'

The sudden concern for her welfare was touching, yet stifling. All those years spent fretting over her children, from that first kick in the womb, to their first day at school, the broken hearts and dented bumpers, David's low sperm count and Jenny's cancer scare. Peggy had been a mother for forty-six years, but overnight the tables had turned. The river of worry and sleepless nights now flowed upstream. And with the worry went the power.

'Let me just check my calendar.'

Peggy stared at the open page. It was a picture of Sam and Emily outside the Opera House, Mel's parents just visible in the corner of the shot. Almost every day was taken up with an appointment of some colour. Wednesday was out. It was there in glitter gold.

Her heart sank. She wasn't trying to be awkward or ungrateful, but that was the only day Jim was free to help the Social Committee look at karaoke machines. With his experience in the music industry, he was the obvious choice, and only too eager to offer his expert opinion when Angie fluttered her eyelashes.

'Mum?'

'Wednesday's tricky.' If she told him the truth, she'd be accused of overdoing things. If she lied and said she had a doctor's appointment, David would worry, or even worse, offer to come with her. Her alibi had to be watertight. Then it came to her. 'I'm seeing Sister Slack on Wednesday. Women's problems.'

It worked, just as it had for his father, the slightest hint of anything to do with the female reproductive system was enough to send Ted scurrying to the garden shed.

'I see,' said David, obviously trying his best not to. 'Do you think you'll be alright for Sam's party next weekend?'

'The Pirates of the Crimean party you mean? I wouldn't miss it for the world.'

'The *Pirates of the Caribbean* party was last year. This one's a *Star Wars* theme.'

Peggy was still in the dark about *Star Wars*, but she would make it her business to find out. She couldn't risk being outdone by Mel's parents again. After all the trouble she'd gone to with that galleon-shaped cake last year, only to be trumped by a dressing-up costume so realistic, it made Sam look like an extra from the movie set.

The conversation might have ended there with fond words of farewell, had David not pulled the pin from the hand grenade. 'Honestly, Mother,' he laughed down the phone. 'You're getting so forgetful.'

Peggy snatched the phone from beside the mushy mango and prodded the red button. She was fuming. It was one thing for her son to query her physical capabilities, but quite another for him to question her mental facilities.

It was time for Peggy to get her shit together in a hurry. Or else she'd better start covering her tracks.

The doorbell rang. Peggy threw the phone onto the kitchen table, and wiping her good hand on a tea towel, trotted towards the front door. Who on earth would be calling in at this hour? She rarely had visitors. What if it was Brian standing on the other side of the closed door armed with a bottle of champagne and a bunch of mixed gerberas? Peggy found her most nonchalant smile and opened the door.

'Hello . . . Christine.' Peggy had been struggling with names recently, even people she saw every day, so it was a relief to see the village manager wearing her name badge.

'Evening. I hope I haven't interrupted dinner.'

Peggy pictured the plastic carton circling inside the microwave. 'Not at all.' She wondered if she should invite

Christine in, but refrained in case she was here to take Basil away.

'Delivery for you. It's been sitting up at reception all day. I thought I'd drop it in to you on my way home.'

'Delivery?' There was nothing in Christine's hands.

Christine stepped to one side to reveal a shiny metal walking frame on wheels. She pushed it up the path towards Peggy.

'I think there must be some mistake. This isn't mine.'

'It has your name on it, see? Mrs Peggy Smart, Unit 24, Jacaranda Retirement Village. The delivery man said there was no-one at home when he called earlier.'

'I don't understand. I didn't order a walking frame. I don't need one.'

Christine unfolded a piece of paper and showed it to Peggy. The invoice was addressed to a J. Smart. *Jenny*. Her own flesh and blood. Peggy had gained five inches round the waist after bringing that child into the world, let alone the damage to her down-belows, and this was how Jenny had decided to repay her.

Peggy noticed a simpering Sheila Martin walk past the end of her path. Oh yes, thought Peggy, she'd love this.

'You are *so lucky* to have such an attentive family,' said Christine, placing Peggy's one free hand around the black rubber handle. 'So many residents are left to their own devices once they move here. It's very sad.' Basil appeared in the doorway. He coughed out a wheezy bark before waddling down the front step. Christine backed up as Basil tottered towards her. 'By the way, I must remind you that you only have three weeks left to find *him* a new home.'

Basil sniffed at one wheel of the walker then cocked his leg and let out a steaming golden stream against a wheel. Peggy stifled a giggle with the tea towel. She was still smiling to herself as she watched Christine drive away. She left the walker in the entrance hall near the front door. Far from the freedom and security it supposedly represented, Peggy saw in those four tiny wheels and shiny red frame the vehicle of her demise. *A hearse.*

Shuffling back into the kitchen, Peggy smelled something. A ping from the microwave made her start. Cripes, the Mongolian Beef! To Peggy's horror there were actual flames behind the tinted glass. It was like looking into one of those fancy gas fires she'd seen on *Better Homes.* Basil limped for cover as Peggy opened the door, filling the kitchen with acrid smoke. The inside of the microwave was covered in wholemeal noodles and molten plastic. Peggy sank onto a kitchen chair and buried her face in the tea towel.

'Oh Ted, why did you have to leave me like that?' she moaned.

~

Her first reaction was to suspect the mince. She was sure she'd defrosted it properly, but there were still a few frozen lumps she'd had to break up with the spatula as it browned in the pan.

Ted loved shepherd's pie, and Peggy had spent fifty years of marriage perfecting her own recipe. Every time she placed the dish on the table, with the steam stealing through the golden potato crust and the meaty sauce bubbling through the cracks like lava, Ted would sigh and say, 'My mother used to make the most wonderful shepherd's pies.' Once, just once, would it have hurt him to lie a little and tell her hers were the best?

Ted had been tossing and turning since midnight. Peggy turned on the bedroom light, and propped herself up on one elbow facing him. He was half asleep, but in the dim yellow light she could see his face, all contorted.

'What's the matter, Ted?' Peggy tried to keep the irritation out of her voice. She knew she'd never get back to sleep now.

Ted groaned.

Peggy tried to wake him with a shake to the shoulder. Perhaps he was having a nightmare. He was always such a sound sleeper; certainly he'd managed to sleep through the crying and night-time feeds when David and Jenny were babies.

'Peggy—'

'I'm here. What is it?'

'Don't leave me.'

'What are you on about?'

'Promise me,' he groaned.

As her eyes adjusted to the light, Peggy could see the sweat soaking through Ted's pyjamas. His face was pale, and he stared blankly through half-closed eyelids. When she touched his forehead, his skin was roasting.

Peggy felt her pulse quicken. The beef mince was past its use-by date. But only by a couple of days and it had smelled fine. What if she'd poisoned him? Given him Salmonella?

'Do you feel sick?'

It seemed to take all Ted's energy for him to even shake his head. 'Not sick . . . pain . . . here.' He pushed the bedcover away and placed one hand over his belly. Peggy noticed it looked swollen. Had he sneaked back for seconds without her knowing?

'Do you need the bathroom, Ted?' It was always the first thing she asked when one of the children told her they had stomach ache. Later in life, the kids had teased her about it, as grown-up children were inclined to do. They'd all be in absolute stitches. 'Broken arm? Run over by a bus? Are you sure you don't need the toilet?'

Ted wasn't smiling. A ripple of panic washed over Peggy. She clambered out of bed, pushed her feet into her waiting slippers and walked round to the other side of the bed. For a moment she wasn't sure what to do. Should she take his temperature? His pulse? Fetch a hot water bottle?

'Should I call the doctor?'

Ted shook his head. *Stubborn old fool.* He hated doctors, going to extraordinary lengths to obtain repeat prescriptions for his prostate pills without ever presenting the offending organ for an actual examination. Peggy began to wonder if old Dr Steele had died of exasperation.

Peggy surveyed Ted's sunken eyes and grey skin. For once, she was going to overrule him. There was something more amiss here than the shepherd's pie.

~

Ted was drowsy from the morphine and didn't stir when Peggy kissed him on the forehead. All manner of wires and tubes snaked from his body. A plastic mask covered most of his face. Peggy could hear the hiss of oxygen flowing through his nose down into his lungs. That was good. Oxygen was good.

They'd wheeled him back from his scan half an hour ago. She'd been trying to catch the young doctor's eye to find out the result, but he looked very busy. All Peggy could do was watch the hands creep round the dial of Ted's watch. It was the one they'd presented him with when he retired from Blake's. It wasn't called Blake's by then, bought by some big department store chain back in the eighties, but he knew every inch of that building, every pipe and light fitting, elevator shaft and emergency exit.

They'd had such grand plans for their retirement, as all couples do. But Ted was content with golf, the garden and simply getting under Peggy's feet at home.

An alarm sounded, startling Peggy. She scanned the squiggles on the monitor, looking for clues, then at Ted to see if he was still breathing. A nurse appeared and pressed a button to silence the alarm. Should she do that? Surely, she should check with the doctor first? Alarms meant something was wrong.

The nurse smiled at Peggy and reassured her the doctor would soon be over to explain. Explain what? Peggy studied the numbers on the screen. 89, 134, 24. The one on the right must be the blood pressure. 93/52. Typical. Ted would live on ginger beer and sausages if she let him, yet here he was with such amazingly low blood pressure. The lower the better. She'd read as much in *Women's Weekly*.

There was a group of doctors huddled around the nurses' station. Peggy could just make out Ted's name written on the big white board, next to his bed number. The doctors stood in a circle, discussing each patient in turn. Some wrote on clipboards, some sipped from water bottles, like players at half-time. One yawned and checked his phone. When they came to Ted, they moved over to an illuminated box on the wall and examined the grainy images that must be the scans of his insides. A doctor pointed to something on the images then glanced over at Peggy. She gripped Ted's hand so tightly, he woke from his groggy stupor and frowned at her.

When the young doctor approached the bed, he could barely meet Peggy's eyes. Gone was the casual banter from when they'd arrived and the joke about the shepherd's pie. The doctor's face was almost as pale as Ted's as he asked her to step outside the curtains.

Sepsis . . . renal failure . . . peritonitis . . . appendicitis. It was a triple-word-score bonanza of medical terms. Peggy watched the doctor's lips move. Every now and again she recognised a word, something that made sense to her, before the incomprehensible syllables reassembled like flies.

There was nothing about food poisoning. Nothing about shepherd's pie. Peggy wasn't sure whether to be relieved, or very, very worried.

When a doctor in blue scrubs joined them, introducing himself as the head of Intensive Care, Peggy realised this wasn't something that could be fixed by a trip to the bathroom.

~

She didn't remember much about the journey home in David's car. It was getting light by that time, and they crawled in the commuter traffic. David fussed with the air-conditioning while Peggy clutched the pink plastic bag containing all that remained of Ted. His pyjamas, and the watch he never took off. She'd always wondered why he wore it at night, always meant to ask him. She'd never know now.

'Why don't you come and stay with us for a few days, Mum?'

'I don't think so, David.'

'You shouldn't be on your own.'

'I've got Basil.' And Ted's side of the bed would still be warm, if they hurried.

'I'm worried about you being all alone.'

'I'll be fine. You drop me off and go home to Mel. She needs you more than I do with the baby on the way.'

'Are you sure?'

'Yes. We'll talk tomorrow. There are arrangements to be made, and I'll need your help.'

Appendicitis.

She still couldn't believe it. Did people of Ted's age even get appendicitis? It was like tonsillitis. No-one ever got that past adolescence. Yet it had shown up on the CAT scan, they told her, clear as day. A radioactive sausage, surrounded by pus. By then, it was too late. Nothing could be done.

It was his age, the doctor explained.

David insisted on coming into the house with her. In truth, she couldn't wait to get rid of her son. She wanted to be alone, wanted to curl up in bed next to Ted, in the sheets still scented with his smell, in the hope she might wake and find him there. She would make him his tea and they would sit side by side in bed, listening to the news and planning their day, as they had every morning for fifty years, after which Peggy would lay the breakfast table. In their respective seats on either side of the round melamine table, she and Ted would butter their toast and take their tablets. Together.

There would be time for grieving and hugging and tears. But not now. It wasn't quite real yet. As long as she held back the tears, there was still a chance it wasn't true. It was only when she saw the empty shepherd's pie dish soaking in the sink that the awful reality hit, and her world collapsed.

16

A Game of Strategy

PEGGY PULLED THE CREAM BLAZER TOGETHER AT THE FRONT
and fastened the button. There was a nip in the air and
she wondered if she should have worn a knit instead. The
wide-leg pants and cream shirt had looked so elegant in the
mirror this morning. It hadn't occurred to her she might be
overdressed. What was she thinking? For heaven's sake, it
was a second-hand book fair in a school gymnasium, not
lunch in Monte Carlo. Peggy unbuttoned the blazer and tried
to push the sleeves as untidily as possible up her forearms.

Any thoughts of rushing back inside her unit to change
were thwarted when the silver Lexus pulled up at the kerb.
Brian climbed out and strode round to the passenger side to
open the door like a footman. David did that for her too,
but only to stop her face planting on the driveway.

'What a glorious morning for it,' said Brian.

If he noticed the new outfit, it didn't register in his
inscrutable smile. Perhaps this whole stupid makeover had

been a waste of time and Brian preferred his women dressed more practically, like Celia in her oil-stained overalls. Peggy imagined Phyllis teaching conjugations in thick woollen tights and a high-necked blouse.

'Here, allow me.' Brian leaned across Peggy and clicked her seatbelt in place. It was an intimate gesture that took her by surprise. She drew an unanticipated breath, inhaling Imperial Leather and Omo. Sneaking another lungful, she detected a hint of something stale and vaguely musty. What Brian needed was someone to air his washing properly. And Peggy prided herself on her airing prowess. Unlike her daughter-in-law, who hung David's freshly ironed shirts straight back in the wardrobe and even put damp sheets back on the bed.

'I'm ready,' was all Peggy could think to say when Brian fastened his own seatbelt.

'I've prepared the backseat for later,' said Brian, as they pulled away.

'Back seat?' Peggy glanced over her shoulder to where Brian had folded down the rear seats of the saloon car and covered them with blankets.

'For the books.'

'*The books.* Yes, of course.' She cringed. They were simply buying books, not jumping into bed together.

The shallow morning sun glazed the windscreen. Peggy felt its heat dampen the back of her neck. Fearful of a full-blown melt, she lowered the electric window.

'Here, allow me.' Brian closed the window again from his control and turned on the air-conditioning.

He stuck rigidly to the speed limit, as expected. Carving through the Saturday traffic, Peggy found herself wishing the high school was further away. In Darwin, for example. The leather seats were deliciously pillowy and the pleasant conversation so effortless that it settled around her shoulders like a soft shawl.

Brian had a knack for putting people at ease. He was the perfect social accessory. Peggy let her mind wander. They were at a cocktail party. She was wearing The Dress and chatting to a group of women.

'Your husband is *so* charming. And so easy to talk to,' one of the women was saying. The other women followed her gaze to where Brian was holding court, his shiny wedding ring catching the light.

He was so expressive. He liked to talk with his hands. So different to Ted, whose work-rough hands were always buried deep in his pockets. Peggy lost track of the number of times she'd mended his trouser seams.

'I was saying, perhaps we could grab some lunch afterwards.'

Peggy wondered if she'd fallen asleep, because when she opened her eyes they were parked outside the school. She'd seen the adverts on TV about micro sleeps. They could be very dangerous in a car. So dangerous, she'd almost missed a lunch invitation from Brian.

'That would be lovely,' she said, grinning in spite of herself.

'Good. Angie suggested a little place not far from the school.'

'Angie?'

'Yes, she's meeting us here. For the book sale. Didn't she tell you?'

~

'I suggest we spread out. That way we'll cover all the genres.'

Angie wore pale cotton trousers with a loose button-up shirt and simple pearls in her ears. She had a cashmere cardigan knotted around her shoulders and yet another handbag. With her dark hair swept back from her forehead, she looked as gorgeous as ever. Utterly and effortlessly gorgeous.

In turn, Peggy felt more self-conscious and awkward than ever, her newfound confidence following the shopping trip already paling. Who was she trying to kid? At the end of the day, the whole exercise had been little more than window-dressing. Deep down, she was still that shy teenager, forever living in Angie's shadow.

Peggy's ice-pick heels click-clacked across the wooden floor. Several people turned to stare. She debated taking them off and plodding barefoot around the school hall. But then she remembered the state of her toenails. Instead, she leaned forward and tiptoed along the aisles of books.

She was surprised how many people were already milling about the hall. The place was filled with rows of trestle tables, each groaning beneath the weight of second-hand books. Boxes and boxes of them. Near the entrance, an army of middle-aged women totted up prices and counted out change. The line of customers, arms laden with hardbacks and paperbacks, threatened to swamp their valiant efforts.

'Brian, why don't you do history and non-fiction,' said Angie. 'I'll do biographies and travel. Peggy, why don't you concentrate on handicrafts and romantic fiction.'

Romantic fiction? How apt. Peggy remembered her little daydream in the car. Fantasy, would be more like it.

She watched Brian follow Angie like a lapdog, laughing at something she'd said. She turned and placed her hand on his arm as she shared the punchline. Brian threw his head back and laughed. Angie had made a career out of marrying eligible men, probably each with an equally eligible portfolio. She only had to click her fingers and they rolled over. It was beginning to get up Peggy's nose.

As if to remind her of her shortcomings, her bladder yawned, stretched and wished her good morning. She hadn't looked at a single book, romantic or otherwise. There was no point in protesting. In this battle of wills, she was destined to come off worse, and with the latchkey incident playing over and over like an annoying jingle in her mind, she couldn't afford to waste time.

'Can I help you?' It was a girl of about sixteen. She looked like one of the high school students.

'As a matter of fact, yes. Can you tell me where the nearest toilets are please?'

'Follow me.'

What a lovely young person. It made such a change from feeling invisible to the younger generation. She was more used to being thoroughly ignored, or addressed via the screen of a mobile phone.

'That's very kind of you.'

'No worries,' replied the girl. 'I'm planning to go to medical school when I leave school.'

'How wonderful,' said Peggy. She thought of Dr Stephen. She wished there were more young doctors like him.

'Yes, I want to be a geriatrician. I work in a nursing home on Saturdays. I'm trying to get as much experience with old people as I can, for my CV.'

Peggy sighed and followed the girl down a long corridor. There was water running somewhere in the distance and Peggy's spikey heels broke into a half-jog.

Clickety-clack. Clickety-clack.

'Here you are,' said the girl. 'Would you like me to wait for you?'

'No. Thank you. I'll be fine.' Peggy smiled and hurried into the first cubicle.

After all that, it was a false alarm. She decided to sit and read the graffiti on the back of the toilet door in the hope the would-be geriatrician would find some other poor old dear to pester.

'Peggy?' It was Angie's voice. 'What are you doing in there?'

Would that woman ever give her a minute's peace? 'Reading poetry,' Peggy replied, sarcastically. Urban poetry. The silent screams of a thousand women just like her, trapped by their own bodies, and the attentions of an overbearing septuagenarian. 'Give me a second.'

When she finally opened the cubicle door, Angie was leaning towards the mirror, applying yet more lipstick. The hairs rose on Peggy's arms, remembering another time and place.

'Want some?' Angie offered the coloured stick.

Peggy shook her head. 'No, thank you.'

'Go on, bring some life to that face.' Angie thrust the lipstick into Peggy's hand.

'I said no.' Peggy thrust it back. 'I prefer a more natural look.'

She daren't look in the mirror. Ted had always told her he liked the 'natural' look. But that was a long time ago now. She hadn't thought to update her face. She changed the blind in the kitchen more often in the past fifty years than her look.

'Suit yourself. I could show you a few tricks if you like? A few things I learned in the trade.'

'One thing at a time, Angie. This is all going too fast for me.'

'But you have to admit, you look amazing.'

Peggy did think she looked amazing. Anything was an improvement after her taupe era. But somehow, the self-confidence she'd expected to go with her new look was still lagging behind, trailing its feet like a truculent child, demanding ice-cream and pulling faces at strangers. She was still a long way from asking Brian over for roast loin with red wine gravy.

'He's a lovely chap, your Brian.'

'What do you mean, *my* Brian?'

'Come off it Pegs. I've known you long enough to know something's going on.'

'Nothing's *going on*. I don't know what you're talking about.'

Peggy felt like she was squabbling with a sister, one who knew her well enough to know when she was lying. Was mind-reading another one of Angie's super-powers? If she admitted how she felt about Brian, Angie Valentine would yet again have the upper hand. The fairytale would be shattered, and Peggy once more resigned to peeping from behind the kitchen curtains.

'If you say so.' Angie clicked the top back onto her lipstick and leaned into the mirror above the sink to check her reflection. Peggy wished it had been a glue stick.

'Brian and I are just friends. We hardly know each other outside the committee.'

Angie's eyes slid sideways. 'What a shame. I'd hate to see a man like Brian go to waste.'

The sand dune began to slide beneath Peggy's feet. She'd seen the way Angie and Brian had looked at each other the other night at the committee meeting. The last thing she wanted was a cat fight, one she was bound to lose. It was most undignified for grown women to compete over a man. When David and Jenny were little, they'd fought over toys, each wanting what the other was playing with. The only solution had been to confiscate the contested item, leaving them both in tears. Did the same apply to handsome widowers?

'Back into battle?' Peggy led the way. She felt a crease in the atmosphere. Something stirred between them. This was about more than refined sugars or sculpting underwear. This was about an old unspoken rivalry. And pride.

~

Brian was struggling with a cardboard box of books when they returned from the toilets.

'I've snapped up their entire selection of large-print novels,' he said.

'What a good idea.' Angie brushed his arm with her fingertips.

'Are you ladies happy to keep going for a while?'

'Absolutely,' said Angie. 'There's plenty of go in me.'

Strumpet.

Peggy felt a head of steam rising in her tank. Enough was enough. The gloves were off.

She pushed the sleeves of her tailored cream blazer up as far as they would go. 'When you've finished in large print, Brian, would you mind giving me a hand?'

He could hardly refuse. Peggy had never wanted to be the damsel in distress, but she had to use every weapon at her disposal. Far from an encumbrance, her broken arm was proving to be an unexpected asset. And if it didn't work on Brian, she could always use it as a cudgel on Angie.

Peggy lassoed Brian with the handles of an empty cloth book bag and began to lead him down the aisle between two tables of women's fiction. 'We'll be a while in Australian romance. Why don't we just see you back at the village?'

Angie set her face. 'I thought we could all go out for a spot of lunch after we're finished here. It's such a lovely day.'

'I think that's a splendid idea,' said Brian. 'How about that little place round the corner you were telling me about?'

Peggy gripped the fabric of the book bag and twisted it into a garrotte between her fingers. The score was 40:40. Her next shot had to be a winner.

'While we're here, I need to find a present for my grand-son's birthday. It's next weekend and I can't drive to the shops with this thing on my arm. I noticed there are some toys and games over there, but I need a man's opinion.'

'I'll see what I can do. It's been a long time since I've played any games!'

Unlike your two female companions.

'But you have grandsons. That makes you the perfect man for the job.'

'Yes, three actually. They're all at university now, but I'll do my best.'

'The party is next Saturday at the adventure park. You know the one by the water with all the climbing frames? I've no idea how I'm going to get there. It'll be weeks before I can drive again . . .' Peggy left it hanging in the air, awaiting the video replay to see if the shot was in or out.

'I can take you,' said Angie.

Out. Peggy pretended not to hear.

'I'd be happy to drive you,' said Brian. 'I wouldn't mind a bit of fresh air.'

On the line.

'Are you sure?' Peggy turned her back on Angie, all smiles now.

Brian stood to attention. 'It would be my pleasure.'

In.

Game. Set. Match.

~

With the last of the boxes stacked in the boot, Brian locked his car doors. Several volunteers, including the would-be geriatrician, had formed a human chain to carry all the books to the Lexus. Not bad for a morning's work, they agreed. The practicalities of unloading, sorting and cataloguing their purchases back at the other end only hit them as they waved off the army of helpers.

The ever-practical Brian suggested they leave the car where it was and walk down to the beachfront. They'd never find parking on a Saturday, he reasoned.

Angie turning to Peggy. 'Do you think you can manage in your condition?'

They exchanged looks. Peggy's nostrils flared.

It was almost midday and muggy as all hell. After all that rifling through paperbacks and carrying heavy boxes, Peggy's skin was prickling under her cast. She'd already slipped off her blazer and in a cunning move, draped it over Brian's passenger seat, thus assuring herself a lift back to the village in his car.

Check.

Ted had taught her to play chess when they'd been going out for only a few weeks. At first, she'd pretended to be clueless but soon developed a knack for predicting his moves. No matter how much he creased his forehead in concentration, Peggy could read him like a book and foiled his elaborate attacks time and time again. In the end, she could see how bruised his ego was, and she let him win. Marriage is all about compromise. Her mother had told her as much.

They set off down the hill towards the beach road, three abreast. Brian, in his Panama, walked on the outside, closest to the road. Angie, in her signature sunglasses and neat straw hat, soon manoeuvred herself into the centre position, forcing Peggy into the inside lane.

'I think we did rather well, don't you, ladies?' Brian, oblivious to the strategic posturing going on beside him, chatted brightly.

'I'd say we make a good team,' said Angie, falling into step with Brian, forcing Peggy to hang back and walk behind.

Peggy trotted forward and squeezed between them. 'The talking books were a stroke of genius.'

She'd taken Angie's castle with her rook, but she'd suffer for it later in her ice-pick heels. Her feet had started to swell like choux buns. Angie had noticed too and gave her a look as if to say, 'What were you thinking?'

The only free table at the busy café – a table for two – was outside in the sun. Fine for Brian and Angie in their hats, but not for the fair-skinned Peggy, who'd forgotten to bring one. Her blouse clung to her damp chest and she noticed Brian deliberately avert his gaze from her bulging cleavage. They borrowed a chair from another table and arranged themselves around the circular tabletop, like three corners of an equilateral triangle. Angie made a big show of giving Peggy her hat, and smirked when it sat on top of her head like a toadstool.

A cloud of white birds erupted from a Norfolk Pine near the beach. A young family sat eating sandwiches on the sand across the road from the café. Everywhere, people moved at a Saturday pace, eating their smashed avocado on toast and smiling in the knowledge that the working week was still far in the future. In some ways, Peggy missed weekends. Retirement afforded the luxury of crowd-less weekdays but there was something about the respite from the nine-to-five that had always made Saturday and Sunday special.

It was such a relief to sit down, and while Brian searched inside for a menu, Peggy levered her shoes off under the table. Loose flaps of skin peeled away with the shoes, leaving blister juice trickling down the back of each heel. There was no point thinking ahead to the walk back to the car. It was time to enjoy the moment, and the first meal she would eat with Brian. If she tilted the hat at the right angle, she could even pretend Angie wasn't sitting there at the table with them.

The conversation was light and bounced between them as they waited for the food to arrive, sharing tiny snippets of their lives. With every anecdote, Peggy slotted another piece of the puzzle into place. She had the corners and edges, and the more time she spent with Brian, the more detail she was able to fill in. She noticed how Angie had shuffled her chair in closer to Brian, throwing the triangle suddenly off balance. As usual, she dominated the conversation, but Angie for once wasn't talking about herself. Instead, she focused her attention on Brian, uncovering tiny nuggets of his past like an archaeologist on a dig. It was verging on the forensic. Far from discussing knee replacements and grandchildren, Angie had him eating out of the palm of her hand. Defeated, Peggy sat and watched the seductress in action.

There was a lull when the waiter arrived with the food. He filled three water glasses and instructed them to enjoy their meals. The plate sitting in front of Peggy was piled high with fried fish and chips. There was a tiny salad garnish sitting to one side, almost by way of apology. Brian, Peggy was relieved to see, was a meat and veg man after all, his own plate barely visible beneath a generous steak and green beans.

'What are you having as a main course?' Peggy stared at the pile of leaves on Angie's plate. It looked as if her meal had blown in on a gust of wind.

'This is it. A mixed salad.'

'What, nothing with it?'

'I don't eat meat or processed foods,' Angie replied. 'The wrong diet can be so *ageing*.'

Peggy paused, a forkful of batter millimetres from her lips. She'd had enough of Angie's sanctimonious digs about her lifestyle habits. 'Aha, that's where you're wrong. Dr Lim told me the other day that women of our age live longer if they carry a little more substance.' Under her breath she added, 'Skinny people are easier to kidnap.'

'Indeed,' said Brian. 'A woman of substance.' He skewered a piece of steak and anchored it to his fork with a crosshatch of French beans. Angie and Peggy exchanged glances, unsure which of them had the upper hand. Perhaps he was referring to one of the books from this morning's exercise. Or, Peggy hoped, he preferred real women with real bodies. Yet it was hard to reconcile the buttoned-up Brian sitting across the table in his dilapidated hat with gravy dribbling down his chin, as a passionate man full of lust and desire.

The waiter reappeared and offered them more iced water. Peggy felt as though he'd thrown it over her. What was she thinking? Were she and Angie really fighting over this thin-faced old man, who used phrases like 'top notch' and began every sentence with 'indeed'? A man who kept a box of Kleenex on his rear parcel shelf?

Suddenly, she had a vision of the future, of pushing Brian around in a wheelchair and scraping porridge from his chin. Life as a full-time carer loomed. She'd seen it before: the women who resigned from the committee and dropped out of Aqua over the course of a few weeks. She'd watched their lives dwindle to little more than nursemaid to their elderly husbands. The lure of the older man, his sophistication and financial security, now paid for in the monotonous routine of washing, dressing and shaving. As if she'd shared the same thought at the same moment, Angie moved her chair back a fraction, balancing the triangle around the table once again.

Brian finished his meal, leaving a frill of trimmed fat grinning around the edge of his gravy-coloured plate. Out of the blue, he started to talk about his wife. 'I nursed Phyllis through Alzheimer's disease. She died a couple of days before her eightieth birthday. It's awful seeing someone you love disintegrate like that.'

'That must have been so painful for you.' Angie's manicured fingers stroked the side of her water glass, and not Brian's arm. 'My husband had cancer. I watched him wither away in a matter of weeks. It was terrible.' Her face was impossible to read beneath her giant sunglasses.

An hour ago, Peggy might have made a point of saying, 'Which husband was that?' How long the unofficial ceasefire would last, Peggy didn't know, but she recognised grief when she saw it. The three of them sat in silence, lost in their own memories of love and loss, oblivious to the impatience of modern life as it played out around them.

The waiter came to clear their plates. A young couple hovered nearby, eyeing the table. Angie had barely touched her salad. Brian passed Peggy's empty plate across the table to the waiter. 'That's what I like to see,' he said. 'A woman who enjoys her food.'

Indeed.

Peggy had polished off the lot, apart from the bits she was now wearing down the front of her blouse.

~

The sun was sinking between the two westerly unit blocks when they arrived back at the village. Outside Peggy's unit, Brian pulled on the handbrake and turned off the engine.

'Thank you so much for the lift.' Peggy reached to undo her seatbelt. She'd placed it strategically over a tartare sauce stain on the front of her blouse. She might be winding down Operation Brian, but she still had her pride.

'Thank *you* for helping with the book selection. I think we worked rather well together.'

Peggy swallowed. 'Shall I meet you later at the library to unpack the books?'

She couldn't *not* offer. There'd be time to change her shoes and pad her heels with Comfeel.

'Don't you worry about that. Celia promised to give me a hand. She was too busy to come with us this morning, but she desperately wants to be involved.'

Celia.

It was difficult to imagine Brian with grease stains, but Celia was certainly a woman of substance and she still had plenty of petrol in her tank. It was time to step aside gracefully.

To Peggy's surprise, Brian opened the door for her and guided her by the hand along the path like a geriatric Mr Darcy. She had an image of him in breeches and felt a tiny puff of desire. Not exactly carnal lust, but a definite stirring in her lower reaches.

The day hadn't gone strictly according to plan, and Peggy was more confused than ever about her feelings for Brian, but the outing had been a huge success on one front. Thanks to the combined efforts of the Jacaranda Village Library Committee, there would be a whole section devoted to Regency romance. Which was just as well. Peggy was getting bored with surgeons.

Across the road, Peggy saw Sheila Martin's curtains twitch.

Brian cleared his throat. 'Right-o, must be off,' he said. 'Don't forget this. Top-notch present.' He handed Peggy the game he'd helped her choose for Sam's birthday. *Star Wars* chess.

'Thank you,' said Peggy. She could feel the stretch in her bladder muscle. The moment she put that key in the lock, it would spring back like a rubber band. She edged closer to the front door. She was hoping to take those pesky nerve endings by surprise, an ambush of sorts. If she left it until the very last moment to handle the key, she could bamboozle her own body and make it into her unit without embarrassment.

But Brian was following her. Was he expecting to come inside? *For afters?*

He cleared his throat. 'What time would you like me to pick you up?'

'Pick me up?'

'Your grandson's party, next Saturday,' said Brian looking confused. 'I wasn't sure if you were accepting my offer of a lift out of politeness. I really don't want to tread on any toes. Who would you prefer, Angie or me?'

It would mean another entry in Brian's diary, another glitter gold square on her calendar. It would also mean spurning Angie, after all she'd done for her. Having been so lonely since she moved to Jacaranda Retirement Village, Peggy now found herself with a new wardrobe, a bustling social schedule and a dilemma. Where did her loyalties lie? With Brian or Angie?

Peggy's fingers closed around the keys inside her bag. The countdown had begun. All she could focus on was getting in through the front door. She couldn't even remember what time the party started, let alone decide where Brian fit into her life or what she owed Angie.

'I'll phone you,' was all she managed as she stabbed the key into the lock and disappeared inside, leaving a perplexed Brian on the doorstep, waiting for his answer.

It was déjà vu, all over again.

17

Champagne and Stormtroopers

THE GAME WAS IN IMMACULATE CONDITION, THE PIECES still sealed inside their plastic bags. In fact, it looked as if it had never been used. A discarded gift? Peggy felt a twinge of anxiety. Would Sam like it? The children were so into their computers and iPod phones these days. The idea of sitting down to play a board game – especially one as slow-paced as chess – might seem awfully dull to a six-year-old. What was she thinking? Clearly more carried away with trying to impress Brian with her intellectualism and outdo Angie than finding something her grandson might actually want to play with.

Peggy was missing her grandchildren. It was only going to get worse as they grew up and Mel enrolled them in every conceivable sport or activity in the unshakeable belief that both Sam and Emily were undiscovered child prodigies at something. In the future, Peggy would have to make an appointment, schedule a slot between Nippers and tennis or karate and Little Athletics.

If only she hadn't told the truth about being exhausted after a full day of babysitting. If only she'd had a reversing camera on her hatchback. If only that nice man from the shopping centre hadn't offered Sam and Emily lollies while she was exchanging insurance details with the Mercedes driver. If only Sam – hyped up after the lollies – hadn't blown the whistle on the whole sorry episode.

The fact that Mel's parents had a large house with a garden, soccer net and an Olympic-sized pool filled with garish inflatable toys, made the whole thing even more unbearable. What's more, they had four fully functioning arms between them. Peggy simply couldn't compete, on pool toys or limbs.

Peggy ripped off a piece of Sellotape with her teeth. It caught on her lip and pulled away a shard of skin. It was more painful than breaking her arm. It was always the little things that hurt the most. Like the cake.

Every year since he turned one, Peggy had made Sam's birthday cake. It became a tradition, in the way that family traditions develop, unnoticed until an alternative came along. In this case, it was Mel and her obsession with organics. Ted would be on Peggy's side, if only because he loved to lick the mixing bowl after she'd finished beating. He'd urge her to make one anyway. 'Go on, love,' he would say. 'Let's put the cat among the pigeons.' He was ever the diplomat in family matters, but he would have hated to see her being treated unfairly. He'd have had a quiet word with David and the matter would be resolved with a tactful invitation for Granny to go ahead and make her usual cake, to be enjoyed by the family with a quiet cup of tea after the main event. Instead, Peggy felt she'd joined the underground resistance, each tiny act of sabotage integral to the fight in the face of tyranny. Courage swelled behind her breastbone, like the acidic aftermath of a beetroot sandwich. Here was her opportunity to stand up, not only for herself but for every voiceless grandmother, for every woman who was sick of biting her tongue.

Peggy Smart, the famous trendsetter and social activist.

In her haste to the fridge, she nearly tripped over Basil. Neither of them could move in a hurry these days, their limbs needing advanced warning.

'What do you think?' Peggy addressed the expectant dog as she surveyed the contents of the fridge. 'Chocolate or vanilla sponge? Buttercream or royal icing? How about some sprinkles on the top?'

Basil tilted his head. His tongue fell out and he panted.

Buttercream *and* sprinkles.

Mel would really hate that.

~

No doubt the village gossip machine would be in overdrive with the silver Lexus parked directly outside Peggy's unit for the second Saturday in a row. There was no sign of life behind Sheila Martin's nets, but the woman had her spies.

Brian held the passenger door open. The supple leather seat beckoned.

'I could get used to this,' said Peggy. She pretended not to notice his hand extending to help her in. She'd managed to whip up a vanilla sponge and a large batch of icing one-handed, so could certainly get into a car unaided. Admittedly

Basil had helped her out, cleaning up the cake mixture spills from the kitchen floor. At least he still appreciated her culinary skills, so much so that he'd had to retire to his basket to recover.

'I can't wait to sample your goodies,' said Brian, placing the Tupperware container on the back seat. He wedged it between a folded tartan blanket and an empty cardboard box.

Peggy grinned. It was nice to be appreciated by a man where it counted: in the kitchen, if not in the bedroom.

'May I say, you look lovely, as always?'

Not thirty minutes previously, wearing only her underwear and a washing-up glove over her cast, she'd been standing at the kitchen bench, putting the last-minute touches to the birthday cake. With her new capsule wardrobe, Peggy had effortlessly pulled together an outfit she hoped would be appropriate for the party. After the book fair fiasco, she'd gone with a pair of straight-leg jeans and an oversized button-up shirt with a thin blue strip. The collar was the only tricky part. Up or down?

'Up,' she heard Ted say, and for one precious moment, he was smiling at her in the mirror. 'Give us a twirl, love.'

'For you my sweet,' Peggy had whispered back to her husband's reflection. She'd spun around like Margot Fonteyn on tiptoes. Overcome by a sudden bout of vertigo, she'd grabbed the chest of drawers for support. The framed photo of her and Ted on their wedding day toppled over, landing face down on the top of the chest with a crash. She'd left it where it had fallen, not ready to face the sight of the cracked glass.

Brian indicated and pulled away from the kerb. He was so sensible behind the wheel, so considerate. Unlike Angie in her Mini. Declining David's offer of a lift to the party had been another tiny act of rebellion. Peggy was looking forward to seeing everyone's faces when she arrived in the Lexus.

'I do hope I'm not putting you out, Brian.'

'Not at all. I'm looking forward to a slice of that wonderful-looking birthday cake!'

'In that case, I'd better warn you. The official version will be egg-, dairy- and nut-free. Half of Sam's friends have allergies of some sort. My daughter-in-law has ordered individual cupcakes instead. They'll no doubt cost a small fortune and she'll pass them off as her own.'

'I'm sure we didn't have all these allergies in our day,' said Brian, pulling out onto the main road. 'I blame the disinfectants. The ones that kill 99.9% of all germs.'

'I couldn't agree more. People these days are so careful. I never worried about having a few harmless orgasms on the kitchen worktop, even when the kids were still living at home. It certainly never did them any harm, being exposed from such an early age. In fact, it probably did them good.'

Brian veered into the next lane and had to swerve to avoid a cyclist. He gripped the steering wheel and cleared his throat.

Peggy continued. 'Shame they never listen to our generation though, isn't it? We could teach them a thing or two.'

'I know, folk today have no idea.'

'They never imagine us young and passionate, raging with hormones, do they?'

'Indeed,' said Brian.

~

Parked cars lined both sides of the road that led to the adventure park. Mostly, they were black tank-like things like Mel's.

'It's a four-wheel drive,' David had explained to his mother. *All cars had four wheels, didn't they?* 'It can go off-road,' he continued.

Peggy was confused. 'I thought the idea was to stay on the road?'

'This car is specially designed to cope with rugged terrain.'

Given Mel's driving comprised exclusively suburban roads, Peggy remained dubious.

There were children everywhere, propelling bicycles and tricycles, skateboards and scooters towards the park. In the distance, Peggy could see balloons and bunting decorating every available picnic table. Saturday was birthday party time, and the chances of their finding a parking space were looking slim.

Unfazed by the traffic, Brian indicated and pulled into the car park. Peggy knew better than to question a man's judgment when it came to navigation or parking, so she kept quiet. There were two empty bays, but they were disabled spots. To Peggy's surprise, Brian pulled into the first space and switched off the engine. He leaned over and opened the glove box.

'Good job my doctor gave me this,' he said, putting a disabled parking permit on the dashboard. 'It's a temporary one, until my knee's better.'

So, there were some advantages to being old and crumbly after all.

'How is the knee?'

'A bit painful today,' said Brian with a wink.

Sam's party was right there in front of them, the table decorated in co-ordinating blue accessories. It was very tasteful and quite dull, Mel's signature style.

Peggy could see her daughter-in-law lining up brown-paper party bags. No doubt they were filled with sugar-free lollies and dolphin-friendly take-home gifts. Hovering close to the table was Emily, wearing her latest princess costume – last year's Christmas present from Granny Smart. Peggy was praying Disney would bring out a new princess in time for this Christmas.

'Hello, darling. Don't you look wonderful,' said Peggy, bending over to give her granddaughter a kiss. Chubby arms locked around her neck and threatened to strangle her. She felt wonderfully weightless in the embrace, and had to stop herself squeezing Emily too tight in return.

'What's this?' Emily released the headlock and pointed to Peggy's arm.

'It's a plaster, sweetie. Silly old Granny broke her arm.'

'Will this make it better?' In Emily's palm was a tiny glass ball streaked through with red and yellow. 'It's for you,' she said, transferring it to Peggy's good hand.

'Thank you, darling, I'm feeling better already.'

Emily looked pleased with herself. 'Daddy said you were losing yours, so I wanted to give you one of my marbles.'

Peggy found a smile and straightened Emily's tiara. She needed to have this out with David, but it wasn't the time or place. She slipped the marble into her pocket, to remind her.

'Granny!' It was Sam, dressed as Luke Spywater, running towards them, wielding a huge glowing wand.

'May the Force be with you, darling,' said Peggy. She stooped to hug him and nearly dropped the container with the birthday cake. 'I do like your *light-saver.*' She congratulated herself. Not wanting to show herself up at the *Star Wars* party, she'd done her homework.

Sam took the gift and tore at the wrapping paper. There was a split second as he stared at the picture on the box, and Peggy held her breath, wondering if she'd committed some unspeakable grandmotherly *faux pas*.

A grin stole over Sam's boyish face. 'Thank you, Granny. I love it!'

Sam's friends gathered around, bemused. There was no screen and no controls. They watched Sam open the lid and pull out the pieces, their eyes widening. What was this retro toy? This was something that none of them had, and the novelty wasn't lost on Sam.

'Cool! Dad, look what Granny got me. A chess set.'

David strolled over to see what all the fuss was about. 'Who's a lucky boy then?' He did a double-take, noticing Brian. 'I'm David.' He extended his hand. 'Peggy's son.'

'I'm sorry, I should have introduced you two. David, this is Brian, my . . .' What was he? Friend? Neighbour? Boyfriend? Fantasy lover? The sentence hovered, untethered in the spring air.

'Brian Cornell. Lovely to meet you, David. And you, Sam.' Brian bent forward to shake Sam's hand.

Sam regarded him for a moment before saying, 'Will you play chess with me later?'

'I'd be delighted to, young man.'

'Cool. Are you my new grandpa?'

David forced a little laugh, but the effort made him cough.

'Are you alright, dear?' asked Peggy. 'Are you coming down with something?'

'No. Yes. No. Why don't you come and say hello to Mel's parents.'

Mike and Geraldine. They were, of course, a perfectly charming couple, which made Peggy feel even worse about her hidden resentment.

Geraldine was a successful psychologist. Peggy had a tendency to ramble on like a mad woman in her presence. Mike, a retired dentist, made her even more nervous. She'd noticed his glance often landed on her overbite, and Peggy felt he was always judging her on her flossing habits rather than her conversation.

'You're looking well,' said Mike, kissing her on both cheeks.

Peggy introduced him to Brian, covering her mouth as she spoke. The men shook hands, exchanged a volley of pleasantries and settled into the small talk of two retired professionals.

Geraldine greeted Peggy like a long-lost friend. Or client. 'How lovely to see you.' She held Peggy at arm's length and inspected her, searching for psychological defects. 'We were worried you wouldn't be able to make it this year.'

'It was a little tricky to beat the eggs one-handed,' replied Peggy, pretending to misunderstand, 'and the sprinkles are clumped in places, but I'm pleased.' She placed the Tupperware container on the paper tablecloth. For once, Peggy was happy to appear a bit dotty. As a strategy for getting her own way, it had potential.

Mel's face was pinched as she gave Peggy a kiss on the cheek. She didn't mention the cake. Geraldine's eyebrows arched as she lifted the lid of the Tupperware container and inspected the ticking time bomb of sugar and preservatives. Peggy saw her exchange glances with Mel.

'So sorry to hear about your *fall*,' whispered Geraldine, as if Peggy had ended up in prison rather than the emergency department.

'It was my own fault. Gin and rollerskates are never a good combination,' said Peggy, smiling.

'You should try yoga – when you're out of plaster, of course. It's very good for posture and balance,' said Geraldine.

'I do my Aqua. That's good for fitness too.'

'But it's not the same, you see. Yoga's all about flexibility and strength.'

Peggy gritted her teeth. She could never win with Geraldine. 'Well, you look very good on it,' she said.

'I try. Do you know I can still do the splits?'

Peggy prayed she wasn't about to demonstrate. She could never compete on suppleness. It was best to play to her strengths. 'Shall I give you a hand with the food?'

'Here you are. You should be taking it easy.' Mike appeared behind her with a fold-out camping chair.

In your condition. Go on, say it, urged Peggy under her breath, as she slumped into the chair under the weight of the unspoken words. It was obvious they considered her old and decrepit. She was only five years older than Mike, but it may as well have been fifty.

Brian pulled up another camping chair. 'I'll keep you company.' He smiled.

'Can I get either of you a drink? We have four different flavours of mineral water on offer,' said Mike.

What sort of party was this? Why weren't children allowed to have a little fun these days? When David and Jenny had birthday parties, Peggy baked for days beforehand. She always made chocolate crackles, piles of fairy bread and served hot sausage rolls to the parents. Yes, the kids ended up hyped-up, running around the house screaming, but they had fun. Good, old-fashioned fun. Pass-the-parcel with proper lollies between the layers, musical statues and a slice of birthday cake wrapped in a napkin to take home.

'Anyone for a pumpkin muffin?' said Geraldine, handing round a paper plate.

Was Mel really expecting the kids to eat these things? They looked like something Basil might find in the hedge. Brian shook his head politely. Even Mike patted his midriff and declined.

David was busy organising the children into two teams for a game, but with so many kids at the park, it looked more like a wild brumby round-up. Meanwhile, Mel was cataloguing the individual gifts in a notebook. Peggy knew Sam would be expected to write individual *Thank You* notes on his own personalised stationery.

Poor kids. Just let them have fun. Before they turn into their parents.

'Why don't you give the party company another call?' shouted David from the melee.

'They're not answering,' snapped Mel. 'I can't leave another message.'

Geraldine explained that the party entertainer – someone called Stormtrooper Steve – hadn't turned up. She'd taken care to enunciate each syllable, as if addressing a hearing-impaired foreigner.

Peggy was bracing herself for Geraldine's professional analysis of her misadventure but so far, she'd been spared. At Ted's funeral, Peggy had managed to survive the platitudes like a boxer deflecting each blow. *At least he didn't suffer. He had a good innings. You're lucky you still have the dog. Time is a healer,* they'd said, as if it was a disease she had instead of a dead husband.

It was Geraldine who'd delivered the winning punch, flooring Peggy with a tilt of her head, and a simple, 'How are you?' She'd maintained the upper hand ever since.

'Listen up, kids!' Mike sprang to life, rubbing his hands together. 'Who's for a game of hide and seek?'

'Not the best idea, Dad,' said Mel, rescuing a pile of *Star Wars* plates before they blew away in the breeze. 'We've got eighteen six-year-olds here, and I'd like to be able to hand seventeen of them back at the end. Or preferably before—'

'There's the cricket set in the back of the car,' shouted David from under a pile of assorted intergalactic characters.

'I knew we should have gone with the petting zoo instead.' Mel batted away several overeager little hands as they turned their attention away from let's-jump-on-Sam's-dad to the food on the table. 'Oi! Hands off. They're for later.'

Under the table, two of Sam's friends were fighting over a sharpened stick. Before Mel could intervene, there was a scream and one boy crawled out holding his head, blood dripping onto his Darth Vader costume.

Emily was crying too, having caught the hem of her princess dress on the picnic table and torn the shimmering fabric. In the midst of the fracas, a cheeky magpie swooped down and stole a muffin from the plate, while Sam stepped in dog poo and trampled the mess across Mel's designer picnic blanket. Peggy wondered if she'd imagined that drop of rain landing on the tip of her nose.

'Perhaps I could show them a magic trick?' said Mike. His expression suggested he liked children, as long as they were strapped to his dentist's chair, under anaesthetic.

'Could you conjure up a bottle of vodka and a couple of Valium?' David limped over, covered in grass. He suddenly looked older than the other fathers in the park. Peggy remembered the struggles he and Mel had had with IVF. It had almost cost them their marriage, as Peggy's miscarriages had a generation before. Looking at her son and her grand-children, Peggy was relieved they'd all persisted.

'The whole thing is a disaster!' Mel looked close to tears. 'Let's just call the parents now and go home.' Peggy felt a minuscule shred of sympathy.

Another raindrop. This time she was sure. What a shame all this expensive inedible food was about to go to waste.

'Look, Dad!'

Sam tugged on David's shirt and pointed to the car park. Peggy heard a throaty roar and turned to see a shiny chrome bumper come to rest millimetres from the disabled sign. The engine revved several times then fell silent.

The bleeding boy stopped crying. 'Wow! Look at that!'

Peggy noted the look on Geraldine's face and vowed to remember it when she was old and frail in her nursing home.

'Coo-ee,' shouted Angie, waving from the driver's seat of the metallic blue convertible. She had a silk scarf knotted around her head Grace Kelly–style. In the passenger seat was rebel-in-search-of-a-cause Jim from the village. He was sporting a pair of Wayfarers and, to Peggy's secret delight, a gold earring.

'If I'm not mistaken, that's a 1965 Mustang,' said Mike removing his spectacles.

Brian hauled himself up out of the camping chair and stood by his side. 'I think you'll find that's a '66. I had one myself. Wish I'd kept hold of it. Worth a fortune nowadays, I believe.'

Jim displayed his disabled sticker on the dashboard before opening the passenger door and almost falling out. 'Bloody sciatica!' he said, clutching the back of his thigh.

Angie untied the scarf and shook her dark hair free. 'That's what I call a car, Jimbo,' she said, tossing the keys towards him. She was carrying a thin parcel tied with ribbon in one hand and a bottle of champagne in the other. When she saw Peggy, she threw back her head and shouted, 'Surprise, surprise!'

Her reaction wasn't what Peggy was expecting to feel. Far from annoyance that Angie had yet again stolen the limelight, she felt a surge of relief at the sight of the two geriatric gatecrashers. They were cool, and now by association, so was she.

'Where's the birthday boy?' said Angie, scanning the stunned faces.

Sam stepped forward and accepted the gift, clearly wary of taking things from strangers. Peggy put one hand on his shoulder and said, 'It's okay, Sam. Angie is a very old friend of mine, from back when we were about your age.'

Sam tore at the paper and pulled out a long plastic package. 'Yesss! Look, Dad, a *Star Wars* kite.'

Sam's friends looked on with envy as he tore away the plastic and began to untangle the strings. 'Cool, it's a stunt kite. Can we fly it now? Please Dad?'

Peggy's insides slumped. It was kind of Angie to bring a gift for Sam, but Peggy couldn't help feeling she'd been trumped yet again. 'Thank you for coming,' she whispered to Angie as they kissed on the cheek. 'It's time my family met my new friends.'

She'd certainly put up with enough of her son's friends in the past. Noisy little boys who turned into even noisier big boys. They emptied her fridge and parked their cars across her driveway. Yet she'd welcomed them into her home and tried hard not to be embarrassing.

'What do you say to Granny's friend?' said David. He edged closer to inspect the present and the surprise guests. He offered his hand to Angie. 'I don't think we've met, I'm—'

'David,' said Angie shaking his hand. 'We spoke on the phone. Peggy has told me so much about you and Mel.' With that she turned and winked at Peggy. 'Hope you don't mind us gatecrashing the party.'

'Of course not. The more the merrier!' David's face wore a pinched smile.

The in-laws stood agog at the glamorous Angie and leather-clad Jim. Before long, stormtroopers, grandparents and several ring-in pirates and fairies from adjacent birthday parties surrounded the car.

'Can I sit in it?' Sam jumped up and down.

'Be my guest.' Jim opened the doors and let the kids climb in.

The grin on Sam's face as he grasped the thin steering wheel in his chubby hands said it all. His friends clambered over the seats to line up in the back. 'This is so cool!' one shouted.

'Nice car,' said David, hands in his pockets, nodding his head in appreciation. 'You don't see many of these in such good condition.'

'I don't get to drive her much these days,' said Jim. 'Any time you want to take her for a spin, just give me a call.'

A smile as wide as Sam's crept across David's face.

Geraldine elbowed her way through the admirers. 'Are you Jim Wilde, by any chance?' she said, unusually animated. When Jim flashed his rock-star smile at her, she added, 'I thought so. I had all your records when I was younger. I even went to one of your concerts, 1961 at The Pavilion.'

Nineteen sixty-one? Either she had snuck into the concert in pigtails and short socks, or the suspiciously pliable Geraldine was older than she let on.

Mike stepped in between his wife and the Mustang's celebrity owner, and tried to steer the conversation back to classic cars. Just when the stormtroopers had discovered the Mustang's horn, another engine roared behind them. It sounded like a Spitfire coming in to land. The engine revved before it backfired, as if a cannon had gone off.

'Whoa!' said David, taking a step back as the ancient motorbike cruised to a halt beside the Mustang. Coated in dull khaki paint, the bike wasn't as gleaming as the convertible, but elicited just as much excitement from the onlookers.

The fully suited rider kicked down the motorbike's stand. A rosy-cheeked Celia emerged from beneath the helmet. Brian greeted her, smiling broadly. Making sure that Geraldine was watching, Peggy trotted over to join them. She'd waited all her life to be 'in with the in-crowd', and she was going to enjoy every moment.

'Royal Enfield,' said Mike, stroking the machine with one hand. 'I rode one of these when I was in the RAAF. Well, well.' He leaned over and introduced himself.

Celia shook his hand and said, 'Bloody nearly came a cropper back there. Some old duffer with an electric scooter pulled out in front of me. Celia Davenport. I'm with Peggy.'

Mike volunteered to co-ordinate the children taking turns to sit on the motorbike while Peggy led her new friends back to the picnic table. They found Mel in a camping chair, staring absently.

'You look like you need a little help,' said Peggy. Brian popped the cork on the champagne while Angie held the *Star Wars* paper cups. 'Anyone for birthday cake?'

Soon, there was a queue of eager stormtroopers and Jedi lining up to collect a slice of cake wrapped in a napkin, albeit a 100% biodegradable, earth-friendly one.

18

The Singing Machine

IT WAS ONLY WEDNESDAY BUT SO FAR THAT WEEK, PEGGY
had answered calls from two energy providers, a security
shutter company, a cancer charity and a man with a foreign
accent claiming to be from the technical department at
Telstra. She was becoming highly irritated by the constant
interruptions.

David had warned her about cold-callers and spammers. But
after the incident with the poor removalist man, she was feeling
guilty and making a special effort to be nice to strangers. She'd
started the week politely declining their requests, telling them
she was a widow on a pension. But they had an answer for
everything, a way of sucking her in, suggesting she pledge small
amounts or buy lottery tickets. Soon, she'd had enough and
started passing the phone to Basil as he snorted and snuffled
in his sleep. It seemed to do the trick.

When the phone rang at eight o'clock that morning, Peggy
let it go straight to message rather than go through the

whole rigmarole all over again. She listened to her special telephone voice – a cross between the Queen and Dame Edna, she now realised to her dismay – followed by a beep. Then Jenny's tinny voice.

'Mother? Are you there? Just checking they delivered the walker. I hope you like the colour I chose. I thought red would be easier to pick out at a distance. Which reminds me, I've made an appointment at the optometrist for the twentieth at ten-thirty. You need to get your maculas checked and some new drops. I thought I could take you to get your ears syringed too, followed by a bite to eat. I'll phone the doctor to arrange a time. Don't forget to use those wax-softening drops I brought you last time. Put two or three drops in each side before bed. Like I showed you. Mind you use an old pillowcase.'

'There is absolutely nothing wrong with my hearing,' Peggy told Basil, who lay on the front door mat snoring. 'Which is more than can be said for you,' she said, stepping around the oblivious dog. As long as there was no background noise, Peggy could carry on a perfectly normal conversation. It was quite acceptable to ask someone to repeat themselves. It was their own fault for mumbling in the first place.

The last thing she needed was hearing aids. They were a perennial topic of conversation at Happy Hour. They cost a fortune and all they did was amplify the noise, not make it any clearer. Peggy remembered her own mother complaining about them. In the end, the old dear had dropped the obscenely overpriced devices into the water glass next to the bed with her dentures, and that was that.

Jenny could stick her eardrops. God made earwax for a purpose, so old people could ignore their interfering families.

Peggy kicked the shiny new walker on the way through the front door. The optometrist could get stuffed too.

But uneasiness had tucked itself around Peggy. With her daughter's visit imminent, it was time to get down to some serious worrying.

~

The shop looked more like the control centre at NASA than an electrical retailer. The committee had deliberately chosen a mid-week mid-morning time, hoping to avoid the crowds. That way they'd have ample time to ask stupid questions.

With wispy down on his chin, the assistant reminded Peggy of a young billy goat.

'Are you looking for anything in particular?' he said.

'We're here for a singing machine,' she said. To her dismay, the other members of the social committee were nowhere to be seen. Somehow, in less than five minutes, Peggy had managed to lose four adult humans. *Honestly, old people are worse than children.*

The assistant looked around nervously, as if searching for a hidden camera or prankster colleagues. It wasn't a good start. At this rate, come the Annual Dinner Dance, they'd all be tucking in to bombe Alaska and shuffling around the Clubhouse to Tony Bennett numbers again. Peggy couldn't even work her mobile phone on her own without checking David's list of instructions, let alone choose a music do-dah. She could just see the top of Brian's balding head in the home computing section, and make out Celia marvelling at the world through a long-lensed camera. Angie was still missing in action, probably reapplying Berry Kiss in personal grooming.

Only Jim had followed her, limping behind like John Wayne in his cowboy boots. His face lit up at the sight of himself on a CD cover in the display, brooding under a Brylcreemed quiff of black hair. With his full lips and smouldering eyes, he must have been quite a catch. He still was. Peggy wondered if Angie thought so. She'd married a photographer, a racing driver, a solicitor and a plastic surgeon. A rock star like Jim seemed the natural progression.

The assistant – Lachlan, according to his name badge – scratched his head. 'Do you mean a sound system? We have a whole section of minis over here.'

Angie had a Mini. They'd parked it on the second floor of the multi-storey car park. No, that wasn't what they were after.

'It's a machine we can all sing along to,' said Peggy. It had a name. It was on the tip of her tongue. 'Jim, what's the name of the thing?'

Jim froze, his mouth half open, like someone had pressed pause.

'Karaoke,' said Angie, appearing beside them. 'Speakers, microphone, amplifier. The complete package.'

Jim looked Angie up and down, as if he was seeing her for the first time. 'The complete package,' he repeated, parrot-like.

'Follow me.' Lachlan led them towards the far corner of the store. Brian and Celia appeared, clutching an armful of brochures each.

There was a pleasing selection of singing machines on the shelves behind Lachlan. At last, they were getting somewhere. Relishing her new role as official spokesperson, Peggy took up poll position. She was all ears. Jim's hearing aids whistled as he adjusted them. Brian clicked the end of his ballpoint pen in anticipation. Even Angie had pushed her sunglasses to the top of her head and was squinting attentively into the artificial lighting. They were under starter's orders.

'The first consideration,' began Lachlan, 'is to decide what you want from your machine.'

'Music,' said Peggy, first off the blocks. 'You know, where the singer sings along to the words on the screen.'

Angie rolled her eyes. 'I think he knows what a karaoke machine does.'

'What about dancing?' Celia pushed her way between Peggy and Brian to the front of the circle. She wiggled her hips and tapped one motorbike boot on the grey carpet tiles.

'Right. I actually meant what sort of features are important to you,' said Lachlan.

'Sturdy, not too complicated, reliable,' said Brian, glancing at Peggy.

The suggestions came thick and fast, a harried Lachlan soon swamped by demands for easy-grip dials, a large-print manual and hearing loop connectivity.

He did a little forced laugh. 'Okay. First, I need an idea of the kind of devices you already have, so we can work out the best format.'

Devices? The committee members all looked at each other. What a strange question.

'Kettle, toaster, vacuum cleaner . . .' Peggy offered.

'I saw a nice new microwave back there,' added Celia.

Lachlan cleared his throat. 'I was thinking more along the lines of technology devices, MP3, Apple or Android, that kind of thing.' Lachlan looked for some hint of recognition. 'Do any of you have a tablet?'

Peggy relaxed a little, sensing her feet on solid ground once more. She knew a thing or two about tablets.

'Bloody dozens of them,' said Celia, before Peggy had the chance to share her expertise.

'Good,' said Lachlan, looking hopeful again. 'This model is compatible with a tablet.'

The seniors looked at the machine dubiously. Taking their silence as a sign they were following, Lachlan proceeded to talk them through a list of seemingly contradictory features on offer: woofers and subwoofers; hard drives and software, wired versus wireless.

The latter drew nods of recognition. They were all familiar with how to operate a wireless.

Lachlan's voice buzzed as Peggy's brain attempted to retune the station. His watery outline oscillated through her field of vision. Suddenly, her skin was on fire. She willed herself to concentrate on his incomprehensible words.

'Are you alright?' said Angie. 'You look a bit pale.'

'I'll be fine.' Peggy removed her jacket. She took several deep breaths, making her even more lightheaded.

Brian was busy writing in his notebook and didn't notice Peggy stagger backwards towards the display cabinet behind them. Jim, too, was oblivious, cupping both ears like a Toby jug, while Celia, arms folded across her chest, challenged Lachlan to explain how music could possibly be stored in a cloud.

'Did you eat breakfast this morning?'

Where Angie had stood only a moment ago, Peggy now saw her mother. What was she doing here, in this place, surrounded by all these ... machines?

'I don't remember.' Peggy's bottom lip quivered. What the hell was this blue thing on her wrist?

'Come and sit down, before you keel over.' It was Angie's face once more. Peggy floated towards a row of seats by the photo-printing desk. She was grateful to sit down.

'You should put your head between your knees,' said Angie next to her.

'I'd have to be a contortionist to do that.' There were parts of her body that Peggy hadn't seen in decades. She was in no hurry to make amends.

'That's more like it. You feeling any better?'

'A little. I'm not sure what happened back there. For a moment, I thought you were my mother.'

'God help us. You know I love you dearly, but let's face it, your mother was a complete battle-axe.'

'She spoke very highly of you too,' Peggy said, half smiling.

'I'm sorry,' said Angie, not looking the least bit sorry, 'but I never understood what she had against me.'

~

If she inhaled any deeper, she'd pass out. Peggy gripped the sides of the bridal car for countertraction as her mother hauled on the zip, as if she was cinching in the girth of a colicky horse.

'Hold still,' said Mrs Weaver through gritted teeth. Peggy noticed for the first time how thin her mother was. Her arms were sinewy, her face long and gaunt.

After her father died, Peggy had taken over the cooking at home. That, or starve. Her mother seemed to survive on the bitterness of her own bile. Her father had also had a sparse physique. Peggy had always considered herself a genetic anomaly, had never understood where her uniquely sturdy frame came from. She was more like her Uncle Bill – her father's handsome older brother – in build, and personality. She had his round chin and blue eyes, even the same laugh.

'That's as far as it'll go.' Peggy's mother gave a snort of derision and adjusted her heavy-rimmed glasses. There was a bubble of white flesh poking out at the top of the zip under Peggy's left arm. It would have to do. Besides, in a few hours Ted would be unzipping her in the hotel room. On their wedding night.

The thought of what lay ahead caused her bladder muscle to contract. She'd deliberately avoided fluids of any sort this morning. For this very reason. Trussed up in a satin circus tent, she was trapped.

It had taken her an hour to get the dress on, even with the help of her mother and Ted's vacant younger sister, June. It was a copy of the fairytale dress Princess Margaret had worn when she walked down the aisle with Antony Armstrong-Jones, and although Ted hadn't even proposed at that stage, Peggy had kept a cutting from the newspaper in a scrapbook.

'Good luck,' shouted a couple of old secretarial college buddies scuttling past, clutching hats and cameras as Peggy grimaced for the photographer.

Good luck. What an odd thing to say at a wedding. It was what you might say before an exam or a cavalry charge. This was marriage. Luck didn't come into it, surely?

The bells tailed off. Beyond the heavy church door, the organ urged the stragglers to hurry. Inside her chest, Peggy's heart sprinted. This was it, the rest of her life. A life with Ted. And the chance to escape her mother once and for all.

Behind her, she heard the sound of heels on the gravel. They'd have to wait another minute for the final guests to go in and find a seat. The last thing she needed was to be upstaged by another latecomer.

'You look divine, sweetie.'

Taken by surprise, Peggy stepped backwards and almost fell off the kerb.

'Angie! I wasn't sure you could make it. I wasn't even sure I had the right address for the invitation.'

'Are you kidding? I wouldn't miss this for the world. I flew back from London especially.' Angie lifted the veil and planted a kiss on both cheeks, in the continental way.

Peggy's mother sniffed.

'Hello, Mrs Weaver,' said Angie, her voice suddenly tight and formal. 'You must be so proud.'

'We must hurry,' said Peggy's mother, sniffing again. 'Do excuse us, Angela.'

Angie replaced the veil over Peggy's face. 'Have fun tonight,' she said and winked.

Peggy saw her mother's pinched face and imagined the invisible steam escaping her splayed nostrils. Transfixed, the bridal party watched Angie sashay towards the church. She wore a pale blue coat that finished below the knee. In spite of the warm day, it was buttoned all the way up to the neck. An interesting choice for Angie – usually one to flaunt her perfect figure – but then, she was anything but predictable.

'Your friend looks just like Audrey Hepburn,' said June.

Mrs Weaver bristled. 'Pick up that train, June, before it gets soiled.' What escaped next was barely audible above her exhaled breath, but Peggy was in no doubt she'd heard correctly.

'*Trollop*,' hissed her mother.

~

'That's it,' said Angie, checking Peggy's pulse on her one good wrist. 'I'll take you down to the hospital, get you checked out in emergency.'

'Please, no,' groaned Peggy. 'I'm sick of being fussed over.'

'Alright, but I'm phoning Dr Lim as soon as we get back to the village.'

'Just leave me alone,' snapped Peggy.

Angie's eyes widened then narrowed. 'What's the matter? I mean, *really* the matter?'

'Nothing. I'm fine.'

'Is it Brian?'

'Angie! Keep your voice down. If you must know, it's my family.'

'What about them?'

'You wouldn't understand.'

'From what I saw on Saturday, they seem a perfectly normal family. That Mel's a little highly strung, but her parents are decent sorts. And if you ask me, David seems to care very much about his mother,' said Angie.

'For the record, I didn't ask your opinion. Of course David seems perfectly charming. You're not related to him. Believe me, Mel has changed him. She's white-anted away his spine. And Jenny's no better. Always trying to take over. They'd all love to see me locked away in some old folks' home, wrapped from head to toe in bubble wrap.'

Angie sniggered and put her arm around Peggy's shoulders. 'Darling, I'd never let that happen to you,' she said. 'Bubble wrap is so last season.'

Brian appeared, face etched with concern. 'Are you alright, Peggy?'

Lachlan offered her a glass of water. 'Don't you worry, madam,' he said. 'The store manager has called an ambulance.'

What a nightmare. For once, she'd wanted to feel consequential. Here was her opportunity to step up and claim her spot, standing shoulder to shoulder with the others – her chance to shine alongside the jet-setting, Channel-swimming, hit-parade-topping professionals.

Instead, she'd had another 'turn', and though she hated to admit it, she still felt most unusual. Even after she'd sculled the water and persuaded the manager to cancel the ambulance, she could tell something was amiss. What's more, the chances of keeping news of her latest episode from Jenny were next to zero.

19

Foggy With a Chance of Falls

THE RADIO ANNOUNCER HEDGED HIS BETS. CLOUDY, WITH sunny spells and a chance of showers; chilly for this time of year, but warming up later.

Some weather forecaster you are. I may as well hang a lump of seaweed on the front door, thought Peggy.

She squinted at the first item on her *To Do* list resting on the kitchen table.

Get dressed.

At first, Peggy had found her new capsule wardrobe a timesaver, but as she discovered the versatility of the mix-and-match pieces, she began setting her alarm half an hour earlier, to allow for extra thinking time. With five new tops, three bottoms and a blazer, not to mention two pairs of extremely unforgiving shoes, and the necklace, there was a myriad of potential combinations. Naturally, Ted would have worked out exactly how many on a piece of paper, using the pencil stub he always kept behind his ear. But without his mathematical prowess to fall back on, Peggy was considering a roster, to make sure she got her – or rather Angie's – money's worth.

Had it really come to this, reminding herself to put clothes on? She'd officially gone ga-ga. In a matter of a few days, she'd apparently developed full-blown dementia. Or maybe she'd had a stroke. Peggy wriggled her toes and played an imaginary piano with her fingers. No, they all seemed to be working fine, in spite of the cast.

It should be a bucket list she was writing, not a pathetic reminder to do basic everyday tasks. Now was the time to be ticking off items such as hot-air ballooning or sky-diving. She'd always wanted to see the pyramids and to ride a motorbike. Perhaps Celia might give her a quick whizz round the village on the back of the Enfield. They could time it to coincide with Jenny's visit next week. It would certainly give them something to talk about over lunch.

One thing at a time.

Make tea.

Her mouth was parched. The memory of Angie daring her to eat a whole packet of cream crackers when they were in fifth grade sprang to mind. If she could remember things like that as though they'd happened yesterday, there couldn't be anything seriously wrong with her memory. Surely?

Basil was lying on the kitchen floor, staring at his bowl. He shot her a look every now and again, the whites of his eyes showing for dramatic effect. Peggy realised she'd forgotten to feed him. She had even forgotten to write it on the list last night before going to bed. What was going on?

Feed Basil, she wrote, then *Take pills*. Now, where were her pills?

David's words echoed in her ears. *You have to be more careful*. He was right. At seventy-nine, it was downhill from all directions.

The phone rang. By the time she'd tracked down the cordless receiver, the caller was gone. It was only when she discovered her Webster-pak in the chiller section, partially obscured by a bunch of wilting celery, that Peggy decided enough was enough.

~

'You're half an hour early but not to worry. I've just had a cancellation.' Dr Stephen ushered Peggy into the consulting room.

'Silly me. I can always come back later.'

'No, come in. Have a seat. How are you?'

'So-so.' In other words, ghastly.

The doctor peered at her through his thick lenses. She imagined him examining her fetlocks and prising open her lips to check her teeth like an old horse.

'You don't seem quite yourself today,' he said, sitting back in his swivel chair.

Peggy looked down and noticed she was wearing odd shoes. One was navy suede with a closed toe, the other a black open-toed sandal. She crossed her ankles under the chair and hoped Dr Stephen wouldn't notice.

'I'm not sure where to begin.'

'Can you be more specific?'

'Well, my eyes are all blurry. I could hardly focus this morning on my . . . list.'

She remembered the all-important list on the kitchen table. There was something else she was meant to bring but she couldn't remember what it was.

'Blurry. Hmm. Anything else?'

'I've been feeling very dizzy.'

'Have you noticed a dry mouth?'

She was astonished, and a little worried. He was onto her.

'Yes, now that you mention it, my tongue feels like a chamois leather.'

'I hope you don't mind me saying this, but you don't seem as on the ball as usual.'

Peggy picked at the seam of her blouse. It was on inside out. 'Do you think I might have dementia, doctor?'

Dr Stephen laughed. 'I doubt that very much.'

'But my memory is shocking. I walk into a room and can't remember why I've gone in there. This morning I found my pills in the fridge.' She decided not to tell him about finding the telephone in the bread bin.

The doctor looked more serious. 'Have you been forgetting anything important?'

'I forget people's names all the time. It usually comes to me around three o'clock the following morning. Then I can't get back to sleep.'

'I can reassure you, that's quite normal for your age. The forgetting names, that is.' Dr Stephen smiled over his father's glasses. 'It's not until you start forgetting more important things that we start to worry.'

'Can you give me an example?'

'How to work the TV remote, passwords, important dates. That sort of thing.'

'I forgot my grandson's birthday party last week. And I haven't been able to use my new electronic telephone because I can't remember the four-digit passcode.'

Dr Stephen hitched one eyebrow. 'That's a little more concerning.'

Peggy quailed. A concerned Dr Stephen scared her. She preferred him light-hearted, sitting back in his chair and telling her not to worry, that it was only her age. What if she did have dementia? How long before she started to show the signs? Would she be the last to recognise it, wandering aimlessly, endlessly repeating herself? Endlessly repeating herself.

'Is there a test I can do?'

'There is something called a mini-mental score. It's quite a basic screening test for dementia. Often, we do need to do more detailed cognitive testing through a specialist.'

Peggy didn't even know what 'cognitive' meant. It sounded like something Ted might have kept on his workbench.

It would be reassuring to take the test and prove her memory was still sound. It was the alternative that scared her. Perhaps it was best not to see the juggernaut before it ran the red light. She could continue to live her life in blissful ignorance, a delightfully dotty old lady. 'She's a bit eccentric,' they might say. Jacaranda Retirement Village was the kind of place where people pretended they hadn't heard the same story yesterday, and gently corrected names. It was a place where allowances were made and like looked out for like.

'Do you think I might have Alzheimer's, Doctor?' Peggy saw the twisted shell of her mother in sheepskin booties.

'Let's not jump ahead of ourselves,' said Dr Stephen. She watched him swallow his Adam's apple. 'There is another possible explanation.'

'What do you mean?'

'You may just be having side effects from the new medication.'

'Which new medication?' She couldn't recall any new tablets in her Webster.

'The one for the urge incontinence. I gave you a prescription last week.'

So much had happened in the past week that Peggy was having trouble keeping up. It was as though Angie had pressed fast-forward on her life. It was hard to believe it had been less than a month since she'd arrived.

'The little white one, you mean?'

The magic bladder bullet.

'Has there been any improvement?'

Peggy's heart sank. 'The only thing that's dried up is my tongue,' she said. And the only organ it had slowed down was her brain.

'In that case, we should stop it.'

'Isn't there anything else we could try?'

'Hmm. There are newer drugs available with potentially fewer side effects, but at the moment they're quite expensive. We sometimes use antidepressants.'

'My bladder isn't depressed. It's just a bit anxious.'

'Have you made the appointment yet with Sister Slack?'

'Who?'

'The continence nurse.'

Sister Slack. The pelvic floor expert.

'I'm going to call as soon as I get home,' lied Peggy.

For someone so young, Dr Stephen looked like he'd heard it all before. 'Look,' he said, 'let's stop the medication and see how you are next week. If your memory is back to normal, there's nothing to worry about. And if not—'

'We'll burn that bridge when we come to it,' said Peggy.

20

Five Dripping Pensioners

THE FICKLE SPRING HAD FURNISHED THE HORIZON WITH a duvet of cloud and turned the ocean battleship grey. Why anyone would find the water enticing on a day like this was beyond Peggy. Yet the water was packed with silver-haired stalwarts oblivious to the foamy waves as they broke over the concrete wall. From a distance, the ocean pool looked like a giant cappuccino.

As if reading Peggy's mind, Angie said, 'You could always skip the swim and wait for us in the café.'

'Not on your life.'

'Are you sure you're up to it?'

'Never felt better.' At least Peggy felt better than yesterday. Her brain was less foggy, and her eyesight had improved enough to spot Brian standing waist-deep in the shallow end. Beside him was Celia in a racerback swimsuit.

'Morning, ladies,' said Brian with a broad grin as they approached the steps.

To Peggy's surprise, Jim was in the water too, adjusting his goggles. His wet grey hair had lost some of its fullness but for a man of his age, it was still a crowning glory. The leanness in his body lent him a certain youthfulness, the muscles of his arms still sculpted from all that strumming. Hands on hips, he surveyed the pool, twitching his pecs like two jellies in a mould whenever he attracted a glance. On Jim's right shoulder, Peggy noticed a tattoo. From a distance, it looked like a stringed instrument.

'Why would Jim have a tattoo of a violin?' she whispered to Angie.

'It's an electric guitar, you wombat.'

'It's a bit daring for a retirement village.'

'Not really,' said Angie with a smile, lifting the elastic of her bathing suit to reveal a blue butterfly on her left buttock.

Nothing about this woman surprised Peggy anymore. It was as though she'd thrown out the operating manual for ageing seniors and written her own. She could be infuriating, not to mention embarrassing, but she was her own woman, something Peggy admired. In many ways, she wanted to emulate Angie, to be more like her. But a wardrobe makeover was one thing. Lying still while some stranger drilled ink into her bottom was quite another.

Keen to avoid another graceless entry into the ocean pool, Peggy descended the ladder side-saddle. She hoped the chilly water might tighten her slack skin, and used a mental image of young Libby to suck in her stomach. Safely in the water, she floated towards the others. Angie, she noted with some annoyance, was still flaunting herself on the side.

'Twenty laps, then lattes all round,' said Brian. He turned and swam off with long strokes, leaving Peggy directly in the path of Celia, who was already on her second lap, slipping through the water like an eel.

'Watch out!' shouted Celia through a mouth full of bubbles. 'You're in the wrong lane.'

Peggy hopped to the side. Sure enough, there were several lanes demarcated for different swimming speeds. Celia was in a lane of her own, naturally. That just left Brian. Peggy watched him trudging up and down the slow lane. There was something mesmerising, almost reassuring about his languid pace, scooping efficient handfuls of water with each stroke.

Ted had been a good swimmer, but like everything he did, he went for efficiency over style. He'd have been surprised to see Peggy in the water on a day like this. Why hadn't she done more when he was alive, tried more new things? They were never exactly joined at the hip, but like two saplings growing side by side, they'd become a single tree, sharing the same roots. The idea of finding a hobby had simply never occurred to her. Now, thanks to her wonderful friends, she was enjoying a whole new lease of life and a bucket list she'd never dreamed of. The possibilities were endless, the world growing smaller by the day. She'd need another ten years to fit it all in. She wondered how much longer they'd all have together as they each faced their own diminishing odds.

Yesterday's mental fog had cleared and to her surprise, Peggy was enjoying the cool silky water as it washed away her cares. She felt almost weightless in this rectangle of captive ocean. A wave of sheer joy swept over her, followed by an actual wave that caught her unaware and made her gasp out loud.

Every time Brian passed her on another lap, he did a funny salute and pretended to sink. Peggy laughed and saluted back.

Slow and steady wins the race.

Finding happiness again, whether through love or friendship, didn't happen overnight. She'd wait for Brian, content to spend these precious times with him, even if they came to nothing. There was more to a relationship than jumping into bed; it was about laughter and shared moments like this. Could she really risk losing all this by asking him out on a date? Suppose he said no, or worse still, accepted out of politeness? It would be a disaster. There would be awkward moments at committee meetings and strained conversations at Happy Hour: they'd soon run out of joints and grandchildren to discuss.

Perhaps Brian wasn't ready for a new relationship, or at least not with her. How could Peggy Not-so-Smart, an intellectual carthorse, compete with Phyllis Cornell, the thoroughbred? Flirting in the library was all very well, but a relationship needed to be built on more than Dylan Thomas.

Jim and Angie were now sitting side by side on the edge of the pool, kicking their legs in the water. They were quite well suited as a couple, thought Peggy. They had a lot in common, not least their shared experiences in the divorce courts. Jim had been married three times, he once told her. It explained why he'd ended up living in a modest villa at Jacaranda Retirement Village rather than some rock-star mansion on the harbour. Perhaps Angie did have her sights set on husband number five after all.

~

Brian insisted on ordering and paying for the coffees. The sun had come out at last and beneath her hat, Peggy could sense her hair drying into a frizzy tangle. Angie was dragging her off to some fancy hairdresser this afternoon. She prayed it wouldn't be as gruelling as the Arabella ordeal, no matter how well that had turned out. To argue would be churlish. Anything for a quiet life.

The light chatter at the table washed over Peggy. She had come to enjoy the company of these dripping pensioners. She craved their light-hearted banter and loved that no-one took themselves too seriously. The others wouldn't allow it. For all their foibles and bickering, they were the first real friends she'd made since she lost Ted.

'Celia, I just wanted to tell you what a hit you were on Sunday, with Sam and his friends. You saved the day with your motorbike.'

'Nah. I just came for the pumpkin muffins,' replied Celia with a wry smile.

'They loved your car too, Jim. Thank you so much for coming.'

'Don't mention it. I love kids,' said Jim. Peggy wondered if anyone was thinking the same as her: that there could be any number of secretly sired Jim Wilde Jnrs out there. She wondered how many of them would emerge from the woodwork, sniffing a potential inheritance in years to come.

Peggy turned to Brian, who was mopping up a spill in his saucer with a napkin. 'Sam wants to know when Grandpa Brian is coming over to play.'

Brian jolted upright, refilling his saucer with latte. 'Indeed.' He fished a notebook and pen from his bag, followed by a calculator. 'Shall we get started with the meeting?'

Peggy stiffened. With or without the Welsh accent, Brian's body language told her all she needed to know. She blew into her coffee and took a sip. It was bitter. She longed to add sugar, but Angie was watching her every move.

'I think we'd all agree that the shopping trip didn't go quite to plan,' said Brian, hooking the arms of his reading glasses over each ear.

'That's an understatement,' said Celia. 'Next time, can we ask for a sales assistant who's out of nappies?'

'I wonder if we're going about this the wrong way,' said Brian, chewing the end of his pen.

Angie leaned her elbows on the table, balancing her long black between slender fingers. 'We have to come up with a plan soon,' she said. 'We can't go back to the next committee meeting without the numbers.'

Madam Chair and Mrs Minutes would love that.

'The last thing we need is a comeback by Jerry and the bloody Toe-tappers.' Celia swatted a fly away before drowning her biscotti in her latte. 'He couldn't remember the words to half the songs last year.'

'Too right,' said Peggy. 'Jerry is out of hospital already. I saw him chatting to Mavis in the foyer.'

'Christ alive,' muttered Celia. She sucked the coffee from the soggy end of her biscotti and crunched the rest.

'The problem is we don't have the foggiest idea what we're actually looking for,' said Angie. 'I don't know about you lot, but I'm even more confused after that debacle in the shop.'

'You're the one who suggested it,' said Peggy. 'It was your idea.'

'And if you'd drunk more water before our outing, we might have avoided another one of your turns and have more of a clue.'

Peggy glared.

'What about eBay?' suggested Jim. 'There might be some good second-hand gear on there.'

'Good idea, Jim.' Angie touched his elbow.

'If you ask me, I think this is all a giant waste of time and money.' Celia yawned and stretched her arms above her head. 'Why don't we just hire a DJ twice a year? It'd be much cheaper and far less hassle.'

Peggy saw the Kenny and Dolly duet flickering like a flame in a draught, their islands sinking rapidly in the stream. Part of her still wanted Brian, or at least the idea of him. She'd tried to convince herself she didn't need the attentions of a man to make her feel attractive, that the whole wardrobe revamp was purely for herself. She'd allowed herself to dream of love and romance. The fantasy had secretly sustained her during the darkest days of her grief. Far from withering on the vine, her life had burst forth with the new shoots of possibility. This pathetic schoolgirl crush was the sole reason she remembered to take her tablets and increasingly, the only reason she knew the day of the week. She wasn't quite ready to give it up.

She and Angie interrupted at the same time. 'No!'

'It'll be so much more fun this way,' said Angie, smiling at Jim. It nearly killed Peggy to admit it, but for once she agreed with her friend, and nemesis.

Celia interrupted. 'Ballpark figure, Jim? What are we talking here?'

'Ballpark?' Jim closed his eyes in concentration. When his mouth slackened, Peggy worried he'd fallen asleep but as she was about to give him a prod, he opened his eyes and announced the magic figure. None of them had the foggiest how accurate it was likely to be.

Taking Jim at his word, Brian tapped away on his calculator. Peggy pictured him sitting at an imposing desk in a smart navy suit, surrounded by framed certificates. After several minutes, he drew a line under a column of numbers. Chewing one arm of his spectacles, he addressed them. 'Based on Jim's rough estimation, by my calculations, it could pay for itself within twelve months, assuming we hire it out three times a year.'

'None of us even knows how to operate it,' Celia grumbled. 'Judging by our collective performance in the hi-fi shop, I'd say we're all complete amateurs.'

'Is there a category below amateur?' Angie muttered into her long black.

Peggy thought out loud. 'What we really need is a teenager.'

'I could ask my grandson, Nathan,' said Brian. 'He works as a DJ on weekends to pay his way through university. He'd know exactly what to buy.'

Peggy smiled, picturing a younger version of Brian grooving away with a giant pair of headphones.

They all agreed it was worth a try.

Over a second round of coffees, they made a list of jobs to be done for the fashion show and allocated them around the group. It went without saying that Peggy would do nibbles. Brian volunteered for ticket sales and crowd control. Celia was tasked with chairs, roping Jim in to set up the stage and the PA. Anything with a hem or a sequin, they all agreed, was Angie's department. To Peggy's relief, managing Arabella also fell on Angie's shoulders.

'Darlings, I could organise a fashion show with my eyes closed,' said Angie, putting a tick next to the final item on the list. *Models*. Peggy was the only one who seemed worried.

To celebrate another successful committee meeting, Celia produced the stainless-steel flask from her beach bag.

'Anyone feeling peaky this morning?'

21

The Caped Crusaders

WHO WAS THAT OLD HAG IN THE MIRROR? PEGGY'S HEART sank as the young assistant fastened the black plastic cape around her neck. Had she really had coffee this morning with Brian and the others looking like this?

Even after her dip in the pool, Angie's hair had remained frustratingly perfect. What was it with this woman? Peggy wished that just once, Angie could look dishevelled. Hell, she'd even settle for under-groomed. Meanwhile, Peggy was about to meet this marvellous new hairdresser wearing what looked like a string bag on her head.

'This is my friend, the one I was telling you about,' said Angie.

'Pleased to meet you, Peggy,' said the olive-skinned face in the mirror.

This must be the famous Alessandro. Judging by his expression, like Arabella, Angie had prepared him for the worst.

'I was thinking something along the lines of this.' Angie held up a copy of *The Australian Women's Weekly*. Helen Mirren smiled back from the front cover.

Alessandro squinted backwards and forwards between Peggy and the magazine, like a portrait painter. A smile crept across his face. 'You know, Angela my darling, I think we might just pull it off!' He clapped his hands together like an excited child. 'But first we get rid of this . . .'

Peggy watched with horror as he removed a strand of seaweed from her head.

'Do I get a say in this?' Peggy addressed the mirror.

'No,' they chorused.

'Leave it to me,' said Alessandro in a suspiciously heavy accent. 'I will help you channel your inner Helen Mirren.'

Peggy had a strong urge to run and hide. Of all Angie's makeover steps, this was by far the most daunting. A new hairstyle wasn't something she could shove to the back of the wardrobe if she didn't like it. If it went wrong, it would be weeks before the hair grew out. She'd never be able to face poor Louise at Dazzling Dos after this. Thirty years of tints and sets, not to mention the cups of instant coffee and ancient magazines, and this was how Peggy repaid her. It was bad enough seeing a new doctor, but a hairdresser? It was like committing adultery. Swapping the steadfastly faithful Louise for a one-night-stand with the glamorous Alessandro.

'Coffee, ma'am?' enquired the assistant.

Ma'am? Did she think she was addressing the Queen?

'Thank you.' Peggy forced a smile.

It wasn't this young girl's fault. Like the would-be geriatrician at the book fair and the removal man with the sofa, she was just trying to be polite, just doing her job. Why was Peggy being so prickly in return? It was all happening so quickly, her days now tumbling into each other like a stack of dominoes. With her timid old life disappearing in its own wake, she was facing a future impatient for change. She could no longer hide behind her inadequacies, holding onto her frumpishness or lack of confidence like a security blanket. It was too late. The Angie juggernaut was unstoppable.

~

Alessandro peeled off his plastic gloves and threw them into the empty dish of hair colour. For thirty agonising minutes, with her bladder fit to burst, Peggy had tried to distract herself by memorising a new salad. Everything about the salon was fancy and upmarket, including the recipes in the magazines. She hadn't the foggiest what pepitas were but was confident the helpful young man at the fruit and veg shop would have some in stock.

She was studiously avoiding the mirror, resisting even a glance. Experience had taught her not to open the oven door before the soufflé was done. With all the fumes from the dye, she was having trouble keeping her smarting eyes open anyway.

'And now we must wait for you to process,' said Alessandro, resting both hands on Peggy's shoulders and addressing her via the mirror.

Process? Like blank photographic paper in a dark room, not knowing what would appear.

'Can I get you another coffee?'

'Absolutely not.' Peggy was desperate to find a toilet but swaddled in the black plastic cape and blinded by bleach fumes, she couldn't risk such an expedition.

She heard Angie's voice beside her. 'Relax. Alessandro is the best.'

'It's hair, Angie, not plastic surgery. There's a limit to what anyone can do with it.'

'Trust me. He can work miracles.'

Like Dr Stephen? His little miracle had left her feeling as if she were trying to do calculus with a hangover. In fact, she was worse off than before, with all the additional worry about her memory. With the threat of the dreaded mini-mental test still looming, she had already worked herself up into a tizzy. The last thing she needed was a catastrophe at the hairdresser's too.

Peggy swivelled in her chair and squinted at Angie sitting at the adjacent mirror. Instead of the elation she'd expected to feel at the sight of her friend with hair plastered to her skull, Peggy was caught off balance. For a split-second, an old lady sat in the place of the perennially groomed Angie Valentine. How would a woman, defined by her looks and the casual fortune that had dealt her those high cheekbones, cope when she could no longer see herself in the mirror? Pity the care assistant whose job it would be to dress the famous fashionista or to brush her hair. Woe betide the poor soul who mixed spots and stripes or chose the wrong heel.

Peggy's stomach clenched. 'Why are you doing this?'

Angie closed her magazine and stared at Peggy in the mirror. 'I'm doing it for you.'

'But why?'

All along, Peggy had been at a loss to explain this unprovoked kindness, too wrapped up in her physical trans-formation to question it. Perhaps Angie wanted an equally glamorous sidekick to hang out with, determined to drag Peggy out of her default drabness to be the perfect accessory.

'I want you to be happy, Peggy.'

'I *am* happy.'

'Sure. The first time I met you, you were scrambling around the floor, searching for your pantyhose.'

No, Peggy wanted to say, the first time you met me was even more embarrassing. She'd tried to forget that day as a shy eight-year-old, the first time Angie had come to her rescue. The shame and humiliation were as raw as they had been seventy years ago. Then she'd met Angie and allowed herself to hope. She'd trusted this woman, this virtual stranger, with not only her wardrobe but with her heart and dreams, only to have her take it all away again.

Beneath the plastic cape, Peggy's skin perspired. 'For the record, I didn't ask for any of this. I was fine before you turned up. Okay, I was a bit beige, but that's not a crime at nearly eighty.'

'Beige? You were so damn neutral, you were virtually invisible.'

'But at least I was being authentic, not injecting my face with botulism and looking like . . .' Peggy stopped herself.

'Go on, say it,' said Angie, impassioned, challenging Peggy with a cold stare. 'Like mutton dressed as lamb. Why don't you say exactly what's on your mind for a change?'

Peggy's gaze dropped to her lap. 'I was going to say that, except it's not true. You look . . . fabulous. You've always looked fabulous.'

Angie rose from her chair and squatted down in front of Peggy, reaching for her hands under the black plastic. 'I just want you to see what you're missing, Pegs. You're a beautiful woman, under all that taupe. All you need is confidence. To believe in yourself again.'

Tears welled in Peggy's eyes again. 'Damn bleach,' she said and tried to wipe them away with the edge of the cape.

'You have to stop thinking like an old person. If you behave like an old biddy, people are going to treat you like one.'

'That's all very well for you to say,' said Peggy, her face close to Angie's. 'Life's easy without children trying to take over your life, treating you like you're completely incapable of anything, assuming you're useless. You were smart not to have kids. No dirty nappies, snotty noses or sleepless nights. Look at you and the fabulous life you've led. You don't know how lucky you are.'

A shadow passed across Angie's motionless face. Peggy saw the change in her eyes, a new expression she didn't recognise. Beneath the cape, Peggy felt a chill. Far from launching a searing comeback, Angie simply stood up and walked away, leaving only a crumpled *Vogue* magazine in her place. Something was very wrong. Whatever she'd said, she'd gone too far.

'Would you like some more magazines, Mrs Smart?' It was the apprentice.

'It's Peggy to you,' said Peggy and, still wearing her plastic cape and a head plastered in foul-smelling stodge, she jumped up and rushed after Angie, past the other heads in various stages of refurbishment, past the bewildered receptionist, and out onto the street.

She scanned to the left and right, spotting Angie in the distance, heading towards the oval. For someone of nearly eighty, Angie was surprisingly quick. Peggy hobbled behind, her stiff knee mercifully loosening with each step, cape billowing behind her like Snow White's evil stepmother.

Heads turned, but Peggy didn't care. Something had upset her friend. Her oldest and dearest friend, she realised, regardless of the years that had passed.

'Angie!' shouted Peggy, crossing the main road without looking. 'Wait for me!' A car screeched to a halt, narrowly missing her. The driver leaned out of the window and shouted an obscenity, but Peggy didn't care. She needed to apologise, to make everything right again. Angie was the only person who saw her for who she really was and not some old crumble to be patronised. In her eyes, she was no different to the Peggy Weaver she'd giggled with at Blake's all those years ago. And perhaps that's how Angie still saw herself. She'd reached out for friendship in the only way she knew. In return, Peggy had slapped Angie across the face with her non-existent family.

It was the furthest Peggy had run since she'd trodden on a bindi and strained a hamstring in the mothers' race when David was in primary school. She would always remember his wounded expression when she limped over the finish line in last place. Angie was leaning against a goalpost in the centre of the oval, her ironed face now creased with pain and disappointment.

'I'm sorry,' said Peggy.

'Don't apologise. You're right.' Angie took a long drag on a cigarette.

Where the hell did she get that? Did Angie carry a secret stash of fags somewhere concealed upon her person?

'I'm so insensitive.' Peggy hung her head, hoping some sort of explanation would fill the silence that followed. If

Angie dropped down dead from a heart attack, it would be her fault. She would have killed her best friend with her ingratitude and petty-minded aversion to ancient grains.

A football rolled towards Angie and she kicked it back to a little boy playing with his father. What a sight we must look, thought Peggy, seeing herself and Angie standing in the middle of the council park in plastic capes.

'I had a son,' said Angie, blowing smoke from one side of her mouth.

'What do you mean? I thought you didn't have any children.'

'I don't, but I did. He died.' One arm folded tightly around her body, she took another long drag on her cigarette. Her hand was shaking.

'Angie, I had no idea. I'm so sorry.'

'Don't be sorry. You weren't to know.'

'I don't understand. How come you've never mentioned this before?'

'It's very personal. You get to our age, and everyone has lost someone they love.' Angie was looking around, at the ground, at the children playing nearby, at the perfect cloudless sky. Anywhere except at Peggy.

'But a child . . . that's different.' Peggy reached out to her friend, hand falling back to her side as Angie flinched away.

'*Simon*. He had the most beautiful smile.' Angie stared off into her memories, her mouth at once both a smile and a grimace. The tears spilled mascara onto her cheeks.

'We don't have to talk about this now.' *Standing in the middle of an oval with our hair plastered in bleach.*

'He was only seven. He contracted a virus while we were travelling. He came everywhere with me. It infected his heart muscle. The doctors in Paris told me there was nothing they could do. He died in my arms.' Angie's voice was barely a whisper, strangled by the memory.

There were so many questions. How did a little boy die from a virus? Where was the justice in this world? Peggy had lost Ted, but they'd shared many happy, contented years together. He'd had what most people considered a good innings. And after the miscarriages, she and Ted had found comfort in each other, united in grief for the babies that barely formed, that they never met. But to lose a child . . .

'Ladies, ladies!' It was Alessandro, running towards them, arms flailing like a human windmill. 'You must come back immediately, otherwise I cannot be responsible for the consequences.' He was still quite a way off, but Peggy could see the panic etched in his face.

'I want to tell you about Simon,' said Angie.

'And I want to hear all about him. I want you to tell me everything, but this isn't the right place.'

Angie gripped Peggy's arm, imploring. 'I need to tell you something important.'

A middle-aged man in football boots blew a whistle nearby and gave them a look.

'We have to go. I think we're blocking the goal, but we'll talk later. I promise.'

Placated, Angie took another drag on the cigarette, as though the smoke held all the answers. Then she hid it behind her back and, wiping away the tears and mascara, shouted at the approaching Alessandro, 'Coming, darling.'

'Keep your tiara on,' she added under her breath, making Peggy smile.

This was more like Angie. Feisty and full of fun. Mistress of the quip. Not bereaved. Not heartbroken and lost. A mother without her child.

Angie was human. Peggy saw it now. Behind the façade, the frailty and vulnerability were as real as in any other resident of Jacaranda Retirement Village. Beneath the Elizabeth Arden and navy palazzo pants, she was ageing too. There was one big difference. Unlike Peggy with her imperfect family, Angie was completely alone.

A police car slowed for a closer look at the two women before driving on.

'We'll be in the paper if we don't hurry back,' said Peggy.

Angie smiled. 'Do you think they'd throw us out of the village for bringing it into disrepute?'

'I think we'd have to try a little harder, don't you?' Peggy took the cigarette from between Angie's fingers, took a drag herself, coughed then stamped it out into the grass.

~

'Would you like the massage chair on?'

Why not? The knots in her back would take some serious kneading, but it was worth a try. The chair reclined to near horizontal and a dozen tiny rolling pins began to gyrate against the muscles in Peggy's back. It wasn't the blissful experience she'd imagined, and did little to stop her ruminating over the incident with Angie.

They'd returned to the salon like errant children without exchanging another word. The atmosphere between them had changed, and Peggy felt crushed by the weight of the unsaid. No amount of coffee or magazines could salve the pain that Peggy felt for Angie.

There was a muted television screen mounted on the ceiling above the basins, showing some awful daytime TV program. A panel of highly coiffed women sat on a curved sofa in a heated discussion about something topical and inconsequential.

'How is that pressure for you?'

'Fine.' Why did women always do that? She wished the girl would dig her fingers in a little harder, but instead, she said it was fine. *Fine.* Another four-letter word to trip up over. Angie was right. Why couldn't she just say what was on her mind? It was time to act the grown-up she was overqualified to be.

'Got any plans for the weekend?' The apprentice ploughed Peggy's lathered hair with her talons.

Was this what they taught at hairdresser school? Part of her wanted to scream, but then she remembered her first day at Blake's, and how naïve she'd been, barely able to tell hosiery from haberdashery, still waiting for Angie to decode the merchandising secrets of the panty girdle.

'My daughter's coming to visit from the country,' said Peggy. Now, was that tomorrow or the next day?

'That'll be nice.'

'Yes,' said Peggy, trying to suppress sarcasm. 'I'm counting down the days.' How many, she wasn't exactly sure and therein lay the problem. How long could she maintain the pretence of normality? She was bound to slip up during Jenny's visit. Were the ear canals simply a ruse, an excuse to wade in and harangue poor Dr Stephen and the crimes of Western medicine?

The massage continued, deep circles at the base of her skull now. 'Does she have kids?'

'Alpacas,' replied Peggy. And a lesbian lover.

'Nice.' The girl continued to chatter about not much, but Peggy found the words soothing and she closed her eyes.

She woke to a snort in the back of her throat. For what had seemed like hours, she'd been eating ice-cream on a beach with Ted and the kids, but it couldn't have been more than a minute or two. The apprentice was drilling Peggy's ears with the corner of a towel. The smiling women on the sofa were gone and the TV was advertising a pre-paid funeral plan instead.

~

A scatter rug of platinum hair covered the floor around the chair. Alessandro came towards her armed with a hairdryer that resembled a machine gun. Where were the rollers and the Viking helmet?

Hot air blasted Peggy's scalp as Alessandro's slender fingers tousled her hair, or rather, what was left of it.

'I'm using mousse,' shouted Alessandro above the whine of the dryer. 'To give you volume.'

Peggy pictured her special double chocolate mousse with fresh whipped cream. It was guaranteed to add volume too. Mainly around the backside.

After what seemed an eternity, Alessandro turned off the hairdryer and stood back to admire his handiwork. All Peggy could think about was getting out of this waterproof cape. It reminded her of that ridiculous plastic slim-suit she'd once worn to bed in the hope of shedding a few pounds. Of course, it hadn't worked, at least not for the weight loss, although it had kept Ted's amorous advances at bay.

'What do you think?' Standing beside Alessandro, Angie was back to her usual glamorous self, shiny dark bob smoothed carefully into place.

'Very nice,' said Peggy.

'Very nice? We're not describing a cup of tea here,' said Angie. 'Try fabulous!'

'I promised you magic!' Alessandro was standing back hugging his arms around himself, as proud as a new father.

They were addressing her, Peggy realised, waiting for her to voice an opinion, the weight of expectation as uncomfortable around her shoulders as the massage chair had been. She hadn't thought to check out her new look in the mirror. Having been quite satisfied with her restyle in 1986, it stood to reason that she should be similarly content with today's do.

'You do look amazing,' said the young apprentice. She unfastened the black cape and spun the chair round to face the mirror. There, to Peggy's surprise, sat Helen Mirren. She let out a little gasp.

Alessandro teased a few strands of hair over the left side of her forehead, forming a soft fringe. 'Stunning, even if I do say so myself.'

Peggy looked at herself. How blue her eyes seemed. How much more colour there was in her skin, even without make-up. Her softly rounded face had lost kilos beneath the layered hair, and for the first time, Peggy admired her own cheekbones. Mute from shock, she brushed a few stray hairs from her top. All she could do was grin.

Goodbye, mousy pensioner. Hello, elegant, confident and utterly fabulous Peggy Smart.

Siren.

Sex kitten.

22

One or Two for the Road

'WHAT A PITY THERE'S NO HAPPY HOUR TONIGHT.' PEGGY primped herself in the Mini's wing mirror. Cinderella, and no ball.

'Tell me about it. All dolled up and nowhere to go,' mused Angie, drumming her shellac fingernails on the steering wheel.

A movie scene unfolded inside Peggy's head. A stylish, platinum-haired woman of mature years knocks on a front door. 'Have dinner with me,' she says to the handsome man who greets her, his expression one of surprise and delight.

Back in the real world, there was no sign of the silver Lexus parked across the road. It looked like another early night with only a cup of Sleepytime tea to keep her warm.

'Thanks for the lift.' She paused, the door of the Mini half open. 'I'm sorry about earlier.'

'There's no need to apologise, Pegs.'

'It was completely insensitive of me. I'm ashamed of myself.'

'We need to talk.' Angie grabbed Peggy's arm, her red nails tightening around the flesh. 'I owe you an explanation, and more.'

More? 'Are you sure you want to?'

'We need to clear the air. My place. I'll give you ten minutes to see to Basil.'

Peggy had forgotten about the poor dog, locked up inside all day. As she fumbled with the key in the lock, she heard him scratching on the other side of the front door.

'Hang on, sweetheart. Mummy's home.'

The door was open barely a crack when a ball of white fluff dashed out between Peggy's legs. He stumbled along the path towards the gardenias.

Leaving the front door ajar, Peggy flung her bag onto the kitchen table and trotted off with equal urgency in the opposite direction, humming 'Frère Jacques' to distract herself.

Seconds later, the screeching of tyres halted Peggy's sweet relief. She heard a car horn followed by the sickening sound of crumpled metal.

Basil.

With barely enough time to arrange herself, Peggy raced to the front door. She could hear voices beyond the hedge.

Please, no.

A crowd had gathered around a red saloon car. Most were familiar faces – casual acquaintances from the village. She also recognised the car. It was Sheila Martin's new Honda.

'He ran out in front of me,' said Sheila, from the epicentre of the group. 'I could have been killed!'

'It doesn't look like there's too much damage,' said Vince Livingstone, examining the front bumper. 'Insurance should cover it. Depends on your excess, of course.'

Peggy's chest burned. How could these heartless monsters stand here discussing car insurance when her poor dog lay squished under the wheels? She pushed her way to the front, fixed Sheila with an icy stare and hissed, 'What have you done to Basil?'

Sheila's eyes narrowed. 'Me? He ran straight into the middle of the road. I had to swerve to avoid him.'

'She clipped the wall with her front bumper,' said Vince running his fingers across a series of scratches in the red paint. But there was no blood and no body.

'It's your fault, Peggy Smart. You know as well as I do the rules about pets in the village. Especially dangerous dogs. Just look at my car.'

'Go stir your cauldron,' snapped Peggy.

'You just wait for tomorrow's residents' committee meeting. It's already on the agenda. Dogs in units. There's going to be a vote.' Sheila appeared to congratulate herself, delivering the winning punch with such ham that under normal circumstances, Peggy would have laughed.

But this was no laughing matter. Peggy felt the words travel through her body, coming to rest in the bottom of her stomach. 'We'll see about that.' She swallowed hard between her gritted teeth.

Vince organised the other residents into a search party, dispatching his wife to check further down the road, and a woman called Hazel to report Basil missing at reception.

'Please hurry,' said Peggy. What if he was lying injured somewhere? A dog of his age could die just from the shock.

The crowd dispersed, checking under hedges and behind walls.

Adrenaline surged through Peggy's varicose veins. She wasn't ready to say goodbye yet. Life was so fragile. How quickly everything could change.

'What about my insurance excess?' Sheila stood with her hands on her hips next to her scratched bumper.

'I've got a suggestion for you,' muttered Peggy as she turned away.

With growing trepidation, Peggy worked her way up the drive, scouring the garden beds and hedges for any trace of white fur or blood. She called his name, but there was no trace of Basil. Eventually, she had to stop, bending forward with hands on knees to catch her breath. Straightening up again, Peggy pressed both hands into the ache of her lower back. It was then she realised she was standing outside Angie's unit.

The front door was ajar. 'Coo-ee,' she called, pushing the door open a fraction wider.

There in the hallway stood Angie. In her arms was a white furry body.

'Is he ... ?' Peggy held her breath as she stared at the bundle.

'Hungry? Yes, he's just wolfed down a wedge of organic goat's cheese, though he didn't like the crackers. I think they were a bit hard for his teeth.'

'Thank goodness.'

'He's done a wee on the kitchen floor though. Don't they make incontinence products for dogs?'

Angie handed Basil to Peggy, his body tense and quivering.

'Come here, old man. You've given Mummy quite a shock.'

'He was here helping himself to my antipasto. I heard the commotion up the road and thought it might be best to keep him out of sight until things calmed down.'

Peggy's hand shot to her mouth. 'I thought I'd lost him.'

'You okay? You look a funny colour.'

'I do feel a bit strange.' Peggy felt herself unravel like a dropped stitch.

'Here, come and sit down.'

Angie led her to a plush velvet sofa. It was the one the removal man had been carrying on his shoulder, the day everything changed. 'Put your feet up,' she said, plumping the cushions at one end.

Basil jumped off Peggy's lap, agile as a puppy, and followed Angie into the kitchen.

There was the clink of glasses, the sound of a cupboard closing and Angie's voice. She must be talking to Basil. It was unlike the old dog to leave Peggy's side. He was very set in his ways and intolerant of new people. Ted was the same, once he retired, content to potter about in the garage. He was never happier than when he was mending things. Sometimes Peggy would deliberately break something, just to keep him occupied.

'Here you are. Drink up. You'll feel better in a minute.' Angie was back, Basil at her heels.

Peggy took the heavy crystal tumbler and brought it to her lips. The smell was oily and she wasn't sure she could drink it. Confronted by the neat spirit, she debated asking Angie for a latte to go with it. But this was an emergency.

The thick amber liquid burned the inside of Peggy's mouth and the top of her gullet. She coughed. Warmth radiated through her body as she let the brandy trickle down. Peggy began to feel better almost immediately. Meanwhile, Angie sat in an elegant French-style armchair, one of those Louis Carthorse replicas.

Everything in the unit was so tasteful. Angie tasteful. With all the expensive furniture, in complementary shades of pale blue, grey and silver, the place looked like a show home. Here they were in a suburban retirement village, and even Angie's unit looked like it should be in a magazine.

Basil had fallen asleep on the mat, a brown and white hide, Peggy noticed. She had a closer look. Yes, there really was a dead cow on the floor. A cloak of weariness descended, and she surrendered to the feather-filled seat cushions. It made her realise how uncomfortable her own sofa was. She'd overruled Ted in the shop. He'd wanted comfort, but she'd seen a photo in a magazine and, in a moment of madness, insisted on an all-cream living room. The whole three-piece suite was looking quite grubby now, as Ted had predicted. And it was very uncomfortable. It always had been.

'Refill Pegs?'

Peggy swallowed the last of the brandy, and hiccupped. 'Why not?' Her muscles had loosened and a lovely weight-lessness had stolen her arms and legs. She accepted the top-up gratefully. 'I don't think I'm ready to let him go just yet,' said Peggy, glancing at Basil, now chasing possums in his dreams. Her words collided as they stumbled from her lips.

'I think I'd better fetch the cheese.' Angie reappeared with a wooden chopping board bearing what looked like olives and strips of something red and shiny flanked by a few rustic-looking biscuits She handed Peggy a side plate. 'Help yourself.'

Peggy's fingers hovered over the assortment, searching for something she recognised. No matter what kind of udders it came from, if she ate this, Dr Stephen was bound to find out and she wasn't up to another list. But desperate times called for desperate measures. She placed a chunk of something white and crumbly onto a biscuit and devoured it.

'You're such a lovely fellow, aren't you, Basil?' Angie leaned down to stroke his head. The dog opened his sleepy eyes at her touch. He yawned, licked his lips then rolled onto his back, exposing his belly. Angie responded with cooing sounds as she circled the pink flesh with her long fingernails. Basil's tail wagged like an excited puppy and he writhed in canine ecstasy. He hadn't done that in months.

'Sheila Martin doesn't think so,' slurred Peggy. 'She complained about him to management and they're holding a vote at the next committee meeting.'

'What sort of vote?'

'A vote to ban dogs. Dangerous dogs. Can you believe it?'

'That's absurd. Basil isn't dangerous. There's no way the committee would vote him out.' She stopped short of adding *would they?*

'There were witnesses. Madam President's cronies. Once word gets out, Basil is as good as gone. She and Sheila will be summoning the henchmen ready for tomorrow night's meeting.'

'I wouldn't worry. There's no way the committee will evict Basil.'

Peggy ran her finger against the pile in the velvet fabric then smoothed it again. If only she could be as confident as Angie about the whole Basil issue. If it came to a vote, it would be close.

'The Livingstones were there,' said Peggy.

'So?'

'It's Sylvia, or rather her cat, Engelbert.'

'You're losing me, Pegs.'

'Basil chased Engelbert up a tree not long after we moved in. The SES had to rescue him with their ladders and there was a big hoo-haa. I'm sure they'll drag it up at the meeting.'

Peggy knew she shouldn't be burdening Angie with the whole Basil-gate business. They were meant to be talking about Simon, not cats in trees. Yet again, Angie had come to Peggy's rescue. The seesaw was skewed, as it always had been: Peggy weighing down her end, leaving the raw-boned Angie high above her at the opposite end. Angie seemed to enjoy having the upper hand in their relationship, as though she relished the power imbalance. When, if ever, would Peggy ever have the chance to rebalance their lopsided relationship?

'Leave it to me,' said Angie, a mischievous grin arriving between two swigs of brandy. 'I have a cunning plan.'

Peggy was surprised to see the bottom of her tumbler so soon, clearly underestimating the power of shock. 'I think I might need another drink,' she said.

'How about one for the road, then I'll walk you home? We've had quite enough excitement for one day.'

Angie poured a thin measure of brandy from the decanter into Peggy's glass. Peggy raised one eyebrow and held out her glass until she was satisfied. 'I could get accustomed to this,' she said, wondering why she'd been so resistant to drinking spirits. There were so many experiences she still hadn't tried, a whole host of vices she had avoided for almost eighty years. It was time to spice up her bucket list with a few debaucheries before it was too late.

'Best go steady,' said Angie, removing a crystal vase just in time when Peggy sat up and swung her plaster cast towards the side table.

'Do you know I've never been drunk before?'

Angie was incredulous. 'What, never?'

'Nope.'

'What not even when you were younger?'

'I was a bit heavy-handed with the sherry in the trifle one Christmas. Does that count?'

'You're going to tell me you've never sworn either.'

Peggy looked down into her lap. 'I used the b-word once, when I dropped a planter box on my toe.' She wasn't sure if she was more ashamed about using the word, or not having used it before.

Angie was laughing now. 'The b-word? What, *bum*? Don't tell me you said *bloody*?'

How absurd, at nearly eighty. Her own naïvety hit Peggy as painfully as the planter box had. There was so much wasted time to make up, starting with a new repertoire of curse words.

'Bugger it!' said Peggy, making Angie recoil momentarily. 'It's about bloody time I started to swear. Better late than never, right?'

The two women clinked glasses in a toast. 'Here's to growing old disgracefully!'

Basil stretched and yawned. He looked from Peggy to Angie and back again, as if trying to decide something.

'Ever tried dope?' whispered Angie.

Peggy was confused. Wasn't that what cyclists did to make them pedal faster?

'You know, pot, weed, cannabis?' Angie offered Basil a piece of cheese. He nibbled it from her fingers.

It wasn't the kind of thing people did at Jacaranda Retirement Village. There was mahjong, quilting and even ukulele advertised in the village newsletter but no pot smoking, as far as Peggy could recall. The village had a coffee shop and a beauty salon, but no drug den that she knew of.

'Isn't it dangerous at our age?'

Angie took a deep breath that nearly doubled her size. 'Not this again. I'm getting incredibly bored with this age obsession of yours. No wonder your kids are behaving the way they are. You're letting them treat you like an old lady and that makes you as bad as they are.'

Neither of them was laughing now. Even Basil had hid his head between his paws, his eyes darting between them. Denial was all very well, thought Peggy, suddenly peeved, but everyone needed to prepare. They were all mortal. Even the imperishable Angie Valentine.

'You can eat all the mulch you like, and stick needles in your face but you have to accept that we're all getting old.'

Angie stood abruptly, sending her side plate clattering to the floor.

'I know that as much as anyone. My heart is completely buggered. Yes, the bodywork is in good nick, but the engine's on borrowed time. It's only a matter of time before they tow me off to the scrap heap. You think I want to sit here and dwell on that? If you think I'm going to spend what little time I have left feeling sorry for myself, then you're mistaken. Now, do you want the last slice of haloumi, or shall I give it to the dog?'

'You're right. Let's make the most of what we have left. It's time to start living.' Peggy took the last slice of whatever haloumi was and ate it.

The deep pillowy sofa had swallowed her and on sitting up, she accidentally knocked a sofa cushion onto the floor with her foot. Basil wandered over towards the discarded cushion. He sniffed it then, without warning, straddled the cushion, and arching his back, began to hump the velvet fabric. Peggy was mortified. Flashes of David and his first girlfriend, writhing half-clothed on his single bed, escaped from her bank of repressed memories.

'You dirty old man, Basil.' In trying to scold the poor dog, Peggy found herself smiling. She saw Angie giggle behind her hand.

Laughter forced Peggy back into the sofa. Helpless, she watched as her beloved pooch made love to Angie's designer cushion. There was a twinkle in his rheumy eyes, and his droopy jowls were pulled into what was most definitely a smile.

'You should take a leaf out of his book,' said Angie, trying to control herself.

It certainly brought new meaning to the phrase *there's life in the old dog yet*.

'I need to pee,' chuckled Peggy, levering herself from the sofa.

Her first steps were like those of a wobbly toddler. The room was warm and it was already dark outside. Where had the sun gone?

'Door on the right. Are you sure you're alright on your own?'

I may be the tiniest bit tipsy, but I don't need anyone to take me to the toilet. Not yet anyway. Peggy felt her way along the dark hallway, bouncing off the walls like an out-of-control zeppelin. She'd always thought it comical, watching drunk people trying to act sober. It was harder than it looked.

There were two doors on the right. To add to the confusion, the first one was closed. A golden glow drew her eye to the second door. Moth-like, she headed towards the light.

This must be Angie's bedroom. The bed rather gave it away. The whole room looked how she imagined a harem would be, the bed adorned with scattered silk cushions and a fur throw. There was a nude hanging on the wall above the bed: a perky-breasted young woman draped over a chaise, with a come-hither expression. Peggy pictured her own bedroom. With its daisy-print duvet cover and the watercolour of the harbour, it was anything but a boudoir.

The brandy urged Peggy to find the ensuite, quickly. It had to be here somewhere. On the far side of the room there was a series of doors with handles. One of them had to be the bathroom.

She pulled the first handle towards her and recoiled. Peggy was looking straight into a mirror. It wasn't pretty. Her new do was undone, and there was a suspicious grease stain down the front of her top. Helen Mirren leaned closer and inspected her with bloodshot eyes.

Peggy Smart, you are drunk.

Sloshed.

Absolutely pickled.

She tried to imagine her children's faces if they could see her now. They'd have her locked away before you could say

Dan Murphy. But instead of shame, Peggy felt a real sense of achievement. She'd finally done it. Peggy Smart had ticked the first item off her bucket list of hedonism. This was the kind of news people liked to share on sociable media. David had already opened her an account on Face-time book as a joke. It was time to start sharing her adventures. If only she could get the camera on her new phone to work, or indeed the phone itself.

The shelf above the mirror was covered in bottles and tubes, pots and containers of every shape and colour, filled with concoctions of face creams, cleansers, serums and balms. Did Angie really use all this stuff? It was like seeing what went into a sausage, making it suddenly less appealing.

On the shelf below was where Angie kept her collection of brushes, combs and hairsprays. Peggy opened the top drawer. Inside, she discovered a kaleidoscope of coloured lipsticks and eye shadows. How did she know which colour went where? Every morning must be like painting by numbers, without the numbers. No wonder the woman was always late.

Like a kid in a sweet shop, Peggy licked her lips and chose a lipstick from the middle of the collection. It was tricky at first, having apparently lost all co-ordination, but somehow, she managed to apply the cherry-red stain. Some even made it onto her lips. In the mirror, she looked like some pouty-lipped porn star.

A cheap tart.

She could hear her mother now: 'You should be ashamed, making a show of yourself, young lady.'

Peggy stared back into the mirror. When her mother died, she'd hoped to bury the disapprovals and put-downs with her. But twenty years on, there was still no sign of the self-confidence her mother had denied her, and the other life she could have lived. At least, not until Angie had arrived on the scene.

'Fuck off, Mother.'

I'm a big girl now. I can do whatever I want.

There was a call from the living room. 'Do you need a hand in there?'

'No, I'm fine,' shouted Peggy.

She searched for a tissue, something to wipe this stupid stuff off her lips. She couldn't let Angie find her playing dress-ups. *Quickly.* There had to be a box in here somewhere. Peggy pulled out the drawers one by one, starting at the top. Silky underwear, stockings, jewellery. More jewellery. No tissues.

The bottom drawer was stiffer than the rest and Peggy had to use her weight to dislodge it, staggering backwards when it gave. The drawer was filled with evening bags: sparkly, sequinny things. Peggy had never owned an evening bag. She'd never needed one. For some reason, she thought of Brian's wife. She wondered what the practically attired teacher had carried to all those Chartered Accountants' balls and fancy dinners. Phyllis didn't sound the kind of woman who owned a whole drawer of black satin bags. Peggy had a feeling she'd have liked Mrs Cornell.

She was about to close the drawer when she noticed something with hard straight edges near the back. It looked like a photo frame, partially hidden by some black feathers. She fished it out and noticed another, smaller one at the very back of the drawer.

Glancing over her shoulder, Peggy inspected the two silver frames. It was difficult in the dim light and without her reading glasses. Squinting, and holding the frame at arm's length, she could just make out the faces.

The largest of the photos was an old black-and-white shot, taken donkey's years ago. Looking at the fashion, it must have been in the late fifties or early sixties. There were three figures, arms linked, all laughing at some shared joke. One of them was unmistakably Angie in her Jean Seberg phase, her hair cropped fashionably short, and a cigarette in one hand. Peggy recognised the other woman as a younger version of herself, shrinking from the camera. She looked so plain in that shapeless knitted jacket, her mousy hair any-old-how. Was it any wonder Angie had attracted all the attention? Flanked by the two women was a man, grinning back at the camera. He was tall, with a full head of dark hair and a distinctive gap between his front teeth.

It was Ted.

She smiled at his fresh face. She'd almost forgotten what he looked like with hair. Why had Angie kept this photo, framed it even, and then hidden it in her bottom drawer?

Peggy turned to the smaller picture frame. It was a faded Kodachrome image of a young child, a boy. He was grinning from behind a birthday cake, a dark-haired Angie in the background. This must be Simon. There were seven candles alight – he was only a year older than Sam was now. He was wearing a cowboy hat and a fringed shirt. Peggy smiled. He reminded her of David at that age. He'd had a cowboy outfit too. In fact, the resemblance was quite striking. Something in that smiling face pricked Peggy's forearms with goosepimples.

This was Angie's son. Her only child. Why would she hide him away in a drawer? Thoughts swarmed like bees inside Peggy's head. Inside Angie's ever-so-tasteful unit, there were no knick-knacks from her supposedly glamorous life of jet-setting. No treasures or mementos, no photographs. Nothing personal at all. No clues to the life she'd led. It was as though the enigmatic Angela Valentine had deliberately concealed her past and her only child.

Peggy stroked the picture. A mother always assumed she'd die before her children. It was the natural way of things. But Angie had said goodbye to her son. With Simon, she'd lost not only a child but also her dreams and her future. Every second person in Jacaranda Retirement Village was a widow or a widower. But how many had outlived their children, enduring a grief that was too silent and painful for a label?

A voice shouted from the living room. 'Good news. I've found a bottle of gin in the cupboard.'

Peggy started and nearly dropped the frames. She had to put these back in the drawer before Angie walked in and found her rifling through her things. It was none of Peggy's business. She had no right to poke her nose in. Returning everything to the way it was, Peggy found the bathroom behind a sliding door on the other wall. She splashed some water on her face and dried her hands on a plush blue towel.

Was this the right time to ask about Simon? Angie obviously wanted to talk about her son, and if it hadn't been for Basil's escapades this afternoon, they would be having that heart to heart right now. Peggy was a good listener. What she lacked in fashion sense or vices, she made up for with a sympathetic ear. It was the least she could do. No more tiptoeing around the subject. She would come straight out with it. There was no time to waste at their age. Besides, she was developing rather a taste for spirits.

By the time Peggy had worked out the sliding door and escaped from the bathroom, Angie was snoring gently on her expensive sofa, Basil lying next to her. The gin stood unopened on the coffee table.

Peggy collected the empty glasses and rinsed them in the kitchen sink, then took the fur throw from Angie's bed and covered them both with it. Closing the front door behind her, she headed back to her unit.

Simon would have to wait a little longer.

23

Angie's Special Brownies

PEGGY STARED AT THE SHAGGY FRINGE OF DUST CLINGING to the blades of the ceiling fan. How she'd love to get up there and give them a good clean, but it wasn't worth it. Her independent life at the village was already hanging by the thinnest of threads. She couldn't risk falling from the stepladder. A broken wrist was one thing, but a fractured hip was quite a different matter. There was no laughing that one off with a waterproof cast. Hips needed operations. Operations needed anaesthetics. And everyone knew what anaesthetics did to geriatric brain cells.

What would Ted have made of last night's antics? He never drank. Never smoked. Never swore, out loud at least. It was only now, almost sixty years after they'd tied the knot, that the irony struck her. Peggy Weaver had finally escaped her straight-laced mother, only to marry the utterly vice-less Edward Smart. Was it any wonder she'd lived such a sheltered life?

Usually, by the time Peggy woke, Basil would be snuffling next to her bed or whimpering from his basket to be let out. But there was no sign of him. Then she remembered: the dirty old man was having a sleepover at Angie's. She recalled the relief of finding him safe and unhurt, followed by the brandy. It got a bit hazy after that. There was something about Basil and a cushion. Peggy chuckled to herself as the memories returned like an incoming tide. Angie was right all along. She should be taking a leaf out of Basil's book.

The phone rang. Peggy raised her head but changed her mind when the room tilted like a boat on a lumpy sea. Her head pulsed in time with the phone. She returned to the safety of her pillow and listened to the caller ring off. Probably just Angie asking what Basil liked for breakfast. He would have to wait. He couldn't expect to have his cake and lie in it. She knew he'd be back eventually. He may have been seduced by Angie's auntie-pasta whatsits, and succumbed to the wiles of her designer scatter cushions, but he knew where home was. That was loyalty. And real love.

Peggy experimented with a sitting position. Her skull felt like the inside of a kettledrum, but at least her bladder was having a lie-in. If her tongue was anything to go by, that was only because she was dehydrated.

Slipping her feet into her sheepskin slippers, Peggy sat on the edge of the bed and waited for the black spots to clear from her vision. She couldn't risk a fall this morning. Not smelling of booze and still wearing yesterday's clothes under her nightie.

Peggy wondered what else had happened last night. What nasty surprises would her short-term memory throw at her as the day unfolded? She cautiously revisited the order of events. Angie had invited her round to talk. About the child who'd never had the chance to grow up like her own two. The child Peggy had so insensitively told her she was better off without. She tried to replay their conversation, but her mind was a blank.

Had they cleared the air, hugged and toasted their friendship? The toasting bit she remembered, but there was no hugging that she could recall. The air felt anything but cleared. There was something about evening bags. A drawer.

The photographs.

Of all the husbands, stepchildren and the many friends she must have collected over her lifetime, why had Angie kept a photo of her and Ted? It didn't make sense. They'd lost touch so long ago, there must have been hundreds of pictures from Angie's glamorous career and her travels, her friends if not her husbands.

But it was the other photo that made Peggy uneasy, the one of Simon. There was something in his smile.

~

After three glasses of water from the kitchen sink, Peggy felt a little better. She'd missed Brian this morning. In fact, she'd missed him several mornings in a row. Operation Brian had finally run its course and it was a relief to know she could now have a proper conversation with the committee treasurer without imagining him naked. If she hadn't plucked up the courage to ask him to dinner by now, she never would. And vice versa. She'd enjoyed it while it lasted, and would always secretly credit Brian for her radical Helen Mirren-isation. But women like Peggy Smart didn't live in fairytales. They lived in one-bedroom units in retirement villages and drove hatchbacks with scratched hubcaps. They did aqua aerobics twice a week and collected endless wee samples for their doctors. If they were lucky, they had a Basil, at least until tonight's committee meeting. Some of them even had a friend like Angie Valentine, who drove them potty but without whom they couldn't contemplate their life ahead. It was time to start acting like a respectable widow instead of a lovelorn teenager. Starting right now, with a cup of tea and a couple of Panadols.

Next to the kettle, Peggy found the agenda for that night's committee meeting. She'd only glanced at it when it appeared in her mailbox yesterday, but there in black and white, after *Fundraising for the entertainment system*, and *Plumbing* was Basil's death sentence.

Clarification of the rules regarding dogs in units.

Peggy tasted bile. That miserable Sheila had had it in for Basil from the start. All along, she'd been waiting for the right ammunition. Peggy could hear her now, regaling the committee with her *near-fatal accident*. Poor Basil had eaten his last supper and smoked his last cigarette. What could she possibly do to save him?

Then she remembered hearing – somewhere between her third and fourth glasses of Napoleon – Angie's words.

Leave it to me.

~

With her arm still incarcerated in plaster, Peggy was getting impatient. There was only so much she could do with the microwave, and she was still wary after the whole beef and noodle fiasco. She was looking forward to some proper baking. She longed to crash the eggs against the side of the bowl and watch nature's perfect miracle inside slip onto the bed of powdery flour. Sam's birthday cake had been a challenge from the start, but she was hoping to produce something a little more sophisticated for the committee meeting, preferably without the fragments of blue fibreglass. She couldn't afford to gamble away Basil's future on icing sugar and sprinkles, but after several false starts and a full workout for her new list of swear words, Peggy had reluctantly settled for a packet of assorted biscuits on a nice plate. Surely the residents' committee would forgive her, just this once? No matter how hard she tried to concentrate on arranging the biscuits – overlapping like petals, in rows, in a random heap – her thoughts returned to Angie and last night. Something was playing on her mind, and it was more than the aftermath of the brandy.

Like looking behind the scenery on stage, she had glimpsed another Angie. Beneath the make-up and accessories was a woman trying to hide.

~

The Clubhouse was filling at an unhurried pace, the default at Jacaranda Retirement Village. Peggy deliberately avoided Brian's gaze but she could feel his eyes following her as she searched for a spare seat. She was nervous about projecting the right image: assertive but not difficult, with a hint of humility. The black pants seemed to fit the bill, along with the blazer over the striped boat-neck. In her ears she wore the simple pearl drop earrings that Ted had given her on their golden wedding anniversary. After last night's lipstick experiment, Peggy had chosen a simple slick of Vaseline on her lips. The hair was a different matter however, and she'd thrown caution to the wind and tousled her tips as Alessandro had instructed. With a final squirt of perfume on her neck, she was ready to face the enemy.

Waving at Jim in the corner, Peggy sat in the chair next to Brian and pretended to notice him for the first time.

'Evening Brian. I didn't see you there. How are you?'

'Very well. Very well indeed. Can I just say you look absolutely stunning tonight?'

Peggy blushed and placed the plate of biscuits in the centre of the table. Mavis did a double-take.

'Not up to your usual standard, Peggy,' said Sheila Martin. Seeing Brian's stern expression, Sheila's face softened and she added, 'Of course, you must let us know if you're having trouble coping in your current predicament. That's what the Village Wellbeing Committee is for.'

'Thank you for the kind offer, Sheila, but I'm managing just fine.' Peggy couldn't help adding, 'With the help of my friend here.' With that, she patted Brian's knee. His whole leg jerked to attention as if she'd been testing his reflexes. Peggy was about to apologise when Angie walked in, carrying a large plate.

Mavis clapped her hands and called the meeting to order. 'Take a seat, everyone. Let's get started.'

Angie removed the cling wrap from her plate to reveal a giant stack of what looked like chocolate brownies. Even Peggy had to admit they looked and smelled divine. It was difficult to imagine Angie in an apron, up to her elbows in brownie mixture, but they certainly appeared homemade. There seemed no end to this woman's talents.

'Goodness gracious. Can we all join in thanking Angie?' Mavis led the applause and pinched a brownie off the top of the stack.

'Help yourselves, everyone,' said Angie passing round the plate. 'Go on, Pegs. You *must* try one. Live a little,' she added with a wink.

Peggy took the gooey rectangle in her good hand and took a bite. Warm from the oven, the brownie melted in her mouth. The flavour was most unusual: earthy, almost grassy.

Sheila was the only one who refused a brownie. 'They're too rich for me.' She opened a small Tupperware container of egg sandwiches and placed them on the table.

'Let's get straight down to business,' said Mavis. 'Sheila, would you kindly distribute the minutes from the last meeting for approval.'

Ignoring the call to order, Jim acted as waiter, handing round Angie's brownies for second and even third helpings. Several members used the minutes as napkins, including Vince Livingstone, who wiped his mouth with a copy.

The more Mavis tried to regain order, the more animated the conversation became. It was only when Brian stood up to give his fundraising report that everyone simmered down again.

Peggy noticed Brian was wearing a new jacket, the tag still hanging from the sleeve. She wondered if she should point it out or simply give it a tug when he wasn't looking. She'd always bought Ted's clothes when he was alive, and made sure he was presentable before they went out. It was the little things that made a marriage, tiny gestures that defined love and belonging. Poor Brian. He might drive a Lexus but what he really needed was a good woman to brush his lint and detach his tags.

By the time it came to the Treasurer's report, Angie's brownies had all but disappeared. Ignoring the fidgeting around him and Mavis's derisive snorts, Brian managed to outline the account balances with barely a hitch. By the time it came to the projected costs for the new entertainment system, however, he was slurring his words. Several times, he appeared to lose his train of thought altogether. He wasn't the only one. Peggy couldn't follow what he was saying, no matter how hard she tried to concentrate on his moving lips. It was the strangest feeling. Not altogether unpleasant. Like being drunk, but slowed down to half speed.

For some reason, Peggy couldn't take her eyes off Brian's teeth. She'd never noticed before how white they were. A fleeting image of him slipping them into a plastic container by the bed hauled her back to the present.

'Is it me or is it getting stuffy in here?' It was Celia, whispering loudly from two seats away. She was right. Brian had already discarded the new jacket and even loosened his tie. Jim's boots lay discarded under his chair and he was sitting across the circle in his socks.

'Is anyone else warm?' said Celia again, interrupting Brian's turbulent flow. She stretched the neckband of her T-shirt and blew upwards lifting her white fringe.

'Where was I?' He flicked backwards and forwards through his pages before abandoning them completely. 'By my calculations, if we make the tickets twenty dollars a head including a drink and nibbles, we should have more than enough for the . . . er . . . what was it called again? The thingamajig . . .'

'The doo-dar—' shouted Celia.

'Whatchamacallit, you mean,' corrected Jim, taking his socks off now.

'So-and-so!'

'The gubbins?'

'Do you mean the doo-bree?'

Soon, there were words flying back and forth across the room, each apparently more hysterical than the last.

Brian was clearly struggling. 'I . . . um . . . where was I?'

Angie rescued him. 'What Brian is saying is that the proceeds from the fashion show will more than cover the costs of the karaoke machine. So we were thinking about giving a donation to charity with any money left over. Any suggestions?'

'How about our very own wellbeing group?' Mavis suggested. Sheila nodded in agreement.

'I think they've killed off more with their casseroles than they've saved,' chuckled Celia.

'The Blind Society?'

'Blind Drunk Society, more like.'

'What about Alzheimer's Australia?'

'Forget them!'

'Better Hearing Australia, eh Jim?'

'What was that?' Jim responded by adjusting the settings on his hearing aids, making them whistle.

Mavis clapped her hands. 'Ladies and gentlemen,' she shouted, raising her voice above the laughter and chatter. 'Let's keep to the agenda. Since you raised the question Angela, do you have a particular charity in mind for this donation?'

'The Heart Foundation,' said Angie.

Fair enough, thought Peggy. She's broken enough of them.

'Very good. Now can we please move on to the next item, which is complaints about excessive flushing of toilets during the night.' Mavis paused and reread the line. 'Yes, that's what it says here.'

The room fell quiet. All eyes were on Mavis as her bottom lip began to quiver. Without warning, Madam Chair slapped her hands hard down on her lap and howled with laughter. This set Celia off, closely followed by Brian and Jim. Peggy joined in. Her sides ached as she struggled to take a breath.

Sheila was the only one not laughing. 'I don't get it,' she said. 'Can someone explain the joke to me?'

'What joke?' said Mavis, and off she went again, giant guffaws gushing from her.

'What's going on?' It was Christine the village manager, standing in the doorway in her red jacket. 'There have been complaints about the noise.'

'We were just discussing the plumbing,' said Brian, stony-faced, before he too crumpled. 'It's number one and two on the agenda.' He slapped his own knee as he delivered the punchline.

Committee meetings were never usually this relaxed. This mellow. This hilarious.

Christine glanced over to the bar and back to the table. There were no indicting bottles or glasses on the table, only an empty white plate and a few crumbs.

Peggy turned to Angie, narrowing her eyes. 'What did you put in those brownies?'

'Never you mind,' she replied. 'Tonight is about Basil.'

The room fell silent again. The teacher had walked in on the class mucking up. Christine scanned the chastened members, searching for the culprits. 'Now that I'm here, perhaps I can read out the remaining items on the agenda. It's past seven o'clock and I need to go home.'

A chorus of sorrys followed. Celia pulled up a spare chair for Christine. Brian offered her Peggy's plate of untouched biscuits.

'Bikkie?' he said, trying not to giggle.

There were several stifled sniggers around the room and some exaggerated whispering.

'Moving on,' said Christine inspecting the list. 'The third item on the agenda is a request for clarification regarding the rules for keeping pets in units. In particular, I believe this applies to dogs.'

Sheila abandoned her egg sandwich and sat to attention.

'As far as the management are concerned, we are prepared to look at this on a case-by-case basis. I have been made aware of a serious incident involving an unleashed dog that caused a head-on collision between a car and a wall. My job is to ensure the health and safety for all residents of this village. The human residents, that is. That said, the statutes on matters of this nature state that it is up to the residents' committee to decide on any change in the regulations.'

Peggy swallowed hard. Basil's fate now lay in the hands of this group of giggling Gerties. Apart from Jim, who had fallen asleep, Peggy noticed everyone staring at her. The entire village knew about the to-do with Sheila's car.

'I suggest we put it to the vote, ladies and gentlemen,' said Christine. 'Those in favour of dogs who are currently resident in the village being allowed to stay – under full supervision at *all* times – please raise your hands.'

Peggy's hand shot straight up, followed by Brian's and Celia's. Angie nudged Jim awake and the two of them put up their hands. That left Sheila, Vince and Sylvia Livingstone, Pat Pritchett who, after her cataract operation, could now spot dog excrement from a mile, and Mavis. It was a draw.

'This is outrageous!' Angie shot up from her seat and swayed a little. 'How could you possibly vote to remove a poor defenceless dog? He's no different to the rest of us. He's old and frail, blind and deaf. Every day he wakes and wonders whether it might be his last. Yes, he sometimes wanders off or doesn't look where he's going. So do half the residents here. Are we suggesting we get rid of them too? So, he's not as fast as he used to be because his knees and hips are stiff. Hands up anyone here who doesn't ache on cold mornings or have to get up ten times a night. Who here hasn't wished they'd make a mobile phone that's easy to use, or write songs with proper words?'

Vince nodded. Mavis stared at her feet.

Angie hadn't finished. 'Who among us hasn't wanted a wider parking spot or wished someone would explain the iCloud? And which of us hear perfectly well as long as other people speak clearly?'

You could hear a pin drop, almost.

'We are already invisible to the rest of society. I say, let's stick together. Let's stand up for one another and celebrate our wisdom and experience. Let's look after each other. Let us show some compassion to humans and dogs alike, and leave the old boy to enjoy his twilight years in peace.'

There was silence around the table. Angie sat down, then suddenly leapt up again.

'And one more thing. If Basil goes, I go.' She picked up the empty plate from the table and added, 'And I'm taking the special brownie recipe with me.'

With that, Mavis's hand shot up.

24

Deny, Deny, Deny

PEGGY WAS TUCKING INTO HER THIRD ROUND OF TOAST when she heard the front door open. She was unusually peckish this morning, and if the empty biscuit packet on the bedside table was anything to go by, during the night as well.

'Hello Mum.'

It was Jenny. She was early. Twenty-four hours early.

'Jenny, darling! I wasn't expecting you until tomorrow.' *Or thereabouts.*

'Slight change of plans. I stayed with Dave and Mel last night. I tried to call you yesterday.'

Peggy was instantly suspicious. They rarely spoke, except at Christmas and on birthdays. It broke Peggy's heart how the siblings had grown apart. Until now. It all seemed a bit too cosy to be accidental. 'Would you like a cup of tea, sweetheart?'

'I'll make it,' said Jenny, bending to kiss her mother on the cheek. 'You just sit there and take it easy.'

Peggy groaned inwardly. Before the day was out, they would be having words.

'How did you get in?' She may have been stoned last night, but Peggy was sure she'd locked her door.

'David and I had keys cut,' replied Jenny, reaching into the cupboard for a spare mug and bringing it to the table.

'What for?'

'Just in case.'

'In case of what?'

'Emergencies, Mum. It's nothing for you to worry about.'

It was all very well, but Peggy wasn't sure she liked the idea of the children walking in unannounced whenever they felt like it.

'You should have asked me first,' she said, helping herself to another slice of toast from the rack. 'About the key.'

Imagine if Jenny had walked in and discovered a trail of discarded clothes: the new jacket with the tag on the sleeve, and the boatneck in a heap. She tried to shake away the image, but it had already snagged itself on her consciousness. She doubted Brian was even capable of strewing clothes. She pictured his pants, neatly folded along the creases, at the foot of her bed.

'In view of recent *events*,' Jenny directed her gaze to the cast on Peggy's wrist, 'I think it's best to be prepared for all eventualities.'

'It was an accident.'

'My very point, Mother. Next time it could be a hip and then you'll really be in trouble.'

'But I'm always so careful.' Peggy wondered if Jenny had spotted the walker gathering dust behind the front door.

'Nan said the same thing before she went into the nursing home.'

'Jenny, darling, for your information, I am not planning another fall.'

'It's not like anyone plans to have a fall, do they? Anyway, I've applied for one of those Vital Call systems to be installed. You wear a button on a cord around your neck at all times.'

Like a noose.

'Why don't you make yourself some toast, Jenny? There's plenty more bread in the freezer.'

'No, thank you. We'd better hurry. Our appointment with Dr Lim is at nine o'clock.'

Whatever did she mean, *our* appointment?

~

'You go ahead and find a seat in the waiting room. I'll catch you up,' said Jenny when they reached the foyer.

'Where are you going?'

'I want to have a word with Christine in the office.'

Peggy's stomach rolled. Something was going on. Something she wasn't privy to. Was this the dreaded day Jenny took her for that little drive, never to return? If that was the case, she wasn't going without a fight. She'd chain herself to the front desk in protest, and shout for equality like a suffragette. *Votes for the elderly! Seniors' rights!* If that failed, she'd phone the Elder Abuse Line. At least they were paid to listen.

The waiting room was empty when Peggy arrived. It was only five to. She opened a magazine and tried not to look at the minute hand marching around the clock on the wall.

There was no sign of the other committee members. She imagined them all having a lie-in after last night's shenanigans. She'd left Jim, Celia and Angie raiding the Clubhouse bar for snacks. Overwhelmed with relief at Basil's stay of execution, Peggy had fallen into a fitful sleep.

Jenny's face was pinched when she returned and sat stiffly next to Peggy. She looked furious.

'It says here that David Attenborough is turning ninety this year,' said Peggy. 'There's a picture of him abseiling. I think I might give it a try.' Her attempts to lighten the mood were met by a stony silence. It was like waiting outside the headmaster's office, not knowing what she'd done wrong.

On the dot of nine, Dr Stephen opened the clinic door. He extended his hand towards Jenny and said, 'Lovely to finally meet you.'

Finally meet her? The sight of the lovely young doctor, usually so reassuring, filled her with a sense of impending doom. All along, he'd been a double agent in disguise.

'Come in, Peggy. Have a seat.' He gestured to the chair closest to his desk. *The hot seat.* 'How have things been?'

Things? What things? Suddenly, she was tiptoeing through a minefield. Now more than ever she needed to be at the top of her ladder.

'Great. Really, really good,' she said, with exaggerated cheer.

'Any problems to report?'

Deny, deny, deny. That was the best piece of advice she'd been given since arriving in the village.

'None. Nil. Zip. Zilch.'

Peggy noticed Dr Stephen glance at Jenny. Evidently, they weren't here about her ears.

'That's not quite true is it, Mother?'

Peggy fiddled with a loose piece of skin on her finger. 'I don't know what you're talking about.'

'I'm worried my mother might be overdoing things, Doctor. Apparently, she's been having a few late nights.'

'It was a committee meeting, darling.'

'And I hear you've been letting Basil run amok. He caused a—'

'Near-fatal accident?' *Not quite fatal enough.* 'It's all been horribly exaggerated. There was a secret plot to evict my little dog. Sheila Martin's to blame. It's really me she's trying to get rid of. Basil is just the escaped goat.'

'I see.' Dr Stephen fingered his chin. 'You do seem a little paranoid,' he said in a calculated tone Peggy hadn't heard him use before. 'Has there been anything else directed against you lately? Any other secret plots for instance?'

'Apart from my children plotting to put me in a nursing home, you mean?'

'That's not true, Mother. We're happy for you to stay here in the village as long as you're safe.'

'I am safe.' Peggy tried to hide her arm cast under her handbag.

'I must admit, I was concerned after the fall,' said Dr Stephen. 'But you seem to be doing fine now.'

Good. He was back on her side.

'Doctor, I'm worried my mother will have another fall and break a hip.'

'We wouldn't want that,' said Dr Stephen. On Jenny's side again.

'I'm fine. Look,' said Peggy, jumping up so quickly from her chair that Dr Stephen recoiled and dropped his pen.

She spread her arms wide to demonstrate her fine-ness. She managed to sit down again just as the blood started to drain from her head.

'Mum, calm down. Look, David and I are worried about you. We've noticed you've been behaving out of character.' Jenny reached into her handbag and pulled out a sheet of paper. She unfolded it and handed it to the doctor. 'Here, this is what I was telling you about.'

Ha! So they had been talking behind her back. Peggy folded her arms and knitted her eyebrows into a frown.

The doctor read without looking up. After a few minutes, he cleared his throat. 'Alright, shall we go through a few of the symptoms, and see if they apply to you?'

'Symptoms of what?' she asked.

'We'll get to that in a moment,' said Jenny. 'Just listen.'

Dr Stephen began. 'It says here, "lack of inhibition", "more extroverted", "socially inappropriate behaviour", "acting impulsively", "spending excessive amounts of money", "increased interest in sex".'

Peggy felt her skin burn. Jenny must have noticed her new wardrobe, and no doubt heard about her new circle of friends. She was sure David and Mel would have also filled her in about Brian.

Dr Stephen read from the list, pausing to study Peggy's expression and tick his list. Craving for sweet foods. Excessive consumption of alcohol or cigarettes. He paused and looked up. 'You don't smoke or drink, do you, Peggy?'

Deny, deny, deny. 'I'm a social drinker only,' she said. *An extremely social drinker.*

Jenny took the piece of paper out of the doctor's hands and leaned over to show him a sentence she had underlined. In red.

'Often the individual will lack insight into the change in their behaviour,' she read.

Dr Stephen seemed at a loss, sinking beneath the weight of evidence.

'Am I allowed to ask what's going on?' asked Peggy. 'What is it that I'm supposed to have?'

'I'm afraid these are the symptoms of Frontal Lobe Dementia.'

'You have all the symptoms, Mum. I looked them up.'

'Dementia? We discussed my memory last week. You told me I was just fuzzy from the new tablets.'

This couldn't be happening. For once, Peggy didn't feel old. So what if she'd lost her inhibitions? She wished she'd lost them years ago. Admittedly, she had been both drunk and stoned this week, but desperate times called for desperate measures. She was having fun at last. As for thinking about sex all the time, if she were twenty-nine instead of seventy-nine, it would be considered completely normal. Talk about hypocritical.

Jenny jumped in. 'Remember how Nan wrote that cheque to the RSPCA and gave all her silver to the cleaning lady?'

Peggy did remember. It had cost them more than the silver was worth just to get it back. Mr Parsons, the family solicitor, had insisted they pursue it. He'd redecorated his office with the proceeds.

'Jenny is right, in the sense that planning for the future would be sensible,' said Dr Stephen. 'Whether you have early dementia, Frontal Lobe or otherwise, it's never too early to set your affairs in order. To begin with, it would be wise to appoint a power of attorney and enduring guardian, while you have full capacity to make your own decisions. I suggest it to all my patients.'

Peggy felt betrayed. They were ganging up on her. She was outnumbered. This time, there was no Angie to save her.

~

The brass bell heralded the end of recess and a crescendo of rattling chains and tumbling water from the overhead cisterns. Peggy held her breath as the last cubicle door slammed and the chatter died away. With only the trickling sound of water as the last cistern filled, Peggy breathed again, releasing a string of sobs.

'Who's in that end one?'

Peggy froze.

'Dunno, but she's been in there for ages.'

'Have a look under the door.'

Peggy's nails bored into her damp palms and she screwed her eyes shut. In her lap, wrapped in white toilet paper, was her shameful secret.

She opened one eye to see a smirking face peering under the bottom of the door.

'It's Peggy Pee-Pants!'

More faces. Squeals of laughter.

'Pee-Pants, Pee-Pants, Pee-Pants', they chanted.

Tears pricked. Peggy curled her toes inside the brown shoes that were a size too small, a hand-me-down from an older girl. 'You'll have to make do for now,' her mother had said. Peggy could almost hear her add, 'blame your father,' his industries as a husband and provider by default falling continually short of his wife's expectations.

Sister Agnes's thunderous rebuke sent the tormentors scurrying back to class. Peggy imagined their sniggers and stares, their sharp rulers in her back, their whispered goading. They were right – she was a freak, a defective. Was it any wonder she had no friends?

Peggy Pee-Pants.

She had to run away. She could hide behind the bike sheds. Squeeze through the gap in the fence. Disappear forever. Never come back to this stupid school.

Peggy eased the cubicle door open and peered out, across to the row of sinks. Someone had left a tap running. Peggy crept out, clutching her underwear.

'You're new, aren't you?'

Peggy spun around. Behind her stood a dark-haired girl she recognised from her class. She'd seen the girl watching her, but she'd been too shy to smile or say hello.

Eyes lowered, Peggy nodded.

'What's that?' The girl pointed to the bundle in Peggy's hand.

'Nothing.'

'Did you have an accident?'

Peggy mumbled, but nothing coherent came out.

'Come with me,' the girl said, taking Peggy's hand in hers. 'I'll take you to the office. The nurse is really nice.'

Peggy's damp thighs rubbed together as they headed towards the school office. The girl's hand was cool, her fingers slender around Peggy's knuckles.

'I'm Angela,' said the girl. 'You can call me Angie.'

~

'We're wasting the doctor's precious time, Jenny.' *And mine.*

The fashion show was only days away and she still hadn't decided on her hot fillings. With hindsight, it had been a mistake to ask about any dietary requirements when people booked their tickets. It was turning out to be more complicated than Sam's birthday party.

Jenny's voice brought her back to the present. 'Are you listening, Mum? This is important. If you do have dementia, David and I will have to make provisions.'

The walking frame, the Vital Call, the duplicate keys. What other instruments of torture would they conjure up between them? Her freedom was slipping away, one independence aid at a time. She felt as if she was looking at her life through the wrong end of a telescope, surveying her lengthening past and her ever-shrinking future.

'There's only one way to settle this, once and for all,' said Peggy. 'Test me.'

'Are you sure?' Dr Stephen looked hesitant.

Stupid mare. Her memory was like a sieve. She'd complained to him about it only a week ago, and still cross-checked her calendar with her Webster-pak every morning. What was she thinking? On the other hand, it might finally give her the chance to prove herself. It was a gamble, but if it paid off, David and Jenny might leave her alone.

'If I pass, will you both agree I'm capable of making my own decisions?'

Dr Stephen nodded. Jenny glanced anxiously between her mother and the doctor.

'We just want you to be safe,' she said.

Safe. There was that word again. Life was full of four-letter words at seventy-nine – safe, slow, pain – each a ball and chain to weigh her down. How much more fun with only three.

Gin. Pot. Sex.

Ted. He was the best three letters of all. What would have been his advice on the matter? *A ship is safe in harbour, but that's not what ships are for.*

'Well,' said Peggy. 'What are we waiting for?'

'Don't be offended if you find some of the questions a little basic,' said Dr Stephen. 'It's a standard test. Same for everyone.'

Peggy adjusted her glasses. 'Ready,' she said enthusiastically. She loved quiz shows and had often imagined herself under a spotlight, one answer away from winning a fortune.

'What day is it?' The test had started.

Not exactly the million-dollar question, but to her dismay, Peggy's mind was blank. She tried to visualise her Webster-pak.

'Thursday?' she said, searching the doctor's face for any reaction.

'What is the season?'

Peggy thought back to her shopping expedition with Angie and Arabella's insistence she return soon to view the new summer collection. 'Spring.'

The doctor ticked his sheet. 'What is the date?'

The nineteenth? Or twenty-something? There was a net curtain between her and the answer. Her eyes found the calendar hanging on the wall behind Dr Stephen's head. She'd never paid much attention to it when Dr Cranky-Pantski was the village doctor. Back then, there was barely time to sit down, let alone admire the walls, before she was calling for the next patient. It was a calendar of European cities, Peggy now saw. There was a moment of sadness as she remembered the brochures she'd pored over, planning a river cruise with Ted. She'd thrown them out as soon as she'd got back from the hospital.

Prague was September's city, judging by the bridges. Now, September rang a bell for some reason. Sam's birthday was in September. That was last weekend. Which made today . . .

'Seventeenth.' Peggy was cautiously optimistic. Strictly speaking, she knew she was cheating, but to cheat properly, she'd have to line up all her marbles in the correct order. Which was even harder than knowing the answer.

She reeled off the answers to the next set of questions using a similar strategy. It was only when they reached the counting section, and Dr Stephen asked her to subtract seven from one hundred, then seven from that number and so on, that she lost her momentum. Ted was the mathematician, not her. Numbers and bills were his department. Letters and words, hers.

Sudoku, Ted.

Crosswords, Peggy.

Bins, Ted.

Laundry, Peggy.

After five answers, Dr Stephen stopped her and wrote something on his paper, his expression impossible to read. He'd have made a good poker player. Jenny's face, however, was taut and strained.

'I'd like you to repeat the three objects I gave you to remember earlier,' said Dr Stephen over the top of his spectacles.

What three objects? She couldn't remember him giving her anything. The spotlight was on her. Peggy Smart was only a couple of questions away from the jackpot. Or a nursing home.

Think, woman. Think.

'Can you name any of them?'

'Apple,' said Peggy.

'Correct.'

Really? She was guessing. 'Table?'

'Good.' Another guess. Another tick. How bizarre.

'And the last one?'

'Penny.' Where had that come from?

Dr Stephen handed over his pen and pushed a blank sheet of paper in front of her. 'I'd like you to write a sentence. Anything you like.'

'A sentence, did you say?'

'Whatever comes to mind.'

Perhaps it was some sort of free-association test. She thought for a moment. How hard was it to string a few words together? She'd always been good at writing at school, praised for her neat cursive hand. Hell, if it hadn't been for her father's stroke, she would have been a teacher.

Today is going to be wet.

The letters were shaky, her handwriting was as leaky as her bladder these days. She hoped Dr Stephen would appreciate her sense of humour and award her bonus marks.

'Last one. A bit of drawing for you. I'd like you to copy this diagram.'

Peggy baulked. She hated drawing. Looking at the two intersecting pentagons on the piece of paper, she felt her palms turn slippery. She could almost feel Ted there, standing behind her. 'Here, leave it to me, love,' he was saying.

It was a little shaky, but the first pentagon emerged from the tip of the ballpoint pen with relative ease. Peggy anchored the paper with her cast.

Concentrate.

One, two, three, four, five. Five sides, five points. It wasn't pretty, but she'd done it.

Dr Stephen ticked the final box and totted up the score.

'Did she pass?' Jenny wriggled impatiently in her chair, like she used to when she was small.

'I have some good news and some bad news.'

'What does that mean?' Peggy was confused. Did she have dementia or not?

'The good news is that according to this test, there's nothing wrong with your memory.'

'And the bad?'

'The bad news is your maths is terrible.'

Peggy threw her arms around Dr Stephen. 'Thank you, thank you.' Peggy's tears tumbled onto his shoulder, proud that she'd found the courage to stand up for herself, first to her mother and now to her daughter.

Game, set, checkmate.

Jenny's face sharpened, puncturing Peggy's victory bubble.

The war was far from won.

25

Nanna Nap

PEGS DARLING, IT'S ME AGAIN. THIS IS GETTING RIDICULOUS. *You really need to start using that mobile phone of yours. I'll pick you up at one so that we can meet Arabella to go through the final selection for the fashion show. Then I'll take you to get that piss-awful thing taken off your arm. Just want to check that the fracture clinic appointment is four-thirty, yeah?*

Morning Maggie, Jim speaking. I can't remember what time we'd arranged to meet to go over the music for the show. Could you give me a call. My number's 9 . . . er. Now hang on a sec . . .

Celia here. Can't get hold of Angie. We need to talk chairs.

Hello, Peggy. I just thought I'd inform you that we've sold all the tickets for the show. I thought you should know

*for the catering. Hope you're well. See you later. Looking
forward to it. The fashion show, that is. And seeing you.
Very much looking forward to seeing you. Goodbye. By the
way, it's Brian Cornell here.*

Peggy played the last message several times then accidentally
deleted it. Darn answerphone machine.

With only a few days left until the fashion show, the
village was a hive of activity. Angie was playing queen bee,
gathering and dispatching her workers on various errands.
'Darling, it will be fabulous. Trust me.'

After hearing Angie proclaim the imminent fabulousness
for the dozenth time, Peggy was beginning to have doubts.
Like everyone else, she'd assumed there were no limits to
her friend's energy and drive. Once or twice, however, Peggy
had caught her nipping back to her unit after lunch. It was
a worry. Angie wasn't the nanna-nap type.

The jitters had started in earnest after the last committee
meeting, hastily convened in Celia's kitchen. With the entire
project so far behind schedule, Celia had brought out the
whole brandy bottle, an afternoon tea of scones and jam
turning into sundowners with savoury snacks as they tried
to smooth out the last-minute wrinkles. Some time later,
having laid waste to the refreshments, both sweet and salty,
they'd agreed to a run-through on the morning of the show,
using Peggy as co-ordinator.

But there was something else playing on Peggy's mind.
The elephant in the room had grown into a woolly mammoth
since the evening of the hidden photographs. It was becoming
harder and harder to broach the subject of Simon and
whatever it was that Angie had wanted to tell her about

him that was so important. With all the last-minute preparations for the fundraiser, getting Angie alone was proving
a challenge.

At least Jenny was staying away. Her last visit had been
mercifully short thanks to a pregnant Alpaca who was due to
give birth imminently. Jenny had rushed back to the farm
to help Eve with the midwifery duties, promising to keep
Peggy updated about the arrival of her first 'grand-Alpaca'.

'Good luck with the fashion show, Mum. I'll call David
and line up an appointment with the solicitor for as soon
as it's over,' Jenny had shouted through the wound-down
window as she waited for the air-conditioning to kick in.
The car was caked in red dust and some bright spark in the
village had written *clean me* on the back window. Peggy had
smiled to herself. It was the kind of thing Celia would do.

As she pulled away Jenny had added, 'There's nothing for
you to worry about.' Up until that moment, Peggy hadn't
been worried.

At last, six weeks were up and she was excited about
having her plaster cast removed. With her hatchback gathering bird droppings at the side of the road, Peggy was
looking forward to getting back behind the wheel. It meant
the end of the lifts in the Lexus for now, but Brian's heated
seat would always be there if her bottom ever got cold.
Ironically, had she not fallen over and broken her arm, she
would never have made the wonderful new friends in the
committee. They were a silver lining in more ways than one.
On the surface, these pensioners had little more in common
than their final address, and yet they would always share
a special bond.

For better, for worse.

For richer, for poorer.

In sickness and in health.

'Til death do us part.

~

Arabella greeted them as if they'd met on the red carpet at Cannes, air kisses for both Angie and Peggy this time.

'Darling! You look simply exquisite. I just love the hair.' Arabella kissed her fingers like a chef inspecting the perfect soufflé. 'Very Helen Mirren.'

'I wasn't sure at first, but it's growing on me.'

'Darling, you're so funny.' Arabella laughed and patted the bemused Peggy on the shoulder. 'I've got just the thing to show it off. Follow me.'

In the centre of the shop the polished mahogany top of the large circular table was covered in piles of neatly folded knitwear. Arabella picked out a yellow cardigan and unfastened the buttons. 'Here, this would look divine on you.'

The cardigan was so soft and so weightless, Peggy feared it might float right out of her hands.

'It comes with a little matching sleeveless top.'

'Twin sets are so this season,' said Angie.

Peggy wondered if Angie remembered that fateful day at Blake's, when Mr Hawley caught her showing off with the Hermès scarf.

'All the way from New York comes this elegant cardigan in pure Merino wool,' said Peggy swinging the cardigan across her shoulders.

To her astonishment, Angie replied, 'Team it with a simple sweater in emerald or Windsor pink.'

She remembered every word. They smiled at each other, lost in the memory. Peggy had no idea at the time that the shy Ted, hovering in the background with his ladder, would eventually become her husband and the father of her children.

'You must have it, Peggy, I insist,' said Angie.

'No,' replied Peggy. 'Not unless I pay for it myself.'

Arabella took the cardigan to the counter. 'I'll work something out for you,' she said. 'Mates' rates. Here, I'll throw in this scarf too.' Peggy wanted to protest. She didn't need charity, but she had to admit the silk scarf went perfectly with the cardigan. 'Let me wrap this up and then I'll show you what I've chosen for the fashion show.'

In the storage area at the back of the shop, Arabella had prepared three racks of clothes.

'This is my signature range. This is my new affordable range, and this is the men's range,' she said, pointing to each in turn.

'Men's range?' Peggy was thrown. She hadn't really thought about dressing the gentlemen of the village. Then she remembered Brian and his hanging tag.

'You'll have to find a couple of willing men to model.'

Jim was the natural choice; he at least had a chest that was still wider than his middle, and Brian always took pride in his appearance. They'd need to make separate changing areas for the men and women, naturally. Peggy saw Angie wilt fractionally, as she added another job to her endless list.

'Arabella darling, you're too generous,' said Angie, flicking through the garments in the racks. 'This is all so perfect for the fashion show.'

'Sweetie, it's not like I'm doing it purely out of the goodness of my heart. I am hoping to launch the two new ranges and bag a few sales on the evening.'

There was so much riding on the success of the fashion show, both for the village social scene and Arabella's business. The ticket sales had already exceeded projected numbers, which boded well for the karaoke machine, but the pressure was on to deliver. Peggy was confident she could handle the catering, once she had two hands again, but didn't know the first thing about the catwalk. None of them did, except Angie. She alone was the life force of the event, but her battery appeared to be running low.

~

It was after six when they finally left the hospital minus the piss-awful cast. Peggy had recoiled at the plaster saw, but once the technician had demonstrated it on his own wrist, she'd relaxed enough for him to go ahead.

The sight of the pale shrivelled skin on her forearm was both a relief and a disappointment. Her wrist bones still looked a little misshapen, but a quick twist and turn revealed the limb was perfectly functional.

Peggy had reached the Mini first, surprised to find Angie dawdling some distance behind. When she did catch up, she struggled to find the car keys in her handbag. Since the latchkey incidents, Peggy had attached her own keys to an old egg whisk. It made it much easier to find them in a hurry, although she'd attracted some funny looks.

It might be her imagination, but Peggy had found a distinct improvement in her bladder-works in the past few weeks. Somehow, she'd accidentally discovered the panacea, some elusive strategy that had evaded her since third grade. She still hadn't called the continence nurse, and the magic bullet had completely missed its target, but something had changed. Whether it was all the laughter with Angie that had toned her pelvic muscles, or simply the fact that she'd been too busy to cave in to the endless demands from her southern regions, she wasn't sure. But like all attention-seeking behaviour, whether it be from small children, puppies or human organs, ignoring it had proved more effective than pandering to it. Peggy felt relaxed, happy and finally in control of her life. And for once, her bladder agreed.

The effort of locating the keys seemed to exhaust Angie. It wasn't surprising, that bag weighed more than she did, thought Peggy. 'What do you keep in that thing?'

'Essentials,' replied Angie, smiling weakly. 'Would you drive, Pegs? I don't feel up to it.'

Peggy adjusted the driver's seat backwards and forwards until she was happy. She was surprised to discover that her legs were several inches longer than Angie's, having always considered herself the dumpy one. All along, she'd mistaken skinniness for tallness. In fact, Angie appeared to be shrinking in front of her eyes, appearing almost childlike in her own passenger seat.

The sporty little engine sprang to life and Peggy couldn't resist shouting 'Woo-hoo!' as the car shot forward under her right foot. This was so much more fun than her boring hatch-back. She sensed a whole new chapter of ageing disgracefully opening up ahead of her.

'I think I might buy myself a two-seater,' she said. 'Do you think I'm too old to go topless?'

'It'd certainly raise a few eyebrows in the village, Pegs.'

Under normal circumstances, Angie would be suggesting they detour immediately via a car showroom, but she seemed to have nodded off in the passenger seat. At the first set of traffic lights, Peggy even leaned over to check she was still breathing. Organising the fashion show was taking it out of her. Even Angie Valentine it seemed, had a limit.

'Do you want me to call Dr Lim when we get back?'

Angie opened her eyes. 'No,' she said, forcing a smile. 'I just need an early night. I'll be fine by tomorrow.'

A sinkhole of unease opened within Peggy and Angie was falling into it. It was the same feeling she'd had while waiting for the results of Ted's scan.

'Do you want me to come in with you?' said Peggy when she stopped the engine outside Angie's unit.

'Stop fussing, woman. I'm fine.'

Deny, deny, deny. She was playing Peggy at her own game.

'I'll call later to see how you're feeling.'

'If it'll make you feel better.'

Some folk at the village talked of nothing but their ailments, treating illness like a competitive sport. Angie was different. She'd breathed new life into the village. It was as though she'd opened the door of a stale room and filled it with fresh air, sticking two fingers up at old age. Hers was a logic that was difficult to argue with.

Dicky knee? Big deal, get a new one.

Grey hair? Embrace it or dye it.

Glass half empty? Pour it into a smaller glass.

The first drops of rain landed like tears on the Mini's dusty windscreen. In the distance, water fell in cloudy stripes from the sky. They were in for a drenching. Best hurry and get Angie inside.

Peggy returned the driver's seat to its original position, made sure all the windows were up and locked the car. Her fingers worried at the key fob as she watched Angie shuffle to her front door, dragging the gargantuan handbag behind her like a wheeled shopping trolley. She looked frail and diminished and, for the first time, old.

26

In Search of a Thirty-Six Waist and a Decent Backside

WITH THE LAST OF THE MINI QUICHES ARRANGED ON A platter and covered with cling wrap, Peggy made herself a congratulatory cup of tea and kicked off her slippers. Sitting at the kitchen table, she surveyed her efforts. Every work surface was filled with plates of food, all ready to go. Her wrist was a little sore after the whipping and chopping, but she felt almost giddy with achievement.

The countdown had begun and with a matter of hours before the start of the fashion show, the social committee was engrossed in the final preparations. With Angie yet to show her face, Brian had stepped in as project manager. He was the obvious choice; all those end-of-financial-year tax returns the perfect training for an unfolding catastrophe. He'd even roped in two handsome grandsons to help, sending Peggy into an unexpected hot flush. One was billeted to tickets and crowd control, the other was helping Jim set up a borrowed PA system in the community centre.

Basil lay in his basket, half asleep. He hadn't been himself either this week. Twice, he'd left his mince and potatoes. Peggy even made gravy and mashed his potatoes with butter, but it hadn't piqued his appetite. She wondered if he might be missing Angie. He always seemed to come to life when she was around. Everyone did. Maybe he just needed some vitamins, or a tonic to perk him up. She remembered her mother asking the doctor for a tonic many years ago. He'd prescribed her something she had made up at the chemist. Nowadays, it was all about talking.

There was no point leaving yet another message. Peggy listened to Angie's chirpy voice, then the beep. She was a fine one to talk about never answering her phone. Peggy had called her last night before she went to bed. Then, at least, Angie had answered and reported feeling a little better. Tired-sounding, but apparently she'd eaten some leftover frittata, whatever that was, and it was working. But Peggy had tossed and turned all night, unable to quell her misgivings. In the end, she must have fallen asleep because she dreamed she'd made Ted a shepherd's pie topped with mashed bananas.

Replacing the handset in its holder, Peggy noticed a bottle of cooking sherry on the open shelf above the fridge. A tiny glass wouldn't do any harm, surely? Dutch courage. She was feeling all fluttery without Angie on hand. It dawned on her how much she'd come to rely on her friend, not just for fashion advice, alcohol and illicit drugs but also for company and moral support.

Peggy blew the dust off one of her Waterford crystal glasses and poured two fat fingers' worth.

Double Dutch.

~

The plan was for the models to meet at five for hair and make-up, and for Arabella to choose each a suitable outfit. There were separate areas curtained off for changing, one for the men and one for the ladies.

It wasn't long before the plan started to unravel. The run-through earlier that day had been a waste of time, without models or clothes. There were only so many times Celia could test the stage and rearrange the plastic chairs while Jim tried to untangle the extension lead. And now Arabella had arrived early, throwing the community centre into chaos. Brian sent his grandsons to carry the industrial-sized racks of clothes from a white van to the changing area. Meanwhile, Arabella set to work ruffling feathers backstage.

Peggy did her best to keep everyone calm. 'What can I do to help?' With Angie still missing-in-action despite a dozen phone calls and an unanswered knock on the front door, the responsibility of managing Arabella had fallen on her shoulders by default.

'Where is my size fourteen?' shouted Arabella, clicking her fingers.

Celia stood to attention. 'That'd be me.'

Without asking, Arabella lifted Celia's loose-fitting top and spun her through a full revolution before tutting. 'Darling, you're a twelve with saddlebags.'

'What's the difference?' Celia crossed her arms in a fit of pique.

'*Gapage*, sweetie. It's fashion we're showing off here, not camping equipment.'

This was a nightmare. Angie was supposed to have arranged all the models and lined up the outfits on the rack so that everyone knew exactly what to wear in which order. Without her, it was one giant muddle of flounced hems and crinkle cotton. Chaos. A shemozzle.

Peggy stepped forward. 'What about me? I could breathe in.'

'I'm not being funny, Peggy. We're talking the activewear collection here. Just stick to the jersey wrap dress like we agreed and find me someone who has actual knees. And while you're at it, find me my size eight.'

'An eight?' Would she like Peggy to conjure up a pink unicorn too?

'Quick, get me a skinny Minnie, now!'

Women like Arabella – like Angie – didn't take no for an answer. It was futile to protest. 'Give me ten minutes,' said Peggy.

'Five, you have precisely five minutes. And send in my first man. I want a thirty-six-inch waist and a decent backside.'

'Don't we all,' said Celia, propping the mirror up against one wall.

'Can I help?' Brian poked his head through the curtains. 'We're all set up out here, so I'm all yours.'

I'm all yours. Was it Peggy's imagination or had Brian held her gaze for a fraction too long?

Suddenly, every sense was heightened. She could hear Jim testing the microphone in one ear, and the chatter of the lorikeets in the grevillea outside in the other. She could smell Brian's aftershave: mint, lavender, coriander and rosemary. Peggy could even taste the peppery bubbles of champagne on her tongue.

'Good,' she said, 'I need you.' *I do need you.*

Brian tensed and, even in the dim light of the changing room, Peggy saw him blush.

'Four minutes,' shouted Arabella from behind one of the racks. 'And counting . . .'

'It's Angie, she's not here yet. She was supposed to organise the models. We're running out of time, and Arabella is about to flip her tiara.'

'Should I go and look for her?' Brian looked worried, which panicked Peggy even more.

'No, it's better that you stay here. I'll find Arabella her models, then head over to Angie's unit.'

'Do you think she's okay?'

She won't be when I get my hands on her, thought Peggy. 'She's probably getting ready as we speak.' She pictured Angie standing in front of her mirror, grouting her face with Estée Lauder. She wished she'd hurry up.

Brian didn't sound convinced. 'I'll key Jim up to act as host. Just in case.'

'Jim? Do you think that's wise?'

'He's spent his whole life on stage. He loves an audience.'

'Yes, but he's not as sharp as he was back in his heyday.'

'It's too late now,' said Brian. 'People have started to arrive.'

He opened the curtains a fraction to show Peggy the gathering crowd. With no fixed seating, the early birds were already jockeying for the best vantage positions. There, sitting in the front row, were Mavis and Sheila.

'This whole thing is a complete fiasco. I'm going to make an executive decision, Brian,' she said. 'Will you back me up?'

'Always,' replied Brian with a smile that turned Peggy's insides into a self-saucing chocolate pudding.

'Three minutes!' called Arabella.

Peggy weaved her way through the chairs towards the front row. She arranged her face into a pastiche of calm and perched on an empty seat next to Mavis.

'Ladies, how are we this evening?'

'Very well, thank you. How is it all going back there, Peggy? Everything under control?'

Typical Mavis. She'd love to see them fail. She must be dying to prove their complete and utter incompetence. Any excuse to step in and take control. It must be killing her, having to sit back and spectate from the sidelines.

'Of course. Absolutely everything is one hundred percent under control.'

'We can't wait to see what you've all come up with,' said Mavis. 'I take it Angie will be compering, as it was all her idea?'

Peggy couldn't tell her they were missing their mistress of ceremonies as well as their models. So far, the guests had paid twenty dollars for a finger-food buffet and a line of coat hangers. At this rate, there would be no fashion show. And no karaoke machine. She had to think of something. Fast.

'We have Jim mainlining tonight,' said Peggy.

Mavis raised her crayoned brows.

Sheila sneered. 'We're looking forward to seeing the models all dressed up, aren't we Mavis? It was such a good idea to include the men.'

The men.

Peggy felt a nibble at her hook. It was starting to make sense now. All along, the unpleasantness over Basil wasn't about the dog. It was about Brian. Peggy wasn't the only one who fantasised about Jacaranda Retirement Village's most eligible widower. The truth arrived with a side order of mischief, as it dawned on Peggy that, quite by accident, she had found her size fourteen and her size eight.

'Would you like to take a look backstage, ladies?'

Mavis and Sheila could barely conceal their excitement, eagerly following Peggy to the changing area. It looked as if Mavis had been to the hairdresser today, her lacquered beehive impenetrable. Even Sheila had abandoned her customary turtleneck and was displaying an unprecedented expanse of skin.

'About time.' Arabella gave Mavis and Sheila the once-over when they arrived in the changing room. She muttered something about beggars and choosers before handing them a laden coat hanger each. The sight of Arabella ordering Madam Chairwoman to strip off under normal circumstances would have filled Peggy with unbridled joy, but time was running out. Jim might have made his fortune out of gyrating his hips on stage, but he didn't know a twinset from a tracksuit.

'Still no sign of her?' Brian appeared. He'd already changed into the first outfit from the rack and looked spiffy in a collarless white shirt and khaki shorts.

Peggy shook her head. She checked her mobile phone again. There were no messages. No missed calls.

'Peggy,' said Brian, clearing his throat, 'I know this isn't the time or place, but there's been something I've been meaning to talk to you about. I've been waiting for the right opportunity, but it never seems to come along.'

'If it's about the food, the vegetarian wraps are the ones on the blue plate. I've marked them with a V.'

'It's not about the wraps.'

'Gluten then? If there are any celeriacs here, they'll have to make do with the chicken wings.'

'It's not about the food, well, not exactly.' Brian fidgeted, loosening his collar with one finger. 'I was wondering if you'd like to . . . that is if you're free one evening . . .'

Peggy looked at her watch. Brian would have to wait. The show was due to start in fifteen minutes.

'Sorry Brian, I've got to find Angie. I'm worried something has happened to her.' She grabbed her redundant mobile phone from her handbag and shoved it into the flimsy pocket of Arabella's signature-range waterfall cardigan in apple green. 'Phone me if she turns up.'

Peggy was already limping by the time she reached the front door of the community centre. Everything depended on her. Suddenly it was 1979 and she was chasing David's kite as it flew towards the powerlines.

'Evening.' It was Dr Stephen, holding the door open for her.

'I'm so glad you could make it,' said Peggy. At first, she was dubious about inviting him to the fashion show, wondering whether it was his thing. Now she was relieved to have him on standby. She wondered if he'd brought his big black bag.

'Everything okay? You look a little puffed.'

'Last-minute technical hitch, nothing serious.'

Now there was an understatement.

27

Pass the Gelignite

PEGGY KNOCKED ON THE FRONT DOOR A SECOND TIME.
A little louder this time.

'Angie. Where are you?'

Darn that woman.

Peggy tried the handle. The door was locked.

'I know you're in there. I can see the Mini parked outside.
You're cutting it a bit fine for the fashion show. Arabella's
losing it and everyone's arriving early. We need you.'

Peggy searched under the front door mat, hoping to find
a key. She thought of Jenny letting herself into her unit after
having a key cut. Though she'd never in a million years admit
it, her daughter might have a point.

The window to her left was Angie's living room. Peggy
peeked through, shielding her eyes with her hand, but the
room was empty. She remembered Angie's bedroom was to
the north side of the unit. Was it possible Angie had taken
a pre-show nap and fallen into a deep sleep? She'd been so

tired yesterday. It was hardly surprising, given how busy she'd been. That was Angie all over. Irons in too many pies.

Peggy made her way down the side of the unit where Angie stored her bins. For all her prowess in the shopping mall or making mind-altering sweet treats, Angie wasn't a gardener. A climbing bougainvillea had taken over in the short time since she'd moved in. Its branches grasped Peggy, a mass of claw-shaped thorns disguised beneath sprays of papery pink flowers. Something snagged the corner of her wrap dress and pulling it free, Peggy heard a tear.

Bugger. There would be hell to pay when Arabella found out.

Surrounded by spiny foliage, Peggy paused to take stock. Should she turn back, and discover what Brian had been working up to asking her? Or press on, risking not only serious injury, but also Arabella's borrowed summer collection ensemble? Peggy picked her way through the branches, ignoring the thin trickles of blood where the spikes had scored her forearms. Suddenly, finding Angie seemed more important than the stupid dress or a few scratches.

The window was covered in cobwebs. Home maintenance really wasn't Angie's thing either. Peggy tried to sweep them away with her hand, succeeding only in transferring them to her head where they sat like a sticky grey hairnet. Less Helen Mirren, more her curmudgeonly great-aunt.

She rubbed away the dust and dirt from one corner of the windowpane and peered in. The room was in near-darkness, but the partially drawn curtains were open just wide enough for her to see the bed. It was empty, apart from a row of scatter cushions standing tastefully to attention.

Peggy slouched with anticlimax. It looked like Angie had deserted them after all. And to think this had all been her idea. It just proved how selfish she was. She'd led them on, Peggy included, with a promise of something exotic and exciting, a chance to escape the mundane. This little escapade showed her true colours. Angie Valentine only ever thought of herself. Everything she'd done was for her own gratification, her own shallow ends. She was not to be relied on, never to be trusted. Someone had turned the lights back on in the middle of the party.

Turning to hobble back to the chaos at the community centre, Peggy noticed that the window was open a fraction. There'd been a story in the newsletter about a break-in at the village last week and the residents had all been reminded to lock their windows when they went out. The Mini was parked outside too. It didn't make sense. Angie wasn't the type to walk anywhere if she could drive.

Peggy's bladder tingled. Something was wrong. With her heart fluttering like a frightened bird, she forced the fingers of her withered left arm through the gap in the open window and released the catch. She paused, listening for any sound from within. All she could hear was tinny music in the distance, a selection of tunes Brian's grandson had put together.

It was too late to call for help. The fashion show had started without them.

Then Peggy heard something. She froze, listening for a sound above the opening bars of 'Honky Tonk Women'. Any minute, Mavis would be strutting her stuff on the catwalk in a Merino two-piece. Surely Angie wouldn't miss something like that on purpose?

Behind her, partially hidden in the bushes, Peggy spied a couple of black plastic recycling boxes. She emptied out the leaves and balanced one on top of the other under the open window. The plan came to a grinding halt when she couldn't bend her waiting-list knee far enough to climb up.

Bloody knee.

Ted was right: she should have persisted with the physio. But it was too late now. It was time for some lateral thinking.

Sitting on the boxes, she leaned back and swung both legs up. With a bit of huffing and puffing she managed to roll over onto her hands and knees. After a few wobbly practice efforts, she stood, clinging to the window for balance. It was a tad precarious, not to mention unladylike, standing wide-legged in her strappy sandals, but at least Peggy was now level with the window. Somewhere inside, she heard a grunt. Then a groan.

'Angie? Can you hear me?'

Peggy heard a tremulous voice call out.

'Why don't you open the front door, you daft mare?'

There it was again. 'Help me.'

There was no witty retort, no scolding comeback or put-down. Angie must be in trouble.

'Hang on, I'm coming.'

It was a long way down from the recycling boxes to the overgrown path below. There was only one direction to head. Prising the window open as far as the hinges would allow, she forced her head through the gap. Standing on tiptoe on the upturned box, she was able to squeeze her upper body through the gap. When she released the window behind her, it slammed into her kidneys, wedging her in place. Winded, she lay there, half in, half out.

What on earth was she doing, climbing through a window at nearly eighty? A whole ream of more sensible alternatives suddenly occurred to her. Imagine Jenny's face if she could see her now. It would be off to that home faster than she could say *apple, table, penny.*

Then Peggy heard the shallow voice again, even weaker this time. 'Peggy. Please help me.'

With a little bounce of her bionic knee, and one arm bent behind her to lift the heavy wooden frame, Peggy propelled herself through the window. With a little help from gravity, she slid down the wall on the other side, managing to unhook her legs just as the window banged shut behind her. She landed in a heap of green jersey, legs akimbo, trailing bougainvillaea and shredded pantyhose from her ankles.

Her daughter's words rang in her ears. *Next time it could be a hip and then you'll really be in trouble.*

Peggy lay on the bedroom carpet, breathing heavily. She waited for the pain, wondering where it would scream from first. With nothing more than the usual aches and pains, her heartbeat began to slow. She wriggled her toes and circled her wrists. The real soreness would come tomorrow, like a hangover in her bruised muscles, but this time at least there was no crunching of broken bones.

'I'm here,' she announced.

'I can see that. I think we need to work on your deportment next,' said a voice from an armchair in the far corner.

Peggy rolled onto her side and tried to gather herself. 'Are you alright?' she said, panting.

'I could ask you the same question,' said Angie.

Peggy struggled to her feet. It was getting dark, but in the dim twilight, she could just make out the frail figure, slumped to one side, face the colour of weak tea. Angie's breathing was laboured and her dark hair clung to the perspiration on her forehead.

'You look like shit,' said Peggy.

'You don't look so crash hot yourself.'

'Should I call an ambulance?'

Angie returned a feeble smile. 'It's too late for that.'

'Too late? What are you talking about?'

'I've been waiting for this.'

'Waiting for what, Angie? What's going on?'

'The Big One. The cardiologists told me they'd done all they could. I've always known the next heart attack would be my last.'

'Don't talk rubbish. Do you have one of those gelignite sprays?'

'Nitrate, you chump. In my handbag, in the kitchen.'

Even in her drunken haze the other night, Peggy had been shocked by the handbags strewn around Angie's kitchen. She had quite a collection of the things. They must be breeding. 'I need more to go on than that.'

'Prada. Black tote with the red lining.'

Peggy stumbled to the kitchen, her good knee suddenly not so good. The pain ripped through her leg with every step. Her hands shook as she rifled through the handbag looking for the spray. She flinched at what she found. For all Angie's elegance and sophistication, the depths of her handbag were caked in mouldy almonds, bits of scrunched-up tissues and a stack of shop receipts. A mountain of them.

This was never going to work. What was she supposed to do? It was miles to the nearest hospital; one of the downsides of the peaceful location the village brochures boasted about.

Calling an ambulance was the logical thing to do, but even with all the lights and sirens, it wouldn't reach Angie in time. She needed a doctor straightaway. With their very own Dr Stephen as guest of honour this evening, Peggy knew exactly where she could find one.

Peggy's hands fell to her sides, patting down her pockets. By some miracle, her mobile had survived the commando entry through the bedroom window. Arabella would have a fit when she saw the state of the delicate knitted fabric, all stretched and misshapen around the heavy telephone, not to mention the snags from the window frame. But Peggy didn't care, not what Arabella thought, nor whether she should be wearing gabardine or gingham, batwings or bell-bottoms. She didn't need a stupid makeover to find love again. It had been in plain sight all along, the kind of love that lasts a lifetime. The love between true friends. The kind of love she couldn't bear to lose a second time. All that mattered was saving Angie. All she had to do was remember four numbers and punch them into the phone. Preferably in the right order.

Every conceivable combination of birthdays and anniversaries ran through Peggy's brain as she limped back to the bedroom, carrying the Prada tote in one hand and her mobile in the other. She handed Angie the bag and watched her turn it upside down emptying the entire contents onto the floor. The red bottle tumbled out. She watched Angie open her mouth and press the nozzle, squirting the mist from the red bottle, directly under her tongue. Angie's eyes rolled back and she sank into the chair, gurgling.

Peggy squinted at the screen of her phone. *What were those numbers?* She remembered her father pushing her on a swing when she was six as if it were yesterday. She remembered the first time she and Ted kissed on the doorstep of 23 Markham Avenue, and the look on her mother's face when she walked in. Peggy remembered the smell of David's head when he was a baby, and Jenny's first word. *Mama.* Why couldn't she remember the code? *Apple, table, penny.* She'd managed to convince Dr Stephen and her daughter there was nothing wrong with her memory, when all along she knew otherwise.

You are a fraud, Peggy Smart. You've pretended to be something that you're not, and you've been found out. Your oldest friend is about to die because you can't see what's staring you in the face. Face it, you are losing your marbles and the time will come when you don't even realise it. Look what happened to your mother.

In the chair, Angie was fading inside her co-ordinated loungewear. Peggy stabbed at the keyboard. The phone shuddered and told her to try again. Her mother had given up, defeated by her own misery. She was an old lady by eighty, dependent and helpless. Peggy would not be beaten. She had to keep going for Angie. It was time to repay her debt.

The code. It would have been something memorable. How ironic. A date perhaps? 1938. No. 1963. Another no. Birthday, perhaps? 16-11. The phone shook in frustration.

'Bloody i-telephone!' It was all Peggy could do not to throw the stupid thing at the wall.

'Language.' Angie opened her eyes and followed the words with a foamy cough. 'Use mine,' she said, gasping for air. 'Coach clutch. In the kitchen.'

'One more try. The numbers are on the tip of my tongue.' David had set the damn thing up for her, but she'd chosen the numbers herself. Something meaningful. Close to her heart.

7 ... 2 ... 7 ... 4. Like magic, the screen opened to reveal an old family photograph. One of the ones David had scanned for her from the old albums.

It was taken on a beach. Ted, with a full head of hair, was standing waist-deep in a hole in the sand. Peggy stood next to him, smiling and holding a bucket. The two children, brown as berries, grinned at the camera, waving red spades. It must have been the late seventies. Happy times. 1972 and 1974. The two happiest years of Peggy's life. After the dashed hopes and false starts of the early tries, the years her two babies were finally born.

Aside from her family, there were only two numbers programmed into the phone. She selected Brian Cornell then pressed the symbol that looked like an old-fangled telephone receiver. Her heart was beating three times the speed of the ring tone. Before she knew what was happening, there was a beep and she was through to his answer message thingy. Trying but failing to mask her mild hysteria, she asked him to come as soon as possible. Peggy's voice trailed off towards the end of the message, knowing it was futile. The music was blaring in the background. He'd never hear his phone over Tom Jones.

She considered running back to the community centre herself, but alarmingly, her knee was starting to swell. The cartridge was torn for sure. Triple zero was the only option. Having learned the numbers as a child, Peggy felt an unexpected thrill at dialling them. Calling the emergency services hadn't exactly been on her bucket list, but there was a first time for everything.

'Dr Lim's on his way,' lied Peggy as she finished speaking to the reassuringly unflustered woman at ambulance control.

What kind of friend couldn't tell the truth, even in their final minutes together?

'I'm going to die,' whispered Angie, eyes rolling back again as she clutched her chest.

Peggy grasped Angie by the shoulders and squeezed until she opened her eyes again. 'Don't talk such rubbish. You're going to be fine. Do you hear me?'

'It's too late.'

'Now you listen to me.' Peggy scraped the damp hair off Angie's face and stroked her forehead. 'You are not going to die. For once, you're going to do what I say. It's about time I got to wear the trousers in this relationship.'

With a half-smile, Angie slurred, 'In that case, make sure they're tailored and skim the ankle.'

'That's more like it. Now, let's get you onto the bed.'

For all her buckwheat scrawniness, Angie was surprisingly heavy. Peggy tried to support the weight over her shoulder, but they only made it halfway across the bedroom before they both collapsed onto the bed. Somehow, Peggy managed to lever her clammy friend up the bed and surrounded her with a lifejacket of cushions. Each precious breath rattled deep inside Angie's chest.

'I need to tell you something,' she said.

'Not now, just breathe.' Peggy took Angie's cool hand in her own. She seemed so slight and insignificant, lying there against the satin sheets.

'Please listen to me. I have to tell you, before it's too late.'

Peggy's insides tumbled. 'What do you have to tell me?'

Angie's gaze turned towards the wardrobe. 'Bottom drawer.'

'You don't have to do this now. We can talk about it later, when you're better. There's half a bottle of cooking sherry left in my cupboard and I can whip up some homemade cheese straws to go with it.'

'Shut up, woman. Just open the drawer.'

Peggy did what Angie instructed, for what could be the last time. There, amidst the satin and sequins, were the two silver picture frames, just as she'd left them. There had been something bothering her since the night she'd found the frames. It was a memory, floating like a piece of litter, always beyond her reach. Whenever she got close, it blew away. She knew now, even before she looked at the photos a second time, what Angie had been trying to tell her, a line racing between the dots.

The little boy in the cowboy outfit smiled at her from the picture frame. Peggy wiped her first tear on the sleeve of her designer cardigan. Between his front teeth was a gap. The same gap as young David grinning at the camera with his spade, before the orthodontist wired up his mouth. The same gap Ted had never bothered to fix.

'I've been looking for you for a long time, Peggy Weaver.'

'Why?' Peggy struggled to process her thoughts. *Why now, after all these years?'*

'To say sorry.'

Peggy stared at the picture of the three adults, their arms linked, the truth slowly dawning. Herself, Angie and Ted, linked in life, and now in death. By a child.

'When?'

'It was after the night at the Odeon cinema. *Breathless.* Just the once, I promise. I was weak and selfish.' The thin words struggled beyond Angie's lips.

Peggy felt as though she'd been shot. 'But you could have had any man you wanted. Why Ted? *My* Ted.'

'I was so insecure, so messed up. I wanted to be you. Ted loved you. I wanted someone to love me too, for who I was.'

Angie was jealous, of her? It didn't make sense. She'd spent so long in Angie's shadow, in awe of everything she did, everything she was. To think that Ted had betrayed her, or had he? He'd chosen her over Angie and lived out his unremarkable life with her. Contentedly, certainly. Happily? Peggy supposed so.

In fifty-four years he'd never breathed a word about the affair, if you could even call it that. Even when Peggy showed him the article she'd ripped out of the podiatrist's magazine, he'd never said a thing. She was the one Ted had pictured growing old with. He'd carried that guilt to the grave, after years of silent atonement. In all that time, he'd played the dutiful husband and father. Never complained, never questioned, never compared. It was as though he'd buried that moment of weakness deep inside and thrown away the map.

'And you never told him about Simon?'

Angie shook her head, the effort exhausting her.

'I was going to tell him before the wedding. I came back from New York because I thought it was the right thing to do. I thought he had a right to know. I realise now I only wanted to clear my own conscience.'

Peggy's memory of that day was sharp and clear, as focused as the day it was formed. She watched Angie heading towards the church, carrying Ted's unborn child beneath that buttoned-up coat. *Trollop*. Her mother had been right all along.

'But you didn't say anything.'

Angie's face sank. 'I watched you promise yourselves to each other and I saw how happy the two of you were. I saw how much you loved each other. I knew I could never do anything to hurt either of you.'

The words seemed to take every last scrap of Angie. She was spent. Too exhausted to hold eye contact, Angie stared into nothingness. Peggy climbed onto the bed next to Angie and held her. She shushed and soothed, as she had with David and Jenny when they were babies. With each breath, Angie faded, the fight to stay alive dwindling with every borrowed heartbeat. She gripped Peggy's hand as if holding on to life itself, as vulnerable as a newborn with its instinctive grasp. No more than a reflex. Hold on and survive.

If only Ted had held on longer. Peggy recalled the moment the muscles in his hand relaxed, his fingers unfolding away from hers. She longed to make good all the times she'd batted him away in public. Peggy tightened her grip on Angie's fleshless hand and breathed into her hair. 'Don't leave me,' she whispered.

From a distance, their rekindled friendship had looked like a perfect line in the sand, dividing the past from the present. Close up, the water ebbing and flowing between them was murky, bestrewn with the flotsam and jetsam of secrets and lies.

After all their years apart, they'd been tied together all along, by one man. He'd given them both the children they loved so deeply. But Angie's child had been taken from her. And Ted had been taken from Peggy. All they had left was each other. It was almost as though Ted had somehow sent Angie to keep her company. To make amends.

None of it mattered now. Before long, where there had been laughter and fun, for one or both of them there would be only pills and strangers. With Angie clinging to each feeble breath, it was time to forgive while she still could. Time to put the lid back on Pandora's box. In the coming years, as the recent memories faded, Peggy would remember only the times before she knew. The truth would be no more, along with the pain and the jealousy.

It was time to let bygones be bygones.

Time to let sleeping ducks lie.

~

Peggy heard a key in the front door then voices.

'Hello, is anyone there?'

'We're in the bedroom. Please hurry.'

The sight of Dr Stephen at the door, carrying his big black bag, filled Peggy with relief. She slumped against the wall, drained. Behind the doctor stood Christine with a master key and Brian, this time quite dashing in a lovely buttoned-down mauve shirt and grey slacks.

28

How Much Is the Coffee?

THE SOLICITOR'S WAITING ROOM WAS MORE LIKE A POSH hotel lobby than an office. Peggy hardly recognised it from the last time she was here, sorting out Ted's affairs. The seats were that nice chenille fabric, rather than the waterproof stuff in Dr Stephen's waiting room, and there was a glass coffee table topped with the kind of glossy architectural magazines that no-one ever read. It seemed such an extravagance. But then, death and divorce were always pricey.

David blustered through the front door and apologised for being late.

'Relax. Mr Parsons is still with another client,' said Jenny, a smile struggling for purchase on her lips.

She'd hardly said a word in the car on the way over. That suited Peggy. She hadn't slept a wink. As soon as it was light, she'd gone round to Angie's unit and packed her a bag for the hospital. She'd watered the plants and arranged the cushions. It was the least she could do.

'Mel couldn't make it, I'm afraid. She was held up in David Jones.'

'What, an armed heist in the shoe department?' smirked Jenny.

Peggy snapped. 'Now, you two, no squabbling.'

Suddenly, they were all in the old station wagon on a hot and sticky road trip up the coast, the children bickering in the back. 'If you can't say anything nice to each other, then don't say anything at all.'

It had worked for her and Ted over the years. At times, they simply ran out of words, ran out of things to remark on. Somehow, the silence worked. When there was nothing to say, it was best to say nothing. What was the point? Nobody listened to her anyway. It was going to take more than a makeover to stop her feeling invisible.

The receptionist looked up. 'Mr Parsons won't be long now,' she said with a faux smile. 'Can I get anyone a coffee while you're waiting?'

'Will that be extra?' said Peggy, mirroring the smile.

'Mo-ther.' Jenny frowned and mouthed something at the receptionist. Apologising, presumably.

That's how old people got. Embarrassing, unreasonable. Just like children. Peggy lost count of the tantrums Jenny had as a toddler. Usually in the supermarket, she recalled. There was no placating her. In the end, Peggy would just walk away and leave her there, pumping the ground with her little fists. David wasn't much better. Always taking his clothes off in public. Then there were the trials and tribulations of the teenage years. It was a miracle they'd managed to navigate that maze. Jenny's smoking and backchat; David's drunken parties and dented cars. Funny how the tables had turned.

'I'm sorry to hear about Angie,' said David. 'Any news from the hospital yet?'

Peggy shook her head and weaved her fingers. Snippets of her conversation with Angie surfaced like bubbles, bursting into her consciousness.

~

It seemed an eternity before the ambulance arrived. Peggy remembered the look on Dr Stephen's face. He wasn't sitting back in his chair, listening patiently as Peggy whinged about her stupid bladder. He was busy being a real doctor with medical bits and pieces strewn across the plain white cotton bedspread. She remembered him pumping the blood pressure cuff around Angie's arm, while Christine offered official reassurance on behalf of the management.

'Help is on the way,' said Christine with a gentle pat of Angie's pallid hand. 'There's nothing to worry about.' Her face said otherwise.

Dr Stephen took the stethoscope out of his ears and sighed. 'Blood pressure's low.'

'That's good, isn't it?' ventured Peggy.

'No, not in this case.' He turned to Christine and said, 'Help me get her flat. Put the pillows under her ankles.'

Peggy had been the one to prop Angie up against the wall of designer pillowslips. In spite of all the medical romance novels she'd devoured over the years, she'd elevated the wrong end. She prayed Angie would live to berate her about it.

'Has she had any of this?' Stephen was inspecting the red gelignite bottle.

'Yes,' said Peggy, wringing her hands.

'Ah, that explains it.'

'I'm sorry.'

'No, that's good. You've done the right thing. It improves the blood flow to the heart, but can lower the blood pressure too. Would someone please fetch me a glass of water?'

'I'll go,' said Brian, heading for the kitchen. He was the perfect man to have in a crisis, thought Peggy. Always so cool, calm and collectable. She'd almost forgotten how solid she felt in his presence.

When Brian handed over the glass, Dr Stephen tore open a foil packet and dropped a white tablet into the water. Peggy wondered if he might have a headache.

'Here, drink this Angie. It's aspirin,' he said. 'To thin your blood.'

'I'd rather have a brandy,' said Angie, frowning at the white chalky liquid.

At that moment Peggy allowed herself to hope. There was a chance Angie would make it after all. It would be rude of her not to. They'd been apart for so many years, and found each other again at a minute to midnight. There was so much lost time to make up.

~

'I'll give you a lift to the hospital when we've finished here,' said David. He'd inched closer to Peggy on the chenille sofa.

'It's no trouble for me either,' said Jenny, her voice soft, gentle even.

'Thank you both, but Brian is coming to pick me up. He's going to take me.'

Peggy wanted to put her arms round them both, and pull them in close to her bosom. She wanted to kiss their heads and breathe in their scents, like she used to when they were asleep in her arms. She thought about Simon in Angie's arms as a baby. Would he have smelled half the same as Jenny and David? He had David's mouth, Jenny's eyes, she now realised. He was a little piece of Ted. A piece of all the people she loved. From nowhere, she felt anger. Not with Angie, not with Simon – only his weak heart and the doctors who couldn't save him.

Before Peggy knew how it happened, they were holding hands. These were her children and they'd lost their father. It was conceivable that they were trying to hold onto their mother for as long as possible.

The only sound came from the click-click of the receptionist's fingernails on her keyboard. No words were necessary. No good would come from telling David and Jenny about their half-brother. Their dead half-brother. They wouldn't understand like she did. Judging their father would only sully their memories of him. Because that's all they had left. Memories. And each other.

'We're only doing this to make life easier for you, Mum,' said David. 'It's only a signature on a piece of paper.'

Birth, death, marriage. When it came down to it, life was little more than a series of forms to fill in. A signature was the most powerful weapon of all, and the most enduring. Peggy's name would live on this dotted line long after she had gone.

Jenny squeezed her mother's hand. 'We want you to keep your independence, as long as possible.'

'Are you sure you're ready, Mum? We don't have to do it right now,' said David. 'We can leave it for another day if you're not feeling up to it.'

'We're here now. Let's just get it over and done with. It's only power of attorney and guardianship I'm signing, isn't it?'

'That's all,' said David. 'Just thinking ahead. Being prepared.'

'So, you're not planning to turn off my life-support machine just yet?'

'Don't tempt me, Mother,' laughed Jenny.

The door opened and Mr Parsons emerged, followed by an elegantly dressed silver-haired woman. Behind them were a younger couple, about David's and Jenny's ages, Peggy guessed. The older woman caught Peggy's eye and smiled. A knowing smile. She looked very prepared. Resigned and world-weary, but prepared.

'Do come through, Mrs Smart,' said Mr Parsons, extending his hand in welcome.

As Peggy tried to stand, her knee gave way and she bounced back onto the seat. David caught her under the arms and tried to haul her up again.

'I can manage,' snapped Peggy, brushing him away. 'I do wish you two would stop mollycoddling me.'

The other woman – now standing at the reception desk in front of her open cheque book – rolled her eyes in sympathy.

'Good luck,' she mouthed.

29

Valentine. As in the Saint

'IT'S AWFULLY GOOD OF YOU, BRIAN.'

'Don't mention it. It's the least I can do.'

Peggy clutched the overnight bag against her chest. There were more bags in Angie's unit than David Jones and Myer combined, in just about every conceivable colour and configuration. Peggy hoped she'd chosen correctly, that her selection of clothes, underwear and toiletries – not to mention the bag itself – would meet Angie's approval.

'Do you think we should be worried?' asked Peggy, glancing at Brian as they walked side by side through the bustling hospital foyer.

'I think we should try to stay positive,' he said. His face looked anything but positive.

The woman at reception stared at her computer screen.

'Valentine, did you say?'

'Yes, Valentine. As in the saint,' said Peggy. *The patron saint of lovers.*

Brian stepped forward. 'Angela Valentine. She was admitted last night.'

'Last night.' The woman scoured her screen, her face pinched as she mouthed the letters, *V-A-L* . . .

Without looking up, she picked up the phone and dialled.

'Good afternoon. Reception here. I have someone enquiring about Angela Valentine. Yes . . . good . . . okay . . . thanks.' She looked up and smiled. 'A nurse will be here in a minute to fetch you.'

'Is everything alright?' asked Peggy. Visitors were usually left to make their own way with muddling instructions about lifts and corridors, rights and lefts.

'Take a seat,' said the receptionist. 'Someone will be with you shortly.' With that, she turned her attention to a grey-haired couple carrying a blue teddy bear and a large bunch of flowers. New grandparents, no doubt. There was so much advice Peggy wanted to offer. Enjoy it, she wanted to tell them. Spoil them but never interfere. Bite your tongue when your daughter-in-law tells you things are different nowadays. Watch *Star Wars*. Install a reversing camera.

Peggy and Brian had barely sat down when the receptionist directed a pale, angular nurse in their direction. She looked like she needed a good feed, poor love. The nurse introduced herself and put her hand on Peggy's shoulder. Her words were as emaciated as the nurse's arms and Peggy couldn't get a firm grip on them.

'Would you like to come up and see her?'

Peggy nodded. Brian had slipped his hand around hers.

They followed the nurse along the bustling corridor. The squeak-squeak of her rubber soles on the shiny floor, still wet from the disinfectant mop, was deafening. Peggy was numb. Gone was the pain in her knee. Her weightless head hovered above her shoulders. The only part of herself she could feel was Brian, their palms connected by a thin film of perspiration.

~

'Stay as long as you want, Mrs Smart.' The nurse placed a chair at the bedside.

Peggy knew the drill. She'd been here before. Around her, a dozen bodies held on, desperate climbers clinging to a mountain face. Peggy saw the bed where Ted had let go. She looked away.

'Here you are, Mr Smart. You have this one.' The nurse placed a second chair next to Peggy's.

Mr Smart? Angie would have loved that.

'He's holding your hand,' she might have said. 'Of course he's interested, you daft ape.'

Peggy tried not to breathe, afraid to contaminate the sterile air.

'Can she hear me?'

The nurse nodded. She explained it all, again. Ventilated, sedated, drugs to keep her heart beating. Tubes and wires to monitor every precious heartbeat. It was touch and go, she told them.

Touch and go.

Peggy reached under the sheet and took Angie's hand. The skin was the colour of raw pastry. She expected it to be as cool, and recoiled at its surprising warmth. There was a chipped nail on one finger. They should go for a manicure together. Peggy had never had her nails done before. They could go to that place in the mall then have a coffee afterwards. And Angie's roots needed a touch up. She'd book an appointment with Alessandro on Monday. There was so much left to do together. There was the European river cruise Peggy had never taken. She would pick up some brochures at the travel agent. They could invite Brian and Jim. It would be a hoot.

Angie lay inert against the white sheets, her lips parted around the clear plastic tube that delivered the rest of her life, one mechanical breath at a time. Her eyelids were half open, as if she were afraid of missing out. That was Angie all over.

Peggy felt her chest tighten, and a sob escaped before she could stifle it with her other hand. Feeling Brian's hand on her back, she turned towards him. 'Do you mind? I just need a moment alone.'

'Of course.' Brian's eyes were full of concern. 'I'll wait over there.'

Peggy reached into her own handbag and retrieved a lipstick from the side pocket. She'd chosen it from Angie's vast collection on the basis of its name rather than the colour. It was the least she could do. Glancing around her, Peggy pulled the top from the lipstick and began to fill in Angie's lips around the ventilator tube with the chosen shade.

Naughty but Nice. If Angie were to die, at least she'd do so looking absolutely fabulous.

Next, she removed the two silver picture frames from the other bag and arranged them on the clinical white cabinet next to the bed.

'Simon's here,' she said softly. *Simon, Ted and me.*

There was no-one else. After nearly eighty years, all Angie had to show for her life was a frail friendship with a woman she hadn't seen for more than fifty years, and an enormous collection of handbags.

The white hospital gown drained Angie's face of life. Avoid everything white, Dr Stephen had said. For once, it was time for Angie to do the listening.

'Now, young lady, it's my turn to be the boss.' Peggy straightened the bed sheets and tucked them in under the mattress. 'I'll tell you what's going to happen. First, you're going to start breathing on your own and put some decent clothes on. White is so ageing, darling. A nice cream colour would suit you better. Then I'm going to take you home and fuss over you. It's payback time. I'm going to force-feed you some proper food and fatten you up a bit. Then you're going to help me choose a new car, something nippy that my children will really disapprove of, and after that we're going to the doggy rescue to find you a little furry friend of your own. Basil is mine, so keep your hands and fancy rubber cheese to yourself.'

She picked up the largest photograph, kissed Ted and replaced it on the cabinet. Then she kissed Angie's stretched forehead.

All that mattered was the here and now.

'And one more thing,' said Peggy. 'These photographs are going out on display. No more hiding Simon away in a drawer. Do you hear me? He was my husband's son too. And we won't discuss it any further. We'll go on as if nothing ever happened, okay?'

They'd discussed just about everything: bladders, pelvic floors, even sex. But there were some things that didn't need to be endlessly dissected.

Some things were better left in the past, not raked over and over.

Some things would always remain unmentionable.

30

Is There a Fire Extinguisher in Here?

'ONE-TWO. ONE-TWO.' THE METALLIC SCREECH ECHOED
between the Clubhouse walls as Jim blew into the microphone.

'Hearing you loud and clear over here,' winced Celia,
dragging a pile of stacking chairs across the floor.

Peggy was busy polishing glasses. 'Did you see if he was
wearing his hearing aids?' she asked.

'I forgot to check,' laughed Celia. 'But if his performance
at the fashion show was anything to go by, I think we'll be
okay. He was quite a hit with the ladies. Want to see?' She
pulled her phone out of her back pocket, squashed her thumb
over a button at the bottom of the screen and ushered Peggy
closer. The video was a bit wobbly and perhaps Celia had
stood too close to the speakers, but there it was replayed
in real time: The Inaugural Jacaranda Retirement Village
Fashion Show.

For all Peggy's misgivings, Jim had been the perfect
compere. Whatever his improvised commentary lacked in

tact or political correctness, it had been made up for with sheer entertainment. It was a pity Angie never got to hear him, or see Christine from management striking a pose on the catwalk wearing leather trousers and a pout.

'This is the best bit,' said Celia, enlarging the screen. 'Watch Mavis.'

Peggy squinted. She didn't want to miss this. From the far right of the shot, a figure appeared wiggling in time to the music. It was Mavis, wearing a pair of black Lycra leggings and a fluoro pink zip-up top. All along, she'd been hiding a surprisingly shapely pair of legs under all that tweed. Peggy wondered if the all-new sporty Mavis would take up jogging or yoga. It didn't bear thinking about. Next up was Sheila modelling a shimmering evening dress, and a pair of high heels that made her walk like a wading bird. Someone had made up her face and backcombed her hair but there was no mistaking the sneer. Peggy heard Celia make a comment from behind the camera and saw Brian snigger before he joined her up on the runway in an immaculate dinner suit. He took Sheila by the hand and escorted her down the steps. Her eyes never left him.

'Where would you like them?' Mavis blustered in with a box of bread rolls.

Peggy took the box from her and smiled. 'Thanks for fetching these. I'll put them on the buffet table.' Mavis moved her attention to the flowers Sheila had just finished arranging, and began to rearrange them. Peggy smiled to herself and turned, almost colliding with Brian, who was carrying a platter of vol-au-vents.

'That was a near miss,' said Brian.

Near miss. Was that all it would ever be between the two of them?

They hadn't had a chance to talk since that day at the hospital. Not properly, anyway. Peggy missed Brian. She missed the touch of his hand and his passenger seat. They stood looking at each other, suspended in an awkward silence. It was as if the words they wanted to say were hovering between them in invisible speech bubbles.

After what seemed like an eternity, Brian said, 'Are you alright?'

'I'm fine, absolutely fine.'

'Really?'

Peggy paused, the ground impalpable beneath her feet. 'No, not really,' she said, crumpling. Brian relieved her of the bread rolls and led her to a quiet corner of the Clubhouse.

The past few weeks had taken so much out of her, both physically and emotionally.

Brian fetched a glass of water. 'Here, drink this.'

The other committee members scurried about the Clubhouse, carrying trays of glasses and platters of food, stepping carefully over the trailing wires that fed the new karaoke machine.

Peggy sipped the water. 'I'd rather have a brandy,' she said with a smile, remembering Angie's words. Brian smiled back and took her hand, his touch coursing pure energy through her veins.

'Can I ask you something?' Peggy reached for Brian's arm, her fingers resting on the sharp crease of his one hundred percent cotton poplin sleeve. 'What were you going to ask me, the night of the fashion show? Backstage? I didn't let you finish.'

Brian swallowed and stood to attention. 'I . . . well . . . that is to say . . .' He cleared his throat several times and Peggy wondered if she should pat him on the back.

'I'm not with you.'

'I think it's important to be upfront with this sort of thing,' said Brian.

'I couldn't agree more.'

'There's no point beating about the bush.'

'None whatsoever.'

'After all, life is short.'

'Very short.' Peggy was getting worried it might be too short.

'I'll get straight to the point.'

'Would you like to have dinner with me?' blurted Peggy.

There, she'd said it. Terrifying as it was, the sky hadn't caved in and she hadn't fallen into the burning fires of hell. It was as though every second of her eight decades had built up to that one question. The syllables stayed there, unsure of where to go next.

'I'm not interrupting anything, am I?'

The voice came from behind them. Brian and Peggy sprang apart like two positively charged magnets. There, shuffling behind Peggy's walking frame, was Angie. She was pale and thin but dressed to the nines, wearing a sequinned dress with matching accessories. There was an oxygen cylinder strapped to the walker, a snake of pale blue tubing ending in two prongs at her nostrils. She stopped and spread her arms wide: Eva Perón on a balcony.

'Happy birthday, Pegs.'

'And happy birthday, Ange.'

A week late for one, and with precious time running out, a month early for the other.

'Eighty, eh? It sounds bloody ancient!'

Peggy laughed. 'I know, let's just call ourselves sixty, with interest.'

The walker was the first of the compromises. It's that or a wheelchair, Peggy had said. Angie also conceded to having Peggy wash and dress her. 'Suck it up, sweetheart. It's me or carers.'

What a strange turn of events. The slingback, wedge-heeled shoe was now firmly on the other foot. They bickered and fought, but laughed much more. Like a married couple.

'You look amazing by the way,' said Angie. 'Great dress.'

Even Peggy had to agree. The inky-blue shift was perfect. Even more perfect now without the cast on her arm. She felt glamorous, confident, invincible even. So much so that she'd just asked Brian out to dinner.

Celia appeared with a tray of champagne glasses. 'How about a drink for the birthday girls?'

'About bloody time,' replied Angie. 'I'm parched.'

It must be all those water tablets, thought Peggy. She'd taken charge of the Webster-pak and battled with her friend daily about taking them. She'd gone along to Angie's last appointment with Dr Stephen, and sat in silence while the truth sank in. It was only a matter of months, a year at best. The poor doctor was so upset as he delivered the prognosis that Peggy ended up handing him the tissue box while Angie patted the back of his hand.

That's the thing with our generation, thought Peggy. We just get on with things. No need to talk ourselves blue in the face. Make the best of it.

Keep calm and carry on.

'Watch out,' said Celia. 'Here come the fun police.'

Mavis appeared, flanked by Sheila.

'There's a problem with the cakes,' said Mavis.

Peggy's back was up already. It had taken her a week to get the individual recipes right. Angie's fat-free version had been the most challenging, the mixture refusing to bind in the mixing bowl. She'd added an extra egg, a sneaky dollop of low-fat cream and hoped for the best. Besides, with any luck, there'd be enough champagne flowing that Princess Paleo wouldn't notice.

'What sort of problem?'

'It's the candles. One hundred and sixty, all alight at the same time. It's a matter of health and safety.'

Brian squared up to Mavis. 'I will take responsibility for the pyrotechnics this evening. I did first aid and fire training when I was a Boy Scout.'

'In that case, I'm holding you personally responsible, Brian Cornell.' With a wink, Madam Chair led Madam Secretary away to inspect the precarious electrical configuration behind the new karaoke machine.

Peggy felt a tug at her skirt. She turned to see Emily standing pigeon-toed in sparkly shoes and a white dress.

'Don't you look gorgeous,' said Peggy, bending down to hug her granddaughter.

Emily pulled back, a coy look on her face. 'I got you a special present, Granny.' From behind her back she produced a green fluffy pencil case. Peggy recognised it as the one from which she'd borrowed the gold glitter pen she used to mark her special Brian-time on the calendar. When she took it from Emily's outstretched hands and opened the zip, she smiled.

'I've been saving them, especially for your birthday,' said Emily. 'Now you have all your marbles back.'

'Thank you, sweetheart.' Tears clouded Peggy's eyes as she caressed the collection of multi-coloured glass balls through the fluffy fabric. 'This is the best present anyone's ever given me.' If only Ted were here to share the moment. Little Emily was so like him. If something was broken, why not fix it? If there was a hole in your life, simply fill it.

Peggy scanned the Clubhouse for the rest of her family. The party was in full swing. Mel was busy giving David a wifely lecture, only noticing in the nick of time when Sam tried to steer an unmanned walking frame towards the edge of the stage. Jenny, already glassy-eyed, was deep in conversation with Christine. Peggy hoped they weren't discussing her. At least they were smiling.

With Celia handing around the champagne and Angie busy playing social butterfly, Peggy looked around for Brian. He hadn't had the chance to reply. After all the build-up, the months and years she'd had to mentally rehearse, the moment had fallen flat on its backside. He hadn't exactly jumped at the offer of dinner, and now he'd disappeared. He was probably hiding in the gents, or emigrated to Canada.

'Ladies and gentlemen, let's hear it for the birthday girls!'

It was Jim, up on stage clapping his microphone between his hands. Peggy saw several guests wince and adjust their hearing aids. She appraised him through the top half of her new bifocals. The leather jacket–clad Jim still looked every inch the ladies' man. As she climbed the makeshift steps onto the stage, he kissed her on the cheek and called her Sandra. They all had their foibles.

'Not so long ago,' said Peggy. She stopped and tapped the microphone. 'Can everyone hear me?' Brian's grandson gave her the thumbs up from behind the console. 'Not so long ago, the thought of standing up here, speaking in front of so many people would have filled me with sheer terror.'

And had me dashing for the nearest toilet.

'But here I am.' Peggy paused until the applause – and Celia's raucous catcalls – died down.

'I have so many people to thank for tonight. My dear friends on the social committee, my children . . .' David saluted his mother with a beer bottle from behind the bar, and Jenny paused to wave a butter knife from the buffet table.

'And not forgetting my wonderful grandchildren, Sam and Emily.' *And baby Lulu, the Alpaca.* Everyone cheered and clapped. Sam brandished his lightsaber and Emily did a curtsey.

'But there are two people here tonight I'd like to thank personally. Firstly, Brian Cornell, for all his help and support over the past few weeks.' There was still no sign of Brian. He had disappeared into thin air, taking his answer with him.

'And not forgetting the one and only Angie Valentine. Without her, we wouldn't have this wonderful singing machine, complete with disco and all-new PA system for the village. The committee is busy planning a series of social events with a more upbeat theme, and plans to introduce a monthly karaoke night. And . . .' Peggy beckoned Jim to join her on the stage, where between them they held up a giant cheque. 'On behalf of the Jacaranda Retirement Village Library and Social Committee, a donation of one thousand dollars to the Heart Foundation.'

Angie, now sitting on her walker in front of the stage, raised her glass and blew Peggy a kiss. The effort in organising the fashion show had almost cost her her life, but only Peggy would ever know the real reason she'd been prepared to sacrifice it.

She continued. 'Please, everyone, welcome the indomitable Angie Valentine to the stage to say a few words.'

With a little assistance from Jim and Celia, Angie made it up onto the stage. Her oxygen prongs lay abandoned on her walker, and it took her several moments to catch her breath. The room fell silent as she donned a pair of turquoise reading glasses.

'Ladies and gentlemen, boys and girls,' she began. 'Friends are precious things. We collect them over our lifetime, different friends for different stages of our lives. Childhood, family friends, work colleagues, friends with similar interests or hobbies. Some are chance encounters, others seem destined to cross our paths. Over the years, it is inevitable that many will fall by the way. Others will come in and out of our lives, and though we may not see each other for years, when we meet again it is as though we have never been apart. In that respect, friends are rather like a dose of herpes.'

Laughter erupted around the Clubhouse.

'In my case, I was lucky enough to find a very dear friend again, after more than fifty years. We met as children and though our lives took very different paths, I never forgot her. Everything I did, I measured against this wonderful lady, and although she never knew it, she was my barometer in life. Meeting her again has been like coming home. She is the closest thing to a family I have ever had or will ever have. And it is to this person that I quite literally owe my life.

I am of course talking about our very own Betty Crocker, the very gorgeous and very funny Peggy Smart. Happy birthday to us, darling!'

A chorus of happy birthdays erupted. Peggy could never have imagined celebrating her eightieth birthday with the mother of her late husband's illegitimate child. But life was like that. In a funny way, theirs was the most modern of blended families.

They both knew it would be Angie's last birthday. The doctors were surprised she'd made this one. But there was no point dwelling on what lay ahead. They would file it away, until the time came.

With Jim already limbering up his vocal cords into the microphone, and Angie racing Celia to the bottom of a champagne bottle, Peggy decided to slip away. She needed to powder her nose and prepare herself to face Brian again.

It was no use pretending. This was no fairytale ending. Like the modern-day Disney princesses, she'd been feisty and forward. But there was no Prince Charming waiting at the door to whisk her away on a white charger, nor a silver Lexus. She'd tried. *A fair heart never won a faint maiden.* Or something like that. In time, she and Brian would laugh off the dinner invitation and move on with their lives. In the meantime, she needed to pee.

Peggy's hand was on the door to the ladies when she sensed someone standing behind her.

'I didn't get the chance to give you my answer.'

For once, there was no spasm in Peggy's bladder. For once, the nerve endings sat to attention, waiting patiently for their turn.

'It's alright, Brian,' said Peggy over her shoulder. 'You don't have to say anything. Let's just pretend it didn't happen.'

'Wait, you don't understand.'

Peggy pushed the door open a fraction. Turning for one final look, she steeled herself for the rejection speech. She'd save him the trouble. 'Don't worry. You're not over Phyllis. I understand. I was way too forward.'

The harsh neon glare from inside shone onto Brian's contorted face. 'Peggy, please.' He ran his fingers through his spartan hair and adjusted his glasses.

'Are you alright? You look rather . . . discombobulated.'

With a quick look over his shoulder, Brian led Peggy down the corridor and guided her behind the bowls trophy cabinet. Leaning closer, he placed his hands on either side of her face. 'I would love to have dinner with you,' he said. He caressed her cheeks as though she were a butterfly between his palms. 'And if I hadn't been so intimidated, I'd have asked you myself, months ago.'

'Intimidated?' Peggy was aghast.

Brian lowered his eyes. 'I wasn't sure an independent, modern woman like you would even look twice at an old fuddy-duddy accountant like me.'

Peggy was as dumbfounded as she was flattered. 'If you're going to kiss me, please hurry up,' she said. For once, it was her impatient heart that was fit to burst.

Brian leaned in towards her. 'May I?'

'You may.' Peggy closed her eyes and allowed Brian Cornell – widower, chartered accountant, Lexus driver – to kiss her. Somewhere deep inside her, the sleeping beast of lust yawned and reached for its slippers. Its best slippers.

Brian's lips were warm and gentle, the taste of him returning to her like a delicious memory. How little the lips age compared to the rest of the body, she thought. What a waste not to kiss with them.

'I'm not so sure about dinner now,' she said, pulling away. She felt his warm breath catch. 'At our age,' she said, 'I don't think we should wait that long.'

'Do you have a better idea?'

'How about we have breakfast together instead?'

Over Brian's shoulder Peggy noticed someone watching them. It was Sheila, her mouth gaping like a giant trout. Realising she'd been spotted, she turned and walked away. Brian and Peggy looked at each other for a moment before disintegrating into helpless giggles.

'Did you see the look on her face?' said Peggy.

'I expect she'll want it recorded in the minutes.'

Brian pulled Peggy towards him. He was taller than Ted, and Peggy had to crane her neck slightly. Sensing her discomfort, Brian cradled the back of her head with his fingers. Close up, Peggy was relieved to see they were indeed all his own teeth.

'I'm so sorry, am I being too forward?' he said.

She'd waited four years. And a lifetime.

No, Peggy wouldn't call that too forward.

31

Tea and a Toast

PEGGY COULDN'T QUITE BELIEVE SHE WAS MARRIED, EVEN as she undid the powder-blue buttons on the front of her jacket, part of the going-away outfit her mother had helped her choose.

Ted had looked so handsome in his morning suit, waiting for her at the altar. Later, while the modest guest list enjoyed roast spring chicken with minted peas at white-clothed tables, Ted introduced her to distant relatives as 'My Wife'. Peggy felt grown up and important. As a married woman, Peggy had joined an exclusive club in which she'd be respected and valued, climbing another rung towards her mother's evasive acceptance.

She and Ted had been going steady for two years. Marriage was the logical next step. With their smooches on the sofa after Mrs Weaver had gone to bed becoming ever more daring and heated, they were venturing into uncharted territory. When Ted slipped his hand inside the cup of her brassiere, Peggy had thought her head might explode. She tried thinking about her mother's braised lamb shanks in the pressure cooker, but as Ted tugged on her earlobe with his lips, and gently squeezed her breast, she felt she was in there with them. She wrestled with the earthy tug of desire. It thrilled her, and terrified her.

Hanging her jacket on the padded coat hanger behind the bathroom door, she whimpered. Beyond that door was her new husband, lying between crisp white hotel sheets, waiting for her. He'd been patient and understanding. Now it was time to go all the way.

She flinched at a noise from the bedroom. It was the pop of a champagne cork. Her stomach heaved like the descent on a rollercoaster. Peggy sucked in a breath and unbuttoned her blouse. So many tiny buttons, one by one, until she let the silky fabric fall from her shoulders onto the bathroom floor. The girls at Blake's had recognised her when she returned to buy her wedding essentials. She was a secretary now, and getting married. They made such a fuss of her, wrapping her lace-edged slip in tissue paper. Even Mr Hawley came out, shook her hand and wished her well.

There was an upturned water glass on the side of the sink. Peggy filled it and took a sip. All the moisture had gone from her mouth. This was it. With a last squirt of Yardley, Peggy looked at herself in the mirror.

'I can do this,' she told herself. 'I am a grown woman. A married woman.'

If only she could believe it. Her skin tingled in anticipation, her little quick breaths told her she wanted Ted with all her being. Peggy stared at the door handle, then back at the white porcelain. The symbol of her oppression.

'Peggy. Are you alright in there?' called Ted softly from the bedroom beyond.

A tear prickled in the corner of her eye. 'I'll be there in a tick,' she said.

Which would she allow to rule her life? Her heart or that enemy buried deep inside her body? Peggy thought of Angie, of the sensuality she exuded, of the power she held over men and women alike.

Just relax and let go.

Try to be more like Angie.

~

The slippers had shrunk since she bought them. They still had the Grace Bros price tag on the bottom, so it had been a good few years. In that time, Peggy's arches must have splayed, because there was now more of her foot hanging over the edges than inside the satin mules. Peggy forced each foot in further, squashing her toes into the pointed end. Weren't slippers meant to be comfortable? She should have worn them when she had the chance, back when her feet were still longer than they were wide. It was never worth keeping things for best. And in future, she wouldn't. She would burn her expensive scented candles, and bathe in her exotic smellies every day of the week.

Wrapping the dressing gown around her middle and securing the silky belt in a bow, Peggy tiptoed to the kitchen. Basil winked at her and yawned. She shushed him and bribed him with a dog treat. She wanted everything to be perfect.

The kitchen blinds were half open, as she'd left them before the party. It was after midnight when the celebrations finally drew to a close. David carried Sam and Emily, one in each arm, to the car while Mel, sober and tight-faced, rearranged car seats to fit inebriated Aunty Jenny in the back. The other residents peeled away, wandering back to their units, Celia still singing 'King of the Road' as she disappeared into the darkness. Jim insisted on walking Angie home. Slowly. She'd winked at Peggy as they set off, the sequins on her dress sparkling under the waxing moon. Everyone agreed it had been a wonderful party. It would certainly make for an interesting debrief session when the social committee next met down at the pool.

The silver Lexus was parked out on the road as usual.

Peggy put the kettle on and set the table. Her grandmother's precious lace tablecloth. The best china. Pulp-free orange juice in Waterford crystal glasses.

'Morning.' Brian stood on the threshold, rubbing his eyes. A sleep-ruffled fluff of hair hovered above his head like mist. He yawned and stretched.

'Sleep well?'

'Like the proverbial log.'

'Me too.' Peggy couldn't remember the last time she'd slept through the whole night without waking. They'd changed into their pyjamas without comment or remark, as if they'd been doing it for years. In the end, all Peggy's misgivings had come to nothing: he didn't snore, he didn't appear to mind her cold feet and, most surprising of all, neither of them had made a trip to the bathroom during the night. The last thing Peggy remembered was Brian's body spooning into hers, his hand resting on the softness of her stomach.

There would be a few sore heads this morning. Peggy thought of a fragile David, waking to the squeals of a miniature Jedi knight and an overtired princess. Mel would roll her eyes and play the martyr while Jenny slept off the night before in the spare room. Peggy just prayed none of them would pay her a surprise visit.

'It was a wonderful party,' said Brian.

'Wonderful.' Peggy smiled back. 'Tea or coffee?'

'Tea, please. Can I help with anything?'

'No, thank you. All under control. Have a seat and help yourself to toast.'

'I must say, I'm quite peckish this morning.'

Peggy carried the teapot to the table. 'Me too, I'm feeling completely ravished.'

She wondered if anyone had noticed Brian return to his unit under the cover of darkness and pack his pyjamas and toothbrush before heading across the road to Peggy's unit. If they had, she didn't care. And neither, it seemed, did Brian. They were both adults, and old enough – quite old enough – to know their own minds.

Brian divided the tea between the two china cups and put a splash of milk in both. He buttered his toast then spread a meticulously gauged layer of orange marmalade over the top. Then he reached into his dressing gown pocket and pulled out a green plastic dosette box, the days of the week printed on each lid. He flicked open Sunday's compartment and spread the tiny family of pills onto the tablecloth.

Peggy fetched her Webster-pak from the cupboard and pushed out her own tablets from today's bubble. They smiled at each other across the breakfast table before swallowing each pill with a swig of tea.

A fall could be a dangerous thing at eighty.

But Peggy Smart was falling.

And it was the most marvellous feeling indeed.

Acknowledgements

As Peggy Smart might say, there have been many wheels in this engine. This is my opportunity to pay tribute to the many talented people behind the scenes who transformed my well-intentioned words into an actual book.

Firstly, my heartfelt thanks to publisher Rebecca Saunders and every single one of the incredible team at Hachette Australia for their passion, vision and unfailing energy in bringing Jacaranda Village to life. From that very first email to the purple cupcakes, I knew my book had found its champion. Also to the team at Hodder & Stoughton in the UK, who shared Rebecca's enthusiasm. A special thank you to Andy Palmer, Ella Chapman and Sarah Brooks for your invaluale roles.

To my editors, especially Karen Ward and Libby Turner, I am so very grateful for your expertise and attention to detail. And especially for turning a blind eye to Peggy's malapropisms.

I am forever indebted to my wonderful agent, Haylee Nash. Thank you for your professionalism and belief in me as a writer.

A special thank you to my mentor Valerie Parv AM for your sage words and encouragement. I am honoured to be your minion.

I'd like to thank The Fellowship of Australian Writers and The Bundanon Trust for the residency that offered the perfect creative space for those first words. A special shout out also to The Australian Writers' Centre for guidance and direction at every step of my writing journey.

Many thanks to Eileen Herbert-Goodall for your insightful comments; also to Kate O'Donnell and Kate Forsyth from Writing NSW for assistance with the early drafts. I'd also like to express my gratitude to David Higham Associates, for permission to publish the Dylan Thomas poem 'Do Not Go Gentle into That Good Night'.

To David Kinley, Catherine Greer, Jules Van Mil, Penelope Janu, Thurza Getzler, Debbie Hawkins, Michelle Barraclough and Carol Flannery: thank you for your advice, support, and friendship. Knowing you were there with the coffee, champagne and/or tissues helped me more than you will ever know.

It is fair to say I couldn't have written this book without the love and forbearance of my wonderful family. To my children William and Charlotte, I am enormously proud of you both. To my husband John: thank you for sharing my dream. As always, you are the gin in my tonic.

To my proud parents, John and Diane Spain: thank you for your unwavering support, and for giving me that first typewriter (and for continuing to store it in your garage).

To my grandparents, Sid and Gladys Spain and Molly and Lol Green: you taught me so much about ageing well, without ever realising it. I only wish you were still here to see this book.

I couldn't have written this novel without my devoted companion and canine muse, Margot. Thank you. Our walks together were always my best thinking time.

Finally, although Jacaranda Retirement Village is a fictional place and all the characters in the book are created purely from my imagination, I must acknowledge and thank the real-life patients who are my elders and betters in so many ways, for their wisdom, stoicism and good humour. You inspire me daily to be a better doctor, writer and person.

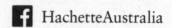